DEVIL KNOWS
A TALE OF MURDER AND MADNESS IN
AMERICA'S FIRST CENTURY

DEVIL KNOWS

A TALE OF MURDER AND MADNESS IN AMERICA'S FIRST CENTURY

DAVID JOSEPH KOLB

GARN PRESS

NEW YORK, NY

Published by Garn Press, LLC
New York, NY
www.garnpress.com

Garn Press and the Chapwoman logo are registered trademarks of Garn Press, LLC

Devil Knows: A Tale of Murder and Madness in America's First Century is a work of fiction closely based on history and geography. References to historical events, real people, or real places are used fictitiously, and are not intended to depict actual events or to change the fictional nature of the work, and all situations, incidents, and dialogues are products of the author's imagination and are not to be construed as real. Other names, characters, places, and events are products of the author's imagination or are used fictitiously, and any resemblance to actual events, locales, or persons, living or dead, is entirely coincidental.

Book and cover design by Benjamin J. Taylor
"Theater of Action: and "Family Tree" illustrations by Scott Rosema

Library of Congress Control Number: 2015946936

Publisher's Cataloging-in-Publication Data

Kolb, David Joseph.
    Devil knows : a tale of murder and madness in America's first century / David Joseph
    Kolb.
        pages cm
    ISBN: 978-1-942146-22-3 (pbk.)
    ISBN: 978-1-942146-23-0 (hardcover)
    ISBN: 978-1-942146-24-7 (e-book)
    1. Salem (Mass.)—History—Colonial period, ca. 1600-
1775—Fiction. 2. Witches—Violence against—
Massachusetts—Salem—Fiction. 3. Trials (Witchcraft)—
Massachusetts—Salem—Fiction. 4. Quaker Women—
Persecutions— Massachusetts—Salem—Fiction. 5.
Pennacook Indians—Fiction   I. Title.
PS3611.O58241 G67 2015
813`.6—dc23
                                    2015946936

Author's Note

Devil Knows: A Tale of Murder and Madness in America's First Century is a work of fiction closely based on history and geography. A few of the names and incidents are the products of the author's imagination or are used fictitiously, and in those cases, any resemblance to actual events, locales, or persons, living or dead, is entirely coincidental.

Several figures are not fictional, however, and of main interest to the reader is that of Mary Bradbury, whose escape from certain death is at the heart of this story. The circumstances surrounding Mrs. Bradbury's remarkable cheating of the hangman – the only convicted "Salem witch" to so succeed – are shrouded in the mists of history. Nor did her great-ancestor, the late author Ray Bradbury, shed any light on her strange story.

For Rosalind

Table of Contents

Part II: A Tale Of Old New England   167

"It is a truth (and it would be a very sad one, but for the higher hopes which it suggests) that no great mistake, whether acted or endured, in our mortal sphere, is ever really set right. Time, the continual vicissitude of circumstances, and the invariable inopportunity of death, render it impossible. If, after long lapse of years, the right seems to be in our power, we find no niche to set it in. The better remedy is for the sufferer to pass on, and leave what he once thought his irreparable ruin far behind him."

Nathaniel Hawthorne

"Go tell the world, What Prays can do beyond all Devils and Witches, and What it is that these Monsters love to do; and through the Demons in the Audience of several standers-by threatned much disgrace to thy Author, if he let thee come abroad, yet venture That, and in this way seek a just Revenge on Them for the Disturbance they have given to such as have called on the Name of God."

The Rev. Mr. Cotton Mather

Frontpiece
Theater of Action, New England c.1692

NEW HAMPSHIRE

Great Stone Face

MAINE

Pennacooks

Cochecho

Dover

Theater of Action: New England c. 1662

Hampton

Salisbury

Newbury Port

Merrimack River

Ipswich

"old road"

Salem

N

Boston

Family Tree
Cotton and Mather Families of the Story

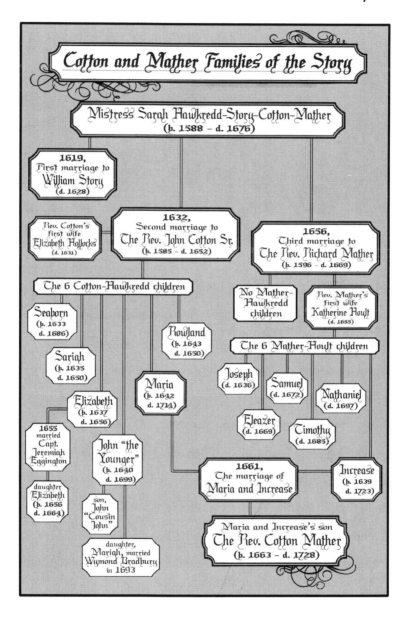

Cotton and Mather Families of the Story

Mistress Sarah Hawkredd-Story-Cotton-Mather
(b. 1588 – d. 1676)

1619,
First marriage to
William Story
(d. 1628)

1632,
Second marriage to
The Rev. John Cotton Sr.
(b. 1585 – d. 1652)

1656,
Third marriage to
The Rev. Richard Mather
(b. 1596 – d. 1669)

Rev. Cotton's
first wife
Elizabeth Hollocks
(d. 1631)

The 6 Cotton-Hawkredd children

No Mather-
Hawkredd
children

Rev. Mather's
first wife
Katherine Hoult
(d. 1655)

Seaborn
(b. 1633
d. 1686)

Rowland
(b. 1643
d. 1650)

The 6 Mather-Hoult children

Sariah
(b. 1635
d. 1650)

Maria
(b. 1642
d. 1714)

Joseph
(d. 1636)

Samuel
(d. 1672)

Nathaniel
(d. 1697)

Elizabeth
(b. 1637
d. 1656)

Eleazer
(d. 1669)

Timothy
(d. 1685)

1655
married
Capt.
Jeremiah
Eggington

John "the
Younger"
(b. 1640
d. 1699)

1661,
The marriage of
Maria and Increase

Increase
(b. 1639
d. 1723)

daughter
Elizabeth
(b. 1656
d. 1664)

son,
John
"Cousin
John"

Maria and Increase's son
The Rev. Cotton Mather
(b. 1663 – d. 1728)

daughter,
Mariah, married
Wymond Bradbury
in 1693

In Order of Appearance

The Personalities

John Arnold, constable of the Boston gaol

Hopestill Foster, an old man

Claude, Constable Arnold's warder

The Rev. Cotton Mather, a pastor of the Gospel

Abigail Cotton, the pastor's wife

Goodman Fain, Constable's Arnold's chief assistant

   Claude Thomson, one of Fain's watchmen

   Eustas Sheen, one of Fain's watchmen

Tizzoo, Cotton Mather's Caribbean slave

The Sandyman Family, soapboilers:

   Henry and Eunice, parents

   Samuel, Landon and Pricilla, their children

   John and Margery Halfield, Eunice's parents

Anne Hutchinson, a goodwife of Boston

John Winthrop, a governor of the Massachusetts Bay Colony

The Rev. John Cotton Sr., Cotton Mather's maternal grandfather

The Rev. John Wilson, senior pastor in John Cotton Sr.'s church

Mary Dyer, an acolyte of Anne Hutchinson

The Rev. John Raynor, pastor of Plymouth Church

The Rev. Thomas Hooker, pastor of the Sandymans' church

Sarah (Hawkredd Story) Cotton, wife of John Cotton Sr., later married to Richard Mather

Jane "Goody" Hawkins, a midwife

Richard Hawkins, Jane's husband, a fisherman

Richard Walderne, a Dover, New Hampshire, businessman and military leader

Peter Coffin, Walderne's secretary

Alice Ambrose, Mary Tomkins and Anne Coleman, Quaker radicals

Constables Roberts and Brike, Puritan officers of Dover and Hampton, respectively

Dogged Pease, a stable boy of Hampton

The Rev. Seaborn Cotton, eldest son of John Cotton Sr. and pastor of Hampton Church

Thomas Bradbury, a selectman of Salisbury in Massachusetts

Robert Pike, a selectman of Salisbury in Massachusetts

Sir Francis Champernowne, a notable resident of Strawberry Banke, Maine

Saunders, an aide to Sir Francis

John Heard, a yeoman carpenter in Sir Francis's employ

Runny Jim Tunkett and Two-Nose Pete, assistants to Goodman Heard

Members of the Pequot raiding band:

Oonoonunkawaee, chief of the band

Quonwehige, brother of Oonoonunkawaee

Borzugwon, brother-in-law to Oonoonunkawaee

Esau Treadway, a homesteader

Members of the Pennacook tribe:

Wonnalancet, second-eldest son of the chief

Passaconnaway, the "Bashaba," or chief of the Pennacook

Nanamacomuck, Passaconnaway's eldest son

Jonny Findus, Passaconnaway's retainer

Kancamagus, Nanamacomuck's son, also known to the English as "John Hogkins"

Thomas Dickinson, Englishman murdered in 1667 at Richard Walderne's truck house

Paul Walderne, Richard Walderne's son

Judge Samuel Sewell, a member of the witch-hunting Court of Oyer and Terminer

Convicted Witches of New England of the Story:

The Rev. George Burroughs

John Willard

Mary Bradbury of Salisbury, wife of Thomas Bradbury

Sarah Good

Dorcas Good, daughter of Sarah

Susannah Martin

Giles Corey

Martha Corey

The Rev. Increase Mather, The Rev. Cotton Mather's father

Leonard Hoar, president of Harvard College

Thomas Sergeant, a Harvard student and classmate of Cotton

Maria Cotton, wife of Increase Mather, mother of Cotton Mather

The Rev. Richard Mather, Cotton Mather's paternal grandfather

The Rev. John Cotton the Younger, youngest son of John Cotton Sr.

Sir Henry Vane, a governor of the Massachusetts Bay Colony

John Cotton, son of John Cotton the Younger

Jeremiah Eggington, a merchant and slaver

Metacomet, also known as "King Philip", a tribal chieftain

Elizabeth Cotton, a daughter of John Cotton Sr., later wife of Capt. Eggington

Thomas Mayhew, a missionary among the Wampanoag of Martha's Vineyard

Bomazeen, chief of the Kennebecs

Charles Frost, a soldier of the Bay Colony

Caleb Boelkins, a Quaker and business associate of Capt. Eggington

Titus, African slave of Sarah (Hawkredd Story Cotton) Mather

Sarah Stockman, Robert Pike's daughter

Colin Edgerly, Robert Pike's orderly

Wymond Bradbury, Sarah's son by her first marriage, grandson to Robert Pike

Mariah Cotton, Wymond's betrothed, daughter of John Cotton the Younger

James and Richard Carr, ferry operators on the Merrimack River

Martha Pike, Robert Pike's second wife

John Harris, Deputy Sheriff of Ipswich

Sagamore Sam, a member of Kancamagus's band

1692: The Witches

"IT'S CLOSE DOWN THERE, I'LL ADMIT," Arnold laughed or, rather, guffawed, to the other. A dreadful sewage stink seeped from the hole he has just bullied open by using his considerable brawn to wrestle aside its heavy lead cover.

At his elbow, maintaining his grim silence, was the midnight visitor to John Arnold's prison, a very tall, strange old man, who had bribed the constable to see the notorious Salisbury witch Mary Bradbury, reputed to have the power to cast a spell on good butter by making it teem with maggots.

"'Suburb of hell' it's been called," again joked the square-headed, boxy form, the burly chief of the ominous structure that haunted Boston's Queen Street.

Taciturn as an Indian, the other man refused to be drawn in to the warm circle of the jailer's humor. He was sick, too, Arnold could tell. Deadly sick. Could hardly stand.

The constable waved the stench of the hole away from his face with the fan of his hand, but he needn't have bothered – in the clammy warmth of the antechamber, the rot of the old jail, the damp earth of the living cemetery below and the rank odor of the nearby harbor that leached out from his own moldy clothes were equally disagreeable.

"Well, then," said Arnold after an uncomfortable silence. "To the matter at hand …" He pulled a torch from its sconce and thrust it at the opening in the dirt floor. The flame flared as it fed on the fetid flow of air from below.

The show of light had its effect. Beneath the men's boots, the sounds of groaning and clamoring for succor grew louder. Some scuffling broke out.

Ordinarily, Arnold would have hurled curses at the mutterings wafting up from the darkness, or even tipped a pot of boiling soup onto the weak voices calling to him from the pit, depending on his mood. But that would not be right in this case, his good sense warned him.

The constable, all too familiar with the scum of the earth, had rarely seen such a hard old bird as his visitor, ailing as he appeared to be. He was no Puritan, this one.

Despite summer's heat and humidity, the stranger wore a long frockcoat, buttoned from his knees to his neck, covering the entirety of his lean frame. A broad, black cloth hat was pulled low over his forehead. There was a disreputable feel about him, the look of a spy maybe. The constable was glad he had called in one of his watchmen to witness the proceedings, just in case.

"Stand back now," Arnold warned him.

The man's eyes narrowed into slits. One large, heavily veined hand gathered his coat's skimpy lapels tightly around his throat. The other was balled into a fist.

Arnold grabbed his club from the guard table. This was a thick, yard-long cudgel with a leather strap hanging from its thinner end that he meticulously wound around his right wrist.

"Wouldn't want to lose you, Billy," he explained without purpose to the thing, giving the stained wood a kiss.

Tentatively, he dipped his foot onto a black step below the level of the ground, measuring in his own mind the advisability of further descent. But, after all, a bargain was a bargain. The thought took the edge off his cheer.

There was a third man in the room, a frightening looking creature with hair as orange as a pumpkin who was absorbed in nibbling his dirty, disgusting fingernails.

"Claude," called back Arnold to his assistant, "stay awake or I'll skin you to the ankles, I swear it."

Arnold went down. The stranger responsible for initiating this illegal and inadvisable journey followed.

There were only eight steps to the bottom. Four feet away, on either side, two passageways loomed, both black beyond the light Arnold's torch threw.

From the left side, there came a hubbub of complaints and shuffling feet, which stopped well short of the men's view, as if those approaching to plead their case dared come no nearer the steps, which, in fact, was the rule. Many a head had suffered the deadly knock of Billy's kiss for coming within the constable's sight.

Arnold's torch pointed to the right.

"Through there," he indicated to the old man, who was now shaking worse than ever. "The chill," he added helpfully, "you get used to it. Now as to the smell …"

"Never mind," snapped the shivering man. "Where is she?"

Arnold ignored the question. A lay of the land, so to speak, must be given first to visitors, distinguished or, in this case, not so distinguished.

"These over here ..." – the constable's torch hand pointed left again – "... these are the real characters. But they'll give ye no trouble."

He looked at his guest, the man's pained face distorted by the flickering fire.

"I see you're shakin' again. No need to worry. They won't come any nearer to me and Billy." He glared over his left shoulder, staring down the narrow passageway, crowded with shapes that could only be felt, not seen.

"AIN'T THAT RIGHT?" Arnold roared at them. The gobbling of the hallway's invisible audience died down to frenzied whisperings.

The constable sidled closer to the old man, nodding in the other direction.

"Your witches are there," he said.

"Witches?" snarled the man. "What do you mean? There's another?"

"A little girl imp of Devil. The mother lies face-down beneath Salem now. Hanged, she was, as yours will be soon enough."

"She's there, you say?"

"The third cell."

"The key?"

"No key. The door is held with a bolt that you pick up. A brazier stays lit further down. It'll give you all the light you need."

"It's not locked?"

"The witches are chained," said Arnold, a proud note in his voice, "iron being proof against their powers. I made the rings special, me being an anchorsmithy back in the home country."

The old man turned to go down the passageway

Arnold called to him. "The ones for the child," he boasted. "They needed some craftwork."

Within a few feet the corridor veered to a sharp turn. It was shored up by crudely mortared stonework that dripped with the humidity collecting within the deep hole out of which this dismal complex had been carved from beneath the main prison.

Just as Arnold foretold, the old man, teeth chattering with fever, came upon a brazier burning in a corner, its thin smoke drawn straight up through a hole above it. At its foot a living skeleton in rags tended the meager flame, hands and face blackened by coal dust, silently squatting in his squalor. Otherwise, the passage was empty. Not even a rat's tail was to be seen.

The visitor ignored the wretch, counting off the cell doors. At the third, he walked up to it and peered through the grate at the top. An overpowering miasma of human scat assaulted his reeling senses.

"Mary Bradbury?" he called into the dark.

There was no answer. Then there was an answer. A chilling child's cry.

"Beware!" gasped a thin, eerie voice from within. Chains rattled.

With shaking hands, the man undid the cell door. Despite the dim glow of the corridor's brazier, it was impossibly black inside.

Yet he thought he could make out human shapes. His eyes may have been deceiving him, but he was certain two forms were cringing against the back wall.

His voiced choked as he called again. "Miss Mary?"

Not until much later did he remember the rest.

Part I

Hopestill

Chapter One

A Victim of the Small Pocks

DARK WAS DEVIL'S CLOAK thrown over Boston. By midnight it very effectively hid from prying eyes a strange procession from the prison's infirmary.

Lit by a torchbearer, the party of six, including the unconscious unfortunate on the litter, wound its way toward the waterfront, stepping across the churned-up filth atop the street stones to the door of a bleak, windowless, featureless house near the Burying Place off Common Street that the Rev. Mr. Cotton Mather had procured for the interrogation.

Uneasily, they awaited an answer to their measured rap.

The litterbearers in the gloom behind Goodman Fain, its leader, were each a member of John Arnold's notorious constabulary. Upon the litter resided a recently risen corpse (or so it had been related to Mather), a victim of the Small pocks. His resurrection, if it could be considered as such, was a remarkable achievement considering the victim's advanced age.

Mather hurriedly finished his devotional, recalling from memory one of his grandfather John Cotton's most treasured passages, Revelation 3:20:

"Behold, I stand at the door and knock. If any man hear my voice and open the door, I will come in to him, and will sup with him and he with me …"

The door squeaked open.

"Pray, inside, Fain," said the bewigged, bandy-legged, fashionably dressed Mather, peering into the empty street as if he were expecting yet another visitor. He felt very blessed to see no one.

Stepping to his left, he motioned the litter crew toward the pinched-off room, indicating a crude pen on the floor, a low-edge box frame filled with fresh straw.

Into it they rolled the undressed, undead man. The constable's assistant carelessly tossed a blanket onto the body.

Although the interior was lit by both the fire in the well-appointed hearth and a variety of tapers around the room, these lights only accentuated the shadows of Arnold's men and their frightening features.

All had been badly scarred by the wicked pocks, hence their assignment to this duty, since they were in no danger of reacquiring the dread disease.

The one on the bed frame? Less fortunate.

To have been stricken with the Small pocks so late in life was generally conceded to be tantamount to a death sentence.

Yet, as Mather carefully explored the exposed flesh of the man's head and neck, and then the hands, he could easily determine that life was far from extinguished in the nearly unconscious body. A mild case, if ever he saw one.

The tall, comatose form appeared to be in his seventies, possessed of a skeletal structure that was slight, almost wraithlike. On the other hand, the victim's pleasantly composed face bespoke to Mather of a happy, perhaps even godly life. This he knew not to be true, further evidenced by the blue-black tattoo of an arrow on the man's chest.

Mather paid little heed to the man's weakness and barely audible moaning. He was intent on the color and shape of the ugly pustules protruding from the flesh.

The pocks were as reported by the constable, which came as a relief to the examiner – red, white, distinct, soft, few, round and sharp-topped.

Had these been bluish-green or black, densely clustered like evil fruit, the prognosis would have been death within days or even hours.

There was some bleeding from the nose, which Mather perceived, again, as a good sign. This was per the advice of the eminent Rev. Thomas Thatcher, whose broadside, *"Brief Rule to Guide the common-people ... in the Small pocks, or measles,"* was one of his treasured volumes.

Old William Bradford, God bless him, had written of the Indians he had seen suffering from the pocks, and his phrase "dying like rotten sheep" had stuck in Mather's mind this horrible summer of the year of Our Lord 1692.

Mather set his sore lips in a tight line. And this malady was just a single, mighty weapon in Devil's arsenal! Just one!

There were so many others.

Goodman Fain interrupted Mather's train of thought by holding out a worn possibles bag finely crafted out of dark hide. A skinner's knife with a horn grip was attached to the strap, and some Indian beads made of tiny, colorful shells adorned the handle of a musket's flash-pan pick, sharp as a pin, that was stuck into and under the flap.

"Ensign Foster's belongin's, sir. There weren't nothin' much in it save a bit of hair tied up, flints, patches, some lead shot and these few papers," Fain said hopefully, holding forth some scraps that he couldn't read, angling for a copper which was not forthcoming.

At the sound of his name, the man in the straw, Hopestill Foster, moved his sweating, feverish head a fraction.

It was a sign that the Rev. Mather took at once as another from God.

Yet of this revelation, the old man, Hopestill, was unaware.

As the minister fussed about him, lifting his eyelids, deducing his pulse rate and estimating his fever (which was increasing), the rough journey on the litter had produced in his unconscious state of mind a sense that he was back in England, a boy of 11, about to embark upon a voyage he had taken 60 years before, to Massachusetts Bay from England in 1632 aboard the miserable Winthrop fleet ship *Lyon*.

This traumatic event came upon him as the fourth unwanted son of a part-time smuggler named Faraday Foster, who sold his slow-witted youngest into indentured service to the Sandyman family. The Sandymans were tradespeople belonging to the Hooker Company, which is to say they were adherents of the Puritan renegade Rev. Mr. Thomas Hooker.

Including the newly acquired Hopestill, there were eight of them in their party going to the New Land – his new master Henry and Henry's wife Eunice; their sons Samuel and Landon; their only daughter, the remarkably fat Priscilla; and Eunice's two gnome-like parents, John and Margery Halfield. These latter, while cold and dismissive to Hopestill, were decidedly not cruel. The boy felt himself fortunate indeed.

The voyage of a duration of six weeks was a storm-wracked ordeal from start to finish, and he remembered it just like that in his nightmare, his wet hair streaming across his face, the choking fear in his throat, his horror-stricken face telling the tale of the journey even though naught but moans passed his lips.

In the dimly lit single room of Mather's house the guards from Arnold's prison watched the old man relive it, struggling with his inner demons. They knew not what he saw, only that it was akin to the terror men face when they are alone and helpless.

"It's a fit. A bad one," remarked Goodman Fain, watching in awe as the prisoner thrashed about on the straw. "Swallow his tongue, he will, you mark me." He looked about his cronies for a reply, received none and shrugged his shoulders.

His employer, a fatigued Rev. Mather, snorted at this fool's ignorance.

In calm, measured tones, as if he were delivering a lecture, Mather observed to the others that Devil or one of his minions was hard at work exciting the aged man who writhed so weakly within the bed frame.

All agreed with this pronouncement.

Mather dropped his head and closed his eyes while Fain and his men shuffled in place and wrung their hats or hands, waiting.

Minutes passed. The minister lifted his face from silent prayer to assess Hopestill Foster's pitiful, almost silent thrashing.

He glanced anew at the struggling old man and wondered if it was all for naught, whether the answers he had been seeking for decades would elude him again with this criminal's death.

Mather shook his shaved head under the wig in defiance of such a possibility. God would not, could not, fail him now.

Yet so many questions needed to be asked, prevented by the seriousness of the ailment and of the man Foster's condition.

Did he assess wrongly? Mather stooped over his writhing patient.

There were not so many pocks upon Hopestill's face, but lifting the thin rag of a blanket covering him revealed a body spotted with evil pustules here and there.

Again, far less than he had ever seen in the worst cases, but enough to make the prognosis up to God.

At his signal, without a word, Tizzoo, his Carib Indian slave given to him by his father, crept over and refilled the minister's cup of chocolate. He dismissed her back to the loft after he tasted the sweet drink and approved.

Mather was determined to stay, at least through this first night, to see if he could influence the outcome of the struggle between Devil and Christ Jesus for Hopestill Foster's life.

The conflict raged before his eyes. He felt blessed with the sight, and if in some small way he could help, well …

"OOOHHHHHH! AAAAAWWWWWW!"

Mather leaped from his chair in almost comic alarm. It clattered away from him.

From his unsuspecting lap, the cup and saucer of chocolate flew off to crash on the few flimsy floorboards within, the thin objects splintering into shards and bits.

The Small pocks victim screamed again.

Then louder once more, in greater agony.

The constable's men looked on in alarm, none daring to act without a direct order. Worried cries called forth from outside in the street.

Wrapped in a shawl, Tizzoo jumped down from the loft ladder barefoot. She, too, shrieked as the shrimp-colored bottoms of her feet were punctured by the broken china pieces from Mather's cup.

Her cries were instantly stifled by the sight that greeted her. Mahogany hands pressed against her open mouth in terror.

Mather cowered inwardly and shrank from the bed and the now-empty chair laying on its side.

For once, he was at a loss for words.

Eyes ablaze, his blanket having fallen away to reveal the full horrors of his naked, diseased body imprinted with that most curious tattoo of an arrow, Hopestill Foster gripped the sides of the bed frame and slowly raised himself up.

Chapter Two

Introductions

WISPS OF BLOODY STRAW drifted to the floor around Hopestill's feet.

Mather reached out his arm and snapped his fingers, motioning impatiently at Tizzoo for her shawl. She removed it from over her shoulders and with a long reach handed it to her master, fearing to step on more fragments.

Eyes intent on the upright man, the minister ordered Fain and his men to retreat to the kitchen side of the house. He warned them, "Give thanks to the Lord God Almighty that you have a soul that is in the care of Christ Jesus."

To his slave he said, "Clean your feet. Then return."

Tizzoo painfully skipped over to the ladder and went up out of the room into the loft.

Mather's attention focused on Hopestill.

The latter stood in place silently as if he had just arisen from first sleep, torpid as a fog from his nocturnal visions.

He was a much taller man than Mather had supposed, tall

and ungainly. His light-yellow hair was almost white with his age. It fell about his head haphazardly, like down feathers sticking out of a bolster.

His tears dried, but his eyes remained pink and crusted – if a long, lean, ancient rabbit had tried to become an old man his eyes might have appeared so. However, behind the pain, they were inquisitive.

Clearing his throat and showing a mouthful of light brown teeth, whether from decay or tobacco it could not be discerned, he inquired politely of Mather, "Have you any beer or ale, sir?"

Hopestill's mild tone suggested an uncertainty as to whether the question might elicit a ringing slap.

"Small beer, yes, yes! I would recommend it warmed but not hot," was Mather's enthusiastic reply to his new patient.

Hopestill nodded slowly. He seemed at a loss as to what to say next.

"How come I here?" he finally asked.

"I s-s-s-sent for you from the hospital where by all accounts you were dying. I had to wait many days even then for your delivery, as it was touch and go with you," Mather answered. His slight stammer had returned, but it went quite unnoticed.

He continued, "It is quite remarkable to have you standing in your extremity, Foster. Pray, may I help you to a chair?"

"'Twould not be advised, I would think," the sickly old rabbit answered. "I cannot say I might sit and then rise after."

His teeth chattered lightly.

"Forgive me," Mather said.

He went over to Hopestill and lightly draped Tizzoo's shawl

around the man's bare shoulders.

"Thankee," said the rabbit Hopestill.

"May I place my hand on your forehead? To assess your condition and the state of the fever?"

"As you wish, sir."

Mather felt the warm but not superheated skin that so often spells imminent decease.

The sweaty dampness of the previous hour had calmed down considerably. Overall, in Mather's opinion, there had been a sudden and remarkable improvement for which he could give no medical account. He gave thanks silently to God that Devil had withdrawn from the battle, if only temporarily.

As Mather fussed over him, Hopestill watched the small fire in silence, contemplating his own situation.

"You know of me, if I take it correctly, sir?"

"I do."

"And you be …?"

"I am Cotton Mather, an ordained minister of the Lord and pastor of the Gospel in Boston. You have no Fox-like objections to that, I pray?"

Hopestill swayed and Mather started, ready to catch him if need be. But it was only a sway.

"Be not insensible to the broken pottery on the floor about your bare feet, my dear fellow," he warned his patient, a cautionary that upon its uttering Mather inwardly deemed specious considering the other was in the throes of the fearsome pocks.

Tizzoo reappeared, limping slightly, in slippers.

She had put on a black dress that covered her from head to toe.

A bright red head tie enwrapped her hair, leaving only her pitted, deeply scarred face with its prominent cheekbones to show.

"Me come, massair," she announced sweetly, careful to not show her sharpened incisors, which, when she was a child, had been filed into dagger points. Mather had warned her harshly never to smile or yawn in company (but privately, he would have her show them to him whenever he needed to fix on an image of a demon or imp).

"Tizzoo, bring a pot of small beer and a cup for Ensign Foster. It must needs be slightly warmed first in the plate as we did for Mr. Howard that time." To Hopestill, he inquired, "It is 'Ensign,' is it not?"

"Aye."

"Aye? Ensign Foster, is it?"

"Major Pike made it so some years back, I reckon."

Without replying to this patent absurdity of an undeserved honor accorded to a traitor, Mather bent down, rather spryly, and uprighted his chair, placing it next to the hearth. He still hoped to cajole Hopestill into sitting down.

The men stood a yard apart, the candles flickering in a set of long, tin canisters that had been placed around the room, bathing them in soft light and bayberry scent. Candles were a luxury too often unseen in Hopestill's eyes. He was mesmerized by the wavering illumination.

"Please, sir." Mather again offered his hand to Hopestill to lead him to the chair but when it wasn't taken, he reached down and petted the seat, almost as if the old man were a young dog able to jump up. The insult was overlooked, yet with some further encouragement, he did coax Hopestill to recline his thin flank upon it, doing so with a deep and painful sigh.

The minister pulled up a crude bench-seat for himself. After settling, he smoothed his stockings, which tended to fall down over his deficient calves. Correctly attired again, he composed his mind and continued his interrogatory.

"You know of me?" Mather asked politely, teeth gritted, echoing Foster's own question.

The two sat before the hearth like old friends, which they were not.

Hopestill turned and scrutinized the pastor, who was gazing at his opposite just as intently. He then turned to look into the fire.

The slight light and heat were refreshing, stimulating. Deep within him, the pain that racked his body was still subsiding.

"All New England knows of you."

"But you, YOU, know of me," Mather asked again, with an edge to his voice.

Foster's voice was decidedly weak, every word a trial for the man. "Thy men spoke of you on the way. I could not move or talk, but I heard. I knew your grandfather, the Rev. John Cotton. He was not so widely known as you, as I recall. But New England wasn't so crowded with folks then, neither."

"My word!" ejaculated Mather in spite of himself, so giddy was he at the anticipation of their interview. Undecided whether to accept the flattery, he rejected it. "Any accomplishments of my own must be w-w-weighed against the miracle of your recovery in just a few short hours. I would have expected as soon as set the linen over your face as we do here now speak."

"Perhaps you might yet. I feel chill."

Tizzoo, who had quietly come with a pan of beer and had set to warming the liquid, poured some in a flip-pot and gave it to Mather first. He sniffed at it and passed it along to Hopestill.

"I need help," Hopestill admitted.

"Certainly." Mather held the pot while the other drank a little.

"'Tis good. I was dry." He drank again, a little more easily.

"You have been with Major Pike these many years, is my understanding," said Mather, perhaps too directly.

"Mmm hmm."

"You have seen much of Devil's work on the frontier, no doubt."

"Devil's work?" For the first time the sick old rabbit seemed genuinely animated. "Labors of Monsieur Le Compte de Frontenac and the Abenakis, I would call it."

"Yes, Devil's work, it is. Most assuredly," snapped Mather, taking offense. He instinctively reacted to the implicit suggestion that it wasn't Lord Lucifer behind the horror, torment and depredations that had ceaselessly afflicted New England since the first planters arrived.

Hopestill ignored the assertion and idly scratched at a pustule on his right arm, which Mather bade him stop, "lest you deeply scar your skin and spread the infection."

"Deer flies itch worse," he told the pastor.

Mather pressed him. "You say Frontenac and yet imply it is not as Satan? He is Louis XIV's agent, no? Have not their hounds gnawed our bones all these years? And Sir William Phips, mind you! He had them in a bottle at Quebec and they escaped. That was no sleight of hand, no finger under the pea cup. Devil's work."

"I meant no hurt, sir."

Mather was solicitous again.

"Of course. Of course. It is ... just that ... (he picked his words very carefully so as not to stammer) … the threat is very real. Devil never sleeps, never sleeps. No. No. In Salem Village you know what is occurring there. His ultimate plan threatens us now, this very instant. We all stand in the gravest peril."

Hopestill wasn't focusing on this important message, Mather realized. He saw that dull, glazed look all too often in the meeting-house in the wandering attention some in the back pews paid to his sermons.

Mather recognized some would rather be elsewhere, doing their Sabbath-breaking behind closed doors and in secret, to get a leg up on the week so as not to be caught flouting the Lord's Day strictures.

Moreover, he could tell what they were thinking when he looked over at them and they, caught by his glance, suddenly brought the theme of the lecture into focus before it was too late and they were called out.

So he knew.

But this wasn't the Sabbath, or Lecture Day, or a talk. This man Hopestill Foster held perhaps the key to the fight of his life against the Wicked King of All Evil, who maimed, tortured and terrified the Chosen People and must be stopped, stopped at all costs.

And then there was the other piece of business, personal business to be sure – the almost certainty that the man knew about the curse on Mather's own family, a curse that would destroy even him.

As Foster stared blankly at him, Mather agonized over how to begin.

He blurted out, "Why did you bribe your way into Arnold's jail to see the witch Mary Bradbury?"

Foster blinked his eyes. A reply formed, and then he began to topple from his perch.

Springing up to steady the man, Mather almost shouted his warning.

"Take care!" He was, in fact, genuinely concerned. He proffered the pot of beer again to Hopestill, who, recovering his balance, smacked his lips to indicate he would like another drink.

The fire in the hearth was dying down. Mather added a small chunk to it. They both watched it snap and sizzle as it was licked by the red coals.

What strange fairies and imps lived inside the flame to attract men's eyes thus, Mather speculated, conceiving a possible missive on the subject. Ah, the subject. He would have to change the subject for now.

He ventured in a lighter tone, quite casually considering the morbidity of the topic, "I have been told you were one of the first to arrive at Cochecho in '89 …"

Hopestill's dulled mind was at first slow to follow the minister's lead. He took a minute to answer before words formed.

"It is to Major Walderne's murder and the massacre to which you inquire?"

"Most anxiously."

Hopestill drew the shawl closer around his frame.

"Oh, aye," Hopestill answered softly, sadly even. "I was there."

Chapter Three

"Go Plant Your Pumpkins"

YES, HE REPEATED SILENTLY to himself, I was there.

There to witness the aftermath of the destruction of the little trading settlement just north of the rude village of Dover, established in the New Hampshire grants some 25 years earlier.

There to see the place called Cochecho, the Indian river name that described the water's raging, frothing wash that beat remorselessly on the boulders over which it dashed, burnt to ashes.

Yes, I was there, he mused, steeped in the bitter gall of his past.

There too late to save any of those doomed that summer's night in '89, three years before, stricken, he was taken prisoner by Mather.

There too late to prevent Chief Kancamagus from finally gaining his revenge on Richard Walderne, Hopestill's former employer – that conniving, cruel, corpulent little man who lorded over Cochecho and Dover like a baron born.

Yet, among all these charnel images sifted through the rank ashes of Walderne's late garrison, Hopestill found her again.

It was to Priscilla that his thoughts turned, his dear fat Priscilla, of all things. His first love and his spirit wife, she was now gone to that better place in the light of the sky and in his heart. A mist of tears blurred his experienced eyes.

Priscilla Sandyman. How he delighted in that silly laugh and sly lust for her "scarecrow," as she called him.

They made a pair, the two of them, newly arrived and thrown together in infant Boston so long ago, scampering around her father's soap boilers, mock-threatening each other with the lye ash shovel.

Priscilla's father and Hopestill's master, Henry Sandyman, had first set up shop on the Roxbury Road, and got right to his business in the hectic months following the landing of the *Lyon* in late May 1632.

Those had been extremely difficult days for the family.

Securing shelter and property was a matter that was largely in the hands of the selectmen and leadership of the Bay Colony and was no easy undertaking, even for ready silver. This was especially so given the influence in civil matters exerted by the powerful First Church, which had been planted in Boston by Gov. John Winthrop and whose growth seemed unstoppable.

Therefore, it was no help at all that the Sandyman loyalties, principally those of Henry's wife Eunice and her aged parents, were known to be in accord with the Rev. Hooker, whose modestly liberal preachments (Minister Hooker was to arrive in New England later in company with the esteemed First Church minister John Cotton) were from the outset regarded with suspicion by the very conservative Puritan element already well-established in that growing city. Tainted Hooker was, as were his people.

Many of the Rev. Hooker's adherents who arrived in advance of their pastor were insulted by their poor reception. So with the blessing of their church elders, they took their worship several long winter miles from Boston and across the Charles River to the place that became known as Newe Town.

There they set up a rudely crafted meetinghouse, just four walls and a slab shake roof with no hearth even, and heard the elders give the sermons every Sunday. All waited patiently until their leader, the beloved Rev. Hooker, might arrive from the home country to meet them in the new land.

One exception was Goodman Sandyman.

Rather than settle in Newe Town, Sandyman, always the businessman, believed himself and his trade better off nearer Boston, even though isolated from his family's congregation.

The best he could do, though, was to secure a rental agreement for a good-sized property just south of town along the way to Roxbury. It was farther away from the city center than Sandyman wanted, but close enough that a good walk would carry customers from both north and south to his door.

Alas, good fortune deserted them with the onset of that first winter.

John Halfield, Eunice's father, who had never truly recovered from the hardship of the voyage, complained of body aches and chills one dreary evening. They put him to bed wrapped in blankets in front of the fire but he was dead and cold on the side away from the flame in the morning, the flannel still tucked in under his whiskers. To Hopestill, he looked like an old stone carving in death.

Margery Halfield went the following winter. She had slipped on the ice during the long walk to Newe Town for the Sunday meeting and could not get to her feet. Carried home to bed by the Sandyman boys and Hopestill, her left leg swelled up and seemed about to burst before she gave leave to see one of the midwives. The old woman was given a special tea, which she choked down, and a nice, smelly poultice to wear on her chest, but a few evenings later Eunice's mother lapsed into a painful, moaning coma from which she never awakened.

Saddened by their losses, the Sandymans and their business plodded on in a half-hearted way. As did their servant.

Soapmaking was a disagreeable profession and not at all to Hopestill's liking. Yet he found it far preferable to the hanging that he supposed was his inevitable fate as a smuggler in his father's gang back in England.

Every day up until Sabbath Eve, then, Hopestill was put to work walking a cart through the streets of Boston to collect wood ashes from the houses to haul back to Sandymans'.

It was thoroughly filthy labor although he did get to see a lot of the small city and its meager sights, which was worth the occasional cuffing he drew for spilling these hard-to-manage loads on floors or stoops.

At Sandymans', the cartloads of ashes were shoveled into ladder-sided barrels onto a thick bed of straw and sticks layered over the bottom. Hopestill would climb up, cover his face with a wet rag and tamp these down with a hickory rake.

One of the Sandyman brothers would then slowly pour water over the ashes as Hopestill worked. Another would stoop below and fill a clay jar with the muddy liquid that oozed out of a little hole in the bottom. This ran around the lip of a groove that had been cut into the stone slab upon which the barrel stood and was the lye they needed to make the soap.

Once or twice a week, the entire family and Hopestill would render animal fat by stirring yellowish chunks of it in the two boiler tubs set over blazing fires until the suet dissolved. There was one tub for beef fat, which rendered tallow, and another for pig fat, which rendered lard.

During this operation it was a miracle no one got seriously scalded, although all carried the scars of blisters from spilled fat or drops of water that exploded in the mixture.

The solid fat that later collected on the surface of the tubs when the rendering was cooled down with more water and allowed to sit overnight or even longer was scraped off and mixed with the lye. This was finally boiled back up to produce Sandyman's liquid soap that was a household staple in many an early New England home.

More to the point, this was what put the coppers into Henry's pocket, because in terms of quality, Sandyman's operation was clean, in that he didn't throw in used cooking fats and thus "taint the tub" with noxious byproducts.

So, many farmers preferred to trade with Sandyman and exchange their fat and some produce and meat for soap, which Eunice would ladle out of a wooden barrel with a dipper into whatever containers were thrust in front of her.

From these plain-spoken and stalwart men and women of the country Hopestill got his first sense of the fine land to the north that was open for the taking. Idle chatter during the exchange of fat for soap was where he learned of the Maine and New Hampshire territories and the upstate frontier then in the forming.

Unhappily, the family's soap business was not the only one in Boston. Worse for Sandyman, the much-smaller Gerrity operation on the peninsula, even though less well-regarded by the locals, enjoyed the distinct favor of the First Church since the Sandymans' connection to the Rev. Hooker's church in Newe Town rendered him somewhat of a less-reputable tradesman in the eyes of those who counted in Boston proper.

And as the Rev. Hooker's stock fell with the Boston Puritans, certain difficulties arose in obtaining the vital wood ashes in the quantity needed for the operation.

He recalled that …

A faraway voice cut at Hopestill like a whiplash.

"Enough of that for now!" snapped the Rev. Mather.

"Eh?" responded a dazed Hopestill.

His return to the present found him half-leaning, or rather half-falling, across the smooth cherry veneer of the finely crafted settle upon which he had been placed, unaware he had been moved. He shook his head to clear it of his dreams.

Across from him, the intelligent face of the minister with its pursed lips and piercing eyes showed annoyance.

"Enough about the soap craft, Mr. Foster. Lye and ash, ash and lye. You said something previously, about Major Walderne and pumpkins. What was that about? You go in and out of things."

"Pumpkins, I said?" Hopestill idly massaged an itchy pustule. He thought he could smell lye soap.

"You said, that Walderne said, to go plant your pumpkins."

"Yes, before the massacre …"

"Yes? Yes?" Again, that tone of dangerous agitation.

"Walderne didn't concern himself …" Hopestill's voice tapered off.

"Go on."

Curiously, to Hopestill, Mather was writing it all down.

The minister had taken off his outer coat and now sat in black vest and white shirt, scribbling and scratching furiously in the heavy journal book opened before him upon the handsome lap table that he balanced atop his knobby knees.

Hopestill fell into silence again.

"Walderne was warned. But he told them to go plant …"

"… their pumpkins … " an agitated Mather finished for him. "All right, then. Hmmmm."

The minister bit at the top of his quill and stared at Hopestill, while the object of his stare felt just well enough to experience a deepening sensation of suspicion about the whole affair, which is to say of his being in this little house with the most learned individual in New England hanging on his every word.

Mather began writing again in his ledger.

"I take it you find me an interesting man," Hopestill ventured cautiously to the famed minister.

Without pause or looking up, scritching away, Mather answered, "Very."

He could see by the expression on the minister's face that Mather was surprised by the account of Walderne's nonchalance about the Indians.

He also noticed that Mather looked behind himself to make sure Fain's men were out of hearing when he asked, "You had dealings with Major Walderne. Many, I'm told. He said nothing of the story of the monstrous births?"

Mather leaned in for his answer.

"I know there's been talk," said Hopestill cautiously. "That's an old story. Walderne and myself didn't see eye to eye on much."

"Balderdash! You know far more than you are telling me," the minister accused him, looking at him straight on. "You will tell it to me, and I want to know about your heretic wife as well."

Mather gestured at his servant. "Tizzoo, give this man more of that beer. Make sure it's warm. Just so." He indicated exactly how warm he wanted it by pressing his thumb and forefinger together so they almost touched.

"Priscilla wasn't my wife, exactly," Hopestill said defensively.

"No?" Mather looked at him contemptuously, all but accusing him of lying.

"She wasn't no heretic, neither."

Hopestill was now feeling somewhat poorly again and it was when he tried to stand that he noticed Goodman Fain had entered from the kitchen area.

Being too weak, Hopestill gave up the attempt to stretch his legs. As he did so, he could not fail to see Fain leaning against the door, barring the exit. Fain's hand tightened over the wooden club he was holding. The muscular warder tapped it lightly against the wall behind him.

Tizzoo stood behind her master. She flashed him a quick smile of her sharp teeth that only he could see.

A chill ran through him as it dawned on him where things now stood.

Nevertheless, he would tell it. He would tell it all.

"I want to talk about Boston," said Mather.

His voice cut like the Indian knives used on Walderne.

"Now!"

Chapter Four

Enter Satan

THE TRUTH BE KNOWN, Henry Sandyman kept Hopestill busy on some First Days behind closed doors, even though it risked his soul – his and the boy's, both. Yet, it was an arrangement the tall, thin youngster found very much to his liking, despite the pain of a whipping and a heavy fine for his master for profaning the Sabbath.

Otherwise, it was sit in the cramped rear pews in the stuffy, windowless Newe Town meetinghouse with the other servants and the only two African blacks, to be watched by the tithingman with his long, knobbed stick ready to rap the skulls of the sleepers.

On church Sundays, the hourglass was turned and then turned again and again as the teacher, Elder Israel Spooner, a close adherent of the Rev. Hooker – normally their minister but absent again having returned to England – blazed forth on the Good Doctrine. The hours went by exceedingly slowly during those Newe Town Sabbaths.

However, God was less on Hopestill's mind in those early years in Boston than was his love for a seemingly unattainable object, Priscilla Sandyman.

His baldly concealed infatuation, which revealed itself whenever Priscilla was within eyeshot, was a source of no little amusement for her two scrawny brothers, who badgered Hopestill relentlessly for his being an outlandish dunderhead. The servant didn't care much for their taunts but took it with the good nature that was an essential part of his make-up.

Landon, the eldest Sandyman son, was by far the more interesting of the two, a redheaded scamp who, while he could hardly lift the heavy family musket along with its iron stanchion, became a decent hunter in time. He supplied the table with a bounty of geese and turkeys, too, once he acquired his shooting eye. The other brother, Samuel, was more of a baby who hated the idea of leaving his mother even to fetch something on an errand. He also coughed incessantly, morning and night.

In spite of the teasing he took from her brothers, almost all of Hopestill's spare thoughts bent to Priscilla, with whom he spent more of his time than the rest of the family supposed and more than he himself had dared to hope.

It was at first a youthful flirtation on his part, kept well under wraps with the help of Priscilla, who admired his sweet nature much as she would a perfect blueberry although with, sadly, sometimes little more regard.

But as the years passed the relationship deepened. Then it began to grow within those private places and secret spaces that could be found wherever lovers looked for them. Those were their hidden but most cherished moments, which they shared with no one.

Still, there were times when it was contentious between them. The friction was religion, a topic of extended interest for the girl but of little import for her servant suitor.

Priscilla often tried to discuss or rather lecture Hopestill on the finer points of Christ's teachings or the intricacies of the Trinity while they worked in the soapboiling yard on this and that chore. He listened to her impassioned arguments but rarely responded, preferring to daydream about her as she talked.

Bulky, assuredly, yet enticingly buxom, Priscilla was light on her pretty little feet and had the most beautiful face, like an angel's face, he mused. He grew to love it, for it was like a thing apart, ensconced as it was inside all that extra flesh. What he saw and cherished was the inner beauty of his friend.

It was when he thought about that inner beauty that he sometimes mused on Elder Spooner's ugly remarks about his own heart – "It's black, boy, black as the Druid's stone, like your father's!" the elder informed him on the voyage to New England and many times thereafter – and whether it was God's place to change that supposed black heart, or his.

Hopestill came to believe it was his choice, that it was within himself, so to speak, that God or a semblance of Him dwelled, that within his breast near his heart was perhaps his own Holy Ghost.

But he kept such views to himself, as he did all his opinions on religion since he was sensible about how touchy an issue these matters were among the Puritans of Boston. His reticence was an ongoing source of annoyance to Priscilla.

So with Hopestill a hopeless sparring partner on dogma, the feisty teen-age girl sought and found a willing ally in the person of a new customer who within a short time became a familiar of the Sandyman family, and especially Priscilla.

Her name was Anne Hutchinson, a devoted adherent of the Rev. John Cotton, the new teacher at the First Church, the foremost house of worship in the colony. Most charmingly, Anne wore a cheerful smile and exhibited a ready wit – unusual traits for the Boston women of that era who tended to be, and often were, either morose or gloomy.

In her very first visit to purchase some soap, the impressive and intelligent Mistress Hutchinson, a tallish woman with dancing, friendly brown eyes, turned the conversation around to the subject of the pastor she championed, John Cotton, whom she and her husband had accompanied from England.

Anne made it clear from the first that she regarded the Rev. Mr. Cotton with outright awe for his gift of interpreting Scripture in a more generous light.

"Isn't it better on the whole," she asked Eunice Sandyman, with Priscilla standing beside her mother looking upon their visitor with more than a touch of veneration, "if we would lift the people up on the Lord's Day to better themselves rather than leaving them crushed under the sentence of their own sins to carry on for another week under such a heavy burden?"

Minister Cotton, who enjoyed the particular favor of Mistress Hutchinson and Anne's husband Will, a wealthy textile merchant but a quiet man of few words, was to Anne and his other newly minted disciples the paragon of the new generation of bright and fervent preachers that had landed in Boston Harbor some two years after the Sandymans had arrived.

Like their own Rev. Hooker, John Cotton had fled the Old World for the new, a separation forced by his vociferous (the authorities were inclined to term it treasonous) rejection of established doctrine back home. Cotton had boarded ship to the Bay Colony, reportedly in women's clothes, disguised so as to fool the King's officers seeking to arrest him in England.

Mistress Hutchinson went on to sing John Cotton's praises to Priscilla as the months passed. Anne was, however, also diplomatically most generous with her compliments for the Rev. Hooker whenever she and Priscilla happened to meet in the soapyard.

Thrilled at being brought into such confidence, Priscilla told Hopestill (even though he wasn't much interested) that her lady friend had related a very private anecdote to her about the popular pastor.

"In her very own words, Hopestill," Priscilla confided, "it is being said that the Lord departed from England when Mr. Cotton was gone from it."

"Well, given our need of Him here, I pray our Lord took ship with the gentleman," was the only rejoinder Hopestill cared to offer.

Mistress Hutchinson's visits to the Sandymans always brought out a new observation from the prominent goodwife although, unlike her good coin, her outspoken opinions were not always as welcome.

She surprised the family, for instance, with her far less generous praise – bordering on actual criticism in Henry's opinion – for the Rev. Mr. Cotton's mentor, First Church senior pastor Rev. John Wilson, when comparing the two men's sermons. Such daring observations made Hopestill's master and his wife cringe.

They were much more frightened of Wilson, though, and not alone in that sentiment, either.

The senior minister was a fearful presence within the community who exuded a fanatic's intolerance of sin and impropriety from the pulpit every Sunday. And when John Wilson looked you in the eye on Lord's Day, you might be headed for the stocks – or worse.

However, the Rev. Wilson was at that moment in 1635 abroad, back in England to fetch his wife who had quailed to sail with him the first time.

This was a circumstance that allowed the stock of the junior minister in tenure at First Church to rise sharply in Boston.

In Wilson's absence, Minister John Cotton handled both sermons and lectures so capably that he accrued renown by the week and attracted numerous visitors from outside his own congregation.

Priscilla had no objection to Miss Hutchinson's pronouncements, however far they bordered on outright dissent.

She became, in time, to the chagrin of her parents and brothers, one of the lady's most loyal acolytes. Hopestill's only concern was that his beloved spent so much time in Boston on the peninsula instead of at home. He moped about when she was away, earning only scorn and derision from her brothers.

The informal gatherings at various homes and cottages around the area that Priscilla attended in train with Anne Hutchinson were the so-called "women's meetings" that gradually become very fashionable.

Their focus, much more so than the innocent gossip of fashion and recipes, was the differences among the many sermons preached in churches throughout Greater Boston within the previous weeks and months. Reports both enthusiastic and less-enthusiastic (outright disapproval was forbidden territory, of course) were offered and commented on with great seriousness during the wide-ranging discussions chaired by the great lady herself.

These sessions were beloved by the God-fearing goodwives since they could speak their minds openly about theological matters without risking criticism – or punishment for straying from their biblical place in society – and soon became so popular that Mistress Hutchinson was moved to offer her own home and garden as the primary venue.

Reflecting the family's wealth and prominence, the Hutchinson House was perfect for these pleasant meetings. This rare, whitewashed, all-brick home stood out in the still-uncluttered, exclusive center of Boston like a perfect tooth, and was considered the handsomest house in the Shawmut, the Indian name by which the city on the peninsula was sometimes referenced. However, its colonial splendor, for those times at least, was in direct opposition, both in architectural style and in location, to the reserved and grave residences of its two closest neighbors.

As it was in spirit.

For just down the dirt path from the Hutchinsons were the Winthrops, whose head of household John was the fleshy, jowly, pushy, nasal-voiced former governor who impatiently chaffed at his successor Henry Vane's ascension to that important post. The younger Vane was a great devotee of Anne Hutchinson, much to the displeasure of Winthrop and his admirers.

In the other direction, also only a moderate stroll from the Hutchinsons' front door, was their next-closest neighbor, the formidable Rev. Wilson, whose abode lay just to the north of where Queen Street cut into the path and whose windows, except for some small cracks, were perpetually covered over by black tar paper, as if their inmates were in mourning or in hiding. Still, some who had to pass by complained of feeling hostile eyes on their necks.

Anne Hutchinson's house was a standing invitation, by contrast.

Into it, the open door and windows allowed the scent of the delicious herbs growing within the spacious garden – cultivated by the mistress for both their medicinal utility and their cooking delectableness – to infiltrate every corner of every room, and in their garden, unlike at the church meeting house, the children were allowed to play with each other and with Anne's brood, which numbered so many she sometimes couldn't remember all their names.

And there was always the aroma of freshly baked bread in the air for, as the good lady loved to contend, "fresh bread has the smell of good Scripture."

Priscilla certainly liked her bread and butter, but she relished more the opportunity to do Mistress Hutchinson's bidding and often volunteered to inform other like-minded women of Boston about the upcoming meetings.

Hopestill's love usually stayed the length of these exceedingly popular afternoon pastimes, during which Priscilla gained a new friend, one of Anne's closest confidants, the bright star of the women's group, Mary Dyer, another extremely opinionated young lady much enamored of Mistress Hutchinson's ways.

Mary, whose fair complexion, summery red hair and good looks were often remarked upon (and sometimes not in a friendly way by those of a jealous nature), was the wife of a London milliner. She, too, was a dedicated adherent of the Rev. John Cotton, and was considered the gayest companion of the younger women in the set, which now included among its intimates the enchanted-to-be-among-them Priscilla.

Priscilla's infatuations with her older peers had all seemed innocuous enough until that day late in mid-summer of 1635 when a stranger arrived, fanning himself with his thin-brimmed black hat.

It had been business as usual in the Sandyman yard when this scruffy Puritan sauntered through their sorry excuse of a gate, announcing himself as from the southern colony of Plymouth, on his way to Boston from Roxbury. Unpleasant as his appearance might be, for his part the man looked none too happy at being so near the untidy, odiferous soapboiling operation.

Apologizing for the stink, Henry said, "It is rather strong today, I fear."

The stranger bowed his head slightly. "The fragrance of hell is far worse, I assure you. I am the Rev. John Raynor, pastor of Plymouth Church."

"Obliged," Henry said, extending a hand to the wickedly thin stick of a man before him and receiving in return the long, bony fingers that might have been snatched from a cadaver.

After accepting a dipper of fresh water and refusing any other refreshment, the visitor let on he was seeking to discern the truth about "tales" of Satan's influence increasing within the heart of the colony "through the conniving" of certain women in Boston.

In particular, Raynor wanted to know if the Sandymans had anything to say about "that clever Hutchinson woman" who, "being one of those women," a point the man stated very strongly, was in danger of being denounced for spreading false doctrine and sowing mistrust among the clergy.

Uncommonly bold and insinuating in his approach, Pastor Raynor told Henry, as Hopestill purposely labored over a leather repair behind him in order to be ignored, that it was only a matter of time before an "evil tide" washed over New England and "carried God away" from the plantations of Christ that had sprouted up on the New World's shores.

"Satan will enter, invited you may be sure, by some who are among us even now," he insisted, watching Master Sandyman closely to ensure Henry's complete attention (Raynor disregarded Eunice's presence). "After all, where will Devil show most malice, but where he is hated, and hated most?"

In Raynor's view there was no worse act than the willful sundering of faith toward the church leadership, even, as he slyly allowed, "if perpetrated through innocent wiles or well-meaning participation."

His prominent cheekbones flushed to their peaks with a purplish blush and his nostrils flared in a most peculiar way as his agitation grew.

"Plans and practices that only devils would approve are as the same as those carried out by the Unholy himself," Raynor ranted. "And then, with Devil's black arts and blasted curate's skirt, the saints will be swept into the low kingdom from where their screams will be as to the delight of the demons of that order."

Satisfied, the lean pastor abruptly stopped his scolding to shoot a hard look at Hopestill, still bent to his harness and suddenly stitching ever more industriously, before casting an eye at Eunice to see if the sole female present dared disagree.

He appeared tempted to say more, but good Christian as he was he refused to give in to the impulse, instead snorting in disgust at the looks of these likely sinners. He rudely took his leave and departed, with both Sandymans mumbling their thanks for his advice, a courtesy the pastor ungraciously failed to acknowledge before turning his back.

Hopestill watched the man saunter away down the road to the peninsula, but it was Henry's face that most concerned him.

The gentle-mannered Henry, whose religious zeal stopped at keeping himself awake and alert during Sunday sermon, appeared stunned by the visitor's pronouncements. In fact, long after the Plymouth pastor left the yard, Hopestill's master quivered like a rabbit marked by a wolf.

Eunice, too, had been equally affected. Watching Raynor until he disappeared, she stood wordlessly alongside her husband, rubbing her thick, sweaty hands as if to screw them off her wrists.

As it happened, it was later discovered their visitor had been engaged in doing some spying on behalf of the absent Minister Wilson.

Chapter Five

Act of God

IT WAS CLEAR FROM WHAT Hopestill had heard that some manner of scandal at best or a case of criminality at worst was being fomented against the vivacious lady who had befriended Priscilla and so many others in Boston.

The boy, weak-minded though he was, felt it was important to speak to his beloved about this matter the next time he saw her, which was later that afternoon, before the family supped.

Priscilla, as was the case increasingly then, had been off visiting the Hutchinsons, this time helping to pick wild garlic flowers and sage stems. Her thick, soft hands smelled pleasantly of both when they met.

"Why, Hopestill!" she told him after he confided his fears to her about Raynor's remarks. "I'll have you know there isn't anything profane about Mistress Hutchinson. She couldn't be no more devoted to our Lord than any pastor. I'd just like to see them try to do her harm! Half the goodwives of Boston would surely object."

"It's not those ladies that I worry about," was his glum reply.

The suspicions raised about the weekly women's meetings

came at a time of mounting concern within the small colony that Satan's influence was indeed expanding there.

Within weeks following Pastor Raynor's appearance, lurid gossip sprung up within the community about episodes of apostasy and opposition to God's will.

Repeating these tales with relish and righteous zeal were those who favored the strict, uncompromising preachments of senior First Church Minister John Wilson, who upon his return to the pulpit proclaimed that the power of darkness was creeping across this newly won corner of the world. His hot words, and the energy of the eager tongue-waggers who spread them, began to damper the ardor of those who had been attending the Hutchinson meetings.

Yet to give all the credit for the lowering of Anne Hutchinson's reputation to John Wilson's powers of persuasion would not be entirely accurate.

His dire sentiments seemed all the more palpable given the dark forests that surrounded Boston and its New England neighbors, densely thick woods through which an omnipresent threat posed by the mortal foes of the English, the far-off French in Canada, might materialize at any moment.

Even more disturbing in terms of end-of-the-world signs were the terrible tales of trouble with the Indians, a race that had never been much of a bother, tales whose telling now became more commonplace.

Notably, the formerly friendly Pequots were said to have turned against the white Puritans, seeking revenge for any number of crimes committed against them, the most sensational of late being the murder of one of their sachems, kidnapped by Dutch traders and treacherously returned as a ransomed corpse.

Farmers told Hopestill, when they came into Boston from

Roxbury and beyond to trade, that things had grown tense on the frontier. Killings combined with horrible mutilations and sometimes even torture had been taking place.

But it wasn't the gloom of the forests or their dangerous denizens that provided the worst blow.

A week of the warmest, most uncomfortable weather had all but shut down the soapboiling, which largely depended on the loads of ashes collected by Hopestill. While fires did continue to burn in the hearths of Boston, these blazed not in a quantity deemed sufficient, for a steady supply of lye ash was necessary to maintaining the putrid aroma of a successful mid-summer soapyard.

In such unhealthy heat, thickly laid and unstirred by any breeze, the constant stink emanating from the Sandyman operations was all but unendurable, even to its proprietors.

Fortunately, the ramshackle Sandyman home was isolated from the general population. Well-situated in Mr. Edward Colburne's fields south of the city proper along the Roxbury road, the family's rented acreage overlooked the salt marshes and farther out, the harbor. On good days, the potent funk of the burning fat and the boiling lye was carried out to seaward to mix with the other noxious taints of the overheated, overly moist city.

Yet these were not good days.

The wind that week in August of 1635 had died down almost absolutely, still as a dream suddenly. In that noiseless vacuum a man's whisper could seem like an explosion.

For the next three days running, morning and evening, apocalyptic hordes of greenbottle flies, gnats and mosquitoes tortured any who dared sit outside in hopes of catching a pleasant draft to ease the steam heat that blasted Boston.

That Sunday and again on Lecture Day, the pastors of the

churches warned of an indefinable threat approaching. Congregations were beseeched to abandon sin and even hope.

But then, amazingly, in mid-afternoon on the fourth day of the stillness, the wind picked up from the south-southeast and began to blow steadily and ever increasingly. The flies and insects were whisked away and the first day of the wind was a day of mass relief from the baking heat.

It was still hot, but the dank swirling air was such a comfort to all. However, as day turned to night, and night turned back into day, the wind, unaccountably, continued to whistle through the yards.

Henry, who rarely talked to Hopestill informally, remarked "I don't like the way things look now." Hopestill just watched the darkening sky. He half-expected to see Devil's face emerging from it.

No sign of Devil, but as each hour passed the next blast of air from seaward was stronger than the one previous.

By the time night fell, the heavy boughs of all the trees were bowing in submission to their new god, wind, only to bend ever lower by morning, which brought on a new phenomenon – eerie whirlpools of dust that rose into the air before exploding into clouds of grit. The boys were sent out regularly to scamper into the yard to fetch the loose shingles flying off the roof.

Three more consecutive days of rising winds rattled the family more than the visit of Pastor Raynor.

Such an intensifying storm was unheard of, visitors told the Sandymans when they came to trade for what little soap Henry had left to sell. No one wore a hat or bonnet on those occasions because these coverings would not stay anchored to heads.

On the fourth evening of the rising wind, the family and Hopestill ventured out onto the single low ridge that bordered the back marshes to watch the ships in the distant harbor roll and sway at their bowers. Before their eyes the sea grew choppier, then frenetic. They collectively gasped when a small vessel was whisked away from its moorings as if by an unseen hand. A lone figure jumped off the stern and was lost from sight. They all spent a most uneasy night, perhaps sensing the unusual shift of the winds before they rose the next morning.

As they assembled for the breakfast that never got served, from out of the northeast came one uninterrupted shrieking blast. Instantly, the temperature dropped. Then all hell broke loose, exactly as the ministers had predicted.

Henry ordered the family to bar the doors, going so far as to allow Hopestill to shelter inside with them, an unheard-of privilege.

The full hurricane crashed into the city with the noon hour.

By late that night, no one dared go to bed. They ate cold soup for supper – fire was forbidden after winds howling down the chimney threatened to send sparks into the walls and burn them out. Then, until it, too, went out, the family huddled by the light of a single candle and prayed.

Hours later, the storm's ferocity increased yet again.

Rain, when it arrived, came in drowning sheets, showering in through the poor remains of the roof.

The tempest of the great ocean just beyond the marshes sounded as if it was about to devour them. Priscilla couldn't stop screaming.

Finally, Henry gave up his ghost of hope.

With their house seemingly coming down around them and the waves crashing into their yard, the patriarch reluctantly gave the order to escape to the safety of higher ground. Into the slashing storm they fled.

They only had a moment to glance into the chaos.

Behind them, to their horror, the tide was lifting over the neck of road that separated the South Bay of the harbor from the Back Bay. They guarded their faces as they ran for their lives for the air was filled with debris and danger. Although they did not know it for a fact, the Shawmut itself was cut off and isolated.

Clinging to each other, with Hopestill last behind Priscilla, they struggled some miles through dark and storm before collapsing in an open bit of pasture, exhausted, completely exposed.

That morning, working in the relentless wind and rain, Henry, Hopestill and the boys were able to lash together a lean-to out of the many large branches that had been knocked down. It gave them a bit of crude shelter but, sharing what little food they had snatched away, these two bare necessities were the only succor they had. For the rest of that night, into the next day, and through most of the following night, they shivered in torment under the tyranny of the elements.

Some hours before dawn, the rain eased to a light, harmless patter, the wind died down and the tides backed off. Suddenly, it was over.

Soaked, hungry, and stupid with fatigue, they left the pasture and in a light drizzle shuffled back like near-drowned dogs through the wide puddles and flowing rivulets.

Their fears of what they would find when they returned were made worse by their apprehension that there would be no soapyard to return to. Or even a Boston.

Along their way, they met streams of neighbors who had fled the peninsula during the worst of the tempest. No one spoke.

As they approached the first settlement houses, many held hands over mouths in first sight of the tidal wave of calamity that had washed across the city.

A vision of hell awaited them first.

The unremitting day-and-a-half deluge and gale, coupled with the wall of flood tides that rose up from the boiling ocean, had disinterred the dead in Boston's graves.

Buried and all but forgotten – except by the Great Storm – the sodden and sunken earthen pudding in which these souls slept in what should have been their final resting places regurgitated the poorly made caskets full of old bones, and these the receding waters scattered about to such a degree that none could say with likely certitude whether the remains be man or woman, white or Indian.

Walking past the boneyards, the pitiless sights grew commonplace.

Sides of houses cruelly caved in. Rooves blown half-off, peeled away and falling across the other half or coming to rest a quarter-mile distant. Chairs, clothing, sheets and all manner of objects found tumbled out of homes. Corpses of friends and neighbors half-buried in the muck.

Worst off were many of those who had stayed put in the city – and lived. Those now-homeless souls were, at storm's height, forced in extremity to rope their waists around trees. Some of the dead, fastened still in their unloosened bonds, hung suspended at crazy angles.

The survivors told of watching helplessly as ships tried to run out the storm far at sea.

Some of these brave and foolish vessels made it beyond man's sight, others were plowed back into the harbor to crumple into wharves, shattering the frail structures into splinters. Weeks later, reports of survivors starving on outlying islands or dead bodies bobbing onto shore came to the general notice.

It was a terrible, terrible time.

At first, the stunned residents of Boston could make nothing of it, other than they had been soundly punished, an idea reinforced by almost all their pastors.

The coffins and bodies vomited from the earth, among them those of Eunice's late parents, were a sure sign that God had not only rejected them and their poor colony, but their dead as well.

For the Sandyman business it was an unmitigated disaster from the moment of their return.

Supplies were tipped over or lost. Important mixtures were spilled. Vats of half-rendered fats were ruined by the rain and spread congealing and disgusting on the ground. Even their existing stockpiles of soap stored in barrels had been contaminated.

Sacks of grain and flour had been wetted through. The small barrel of gunpowder Henry kept in Hopestill's shed had let in much damp.

Surprisingly, the house, which wasn't much to begin with, had survived, although many of Eunice's little fineries that she had carried from England, like her Belgian lace doilies, had been defiled by the mud beneath which they were found.

After beholding his ruin, poor Henry Sandyman was beside himself, weeping and holding on to Eunice.

For days afterwards they spread all their dry goods out in the sun in hopes of saving what they could, which wasn't much.

None escaped unscathed from this storm, but it was more than just the loss of possessions that unnerved so many in the days and weeks that followed.

They had all been witness to an act of God so terrible that it seemed as if it had been directed at them personally, to each individually, as if he or she had been singled out for some unique retribution.

Nor could they find solace in the days ahead.

The survivors discovered to their horror that harvests in the fields were blown down and nearly swept away in their entirety. The roiled seas for weeks gave up few fish. Not even small game could be seen in the woods in the aftermath and hunters had to go far afield, even into Indian territory, to come home with a little fresh meat.

With the onset of winter only months away the prospect of starvation and want loomed large.

Yet all of this they deserved, their ministers and teachers of The Word informed them.

All of this misery they had brought down upon their own heads, and there would be more of it to come.

Every Sunday, they heard the same message delivered from every pulpit, and every Sunday they struggled back to their poorly repaired, crude little houses to await the further judgment.

For on Sabbath Day, there was nothing else that could legally be done except to sit with bowed heads before their stone hearths with their Bibles in their hands and perhaps a bit of soup in the pot to reflect on the certain, greater horrors that surely lay ahead for each and every one of them.

Chapter Six

The Women's Meetings

COTTON MATHER LISTENED TO THE TALE transfixed, angered, amazed, appalled.

Before him, Hopestill Foster stared off into space, dreaming, not quite there, but there when Mather remarked, "You say your wife was not a heretic, but now we have your word she was."

Those old, sick rabbit eyes blinked shut, then reopened.

"A heretic? Priscilla? Never. A child of God she was."

The minister allowed a smile to show.

"A familiar of Anne Hutchinson is pre-judged," he said.

Hopestill, rather than argue, shrugged. What difference did it make now?

Mather stood up and stretched. They were alone again.

Throughout Hopestill's narrative, which was mostly coherent, Goodman Fain's men came and went, as did Tizzoo, passing in and out of the room on minor errands. Now they had all disappeared for the time being. Mather could hear the guards beyond the front door, talking amongst themselves outside in lowered voices.

The minister could barely contain his ecstasy. Listening to the man before him was like opening up one of the ancient volumes in his father's library and being transported back in history to the days of the Greeks or the Etruscans.

Yet he knew what was to come would be ever more dangerous to him than what he had already learned.

He said, "It seems the esteemed Rev. Wilson, God bless his memory, was right. The sins of the few had to be paid by the many through that storm and in the months and years ahead."

"Many died," answered Hopestill, listlessly.

"The wages of sin ARE death," retorted Mather, "but do proceed."

The rabbit's eyes closed again.

Many did die that terrible winter after the cruel hurricane, but spring's scent, a fecund mixture of rich loam and delicious air, lifted all their spirits.

Coinciding with spring and the breaking of the ice on the rivers came a flood tide of ships from England bringing the godsend of supplies, new faces and a return of hope.

Setting foot on dry land after their arduous voyages, all the latest arrivals from overseas dropped to their knees in prayerful thanks. Many among them, though, hesitated to go ashore at first, stunned by the raw sight of infant Boston, much of it still in ruinous disorder as it unfolded before their eyes while their vessels glided into the shattered harbor.

The newcomers were taken aback even more by the towering forests populating the distance.

Nothing they had heard back in England about the American continent prepared them for the spectacle of this fantastic vermillion fence that hemmed them in as far as they could see, and stupefaction soon replaced astonishment as they took in the immediate perplexities of their new world before setting out to find their place in it. Nevertheless, they kept coming, stepping off onto the wharves of King Street in ever-increasing numbers with their boxes, bundles, animals and families.

Within Boston and its surrounding suburbs something indefinable was also certainly in the air besides the joy of seeing new blood, and this intangible presence brought out more smiles among the older residents than had been seen in many a month.

Citizens mentioned to each other that they just felt better about things, that they could feel a bit of their oppression lifting, even though they had been laid low as much by adversity as by the increasingly hard line and grim tone set by the hard, grim men who governed the Commonwealth through the mighty Great and General Court, and who lashed them with harsh words every Sunday.

One individual in particular seemed to be at the source of this newly flowing wellspring of optimism, the Rev. John Cotton.

Hopestill was given to understand by Priscilla that the Rev. Cotton had delivered a mighty sermon about the Great Storm on the first day of spring with a message that spoke to them all not of blame and retribution, but of hope.

Not that the young servant himself had heard this great and wonderful talk by the acclaimed pastor.

As usual, except when it could not be overlooked, during services at the Newe Town chapel, Hopestill remained secluded inside the Sandyman house, or rather the caved-in remnants of the original decrepit dwelling.

There, he attended as silently as humanly possible in dark corners and out-of-the-way places the business of repairs or such other noiseless work assigned to him by Henry Sandyman. His master had even fashioned a little hidey-hole for which Hopestill was to repair with undue haste had any but Henry called out his name on a Sunday.

The servant knew that all of Priscilla's excited chatter about the Rev. Cotton was undoubtedly the result of the women's meetings his young love had resumed attending with regularity at Mistress Hutchinson's house.

Originally damped down by the fomentations of the Rev. Wilson and his lackey Pastor Raynor, these had quietly been growing in size and scope once more. And, once again, they were taking place within the damaged but still handsome Shawmut home of the Hutchinsons with its curious – and repaired – diamond-shaped windows.

Priscilla's reinvolvement with the group did not sit well at home.

The girl's parents, still unsettled by that strange pastor Raynor as well as the worrisome gossip – and, more ominously, a growing official displeasure with the women's meetings – nursed as many uneasy expectations about Priscilla's friend Anne as they did a return call by the Puritan Rev. Raynor from Plymouth.

Eunice pleaded with Henry to forbid her daughter from attending the meetings and mingling with the Hutchinsons, but Henry was most reluctant to cut ties with one of his best customers, so there things stood.

As it was, though, as if to balance things, the Sandymans' own minister, the Rev. Hooker, began to receive almost as many laudatory compliments by the Hutchison-led women's group, which soothed Eunice enough somewhat to put aside her persistent nagging.

Yet no one's light shined as luminously within the group as that of the Rev. Cotton.

In a place where no one's reputation was safe and where human corn was ground into the shape of real or imagined enemies, both internal and foreign, somehow, some way, the person of John Cotton remained above the increasingly contentious tug-of-war over his sermons.

This might have been because Cotton's messages could be read in more than one light (as the Rev. Wilson, mindful of Cotton's popularity, chose to do).

It might have been because the brilliant speaker deigned never to involve himself directly in the women's meetings, and avoided all comment on them, even though these were lavish in their praise for him.

Or it might have been that the Rev. Cotton cut a very sharp figure in the city of Boston.

With his wavy, auburn locks, neatly trimmed facial hair, stylish skull cap and a flashing smile, the minister appeared to be enjoying himself immensely since he came to America. This was unusual in that a cheerful demeanor was a rare exception after residence had been established in the New World and the brutal reality of one's continental isolation took hold.

More than a few looks were sent the reverend's way by the ladies of Boston, which he appeared not to notice. On the other hand, Hopestill did catch sight of a few of these sly glances thrown at the minister, often as it happened, since the lanky servant spent many hours lugging his grimy ash cart through the streets. Boston was not so large that most men's paths did not cross frequently.

Cotton, whenever Hopestill happened upon him, carried an open Bible. From this the pastor would read and preach aloud to himself while wandering about in the open air, often in the vicinity of the ocher-stained whipping post or near the stockade that served as a prison while the permanent one was under construction. Hopestill would smile and nod when they crossed paths but the Rev. Cotton would merely look up from the Good Book and eye him over as if looking for someone else, then grin meaninglessly and go back to reading.

Once, Hopestill had dared to speak to the famous pastor, but was received rather curtly for his trouble, after which he troubled him no more.

Dismissal, too, was Hopestill's fate when he presented himself to the other half of the ministerial equation, Mistress Sarah Cotton, one of the few who denied the soapboiler's servant the ashes of their large, impressive hearth.

The minister's wife was a tall woman with big, red, ungainly hands that the boy imagined might prove very effective in throttling Sunday dinner hens. The rest of her was mannish, with her small bosom barely touching cloth and her thin hips presenting a seemingly impossible portal through which had passed a healthy son, Seaborn, who had arrived bawling into the world aboard a Winthrop ship during the middle of an Atlantic storm.

Goodwife Cotton haughtily told the gawky servant that her household's precious cinders properly belonged to the Gerrity soap operation, run by a First Church family.

Furthermore, she informed him, she didn't like being pestered by servant boys and that his tattered, filthy clothing was "savagely unbecoming for a Christian."

Hopestill shrugged his thin shoulders and backed away from the front door she had shut in his face. Seconds later, behind him, the wooden slab reopened and she called him back. He feared to approach this stern woman a second time.

"My husband's ministry is not a source for your women's gossip," she snapped, and shut the door again in his face.

Priscilla, to whom Hopestill related his unpleasant encounter, laughed off the episode.

"Mistress Cotton doesn't speak for us from the lectern," she informed him, then patted his forearm.

"You see, Hopestill," she told her secret lover, "it wasn't Mistress Cotton who tells us it's not enough to do good works, to attend to the Sabbath, to love thy neighbor, to prepare for Christ's return. These good works are only part of what we need."

"We need a lot more ashes, too," he answered.

Priscilla always grimaced when Hopestill made such numb-skull remarks.

"We also need grace," she continued politely but insistently. "We need to attain that."

She waited patiently for his response.

Hopestill cleared his throat. "Yes," he admitted. "We need that."

"The other pastors all teach works," Priscilla went on. "It is all about doing, or not doing, but they never talk about what's inside of us, Hopestill," and here she touched her heart.

As it so happened, the core of Priscilla's lecture to Hopestill regarding who was preaching what became the epicenter of a controversy that precipitated first a debate that fall, and then a full-blown outcry through the winter of 1636 and into the early spring of '37.

According to Mistress Hutchinson's supporters, the core of the argument lay in the question of which minister was supporting "a covenant of grace" as opposed to who was advocating a mere "covenant of works."

The Hutchinsonians, of whom Priscilla was a dedicated adherent, were of the decided opinion that God's grace was not to be found within the mere "letter of the law" or the "covenant of works" that is Scripture. Nor was it to be found even in the admonitions of the Lord's pastoral representatives on Earth.

It was *already* there, grace that is, within and inside each and every person.

"Religion is not mere legalism, a legal system of religion, a thing of beggarly elements," Hopestill and the Sandymans heard the learned Hutchinson woman proclaim more than once.

"If it were, God would no longer be our friend, but merely a judge to condemn us for wandering too far afield from the rules."

Most important, Mistress Hutchinson urged in arguing for a "covenant of grace," was to have a unique and personal relationship with Christ himself.

"If we part with Christ," she warned, quoting another favored minister, the Rev. John Wheelwright, "we part with our life, for Christ is our life."

Needless to say, those other ministers standing accused (or so they saw themselves) by Mrs. Hutchinson and her supporters of promoting their supposedly selfish "covenant of works" without a corresponding nod to the element of personal grace were deeply offended.

Indeed, they felt scandalized by the debate that continued to persist in the face of official displeasure, and by the women's meetings discussions that remained a consuming topic of conversation around town.

Chief among the objections of those in the camp of ex-Gov. Winthrop and the Rev. Wilson was that to take these dissenters at their word was to consider that the individual ceased to exist –

literally, they supposed.

They argued that Christians who adopted this view, who claimed they had Christ within themselves, had come to think of themselves as the "Holy Ghost himself." Such a cataclysmic error of faith could not stand, they swore. The dreaded word "heresy" began to be whispered, then shouted.

Residents took sides as to who was right. So many arguments were heard about grace and covenants that sometimes purchasers on either side of the issue who arrived at Sandyman's to fill their soap containers had to be restrained from breaking their clay vessels over the other's skulls.

Arriving in the soapyard, too, was the unwelcome news of the anger that other ministers had been voicing over the women's meetings.

One traveler might bring the word that "Mistress Hutchinson's temerity is going to cost her, mark me now!"

Another would tell of the bad blood between the present governor, the young and inexperienced Sir Henry Vane, a Hutchinson supporter, and the former governor, John Winthrop, a wealthy, crafty, and mean-spirited man who led the Hutchinson opposition, even though he was virtually a next-door neighbor to the women's leader.

Still another might warn that "Devil has his very hand in it," stirring the pot.

Devil seemed to have had a hand in hurting Henry's business prospects, too, or so it seemed.

Inasmuch as the Sandymans lived rather far out along the Roxbury road, Puritans traveling into or out of the Shawmut peninsula to head into Boston proper or leave it from the south usually passed by the soapworks.

Sadly, this didn't increase business as much as Henry would have liked since cash money was still very scarce, and most travelers had precious little. So they bartered, and as a result, Sandyman's yard began filling up with all manner of people's junk-in-trade.

In piles lumped up in varying sizes were pots with holes in them, a broken ox yoke, capes with the lining torn out and rat droppings ground into them, and barrels with gaps and rusted cleats. There were belts with tongues and no buckles or tongueless buckles attached to half a belt. Bricks, when they had them, were to be found broken. Here and there were shapeless hats that looked as if a coyote had gnawed at them, and the odd book or two with covers made out of dried codskin, although these last were in demand for the few paper pages they held, good for starting fires or wiping at the privy since they could be washed and reused many a time.

It was one of Hopestill's jobs to sort through the garbage that Eunice allowed Henry to take in trade and then to refurbish it so that it was mostly serviceable.

The happy part of such labor was that the boy was able to assemble a fairly complete kit for himself out of the leftovers, rags and scraps of cloth and metal, including a dandy dagger made out of a long piece of iron hoop.

Sometimes Priscilla joined the servant when he took his accustomed seat on a homemade chair that he had fashioned with his awl and ax.

While Hopestill bent over some piece of material balanced on his leather apron and worked his magic with needle and sinew, they would talk about what they wanted to do with their lives, and how they hoped to have a place of their own when they could openly declare their affections, a conversation that never failed to end in long, meaningful glances into each other's eyes.

Henry, of course, as Priscilla's father and the boy's master, had every right to beat Hopestill brainless over his servant's attentions to his daughter, but Henry was not that kind of man.

He was adrift in debt by this time, with no means of returning to England and a lifetime ahead of him in this Puritan wilderness.

Besides, any meanness that may have existed in some far corner of his being, and there wasn't much to begin with, had picked up and wandered away somewhere. Mostly Henry just ambled about with his hands playing with each other behind his back as he watched the boys work.

Eunice was more hard-scrabble about things. Although she tolerated Hopestill as a person, she frowned on Priscilla's fondness for the fool. It worried her that the only boy she appeared to be interested in was the too-thin servant they had chosen from Mr. Mosby back in Exeter.

Yet it proved to all be an idyll.

One spring evening, Priscilla's happy demeanor left her, and without account, her health deteriorated at a rapid pace.

Within a matter of weeks the girl, who normally would eat off other people's plates and raid the buttery when no one was looking, had all but lost her appetite. This was an almost unheard-of condition for Henry and Eunice's hefty daughter, although it had to be admitted that the more weight Priscilla lost the prettier she looked.

As additional weeks sped by the girl could keep little down. She had also been of late disdaining away any and all offers of assistance, and refusing to listen to entreaties of concern. Even Hopestill's frequent expressions of kindness were met with stony silence, a turn of events that left him darkly subdued.

Priscilla finally asked to be taken to see Anne Hutchinson.

On a fine afternoon, with a fair wind blowing out to sea, Eunice escorted the girl to Boston proper. Eunice went with great reluctance, as her daughter's mentor was at that time under a great cloud of suspicion among the clergy, and that a trial for heresy loomed.

Mistress Anne listened politely as Eunice took pains to allow, to inquiries about her daughter's pale complexion, that everything was normal and that Priscilla's unsteadiness in her mother's arm was the result of a touch of moon fever, certainly nothing more serious.

Anne asked if Priscilla and she might have a few moments alone.

"Aye," said Eunice, relieved. She went into the garden.

It was Eunice's habit, on the rare occasion when she happened to be present at the Hutchinson home, to pretend to admire the view from each corner of the oblong, handsome property. She had to admit to herself, deep down, that things looked in a better sight when seen from this rich woman's property than from her own.

It was while she was so engaged in self-delusion that Mistress Hutchinson's daughter Katharine, a fair-haired beauty with sky-blue eyes, ran to inform Mrs. Sandyman that Priscilla had collapsed but was resting comfortably within the parlor and to please hurry.

Chapter Seven

A Blow is Struck

ON THE MORNING FOLLOWING Priscilla's collapse, the family was bereft of answers. They could discern no plausible explanation for such a demonic attack on a healthy young girl.

An overwrought Eunice had insisted upon Priscilla's leaving the Hutchinson house directly after. Rudely brushing away Anne's helping hand, the mother bullied her dazed and weakened daughter to her feet and hustled her down the Roxbury road a little more than an hour after her swoon.

That same unpleasant afternoon, Henry and Eunice stood nose-to-nose in the southeast corner of their long, mushy yard where the endless cords of split hardwood were stacked to cure. The parents maneuvered around each other during their argument like enemy frigates seeking the weather gage.

Watching from afar was a hopelessly muddled Hopestill who, while unable to discern the words, correctly estimated the emotional scale of it to be considerable.

He knew he had done wrong by Priscilla and was certain he was the cause of her suffering, a guilt that weighed on him as heavily as a smuggled chest of ill-begotten goods. But lacking the means to repair the damage or the wits to ascertain whether that was even in his power, the boy preferred to bank his faith in the hope that maybe, perhaps, this had nothing whatsoever to do with him at all.

Priscilla's parents walked the length of the firewood stack, a considerable avenue of drying wood, and changed positions only to walk it again. Hopestill dared to steal only sidelong glances at the confabulation while stirring a burbling tub of yellow ox fat with a flat board as long as an oar. When next he spied, Eunice was blundering away, windmilling her mottled arms and shrieking more to herself than to Henry. Such an open break between these two ordinarily docile individuals was an extraordinary occurrence and it discomfited Hopestill more than he understood.

What transpired next was Henry's calling for young Samuel to dash up the Shawmut with a message (with the sharpest admonition to say nothing to anyone) and to beg Anne Hutchinson's pardon. Samuel returned with a short note promising aid and reassurance on the morrow, toward evening.

The good lady arrived just before their meal of garlic and onion stew was ready for their bowls, but Anne begged to decline to sup with them in order to tend to Priscilla.

Henry, the boys and Hopestill watched as she visited with the girl, who had now taken to bed, refusing to get up even to tend to her necessaries. When the two women touched hands, Eunice left the room with a sour look and went outside.

Anne labored for some hours, with Henry on call to fetch this and that to make the girl comfortable, but there was only so much she could accomplish with a case that, she maintained, presented so few familiar symptoms. The day waned and night came on and Anne announced she wished to return home. She looked tired and more than a little discouraged. As the lady tied her cloak, she strongly counseled Henry to speak little of this to anyone for the present. He promised to comply and bid Landon and Samuel to accompany Anne back to her home on the peninsula.

In the days following, Anne brought living gifts from her garden, the green kind, and little by little, the rough-hewn box that lay beside Priscilla's bed was filled with a variety of fragrant, some quite pungent, herbs and unguents. The stricken girl would run her hand over these and savor the scent but was otherwise unmoved.

Try as Anne might to get Eunice involved in the caring process, after that anxious first night Eunice remained mostly a stranger at her daughter's bedside. The mother could not sit for long periods by her ailing Priscilla, nor did she go out of her way to pamper her child.

Henry could not get his wife to talk about her fears and he was reduced to shaking his head at Eunice's inward turn. Once he muttered "she knows more than she tells" after leaving her side but declined to press her. It seemed to him to do so might uncover some horrible fact.

Whenever Mistress Hutchinson called in the weeks to come, the mother withdrew into herself. Rather than engage her visitor, Eunice would walk a tight circle around the hearth while waiting for the ubiquitous kettle of water to boil. This Anne used to dab a pleasant fragrance, smelling faintly of lemon and thyme, onto Priscilla's chest and throat with a hot, wet cloth.

After the water was poured into the bowl by the bedside, Eunice would move outside and walk to the marsh grass at the far end of the lot. Through one of the large cracks that had opened in the east wall, Henry would watch her in silence. To Hopestill, who was now burdened with a lion's share of the work, the wife cut a tragic figure, seeming to ponder the random cries of the seafowl that echoed from the bay yet reacting to them with a disquieting emptiness.

Anne, often accompanied by pretty Mary Dyer from the women's meetings, attended the girl as often as she could. When she could not, their substitute visitor was a strange creation named Jane Hawkins, a midwife said to be skilled in the healing arts who had arrived some years before from St. Ives under curious circumstances tainted by a suspicious past.

The midwife's husband, Richard Hawkins, an itinerant fisherman and fish-monger with tattooed hands and a smile that uncomfortably suggested a sneer, was held in equal ill-repute by many in Boston, with the couple suspected of being free-thinkers or, worse, familists belonging to an alleged free love cult.

Naturally, Eunice would have nothing to do with this new face in the house, going so far as to complain to Henry (and anyone else, including Hopestill, who was within earshot) that she "sniffed a whiff of the witch" in the woman.

Goody Hawkins ignored the mother's shunning.

When Midwife spoke, which is to say *if* she spoke, which was rare, it was to denigrate a full range of departed church elders, although she often made an allowance for the late Deacon Samuel Fuller, whom she praised as "a learned man rather than a purloiner of souls." This endeared her somewhat to Henry, who remembered the old man's noxious boluses, some of which even answered for his bouts with the flux.

Yet Deacon Fuller had been mighty fond of the practice of venesection, and this, too, was advanced by Henry, who wished to see Priscilla bled until white, not out of any malice but because it was a medical strategy he claimed worked for his grandfather.

Midwife would have none of it.

"You want her alive not dead, I fancy?" asked Goody Hawkins

in a tone bordering on the malicious, and Henry quietly backed off his suggestion.

In the period that followed, Hopestill, when he dared to venture inside during the ongoing crisis, would limit his physical presence to a corner of the sprawling single-room Sandyman dwelling. He often found himself shaking, for as frightened as he was for his love, coward that he was, he was more frightened for himself.

Yet long before, she had withdrawn even from him.

He had had no intimation that Priscilla had been seriously ill in those weeks before her collapse, taking her "strangenesses," as he called them, for one of the usual bouts of illness or depression, both mild and moderate, that all of them suffered through a good part of each season.

With her collapse, though, it was clear to even one as slow of mind as Hopestill that this case was quite different, and that Priscilla's sudden change of personality was the manifestation of a baneful ailment.

The girl, weakened by her refusal to eat or drink much except when the throat-scratch of thirst was upon her, would mostly groan and moan while awake. Only the sight of her friends, Mistresses Hutchinson and Dyer, brought her some little cheer.

At Anne's urging, Priscilla would reluctantly rise up from her sickbed to stand unsteadily on bare feet. Anne would then shuffle her around the room while the rest of them watched. That was all they did – watch. When Mistress Hutchinson took one of Priscilla's hands in hers, and Mistress Dyer took the other and the three prayed, bowed to nearly touching the large Bible that Anne held in her lap, the family participating behind them mouthed the words but added slight enthusiasm.

They were all sick with fear. A deep foreboding kept them from attending with full devotion their daily tasks, or getting out much into the community except on Sabbath Day.

It was true that a suggestion of a new plague or unknown affliction in their midst might well leave them open to ostracism or scorn, since it was known that God visited sinners with signs of his displeasure. Should the family become so marked, it could mean Henry's business would dry up, or worse, their expulsion from the colony.

Even so, that was not their chief unspoken fear.

Priscilla's unnamed illness represented a possibility of something worse than even disease, a scandal whose roots might reach down who knows how deep and change the very substance of their existence on this earth, which was Boston and all they knew. Whatever Mistress Hutchinson thought, whatever Eunice feared, whatever Goody Hawkins suspected, all this was left unsaid.

So the pattern of clandestine visits went on for more months with little variation, although, after noting Priscilla's absence from Sunday meeting for several weeks running, the Rev. Hooker finally paid his duty call to the Sandymans as summer at last turned to fall.

Hooker was at the time in his early 50s, a robust fellow with a kindly, intelligent face and a longish, white beard that puffed out like dog's fur across his chest. The minister wore the small, round black skullcap that was a visible sign of his ordination.

It was said of Hooker that he was dismayed with the Massachusetts colony's intermingling of government and religion, and that he was even now casting about for the means of removing himself and his flock from Boston, but such things were only whispered about and not a subject of open conversation. Certainly, Minister Hooker did not himself make reference to such things.

Henry and Eunice held him in uncommon esteem, however,

they blenched at their pastor's appearance when he showed up in their yard one early morning. Nervously, Eunice offered him a biscuit and hot water with lemon, which he quaffed with good humor as both of Priscilla's parents strove to put the great man at ease about the uncertain nature of their daughter's affliction.

In he came to the girl's side, rather hesitantly. Yet there was no concealing the creases of concern in his wide brow at viewing Priscilla in such an obviously unhealthy state that mimicked no easily understood disorder. He put the heavy mug down untasted and gazed at her for a long while.

Finally, he said, breaking his silence, "I will ask for God's intercession on your behalf, Priscilla."

His concession might have lifted another, but the girl for her part could hardly bear to look at her minister, and would shift so as to face the wall when he voiced a few perfunctory pleasantries. Her fleshy hand gripped the faded quilts that covered her as if she believed they might be snatched away.

Rev. Hooker chose to ignore these outward signs of rejection. He prayed over Priscilla, and then comforted the family as best he could with some parsimonious words that he parted with as reluctantly as coins. He left rather sooner than they would have expected, but given his long walk back to Newe Town his eager departure was perfectly understandable, especially as he said he had business to attend to at home. He politely but firmly took his leave after a slice of wine cake and a glass of warmed ale were offered and tasted.

Weeks passed. The skies now darkened earlier as November's days dwindled down to a mere few and dissolved into early December. Priscilla's pallor whitened into a frightening mask. A terrible tension gripped the family.

On a late and cold afternoon Hopestill was in the yard cleaning himself off after the day's work. He always saved a little hot water from the smaller copper kettle and, of course, enough soap could always be gotten out of an empty pail to scrub down.

He washed with a will as the weather of late had turned bitterly cold, with blasts of frost and freezing rain. An unheralded snowstorm the previous week had put a white coat on everything. Then, just as suddenly, the storms and cold abated, as if to draw strength in preparation for a more intense blast of the future winter's breath.

Unbeknownst to the boy bent over the kettle, Eunice had left the house and was striding toward him when she stopped, bent down and picked up a large knotted branch that lay in her path. She weighed it thoughtfully in her right hand. With a stern, set face, she came up behind the lathered servant, lifted the cudgel above her head, and brought it down with all her force across the top of Hopestill's shoulder, shattering the partly rotted wood.

The boy screamed from the pain of the blow and dropped to the ground on his knees. Eunice looked frantically around for another solid implement with which to bludgeon the lad. Unable to see anything of immediate utility, she gazed stupidly at the broken hilt of stick she was still holding.

She screeched at him, crushing her hands to both ears so she couldn't hear her own words.

"Fornicator!"

"Bastard!"

Henry and the boys spilled from the doorway to stare, with Henry having the sense to run to his wife and restrain her. Hopestill lay where he fell, his right arm bursting with agony, already beginning to purple up at the point where he had been struck. His dull wits could not comprehend the meaning of the attack.

He crabbed away in the dirt as Eunice tried to break away from her husband to get at him again. Landon, his wild red hair flying, pulled Hopestill up by his wet, tangled, yellow locks and wordlessly took a swing at him, knocking him down again.

Henry called forcefully to his son. "Enough." Landon returned to his mother's side. Samuel stood at her left. She had slumped in their arms and her face was wet with cold sweat. The boys turned her around and led her back to the house.

Now it was Henry who faced Hopestill. He had cut his ear shaving when he heard Eunice scream and his shirt was spotted with drips of bright blood. Absurdly, a chicken feather was sticking to his neck.

"The girl is going to bear a child, as you know," he said to the boy in a grim, unvaried tone.

Hopestill frequently misunderstood what people were getting on about while they were talking to him, but there was no mistaking that something had changed Henry, aged him, altered his internal fabric into a new kind of cloth, so to speak, in just a matter of minutes.

Having never quite feared Henry before, certainly not anything like the cold dread he held for one of his father Faraday's like moods, Hopestill fancied he might be murdered right where he stood. His bare toes squished in the rabbit's kidney that had dropped out of the skin Landon brought home yesterday. He jumped away from it.

"Why, sir! Mr. Henry, sir! You can't say that, sir! We … we … were … never …"

It was all of the lie he could force out of his mouth, unable in his insipid panic to so much as think of the proper word for the thing he wanted to assert he was innocent of. And he stated it with such earnestness and conviction in his guileless face – now pale as fresh snow – that Priscilla's father almost believed him.

Then Henry hardened again, his ordinarily serene face darkening with both the effort to control his emotions and the raging questions that still raced through his mind.

"Stay in the shack," he said, brushing his hand at the little shed where Hopestill slept on a strawpile covered with a sailcloth. Without another word or look, Henry turned back to Eunice being led into the house.

Chapter Eight

Spawn

HOPESTILL'S REMAINING DAYS with the Sandymans were unhappy ones.

Cold as it was, the boy was allowed out of his little shelter only to do his chores at a distance from the house. No one spoke to him again in a friendly manner. He was disallowed from the moment the blow was struck to address any of the family, especially Eunice. Furthermore, Henry told him, if the boy breathed a single word about matters at home to anyone, "I will have the back off you, lad, for the sure of it."

Those were harsh words from Henry, who had been as mild a master as any servant could have wished – even a cuffing was a rarity. But along with his warning the master brought a bowl of hot corn soup for Hopestill to sup, and from then on he continued to bring out the boy's meals, and these were served out in good measure almost as if the boy was still part of the family.

Alone in this new world, the servant naturally feared for his daily bread and the modest roof over his head.

Hopestill at times felt as doomed as when he was back in the clutches of his father Faraday's gang, given all the bad will exhibited him. Even so, the boy's personal concern for his own well-being was overshadowed by his dread for the fate of Priscilla, with whom he was not, at his peril as he was warned, allowed to so much as gaze upon. The ban was meaningless – Priscilla wouldn't see him or speak to him. The few times he managed to sneak inside she had averted her eyes from his face and remained like a stone until he left.

After the blow, there things sat for four long days, short as they were in early December. A thaw had stilled the winds, turned the snow to slush and the ground to mud. The thin ice that had formed here and there began to crack apart.

Hopestill nursed his wounded shoulder by himself, enduring the throbbing pain with an inner stoicism bolstered by a sort of dumb confusion and disbelief in the miserable circumstances that wound about him like an angry snake.

He was not so stupid that he did not accept the blame that was due him, blame that obliterated any resentment he might have felt. But his hopes that through acceptance of his guilt Priscilla might somehow endure her nightmare with less pain was, alas, delusion.

On the fourth night, he slept through the arrival of Anne Hutchinson and her intimate friend and close companion Mary Dyer, who were accompanied by the midwife Goody Hawkins. The trio of women hustled onto the property by the dim glow of the stars and what was left of the moon, their long shawls sweeping across the yard like witch's shadows.

The women must have been fetched by Landon, he later reckoned, and must have sneaked past him earlier, which was no great trick really, as Hopestill at that time in his young life, before he lived among the Pennacooks, turned in after supper and was a heavy sleeper given to loud snoring. Moreover, Landon could be quiet as an Indian, and swift as a marten.

After their arrival, Priscilla began screaming.

Hopestill was already awake. He was folded tightly into a fetal ball, heart pounding insanely, his back pressed against the sharp corners of his shed, cowering like a child who fears a goblin is in his room.

In those minutes before he heard Priscilla's terrible cries, an unnatural presentiment of his death – a dream of himself half-buried in the cold dirt of an open grave – had disturbed his slumber and caused his eyes to flutter wildly in the gloom.

He woke, sweating and terrified.

Somehow, through his terror, the voices of the Boston women in the Sandyman house, conferring amongst themselves in low, frightened whispers, too low to be heard distinctly, reached his ears.

Hopestill shook the fearful vision from his mind.

He crept on his knees from beneath the rough canvas that served as his night cover and peeked out from the narrow opening of his coffin-like abode.

It had been a cold, clear night, but still he had slept with his heaviest jacket under his head rather than around him. Now he pulled it on as he leaned out and sniffed the cold, cutting air.

It was then Priscilla shrieked anew. Now came a second cry and then a third and then there followed little whimpering moans. Hopestill listened intently as the women soothed her, but he was petrified for the girl.

It was her time now. Or had he slept through it?

In another corner of the yard he could just make out Samuel grabbing logs and branches for the fire. He swiveled his head. The door to the main house was open and a rectangle of flickering light filled with black images poured out onto the yard.

Eunice, he could see from the backlit penumbra of her form, was holding her head in both hands and rocking to and fro by the table board.

He crawled out a little bit so he could see inside. Next to the mother on the floor lay a bundle of what looked like old rags.

Hopestill crept nearer to the long, low house. This was a clear violation of the rules that Mr. Henry had laid down the day the boy was accused by Eunice, but his renewed apprehension for Priscilla finally obliterated his own fears.

Silently, he worked his way over to roughly where he knew the girl to be.

There was a hole covered by oiled paper cut into that side of the wall. It was to that dim yellow spot that he worked, to the voices and the moans.

As he rose up for a better look, a strong hand clamped his injured shoulder. The squeeze was aggressive enough to make him wince.

Hopestill jumped within himself and came face-to-face with Henry in the darkness.

"Come away with me now, boy," Henry ordered. His tone of voice left no room for the slightest protest.

The older man marched Hopestill to the very boundary of the soapworks, far from the house, stepping around the snow-topped piles of junk and lumber they had been collecting over the years.

The moon was low in the sky, in its last quarter, an orange fingernail hanging lopsided like a wounded grin. Henry led Hopestill farther, and then farther yet again from the house, saying nothing but continuing to seize the boy by his painful shoulder.

They had walked very close to the road. Within minutes,

Landon hurried up to his father's side.

The red-haired boy handed Henry the rolled-up sail canvas that had covered Hopestill less than an hour before. Landon informed his father in a voice as chilled as the night air that it contained the servant's clothes and all his other belongings from the shack.

Hopestill didn't much care what was in the roll that Henry held out to him – there was not much of value to account for, as Hopestill had managed to save very little and had acquired even less. He depended on the Sandymans for everything, and for what little extras or comforts he received, it was Priscilla who provided them.

"A terrible thing has happened tonight, Hopestill," Henry quietly told him, the father's voice in the man breaking.

"Priscilla!" Hopestill blurted out miserably. He was brought up short by the hard grip that clamped on. He asked, "Is she going to die?"

Hopestill understood so little of pregnancies or childbirth that he conceived of the state as a sort of illness, an illness for which death was a distinct possibility.

With a sharp word, Henry sent Landon away into the night and the eldest son disappeared. Whatever they had arranged had all been discussed previously, and even to Hopestill it became obvious that a plan had been formed, a plan of which he was the unwitting object – a plan in which he was to have no say.

"Look ye," Henry finally spoke. "Priscilla has delivered, as ye might have expected. Come. You are not so dimwitted as all that, are you now?"

"Many die in that state, sir. I have seen it with my own eyes."

"Would it were so, and I say that as one who is cursed. For my dear daughter states you are the father ..."

"Not I, Mr. Henry!" Hopestill exclaimed in alarm and wounded innocence without realizing he was harming Priscilla further. "Not I! You must believe me."

Henry didn't answer the lie, and again they walked on a fair piece before stopping. Henry handed Hopestill the sailcloth bedroll and once more they stopped.

"Listen to me. The babe was born a monster. It came out stillborn, which means it was dead e'er it left the mother's womb."

Hopestill went sick to the pit of his stomach. He doubled over as to empty his gut but nothing came forth except a dribble of the bitterest bile.

Henry could now barely speak his words.

"'Twas the most devilish thing ever entered my eyes, Hopestill. Flaps of skin, leathern skin, not hands, but like a turtle. No head, but a face, a face, mind you, on its chest, seeming, like! And its brain, its poor brain ... Midwife warned us it would be bad, but we had no idea."

He paused, then continued thoughtfully, "It is the end of us here. They would account us all as sinners or worse, witches."

Henry's voice trailed off, trying to make sense of things, perhaps to an invisible other with more understanding. However, it was only he and Hopestill standing there.

"I've arranged for you to go off ..." Henry began again.

"To go off?" Hopestill sickened inside. "To go off? Where would I go, sir? I have no one. I have nothing."

Without shame, he sank to his knees before his master.

"Please sir. Please. I have never begged of you. I have done all you could ask. Don't send me away. Don't send me away."

They were in the semi-darkness, well across the open field by now, not down the Roxbury road but across it to the northeast, to where the big and broad Back Bay opened up behind the peninsula. Sheets of broken white ice, motionless, shined their reflected light back at the thin moon.

Hopestill knelt his forehead into his bedroll, now half-buried in the freezing muck of the marshland.

"We are leaving, too, boy. As soon as we can. Pastor Hooker cannot abide the tight grip of the Puritan church here. He says he feels it like a hand around his throat. He has guessed at our troubles and has asked us to go south, far south to a new colony into which our church will pass before long. We will be among the first there. God only knows what will become of us."

Henry lent a hand, pulling Hopestill up. He bent over, plucked up the bedroll from the mud and placed it under the arm beneath the boy's good shoulder.

The sad, lonely, bereft pair stepped off into the marshy silt of Back Bay, a vast, low-lying area surrounded by the fens. Its navigation required the most careful touch to move among its shallow channels even in fair weather.

Henry cleared his throat. "I've made it for you to go off with Goodman Hawkins in his shallop, which will rendezvous with us." Henry pointed to an inlet. "You must go with him and remain where he takes you, which I fear is a long, long ways from Boston. You will need what little wits you have about you to survive in that wilderness."

Taking a crackling paper from his coat and handing it to Hopestill, Henry went on. "I'm giving you your liberty. That and a few shillings are all I can do for you, boy. We can never meet again and you must never search for us, otherwise I'm afraid it will come to great grief for all of us and especially for poor Priscilla."

Sandyman called out in a long drawl, "Hawk … ins!" His breath steamed in the air.

"Aloooooo!" came the answer from a distance, followed by a distinct sound of splashing.

Hopestill clutched at his master's coat sleeve.

"Oh, Mr. Sandyman, don't send me away. I beg you again." But Henry turned away to leave.

Hopestill, in a frenzy of guilt, confronted his master.

"Punish me!" He held out his right arm. "Chop it off with your ax. I am ashamed. I will never sin again! I swear to you, sir!"

"I will not take your arm, Hopestill, since I want no part of you." He looked hard into the boy's eyes and told him, "Part we must, and forever."

Out of the night gloom rose a burly man, reeking of salt water and dried fish.

Henry went to greet this presence, whom Hopestill took correctly as Hawkins, the midwife's husband.

The men clasped hands and, their eyes now well-accustomed to the dark, turned to look at the tall, thin boy, who felt his life slipping away. He had no one to look after him from here on.

"Come," said Hawkins. "We have gotten a break with this spate of fair winter weather. Now we must make tide and get around Fort Hill afore the moon rises to its height. Mind you don't stand in the muck too long or you'll lose your boots."

"But I have no boots on, sir," replied Hopestill. His feet were almost frozen.

"Take mine," said Henry, removing his. "I have others that you made for me. Now I go."

The older Sandyman turned away and went back up the path toward the road without another word. Soon he was lost to sight.

Hawkins's hand found Hopestill's shirt.

"Haste now," he urged the boy, pulling.

Hopestill had other ideas. He wrested his shirt away from Hawkins and ran off in pursuit of his master, boots in hand. He simply could not accept the gift of Mr. Sandyman's boots.

"Boy!" Hawkins hissed at him from behind.

However, Hopestill only went a short distance before something stopped him in his tracks. He listened. He heard voices. Distinct voices. One was Henry's.

His former master, dimly made out as a silhouette in the dirt-black night, was talking to another man, whom Hopestill could not immediately recognize.

It was most certainly not Landon, but an adult, a larger presence with a most distinctive way of speaking, in some ways very distinctive. Could it be? The Rev. Cotton?

Some deep-rooted doubt warned Hopestill against drawing any closer.

His ears strained to catch the drift of the conversation at the edge of the field that led to the soapworks. He sensed what was being said was vital, of the utmost importance, but the words spoken by the man with whom Henry was meeting mostly did not signify, excepting a few.

"Consecrated ground," he heard.

"Cursed" chilled his soul.

"Hopeless … failing" was another snatch of words he caught.

At the words "Devil's spawn," Hopestill winced in visible pain, tears forming.

He turned and without looking back rushed through the slimy weeds and whipping marsh grass and splashed up to the small neat craft eager to pull away. Hawkins hauled him in by his coat, along with the boots and bedroll.

Noiselessly, with barely a creak of the push-pole against the gunwales, the little ship slipped into the bay and was pulled along by the ebbing tide.

Chapter Nine

A Gift of Venison

MATHER SAID TO NO ONE in particular, "Ach. He's gone out again." He put aside his writing tray and stood up over the old man, who had suddenly dropped off yet sat straight in the settle as if awake. Curious. It was fortunate to have thought of the settle to bring in, mused the minister.

Late as the night was, Mather felt himself aglow with energy. During Hopestill's rambling recounting of his nefarious past, Goodman Fain's men from the prison detail were kept busy jumping to Mather's orders.

An hour previous, with Hopestill drooping in the small chair by the hearth where his frail figure earlier had been installed, Mather set his hired dullards hurrying to his father Increase's house at Hanover Street, just below Bennett Street, to fetch the tall settle there from the parlor.

With its solid back the settle was just the thing for Hopestill to lean against without falling over, as he seemed prone to do in Mather's former chair more than once during his oft-broken monologue.

At another point in Hopestill's narration, the minister had Fain's men race to his own house and return with his personal writing stand, inkwells and a fresh supply of quills. Mather realized he had been sadly mistaken about the wealth of information that he was now gleaning, with God's good grace, from what might well have been a dead man.

Mather had been taken aback by Hopestill's admission that this man had known Grandfather Cotton. Until he had thought it through.

Well, of course he had known the Patriarch. Who in ancient Boston did not know of the Great Man?

Yet he himself had been denied that privilege, he thought with rueful sorrow. The Lord had taken The Rev. Mr. John Cotton from this world long before he, Cotton Mather, had come into it. And this creature before him, this tool of Devil, instead had enjoyed the privilege although he had no doubt disdained it.

"Ach!" he exclaimed again, as if to spit the thought from his mind.

Watching the weak tide of life flow back into Hopestill, Mather recognized the self-pity inherent in his thoughts even as he obstinately and yes, selfishly, indulged himself. What he might have learned from his grandfather!

Abruptly, the minister grew ruthless with himself again. This is, and was, God's plan, he realized. It must not be questioned. He sat back and stared malignantly at Hopestill, who alternately mumbled and dozed.

When the men brought everything he needed, including the provisions that Mather demanded Tizzoo prepare, he shooed them outside.

He had to be careful now, with the interrogation threatening to double back so soon to the scandalous years of which he knew so little about, only surmised.

Fain and his men were dolts, but little pitchers have big ears, don't we know?

"Ensign?" he inquired politely. Hopestill's eyes were closed.

When no answer was forthcoming, Mather prodded Hopestill's bare foot gently with the toe of his shoe. The man fluttered awake. Then dropped off.

With a feeling of loathing strong enough to make his skin crawl – not from Foster's outwardly diseased state but rather from Mather's suspicion that his prisoner was an intimate of Devil – the minister disgustedly lifted one old, pock-marked arm as if it were a piece of carrion.

He felt for the beat of the heart in the artery there. Strong. The man's pallor was good. Skin dry. Good. Hopestill's closed eyelids shuddered ever so delicately. Mather returned to his seat and steepled his fingers, musing.

Where did he disappear to, this sorcerer, in his unconscious state? What was his dream?

Hopestill's dream was of himself.

The old man struggled for images of his Indian wife and children, long dead by then but alive in his heart, yet they would not come forth from his fevered memory to greet him.

So he dreamed of himself as a butter-haired man of early middle age, standing at the edge of the unfathomably dense hardwood forest, the way it was so many years before in the year of 1662, the year of the great Quaker persecutions by the Puritans.

That man who had once been Hopestill Foster stepped forth and paused. He had once witnessed a brother cut down in cold blood who emerged from a clearing without paying heed to the inevitable watchers.

The flood of woods before him emptied into a sea of rippling grassland that in turn gave way to the flowing Indian corn ground above the Cochecho near Dover in the New Hampshire grants. Into this knee-high wilderness painted with viridian and umber, the Hopestill of his past waded, moving ever closer to the absurdly small settlement at the water's edge. The clash of raging river water spilling over the stones near the little falls roared ever louder with his approach.

Slung over his back was a gutted doe stuffed with sweet grasses. With every stride the inert head of the deflated animal bobbed and slapped against the traveler's stained buckskin shirt. This was cut Indian-fashion, with long panels hanging to the man's knees that allowed him to take his ease in the woods without a second's delay since beneath he wore no small clothes. His legs were covered of a fashion very much like a soldier's spatterdashes but not of cloth – rather of deerskin, softened to velvet by the teeth of squaws and the liberal application of fresh deer brains.

No snaphaunce was in hand, nor cartridge belt over his neck for weapon and ammunition, only a fringed quiver stuffed with an assortment of ironwood arrows served notice that here was a deadly foe. He carried with one free hand a slender, supple bow with its loose gut string waving freely. Tucked in the rope of brightly colored wampum around his waist was a hickory-handled tomahawk. These were his visible arms, although if one looked closely there was a wickedly sharp poniard fashioned out of an old iron hoop strapped to the inside of one leg.

Swiftly yet with silent grace his feet hastened him along, encased in moccasins trimmed with bits of pale whelk shell distinctive to the tribe of his adopted family, although his current footwear lacked the holes in the bottoms cut into his first pair. When he was deemed to have been reborn, the stitched deerskin was pulled over his toes along with the accompaniment of a great deal of laughter by his adoptive mother Chibaiskwa, who told him that when a child as old as he is breached it is still not yet fully human and an entryway must be allowed for into which the Great Spirit can whisper His wisdom.

Watching him cross the tall grass were two men, one big-gutted with a heavy black beard and the second hard-faced and dumpy in stature, crowned with a white plantation hat and a gentleman's coat for a robe.

Without changing expression, the big man watched Hopestill come up close. He put his hands on his hips and said to white hat in a voice loud enough to be heard, "Here comes the simpleton, now, in a savage's garb. Why, it's a wonder they ain't boiled him yet."

The object of his gibe declined to be insulted, for Hopestill had come to believe it was his right to take umbrage when he chose, which was rare. He understood many whites thought of him as dull-witted – certainly poor Priscilla and her family had – and he would rather folk think of him in that way than worry about his cleverness.

White-hatted Richard Walderne, a major and magistrate in His Majesty's Bay Colony service, a man who employed him here and there, stepped into the dirt out of the shade of the doorframe to his trading house, which Hopestill could see was growing a blockhouse above the ground floor since his last visit. That brooding edifice jutted over the window below like the brow of a concerned god.

Walderne walked out with a brisk stride to greet his new arrival.

"A very pretty juniper-jumper, Foster, I must say," Walderne complimented him.

The squat, frumpy magistrate, with an ironic stare, stepped behind Hopestill. Lifting the flaccid skin of the doe's head with two fat, fussy fingers, he peered into its glazed eyes, examining them as if searching for the missing spark of life. He sniffed to judge its freshness, then exhaled noisily a second time to clear his nostrils. Dissatisfied with the attempt, he fumbled for his snuff box.

Hopestill laid down his burden outside the long, low cabin with its new blockhouse that served as the business office of Walderne, the most powerful white man in the New Hampshire province of the Massachusetts Bay Colony.

Behind it, close by at water's edge, under construction was a companion mill to its working twin on the other side of the Cochecho. Although Hopestill had been gone for weeks on his mission to treat with Chief Passaconnaway, he could see that Walderne, now elected as magistrate of Dover, was wasting no time in expanding his already impressive operations on the edge of the great northern wilderness of New Hampshire.

"This is from the Bashaba," Hopestill said. "A gift. He knows the major fancies his bit of venison."

The hulking form of Peter Coffin, Walderne's secretary and right-hand man, remained in the doorway, nearly filling its frame. A crazy bushy beard, black as lantern soot, clambered over his face, strangely unrelated to the shape of it, like a wild vine topping a stump. Coffin scratched at the growth, closely looking Hopestill Foster over with his smallish, contemptuous eyes.

"Who's come back from Pennacook?" Coffin told himself more than anyone else. "Why, it's Red White Man. Har, har, har." He spat a brownish glob out of the side of his mouth. "Fetch me over one of them arrows, Foster. I need to clean my teeth."

Hopestill refused to acknowledge the big man's presence. Instead, he addressed Walderne, who was slowly drumming his fingers on his sleeve, deliberating.

In his dream of 30 years past, Walderne's face, clean-shaven, twice actually, bare and pink, was directly in front of him, as if it really were there, alive, not butchered in some subsequent massacre. He could in his mind see the major's close-set eyes, too, braced by slanting brows, lending to an otherwise intelligent face a perpetually quizzical look. He recalled in detail that thicket of dark brown hair, handsomely swept back and amply pommaded.

Hopestill offered, "The Bashaba wanted you to know he is still thinking about your plans for the second trade-house."

"When will he decide, is your guess?" Walderne asked sharply.

"The council is divided, with much debate." Hopestill's eyes went blank after delivering the purposely noncommittal answer, the way an Indian's does when nothing is to be revealed to an enemy.

Walderne waited for him to go on, but in vain. Finally, the major cried out in exasperation.

"That picaroon! He proclaims his love for the English but keeps me at arm's length. This cannot go on indefinitely! When will that filthy old devil die, eh? I say, when?"

Hopestill looked straight ahead. He knew this wasn't a question to be answered since it had been asked with assorted shades of vexation many times by this same person.

"Major, begging your pardon." Coffin handed Walderne some sheets of brownish, rough-cut paper. "I have finished those papers you ordered for your sig' 'n' seal."

Coffin turned and leered at Hopestill. "Your Quaker friends will be none too pleased, you half-savage bastard. Those Ranters have come mighty high at it these few months."

Hopestill replied inoffensively, no more provoked than a bird,

"Quakers ain't Ranters and Ranters ain't Quakers."

"They'll not 'thou' and 'thee' when the lash whistles its tune, will they, Major?" crowed Coffin.

"I want an answer from Passaconnaway," Walderne demanded of Hopestill, pointedly ignoring both remarks. "What course do you suggest?"

He flicked his secretary away. With a heavy sigh of disgust augmented by a sour relish of muttering, the big, unkempt Coffin lumbered back inside the cabin.

It was a stunning late fall's day, as Hopestill remembered it in his disordered mind, the wind's breath capricious and light. In such pure blue skies the cloud puffs hung in place like pictures tacked up on heaven's stairwell.

He squatted down before the dead deer, drew out his dagger and idly scratched around in the dirt, thinking of the sachem Walderne was continuing to revile – Passaconnaway, the acknowledged chief of all the northern Pennacooks who remained, at perhaps 70 years old, a legendary figure among the tribes of the northeast.

But Hopestill remembered him as the man who saved his life and became his father.

Passaconnaway was a shrewd leader, a far-sight more intelligent man than the craven Walderne. Nevertheless, the major was not disrespected by the Bashaba – Walderne may have been a relative latecomer to these parts, but he was one whose industry and ambition drew much attention from the keen old man of the woods.

Hopestill looked up directly into Walderne's badger-sly face.

"I don't know what course is the rightest one, major. He don't confide in me excepting he tells me what to pass on to you and I do it. I don't take sides, and he knows it and you know it. I can tell you the old men are worried about the people getting the strong water there, like they gets in trade from the Dutch and the Frenchies."

In his dream, Hopestill shrank into himself at the memory of his intermediary dealings between Walderne and the old chief, which ultimately turned to tragic misfortune for all.

He knew Walderne was certainly not deceived by any son of Passaconnaway, red or white. He was certainly not deceived by the gift of venison.

Nor was Passaconnaway deceived by Walderne or any white man. The old chief often said he only knew what he knew, that the Indians had no hope of sweeping the men of the white race into the great sea and cleansing the land.

With a smile, Walderne told Hopestill he had a new job for him.

But first, he insulted him. He told him he believed him to be an insolent man and the tribe of the Pennacook to be an insolent people.

To demonstrate more forcibly what the rewards for insolence might be, Hopestill was to drive the cart to be used to transport three Quaker women that Walderne – as Puritan magistrate – had recently sentenced to be whipped through the colony to Boston.

Furthermore, Walderne told him, he was to wear white man's clothes again in the company of white men.

"And burn those filthy Indian rags, you disgraceful degenerate," he ordered.

Walderne twirled his fingers behind his back as he tried to count up the excessive number of lashes the women would receive, ten per village and town, but soon gave the exercise up as it bored him.

He decided it would be a good lesson in how Dover's enemies

were treated, maybe one that would get back to Passaconnaway, that old dog.

The major was, however, getting hungry.

The dead deer at his feet would go down very tasty when it was roasted to a turn on the spit.

Better get started. "Coffin!" he yelled.

"Tizzoo!" shouted Mather, a second time, his voice undercutting Hopestill's fever-dream, yet not quite.

The smell of red hot flip, broiled with a fiery poker in a tankard, tickled Hopestill's ravaged senses, but the rank smell of Goodman Fain's men, called inside the house and crowding near him to receive their share of the boiling refreshment served out by the black slave, made him want to gag.

Hopestill heard the men laughing as they swilled their drink. In his mind he also heard the noise of cartwheels churning, churning.

Then the sounds of weeping, weeping.

Chapter Ten

Walderne's Warrant

THE WIDE DUNG CART rattled like a cage as Hopestill, driving it, picked a path through his fevered imagination that followed the ruts of the old Hampton Road. Behind him, huddled together on the coarse planks of its bed, were the three miserable Quaker women, one sobbing, the other two consoling.

"You there, stop that noise," said Constable Roberts, the flogger. He spoke without much passion or conviction, since after all he had been repeating himself in much the same way since they had left the dubious comfort of Capt. Wiggin's Stratham farm that morning in 1662.

"No more of that. Bear up. Bear up."

A few lengths behind, expressionless and bored, rode two threadbare Puritan cavalry guards, assigned to accompany the cart and its prisoners to the ferry across from Newbury Port, where they might be relieved by true Massachusetts men. Their horses plopped along in the muck and accumulated manure of the years, scattering clods of the stuff behind them into the gloom of the sharp-set day.

The road, empty as the sea, at times led them through whale-sized dunes almost within sight of the great ocean, whose distant salty groans echoed those of the women slumped in the cart – Alice Ambrose, Mary Tomkins and Anne Coleman.

Nearing Hampton, the tangy rot from tidal pools and the nearby marshes, beaten down by the frosty, wet weather of late, invaded their nostrils. They were now within short reach of the town.

Constable Roberts ordered, "Foster, stop this cart," upon which Hopestill pulled back on the reins.

The mid-December wind blew across the road and ruffled the mostly denuded treetops around them. This mild fall would pass into something winter-worse from the icy feel of it, and soon.

"Get down," said the constable to the women.

The two cavalrymen rode up to the cart and signaled to the women to climb out. That these frail forms were able to obey was due to an act of small mercy. In the wagon, their hands had been shackled together but not bolted to the floor ring because the constable, driven to distraction by Hopestill's nagging, had taken pity and unlocked the clasp. But no leniency could be shown in sight of Hampton, a town renowned in the colony for its fervent Puritanism and hatred of the heretic Quakers.

The constable got out of the cart and stepped into the partly frozen road with a grimace of renewed disgust at the clawing mud that was seeping inside of his shoes.

He attached each woman's wrist irons to a long chain and locked the steel links to a hoop stapled fast into the cart's ramp gate.

The Quakers' dark cloaks hung about their ankles like forlorn curtains.

The cart continued on, lurching down the road at a slow pace, with the captives trailing behind. Soon, it passed into what was called the Ring Swamp and then into the common way. Three, then four, then six boys ran alongside gleefully shouting to all, "The Quakers have come!" More townspeople soon joined the growing procession until it reached the wide green, where it halted.

The cavalrymen dismounted and took up positions on each side of the cart. The constable herded the women, led by the tallest of them, Alice Ambrose, to their places in advance of the declaration of their guilt.

Hopestill stepped off the carriage and stretched his arms as a large fellow, the town blacksmith, approached him.

"Is Dog within?" asked Hopestill. The blacksmith looked around him to see if anyone was listening. Then the two held a hushed conversation, into which joined a barefoot lad in tattered buckskins. After its completion, the boy walked out from the back of the smithy's barn and sauntered away from the scene.

A crowd, mostly from families living nearest the commons, swelled around the little knot of travelers. There was much murmuring, but the Hamptoners mostly kept their distance from the Quaker women, fearing bewitchment.

Constable Roberts called out.

"Constable Brike!"

"'e's coming along!" shouted one of the men. In fact, several men on horseback could now be seen riding in from a narrow path that led to the green from a swampy area bordering on the westernmost strip of forest.

The lead rider, a strapping but ugly man in his late thirties, rode directly to the cart, the crowd parting for his horse. His black, plain clothing was made darker by the sweat that had clearly flowed freely that morning in spite of the cold. His huge hands were calloused and stained. His face was punctuated by old pocks scars.

"Constable," the rider said in a sullen voice, acknowledging his sour-looking counterpart from Dover.

"Constable Brike." Roberts nodded in turn to Manneasseth Brike.

"Pray read your warrant, Mr. Roberts," said Brike, having dismounted and brushed off his jacket.

The villagers were struck dumb by this official show, the prelude to judicial violence.

The constable leaned into the cart and took out the legal papers he had received from the very hands of the esteemed Richard Walderne, the Dover magistrate, Hopestill's employer. Roberts unrolled one sheet and read from it:

"Whereas there is a cursed set of heretics lately risen up in the world, which are commonly called Quakers, who take upon them to be immediately sent of God, and infallibly assisted by the Spirit …" he paused significantly, looking about to discern the level of attention from his listeners.

Pleased to note it was rapt, Constable Roberts continued on:

"… to speak and write blasphemous opinions – despising government, and the order of God in church and Commonwealth, speaking evil of dignities, reproaching and reviling magistrates and ministers, seeking to turn people from the faith, and gain proselytes to their pernicious ways – the court doth hereby order …"

Here he was forced to pause again.

The rest of it was on another parchment.

As the men and women of Hampton moved in closer to the accused women, a few daring to hiss at them, Constable Roberts carefully rolled up the first sheet and spoke the words from the second:

"To the constables of Dover, Hampton, Salisbury, Newbury, Rowley, Ipswich, Wenham, Lynn, Boston, Roxbury, Dedham, and until these vagabond Quakers are out of this jurisdiction …"

He halted dramatically to clear his voice for the big pronouncement that he knew would elicit a collective gasp of sexual excitement, awe and revulsion.

"You and every of you are required in the King's Majesty's name to take these vagabond Quakers, Anne Coleman, Mary Tomkins and Alice Ambrose, and make them fast to the cart's tail; and drawing the cart through your several towns, to whip them upon their naked backs, not exceeding ten stripes apiece on each of them, in each town; and so convey them from constable to constable till they are out of this jurisdiction, as you will answer it at your peril. Per me, Richard Walderne."

A chorus of angry voices rose at the reading of the charges. The Quaker women hugged each other and prayed with silent moving lips against the prospect of the ordeal to come.

"QUIET!" thundered Constable Brike. There was immediate silence as if a cover had been dropped on a cage.

He spread his muscular arms wide to part the crowd. The cavalrymen went among the villagers, pushing them back. At the front of the cart, Hopestill Foster was tending the horses, patting them down with rags and soothing them with words.

Brike sternly addressed Alice Ambrose, who showed the least fear and the most fire in her eyes.

He asked her boldly, without a hint of courtesy, "You own yourselves to be such as are commonly known as Quakers?"

"We are so called. We are all of one mind," she answered in a steady voice.

"You brought not over hither …" Brike pointed north to Dover, "several books wherein are contained the several opinions of the sect, or people?"

"Yea. Those were taken from us."

"Wherefore came you unto these parts?"

Unexpectedly finding strength in their reply, the three women looked each other in the eyes and answered as a group:

"To do the will of God, whatever He should make known to be His will."

The constable turned around and around in a circle, glaring at the villagers. The increasingly hostile tone of the grumbling behind him was becoming a mob's voice.

With his upturned hands, he motioned for complete silence.

He returned to the questioning.

"How do you make it appear your God called you hither?"

Alice answered for herself and the others. "I would not have come but the Lord hath brought me down to obey Him in His call."

A short man in work clothes, a coat of skins and low-buckled shoes stepped out from the encircling ring of men and women. He had just come in from his forest work.

"I would have questions for the prisoners, Manneasseth Brike."

Adorning the man's head was a little cap made out of two squirrel pelts stitched together with the twin grey heads of the little beasts joined at their cheeks. His neat black beard was trimmed to a sharp point at the very tip; it seemed to jab at his throat whenever his lower jaw opened.

He bowed slightly to Constable Roberts, who returned the honor.

"By your leave, parson," said Constable Brike. He folded his arms.

The Rev. Seaborn Cotton, eldest son of the renowned Boston minister, the late Rev. John Cotton, looked the women over and they in turn locked a gaze with him. Hopestill examined the face of this other Rev. Cotton carefully, noting within it the resemblance to the father, with the exception of the addition of a cruel mouth.

"Do ye acknowledge the existence of God and man in one person?" demanded Seaborn Cotton.

The women's hands gripped together on the chain that attached them. They answered not.

The parson's voice rose in tenor. "Do ye acknowledge one God subsisting in three persons – Father, Son and Holy Ghost?"

No answer escaped their lips.

He all but screamed at them.

"Do you acknowledge God and man in one person remain forever a distinct person from God the Father and God the Holy Ghost and from the saints, notwithstanding their union and communion with him?"

Nothing but silence from the women, who quivered in terror at the direction the inquisition was taking.

"Do you acknowledge yourselves sinners?"

Gaze met gaze.

Pastor Cotton thought a moment and tried a different tack. He lowered his tone.

"Do you acknowledge baptism with water to be an ordinance of God?"

Nothing.

"Fie!" he exclaimed, turning away and throwing up his hands.

"I have nay more to ask of these heretics."

The Quaker women cried out together in anguish and fear.

Roberts handed Constable Brike his terrible whip of three long and heavy knotted cords of dried leather, which he had already unwrapped from its cloth bag, it being customary for the resident official to carry out the punishment.

He unshackled Anne and Mary from their common chain and handed each of them off to a cavalryman. Alice remained locked to the cart chain. Brike removed her cloak.

"If you will consider, constable," suggested the Dover official hopefully to the Hampton official, "might her nakedness not be immodest inasmuch as the day still endures?"

He and Brike looked around at the many eager faces anticipating the whipping.

Brike then allowed that he was amenable to the suggestion.

Alice Ambrose was not.

"Set us free, or do according to thine order," she told him.

Her reply shocked and angered him.

"Sarie Penniman!" demanded the constable of the bird-faced, graying midwife hanging at the edge of the crowd. "Come hither and strip the clothes of this Quaker."

"It pleases me not, constable, and I would not obey, not for all that is in this world, to do this thing," the midwife replied in a firm voice.

Without further word, Midwife Penniman turned away and left them all. Hopestill watched as she hurried up the road to fetch her servant from the community smokehouse, the boy from the blacksmith's barn, swift little bushy-haired Dogged Pease, whom everyone called "Dog." He was lean as a hound, never wore shoes and was as eager to please as his namesake.

After a few words with him, during which Dog relayed to her the message he received from Hopestill via the blacksmith, she sent the boy speeding on his way as fast as he could run, south to the town of Salisbury with an urgent message for that place's esteemed selectman, Lt. Robert Pike or, in the event of Pike's absence, his noted second, Mr. Thomas Bradbury.

Chapter Eleven

An Insurrection

THE MIDWIFE HAVING DESERTED, Constable Brike tore open the back of Alice Ambrose's dress. The covering fell easily away since it was mostly open to the air under her cloak. It had been ripped previously in Dover.

Its removal revealed a purple pond that spread across the woman's back and shoulders and flowed painfully around islands of puffed-up welts and bluish bruises. Alice held fast to the cart's ramp and drew in her breath, awaiting the fall of the lash.

The constable shook out and disentangled the tails of the long-handled, three-pronged whip. This cruel scourge had been especially designated by Magistrate Walderne for use on the blasphemers.

Constable Roberts nodded to the town drummer, who commenced a loud but mournful tattoo.

With shocking force, Brike struck the woman with the lash, drawing blood at the very first blow from her unhealed, pulpy back. Alice screamed in unfettered agony and slowly sank to her knees.

At the second blow, Alice collapsed full-face into the slop

below the wheels of the cart. Still, the constable lashed her again and again, oblivious to her guttural screams.

"Oh, spare, mercy," wailed Lydia Goodspeed, an onlooker and farmer's wife. She chewed on her white neckerchief and watched in horror as the heavy whip tails rose and fell again and again and the drum roll increased in its tempo to a mindless cacophony of noise.

"No pity for these wretches!" cried out one Hamptoner.

"Aye," shouted another voice from the safety of the many. "It is only fair. They have beaten the Gospel black and blue!"

That drew a nervous laugh.

When ten had been counted out, Constable Brike handed the whip over to Constable Roberts, who wiped off the bits of flesh and garment clinging to the knots. Brike delicately dabbed at the sweat from his brow with the back of his wrist. Flecks of Alice's blood spotted his cheek.

At the men's feet, the woman groveled hopelessly in the sodden earth of the commons amid clumps of mildewed straw, loose grain, chicken filth and refuse, clawing for escape.

The cavalrymen lifted the wounded Quaker out of the mire. They half-dragged her onto the floorboards of the open cart. Hopestill reached in and spread her cloak over her torn shoulders, tucking her in with it as if she were a child. She moaned with the pain of its touch.

Within minutes, the drumming began anew.

The constable did his duty on both Anne and Mary, neither of whom bore up well under the torture. It was a ghastly scene, three cold, half-naked women brutalized in such a manner. Yet when it was over some in the crowd wanted more.

"Kill them!" one goodwife screeched.

The constables would have none of that. They pushed at the people to break them up into smaller groupings. Heavy snow was in the air of the now late afternoon and there was still hard work yet for all.

More importantly, Salisbury lay ahead many long miles down the horrible road.

A weather-beaten barn was procured for the party for the night at the edge of the commons. Refreshments sent for the sake of the Quakers were refused by them, and all visitors and hecklers were rudely turned away for the evening. The women were herded into one corner of the barn and left to fend for themselves.

The guards and Roberts stood watch in shifts. Hopestill, to the constable a notorious Dover personality and Indian lover, disappeared for many hours. From long experience, Roberts knew it was futile to seek him out.

Night fell without the promise of heavy weather fulfilled, but the cold of it made for a long ordeal not conducive to sleep. Also, the straw wasn't clean.

When dawn finally broke, it was some time before the Quakers could be coaxed up from their agonizing respite. Hopestill, who on his return had nestled deep inside a filthy hay pile like an animal, was the last to rise.

A meal of cold milk, warm oats and black bread for all was brought over by Pastor Seaborn Cotton's wife and two other equally stern-faced women. It was consumed without words being spoken. When finished, the Quakers were allowed to attend to their morning toilet in a horse stall, then ordered outside and shackled again to the end of the long chain at the cart's end.

Secured, they were led shuffling like broken dolls behind the dung cart to the jeering of the men, women and village brats of

Hampton, who had arrived once more with the breaking of the day because they couldn't get enough of the entertainment.

The Hamptoners pelted the departing Quaker women with garbage and ran alongside them shaking the scratchy tops of rotting corn stooks in their faces. Neither of the cavalrymen interfered, walking their horses around the tormenters rather than scattering them.

This went on for almost a full mile, after which the mob members melted away, trudging back to the village with the happy chatter of those who have enjoyed a pleasant respite from their ordinary routine.

Hopestill halted the horses, and he and the constable unshackled the women and helped the Quakers to climb back in. The party then rode on in silence for several more dull, freezing miles in the lurching cart.

As the afternoon came on, the sky turned once more uncommonly dark and threatening and Roberts ordered the cart halted. After offering the Quakers water from a wooden keg – ice-cold, as was the air – the constable directed the men to repair to the side of the road to share a light meal of hard ship's cheese, bread and cider. The Quakers would eat none of the remains, although two of them reluctantly quaffed a few swallows of the cider. They prayed in a huddle, heads bowed.

Sodden snow started to pelt down in the form of heavy flakes, wet and wide as fox eyes. The temperature plummeted. A mile after it began, the carpet of white slush was ankle deep on the road, slowing them down considerably, but not enough to prevent them at the pace they were on from reaching Salisbury before dark.

This was agreeable to neither the constable, Hopestill nor the cavalrymen. Conferring among themselves, it was decided to slow the cart's pace so it would be after dark when they arrived.

This would spare the Quaker women their day's punishment, but it would have the beneficial effect of hastening the men's own supper and bed. That way, in the morning, after the next whipping, as they agreed, they could then drive to Carr's ferry and cross the Merrimack for the longest part of their journey.

However, over the next several hours, conditions worsened. The snow gave way completely to sleet and the wheels churned with difficulty in the slippery, icy soup of the road.

The women lay soaked and nearly insensate on the blood-smeared wood of the cart's freezing bed.

Constable Roberts told Hopestill in a worried tone that he feared for the women's lives. So, as they lurched along, he poked them with his shoe every now and then to console himself with the sound of a healthy moan.

As Roberts was engaged in so doing, Hopestill stood up off his bench seat and, without warning, jerked back on the reins.

The heads of the horses flapped in the air, startled by the stop. In the fading light, a half-mile distant, was a line of men on foot blocking the road into the town of Salisbury. These were augmented by two mounted officers positioned at the ends.

Constable Roberts urged with his feet and hands for the prone women to get up, to get up, to get out, to get out! The Quakers half-rolled to the end of the wagon.

"Quickly, now! Quickly, now!"

The sufferers were propped up in the cold clay of the road and the long chain was again attached to their wrist manacles. Tying their cloaks to their necks, Roberts climbed back in and resumed his seat, fanning himself with his hat. Vapors of sweat steamed off his fat face in the chill air.

"Go on now," he nervously ordered Hopestill. The cart pitched forward anew, the three women stumbling forward as best they could. Hopestill held the reins tight, strangling the pace to a creep.

"There's Mr. Bradbury," he said, a note of expectation in his voice.

"Eh?" said Roberts.

Hopestill, grinning like a fool, indicated to the constable with his switch the shorter of the two men on horseback. This was the one with the cocked hat coming toward them at a canter. Bradbury was a very educated man.

"And Robert Pike," Hopestill added of the other horseman, a large, impressive man in breastplate and helmet.

"I dare say," was the worried answer from the constable when Hopestill pointed them all out. Roberts very much disliked Salisbury men.

Astride his fine chestnut gelding, the officer named Bradbury splashed up to them in a brisk spattering of road mud. He turned his mount smartly, following the cart as it plodded forward to the roadblock.

"Good afternoon, Master Constable. And upon my word, Hopestill Foster! Truly, God is merciful today, is He not?"

Hopestill laughed. Behind him, the shaken Roberts spoke up hopefully, "Assuredly, good Mr. Bradbury. He is always merciful."

But the constable was extremely unsettled in his mind now. The men ahead, all armed in some fashion, did not move to make way.

Bradbury showed a delighted twinkle in his grey eyes.

"More than we know. More than we know."

"We are hence to Salisbury with these prisoners," Roberts

shouted across to his new companion above the noise of cartwheels and horse whinnies. His voice's authority had returned along with a sudden desire to bluff his way through.

"Whoa!" yelled Hopestill and the cart stopped short again. The animals would proceed no farther in the road filled with men. He spoke soothingly to the horses as they shook their bridled heads and stamped impatiently.

Suddenly, ahead of them, the tall, helmeted Lt. Pike burst from the line of men. Putting spur with his fine boots to his black horse, he shot past the cart to confront the two rear-guard Puritan cavalry. These had stopped dead in their tracks a ways back.

The trio conferred for several minutes. As Roberts gaped in astonishment, the cavalrymen then broke away from Pike and passed the cart at a fast clip down the roadside, taking their leave of duty without even acknowledging the slack-jawed constable. Picking up speed, the two riders passed through the roadblock and disappeared around the bend toward Salisbury town.

Pike's black horse with its rider cantered up to the motion-less cart. In the saddle was a tall, impressive soldier, clean-shaven, perhaps in his early 40s, and possessed of an unhappy countenance.

"I am the authority here," he announced to the now speechless Constable Roberts. "I have taken the liberty of relieving your men and sending them on their way."

He paused to hear any objections. There were none from the astonished Dover official.

The soldier continued. "They, and you, have no further official business in the good town of Salisbury."

"May I introduce Lt. Robert Pike, Master Constable?" interrupted Mr. Bradbury, sweeping his cap in deference. "You may have heard of his good service in the late Indian troubles to our brethren in Haverhill?"

The constable stood up hastily, wobbling in the cart.

"Yes, yes, of course!" he insisted. "Upon my honor, sir."

Pike would have none of it.

"Show me your warrant."

The constable dived down into his bag and tremblingly brought forth the papers from Dover.

As Pike read them a fire lit his eyes.

"This warrant means murder."

He crushed the parchments in his fist.

"I won't have it, sir. No, I will not."

Roberts shook as he stood in the cart. Hat still in hand, he had no idea what to make of this sudden calamity greeting him from the men of Salisbury.

Bradbury smiled at the constable's alarm and reached into his coat pocket. Drawing out a clean, yellow sheet of paper, he said, "Fear not, good Master Constable Roberts. Here is your new warrant, drawn up in my exceedingly clear hand. Lt. Pike and his trainband …" He turned and smiled at the men behind him. "… will be taking charge of the prisoners. Pray release them from their chains."

Without waiting for an answer, Bradbury dismounted and began helping the Quakers. They fell to their knees in the freezing mud, pressing his hand and weeping with relief. He tsk-tsked at their condition and tried to reassure them.

The constable clumsily did what he could to assist.

"But the warrant …" Roberts said anxiously, looking at the wadded up mess of the Dover magistrate's orders now soaking in the road.

"Your warrant? Here is a newer one. Pray present it to Mr. Walderne with my compliments and those of Lt. Pike and the selectmen of Salisbury, and assure him the prisoners will be well taken care of. This other document …"

Bradbury handed forth a second.

"… shows that I have been deputized in the service of this good order."

"But this warrant …" persisted the constable, pointing at the crumpled, sodden remains of Magistrate Walderne's papers.

"… is no good," replied Bradbury, finishing the constable's sentence. "Surely you recall passing Boundary House?"

"I do, good sir, I do."

"Yonder is Salisbury. It is the lieutenant's charge. You understand, I'm fair certain."

"Aye. I do. I do."

At the mention of his name, Lt. Pike drove his snorting horse around the cart and bent his helmeted head to within three inches of Constable Roberts's face.

"No warrant is good, even though backed by the Crown, for whipping these women in Salisbury," Pike told the constable evenly. "I won't have it. It is cowardly."

"They have been cruelly treated," Hopestill chimed in from his driver's seat. He touched his cap to Pike. "Compliments, lieutenant."

"Mr. Foster," said Pike respectfully. "Thank you again for your timely warning."

Constable Roberts now understood in whose camp his driver's tent was pitched.

"Come, let us all go anon to our good town, Robert, and leave this road," suggested Bradbury to Pike. "A hot supper and a warm hearth await us in my Mary's kitchen, a better place than this frigid road."

He mounted up and smiled at the Quakers, who hugged and kissed each other, and shed many tears.

Lt. Pike called over to Roberts from the other side of the cart. He pointed to the darkening sky. "Time is short, constable. Let us get these poor souls into Mistress Bradbury's healing hands."

"The Lord is indeed merciful," suggested Bradbury to the bewildered, though newly compliant constable. With a look skyward, he added, "But the weather will be wanting in that quality this eve, I fear."

The contingent of men, cart and Quakers turned up their collars and cloaks to follow Pike and Bradbury. Needles of ice rain blew sideways, stinging their faces. The storm deepened behind them.

Chapter Twelve

Orphan of the Woods

ALAS, THE QUAKER WOMEN WERE DOOMED, of course. Their fanatic's devotion to faith led them to repeat the forlorn hope of committing additional religious liberty follies in Walderne's Puritan New Hampshire, a fatal indulgence. They prayed to be doomed, and they were.

When next they set foot in Dover the following year of 1663, once their shocking wounds were healed by the ministrations of kindly Mary Bradbury in the safety of Salisbury, they were brutalized anew by Walderne's deputies and exiled from Massachusetts, this time by vessel.

Mary Tomkins and Anne Coleman vanished as if they had never been. Alice Ambrose was taken in chains to the Virginia colony where she fomented a new insurrection for which, Hopestill learned from the laughing lips of Walderne himself many years after, she was lashed into a state of permanent insanity.

Momentarily lucid at the memory of the poor Quakers, Hopestill's body, gripped in a renewed bout of pocks fever, made him writhe in his settle-seat by Cotton Mather's hearth like a man on fire.

"I burn," he managed to croak.

The Rev. Mather watched the old man's struggle with a technician's eyes, calculating how and when to intervene should it prove necessary.

"Take a cloth and wipe his brow," he ordered his slave.

Behind him, the minister could sense a building interest in Fain's men as to the outcome of the interrogation. Wagers were entertained among the prison detail in guarded whispers as to whether the old renegade would live the night. Mather chose to disregard the various forms of blasphemy he knew for a certainty were being expressed.

Tizzoo applied a soothing cloth to Hopestill's forehead, his threshing almost immediately becoming less agitated. When it was withdrawn, the lingering coolness was reflected in his changing dream.

It became a vision in which he saw himself wading through the slush of spring after the great cracking thaw loosened the grip of winter that followed the freeing of the Quaker women. He had left the hospitality of the Pikes and the Bradburys in Salisbury to return to his amazingly ordered little cabin tucked into the northern woods far up the river beyond Dover and Cochecho.

As he walked, weighed down with the presents his friends had gifted him, Hopestill skirted the settlements out of fear of retribution for his part in the rescue of the women, which he knew Constable Roberts had reported to Walderne, no doubt in colorful terms. Indeed, although Hopestill continued to work for Walderne, his part in that little insurrection was never forgotten by the volcanic-tempered magistrate.

Hopestill took his leisure traveling north.

He chose to dawdle at familiar old landmarks, stopping to

check if his hidden caches of supplies and personal treasures were still in good order. Of these last he had but a few, among them the tattered letter declaring him to be a free man signed by Henry Sandyman.

Another was a precious clipping of chestnut hair tied with a sliver-thin shred of sinew that he kept very well hidden so as not to be accused of taking a scalp. This was all he had of Priscilla to remember now that she was gone, buried in an unmarked grave unknown to him. She had died from the effects of childbirth a few days after he was driven from Boston that dark night in early December 1637.

He heard about his love's death from a counterfeiter who passed through from other parts and had a bit of familiarity with the Rev. Hooker's congregation, since resettled in the colony of Connecticut.

From the same rogue Hopestill learned of Anne Hutchinson's subsequent trial, expulsion, and tragic death, and of Mary Dyer's conversion to Quakerism and her later being hung by the Puritans as a martyr to her new faith.

Most amazing to Hopestill, there was a lurid "monster baby" story attached to each of the latter two women, but not to his Priscilla.

He shrugged. What did it matter now? The poor women! And the Quakers, too. All were victims in their own way of Puritan hate-lust, he mused dreamily. They had paid the onerous price that Massachusetts set for those who dared presume there was another way to love God.

He hung his head, both in his dream and upon Mather's tall oak settle, when he thought of Priscilla. Through his mind played the reanimated fantasies of the life they might have shared together.

And in his mind, the years flew backwards again, back to that horrible December night in 1637 when he scampered, sobbing, aboard Goodman Hawkins's stinking shallop which ran before the icy wind, stealthily passing the watchers on Fort Hill on the way out of the city of Boston.

A short but harrowing voyage had deposited the bewildered boy – along with a few words of comfort and best wishes – at tiny Braveboat Harbor on the shores of Strawberry Banke, Maine, where he was met by one of Hawkins's acquaintances.

From there, Hopestill was taken to the rambling Greenland estate of the exalted Sir Francis Champernowne, a notable personality of his time. As he and his escort approached the solitary house, which at a distance was backlit by the red dusk of evening, Hopestill was struck by how much it resembled a gigantic lump of coal cooling in a hearth.

Hawkins, the boy's deliverer, had a long-standing and clandestine relationship with Sir Francis and his cronies, and Hopestill wasn't the first nor was he the last human cargo carried by the fisherman to the northern extremities of the Bay Colony.

Champernowne, then in his prime, was through and through a King's man, known to be keen on anyone who wasn't in the pay of, or in sympathy with, the long arm of the Massachusetts Bay Puritans. So any extra hands who passed his scrutiny were welcome so long as they didn't eat too much, did as they were told, and kept out of his way.

Hopestill was taken before Champernowne, mildly belligerent and somewhat drunk, after that evening's meal. The boy was probed about his loyalty to the King, his political ideas and his skill sets. He feared he was on the verge of being dismissed, but Sir Francis wasn't finished with him quite yet.

"You have a father in England, I presume?" Champernowne

asked in a leading tone, hiding his mouth by imbibing with gusto from an oversized silver tankard engraved with a coat of arms. His face with its drooping eyes in some ways resembled that of a hound.

Hopestill nodded.

"What was his name?"

The boy thought it best at this time, when so much depended on his being accepted into this strange new community, to deliver a misleading answer rather than to be entirely frank about his youthful connection with his father Faraday's smuggling ring.

"I don't know, sir. Aye, I had a father …"

At this Champernowne, and also the ruddy faced man who came into the room to stand next to him, a man named Saunders, both laughed heartily. "Well, of course you had, lad …"

"… but I don't, didn't know of him that much. I have been a servant all my life …"

"And now you're an orphan again, I see, I see. Why was it they turned you out of, of, of …?"

Appearing to stumble, the man called Saunders lent a hand, leaning over and saying "I believe it was Sandyman, Sir Francis."

Champernowne brightened. "Yes, Sandyman the soapboiler."

"Yes, sir," answered Hopestill. "He is leaving Boston and did not wish to take me with him."

"A valuable boy like yourself? I can hardly believe it."

"He is a poor man and has had a hard time of it," Hopestill said. "I was a burden to him, he said."

"Yet he did not sell you to another. Very curious, indeed. I certainly should have done so, under the circumstances. You did not run afoul of the law? I have your word on that, sir? Some clergyman hasn't taken a disliking to you, or Gov. Winthrop himself? You are not a wanted man by any law?"

"No, sir. Not that I know, sir. Except by you, sir. I hope, sir."

Hopestill felt ashamed of himself for having dissembled so easily to the handsome gentleman who had accepted him without too many questions asked, but Sir Francis, as it turned out, had an ulterior motive, which was to provide a new set of hands for his grouchy and complaining carpenter, Mr. John Heard, to whom the boy was soon attached as a sort of apprentice.

It was an appropriate placement. Among the many negotiable skills Hopestill had acquired with the Sandymans was an ability to do a little minor forge work, and with a proper anvil and a decent sledge he could turn out a reasonable supply of nails, a necessity in desperately short supply on the Maine-New Hampshire border, which was the outer limits of the English settlements in New England.

And in that, more than two years – not unpleasant ones, either – passed. Hopestill might even have made his fortune in the nail trade had that day not arrived in the fall of 1640 when he was first taken to the vicinity of Dover in the New Hampshire colony with a load of tools, accompanied by Mr. Heard and two others.

All the party were allied with Goodman Heard in some fashion at Champernowne's estate, but on this day they were to labor on the carpenter's long-term personal project, one for which the man and his crew had taken their leave of Sir Francis for a few weeks that unusually warm autumn of 1640.

Mr. Heard, by virtue of the largesse of Sir Francis, had acquired several large, wooded lots to the north of a prominent hill that topped the terrain for miles around near Dover above the Cochecho River. The four of them, including Heard's hired men Runny Jim and Two-Nose Pete, were to stake and clear the immediate vicinity for the carpenter's future garrison home.

It was a joyous even though strenuous outing for Hopestill, as his fascination with the deep forest was a long-standing one, dating back to happier days with the Sandymans. On occasion Landon Sandyman had taken him hunting well beyond the Boston commons and into the new fields beyond that, past even where the massive stands along the tree line, interrupted by the incessant felling then taking place, had stood shoulder to shoulder again, like sentinels guarding some dark castle keep. There, the pair kept one eye open for game and another for Indians, even though these last were not at that time openly hostile in the vicinity of the Puritan stronghold. Still, the thought of being ambushed by those strange and frightening people put the creep on them and kept it there.

Hopestill felt that same odd mixture of thrill and chill when he was with Heard's gang that day in New Hampshire. They were north of the little Dover settlement, across the Cochecho, on the work site before dawn, pulling up stones and piling the massive shapes in heaps for the future foundation and chimneys.

Heard's house was as yet still only the carpenter's phantom, and they were a full season away from even framing in the lower supports. The finish to the job, let alone that long day's work, loomed far, far ahead.

Despite his misgivings about Indians, Hopestill felt little cause for immediate concern.

Relations with the local Indians, the Pennacooks, were on an even keel. A fair amount of trade between the races was ingrained in the community, and the great hostilities of recent years had all taken place much further to the south, before Hopestill had been spirited away from Boston.

So when the crew broke for their mid-morning meal of ale and slabs of cold meat, the boy took his handkerchief of food and beverage pot and walked a fair distance away from the other men, entering after a brief hike into the relatively cooler shade of a thick growth of red maple, his favorite tree. The beautiful burgundy leaves were just starting to shrink and curl back into themselves before their inevitable fall.

He was taken at the instant he stepped into the welcome darkness, and hauled down by his neck. Before he could gather his wits about him, a huge Indian bent a knee into his chest and brandished a tomahawk about his face, daring him to cry out. The Indian's eyes belonged to a mad man.

He lay on his back, supine as a sacrificial Isaac, as the woods around them erupted with the ferocious yet dismal war cry, a cry unlike that of any single terrible animal but rather a combination of them, which, given voice, produces a most terrifying effect.

The Indian who had taken him jumped up and stood astride the prostrate Hopestill. His strong trunk was decorated with wild squibs and lines of black lead. He reeked of sweat and grease.

Brandishing his hatchet, he screamed at the young man, demanding in halting but understandable English (although noticeably devoid of the ability to pronounce the letters "r" or "l") "Weah mo you? Weah mo you!"

Hopestill, stunned, defenseless, on the ground, pointed to where he had been, to the site they had been clearing of rocks. "We're there!" was the best answer he could muster to the question he supposed in his terror to be "Where are there more of you?"

Immediately after he spoke, the bass cough of a musket boomed out from that general direction from a scene Hopestill, his back pinned to the ground, could not witness. This was followed by additional peals of fierce yelling from distant savage throats.

Within minutes the screaming ceased and there followed

shouting in a tongue he couldn't understand from voices close by.

Suddenly Hopestill was yanked up from the forest floor by the clutch of a fist that gathered up his shirt around his throat. Kicked and half-dragged along by his captor into the depths of the forest, they joined a headlong flight with the other warriors.

The men hallooed at each other joyously as they ran. An Indian sped to Hopestill's side, panting, a maniacal grin on his painted face. In his fist he held out a dripping red disk of hair, a scalp streaked with grey torn from, almost certainly, Runny Jim's head.

Away they flew at breakneck speed. Hopestill was carried along, almost lifted off his feet at times by the giant Indian who had captured him. Another, a whiplash thin warrior bedaubed with a lunatic scrawl of green and white squiggles, also held him fast. Each had seized the lightly built young man by the upper arm with their iron grips, easily manhandling him along, forcing his feet to conform to their pace and gait.

Very quickly now they all but flew through the cathedral of trees, the intermittent sunlight flashing down on them through the canopy as they fled from the ambush, the filtered rays alternately lighting up their bodies and faces.

To the mind of their shocked victim, this mad dash through the woods and undergrowth seemed to go on forever. There was no telling where they were headed except it was obviously as far away as possible from the scene of the murderous encounter with Heard and his men.

When it seemed his heart might explode from fright and exertion, Hopestill was launched onto his face into a small clearing where the attackers had earlier encamped. There they had deposited in the brush a variety of tools and kettles, and large packages of wet skins and slimy hides tied up with sinew and bulging with heavy haunches of still-dripping meat.

These they heaped on him, now lifted up and thoroughly dazed, as if he were a pack horse. After the rest took up the remaining goods, the ferocious Indian with the black paint lifted a large stick and beat Hopestill around his shoulders and head.

Thus compelled, he took off wobbling after the lead Indians, trying to fight past the sickening spasms of pain and exhaustion. A tremendous kick into the small of his back sent him and his load sprawling into the leaves on the ground once more.

They picked him up a second time, very roughly, jeering at him in angry voices. Then they marched him away, burdened anew, at a somewhat more moderate pace. Deeper into the wilderness they went, away from everything he knew, to where he knew not, but to a destination in which it now dawned on him was completely without hope, a destination that he knew to be certain death.

Chapter Thirteen

Man and Mouse

THE RAIDERS WERE PEQUOTS, desperate as they were dangerous. They were themselves hunted, despised, outlaws among the northern tribes and constantly on the move, as they were again after they ambushed John Heard's party.

As his nightmare assumed vivid form, Hopestill cried out and thrashed wildly to Mather's alarm. Fain's men held him down as he raved.

"What is he is saying? What is he saying?" The minister asked in vain of the stupid, tipsy men around him. They gaped back into the alarmed face of their leader without answer. Each took hold of a quivering limb.

Hopestill was, however, helpless in the greater grip of a nightmare.

The Pequot leader was Oonoonunkawaee, or Chop the Cloud, the huge warrior who had taken charge of Hopestill and who, as they ran from the scene, continued to beat the young man remorselessly on every part of his body not covered by the burden of skins and meat he carried.

Blood now oozed from numerous wounds on Hopestill's head and arms, and it streamed from his cut-up buttocks and legs, yet he knew instinctively that he must keep up with his captors or die where he might fall.

The band that had taken him and murdered Runny Jim were remnants of the infamous slaughter that had destroyed the Pequot redoubt years before at Misistuck. They were among the very few survivors of the late war that had all but wiped out their clan.

In their tree-walled strongpoint on the Mystic River in the heart of tribal territory far to the south of Boston, hundreds of followers of Chief Sassacus were savagely butchered by the Puritans and their Narragansett and Mohegan allies (along to settle old scores). Scarcely a dog escaped the gunfire and flames in the frenzy that ensued after that Indian castle fell. The cowering Pequots, women and children mostly, who were still alive after the assault were then subjected to a second onslaught, sliced and hacked to death with swords and pikes in an orgy of killing that left the rejoicing victors drenched in blood.

Oonoonunkawaee's band of five included his brother, brother-in-law and two other warriors of the porcupine clan to which they all belonged. They had been raiding far afield during the disaster at Misistuck when, learning of the tribe's misfortune, they had slipped through the closing net around the surviving Pequots.

At first they ran south, and raided Dutch farms in New York. They then became the prey. Yet, through three summers and part of a third autumn, by adroit maneuvering and luck, they had managed to stay one step ahead of their pursuers in spite of the fact that the Mohawks had joined in the hunt. Nothing struck horror into their hearts more than the possibility of being caught and boiled by the man-eaters.

They were not about to get caught this time, either. Throughout the summer before the raid that had taken Hopestill, the band had worked itself ever farther north into the land of the Pennacooks. This was a daring and deliberate strategy carried out in spite of misgivings from Quonwehige, Oonoonunkawaee's brother and an equally terrifying personality.

Oonoonunkawaee's plan, which they adopted, was to kill more English, steal their goods and then escape to Saint Francis far to the north in Canada where their leader asserted they could feel certain of receiving a friendly reception from the French and the western Abenakis, the Arsigantegoks, among whom he was purportedly known.

After a few hours of running with their new captive, the raiding party settled down to a brisk walk. Convinced there would be no further pursuit, Quonwehige and his brother continued the argument about their next move. Oftentimes, they struck each other with the sticks they carried, although not with any real force. This, their unresolved brutality toward each other, they reserved for Hopestill.

When the party came to a halt the Pequots divested the frightened young man of his burden, tied his arms around a tree and beat him steadily, so often and with so much force that he could feel the life literally draining from him. Quonwehige, who was the smallest warrior in the band, told Hopestill through his brother, who spoke a smidgen of English, that if he dared tried to escape they would hunt him down and burn him on every part of his body with hot coals.

For several days they traveled in what Hopestill believed was a northeasterly direction. It seemed to him that they were looping back to the English settlements again.

Instinctively, the captive felt they had not left the immediacy of New Hampshire since they had not crossed any great river, but he did think it possible they were perhaps in Maine, where there were a few small hamlets along the frontier. This was when he thought he smelled the great ocean, which was a comfort to him.

He felt more hopeful as the days went by since the band did not follow through with its threats to kill him. And while the Pequots did not lessen their cruelty to him to any measureable degree, they did allow him a morsel of freedom when at rest in the day by not binding his hands behind him around a tree, a night-time practice that caused his fingers to swell up like sausages.

Hopestill intuitively understood that if he tried as hard as he could to please he might continue to be allowed to live, so that is how he conducted himself, staying as submissive as any slave. More importantly, despite several opportunities he felt were balanced in favor of making a run for it, he stayed put every time in the belief they were waiting for him to try an escape in order to put him to the torture they had so often threatened.

Thus, Hopestill remained their beast of burden as they tramped through the woods, with all growing more miserable as each day passed. The weather, at first frenetically then desultorily, turned uglier and much colder, and here and there snowflakes swirled about in a frenzied prelude to a storm that never materialized.

The Pequots eventually covered up with skins they tossed over their shoulders but their captive was given nothing to ward off the increasing chill. His clothing had degenerated into a serious state of disorder, ripped in numerous places and caked with his own dried blood. The boots on his feet that once belonged to the fondly remembered Henry Sandyman still held up, and for this he gave thanks every night under his breath.

Such was his lot the afternoon they skulked about the out-skirts of a poorly constructed dwelling near Berwick, Maine, that exhibited all the signs of a farm on the verge of ruin. After surveying the place for some hours from the safety of cover, they retreated back into the hidden recesses of the wood fully informed about the home's paltry defenses, which consisted of an older man, his plain wife and five children, two of them very small girls, possibly twins.

The Pequots attacked the homestead just after the sun broke through into the frosty dawn the following morning.

With Hopestill watching in a state of dread, two warriors seized the man as soon as he passed out of his cabin's doorframe, stooping low, apparently to check as to why his animals had gone so quiet in the night. These had been silently butchered, which of course he could not have known, and lay in the field like moored boats in the calm of their own gore.

After stunning the man with the flat of a hatchet before he could cry out, the raiders rushed into the cabin and loudly massacred his family. The pitiful screams and entreaties for nonexistent mercy that issued from within that house of death, mixed with the hideous war whoop, were as unbearable for Hopestill as they were for his dazed companion, who was dragged to his side and dumped beside him.

The man, a rather thin fellow with sparse black hair beginning to turn grey, upon regaining his senses and attaining a renewed understanding of the fate of his beloved family, begged his guard to put an end to him.

This most earnest wish for release from life was expressed in a manner that should have melted the heart of the most depraved killer. Instead, it was met with kicks and mockery, and before the destroying flames had reached their zenith, obliterating in clouds of greasy smoke the remains of those poor souls inside and all the man's worldly goods, the farmer was piled high with the remnants of his humble possessions, the booty of the raid.

The two Englishmen staggered under their outrageous loads, goaded back into the wilderness with heartless threats and taunts by their joyous captors, now adorned with stolen clothing thrown over their backs or worn upon their heads in a manner that would have seemed ridiculous were the circumstances not so very hideous. The Indian Hopestill had come to identify as Borzugwon had taken a particular fancy to the dead wife's black shawl and girlishly twirled it about his shoulders in order to elicit comment and praise from his brethren.

In gasping bursts swiftly punished by brutal blows, the farmer managed to relate to Hopestill that he was Esau Treadway of Marylebone, London, and that the name of one of his slain daughters was Zipporah. Having gotten out this small bit of information, he could relate nothing further as his misery choked him.

For the rest of that terrible day the weight of Treadway's grief so darkened the man's mind and so crushed his spirit that he could not utter another coherent thought. He wept and moaned constantly as they moved back into the deepest haunts of the endless forest. Yet as much as the man's unhinged despair at his personal loss and complete ruination amused them, it annoyed the Pequots even more. Ominously, no amount of stick-beating or verbal torment could reduce Treadway to the absolute silence they increasingly demanded of him.

That evening when they finally stopped was the coldest night since Hopestill's capture. Members of the band raced to and fro in an uncharacteristic frenzy, gathering logs and sticks and piling them in a heap in the center of their new camp, which might have been anywhere as it was unrecognizable territory. Soon a kettle of water was set to boiling and pieces of rotting meat and organs were thrown into it only to be snatched out well before this inedible sustenance was anywhere near done.

The warriors sat around the fire contemplatively after their disgusting meal, belching appreciatively, pointing and talking amiably among themselves, all previous arguments now resolved or put aside. Only the gnawed fragments of discarded half-raw cow, flung at their heads, was offered the dead-tired and dispirited captives, who lacked any appetite.

After a bit of leisurely stretching and laughter, the band jumped around anew, capering with glee as they piled more wood upon the roaring fire. The sparks from the mostly rotten pine trunks they threw onto the blaze exploded like whip cracks.

The shawl-wearing Borzugwon took charge of the new prisoner. He angrily kicked Hopestill over to a large tree and stood glaring at him, which the young man understood was a sign to remain where he was placed. The unfortunate Londoner in his turn, even though not offering the slightest resistance, was then manhandled by Borzugwon to the ground. Thick cords of dried rawhide were expertly knotted deep into the tender flesh of Treadway's wrists.

The others watched this exercise with a sort of detached curiosity, still ruminating contently on the remains of their loathsome repast or unconcernedly going about their tasks, which now included digging with the aid of large clam shells a pit in the earth near the fire almost as deep as the length of a man.

When they had finished, they rolled the terrified Treadwell to its edge where Borzugwon slowly cut into the forehead of the now screeching man. The Pequot tore away his scalp with a single muscular rip that elicited an unearthly howl of pain.

The Indians digging the pit dropped to the ground and collapsed with stomach-hugging hilarity at the sight of their bound victim's bewildered suffering, which left him jerking and thrashing helplessly from the shocking agony. They reveled in it for some minutes as he writhed like a worm on the hook.

But once Treadway's worst convulsions abated they all piled onto him. Soon they had him rolled into a cocoon of raw cow hides from the neck down as neatly as a cigar, unable to so much as wiggle. Hopestill saw the man's jaws working as they secured him but no sound came out. Worse, the horrible face had lost its human aspect somehow amid the exposed, throbbing, vulnerable mass of profusely damaged tissue and muscle.

Lifting up and dropping their scalped bundle into the pit, they buried it up to its neck, kicking loose dirt to fill in all the cracks and then stamping the earth into a hard pack. With pieces of bark they used like small brooms they swept a low bank of burning coals into a ring around Treadway's head, just far enough away to slowly bake his skull but not kill him.

Treadway's head began shrieking almost immediately that his very brains were boiling. He implored God to let him die, to let him die, to let him die. At that point the Indians scrupulously brushed the red embers back and began the roasting again at a safer distance.

Intent on the horror before him, Hopestill became aware of Oonoonunkawaee now beside him.

The huge Pequot had squatted down and was leaning on the resinous pine against which the young man was braced. In his hand he held a glowing firebrand, which he used to slowly brush across Hopestill's tear-stained cheeks while Treadway screamed into the night.

"Face wet. I fix," the Indian said, much as a solicitous parent might, touching the dots of salty water streaking Hopestill's face with the smoking hot stick.

As an intention to physically discomfort him, this was a failure. For some minutes now, Hopestill had been enveloped by an insensate numbness that threw a calming curtain over the ghastly scenes and sounds before him. With the noise of the strangled bleating of the tortured man fading in his roaring ears, the young man's mind spirited him away.

He imagined himself once again climbing the rude ladder to the airless loft above the Sandymans' sleeping quarters, which the family used for storage of their grain supply to keep it off the dirt floor.

They had woefully underestimated the determination of the vermin to get at this desirable bounty. So in another life long ago it was Hopestill's job to catch and kill the mice that plagued these precious stores.

Not so easy, that job was. Blessed as they were with an inherent deviousness, the rodents got into everything edible with ridiculous ease. No plugging, patching or reconnaissance could thwart them. There seemed to be no way to kill them except to catch them unawares, which was very difficult – every evening after dark the maddening and unstoppable scritching and chewing could be heard upstairs.

So Hopestill experimented with a sort of glue he obtained by boiling pieces of calf hoof. This he cut with pine resin and spread on rectangles of bark. A sprinkle of grain for bait completed the trap.

This was no panacea but he did manage to catch a few mice and gain a word of praise from his master whenever he climbed down waving the evidence that another little grey thief had foundered and expired in the gooey mess that protected Sandyman's grain.

Considering the extent of the damage and the sheer volume of droppings, it was clear that the elimination of a mouse or two was not going to end the pilfering. And since success was rarely achieved anyway, Hopestill only checked on his glue traps when he had to go up into the oppressively hot loft to get something. So it might be days between visits.

One very miserable, humid late afternoon he was sent by Henry to patch a leak that was impossible to ignore now that it threatened the integrity of the main chimney and its precious flue.

Emerging into the loft with his sack of wet mortar Hopestill was greeted by a blast of ferocious heat in the stuffy, pent-up room. Sweat poured out of him as if a shuttle-cock had been opened.

As he smeared his gushing forehead, a glint of movement and a hint of moistness in the center of a piece of bark caught his eye. He furrowed his brow and crawled over to it, shedding his load.

Here and there bits of sunlight lent some dusty illumination but the room was still almost as dark as a pit. Hopestill stooped over his trap and peered; in response, it seemed, the almost unidentifiable, gelatinous mass quivered ever so slightly in the grasp of the hardened glue.

It was a mouse or what was left of a mouse.

In its efforts to get free, which had become exceedingly more insane as the intense heat and its own maddening thirst took their toll, the animal, the mutilated thing that was now cemented to the sheet of bark, had gnawed itself open, all to no avail. It should have been dead long before now yet somehow it had painfully lingered, barely alive, with no strength or will left.

Except that it could see.

With its one remaining damp open eye it was looking directly at Hopestill, and there was no question in the boy's mind that it was trying to communicate with him on the most elemental level, a primal thought really, from one creature to another.

Their eyes met, and man and mouse understood each other sweetly and perfectly. In those strange, otherworldly seconds all was clear to both.

Hopestill crushed it underfoot. His ears buzzed with the wings of a billion insects in the shimmering, maddening oven of a room, and an overwhelming sadness flooded his heart.

Chapter Fourteen

Robinhood

A BARELY CONSCIOUS HOPESTILL now slumped on the settle in the wharf house procured by Cotton Mather.

The deathlike film gathering over the old man's unfocused eyes had glazed this window into the dangerous state of his unwellness, but his teeth could not hide the fact of it. These clicked away, making a noise like shattered ice falling onto rocks.

Nonetheless, outside the painless, dreamlike state in which he was ensconced, Hopestill remained sensible of voices even though he could not make out exactly what was being said. He was also vaguely aware of a wet eye scrutinizing him.

"Eh? What did he say? What did he say?"

The Rev. Mather, wig removed, unbuttoned at the collar now, sweating lightly in spite of the night's moderate cool, looked wildly around him at Goodman Fain and his men for some interpretation or insight. Naturally, there was none to be had.

These six, without orders, had remained in the close room, crowded together so as to better hear the story of Indian cruelty, a theme to which they were perversely devoted, being New Englanders.

Such tales added to the growing legend of the red people, who, truth be told, few had actually met in the wild.

Most city dwellers rarely left the confines of their immediate neighborhoods and when they did encounter the odd Indian, this was generally speaking some poor wretch fallen on hard times, an object of derision or more often scorn.

Encountering one of these scroyles, stretched out in an alleyway or near the wharf, who could barely stand up when blindly under the influence, one was hard put to imagine them as Beelzebub's helpmates.

On the other hand, the Indian of their imagination, the Indian of the incessant, lurid gossip to which they were given, was a fiendish figure.

Employed along with the French Papists of Canada these frightful agents almost certainly worked in league with Satan to destroy the chosen people of the Lord, namely themselves, by driving them into the sea – but only after they had feasted on their banquet of blood and torture.

"Hear him tell it," one of the pox-faced guards gasped in amazement at a particularly grisly moment in Hopestill's account.

"Ooooooo," marveled the short, swarthy man standing next to him. "'is wery eyes gooshin' out of 'is head! I wou' ha' seen that if I could."

This observation spawned a spirited debate.

Goodman Fain's men relived the final moments of poor Treadway, arguing with a certain degree of peasant logic the relative merits of harsh mistreatment in English jails compared to that while in the clutches of Devil's red imps.

Ultimately, a common consensus was reached that Tread-way's martyrdom was the most unhappy when considering that the Pequots' victim in this instance did not get his fair trial, such as those that the accursed witches were currently getting in Salem Village, a point that occasioned a new round of discussion.

They didn't get quite all the narrator's story, though.

Toward its finish, Hopestill had lapsed into the incomprehensible tongue of Pennacook Algonquin that he spoke fluently. This had confounded them just as the sick old man's account had reached an especially hair-raising passage.

"'e's speakin' Injun. 'e's a bleedin' Injun!" remarked the tallest of the stretcher-bearers, Claude Thomson.

Had it not been for the unnatural crook of his back, Thomson would have stood taller still. Thomson's funny, rusty colored hair, which rather matched the shade of his grave-digging fingernails, earned him the nickname of "Orange'ead," an appellation he very generously took, no harm meant, as a nod to His Royal Highness King William.

The guard made as if to touch Hopestill, to examine him like a horse, before he was warned away with a violent look from Fain, who himself was a very nasty customer indeed.

The swarthy guard, Eustas Sheen, snorted in derision. "The bloke is white, Orange'ead. Look at 'im at now and tell me 'e's not."

"Well then, Mister 'igh 'n' Mighty, who else 'as them a blinkin' arrow inked onto their chests, eh?" retorted Orangehead Thomson with more than a modicum of satisfaction, pointing at the blue tattoo of a horizontal shaft nestled among Hopestill's oozing pocks sores.

Once again, argumentation resumed as to whether the sick man was red or white, with opinions sharply divided, but they returned to the subject of witches again since the man on the settle had apparently fainted.

"Enough!" snapped the minister at the gawking guards. "Silence!"

Cotton Mather rose, his knees creaking after the hours spent in bearing up the heavy writing desk. Upon it lay the scattered papers, quills and ink pots from the (more or less) transcription of remarks and observations by the man known as Hopestill Foster, who had somehow become an ensign or former ensign with the Old Norfolk Regiment. There he served under, Mather believed, that testy Methuselah, Major Robert Pike.

What Foster was doing in Boston at this time remained a mystery, still to be unlocked from a brain twisted in fever. Yet Mather knew a proverb or two about a dog and a bone and persistence when it mattered. It certainly mattered in this instance, a thought that occurred to him now that the ugly subject of the witches had been revived by these ignoramus guardsmen of Fain's.

The witches of Salem!

It reddened his ears to hear this disturbing inner voice weigh in once more, but how he wished he had never heard of these cursed cases!

Of late, the judges had turned to him, Mather, their philosophical and ecumenical touchstone, for the security of a learned opinion on the points of law upon which this serious, deadly serious, affair was now turning.

Their fear was shockingly palpable that public opinion would rebound on them in this delicate phase, as the hunt necessarily widened to net all the Feared One's agents.

Already some grumbling had been heard in court, some ill looks cast, but as yet there was no concerted revolt, no revolution of thinking, thank the Good Lord.

From under heavy lidded eyes Mather looked at the muttering man across from him, who just minutes before had fainted away.

He knew of the man's dastardly relations with the Indians of the north, and of Foster's reputation as the son of a red sorcerer.

Now he knew of his godless background and his ties to the hated Hutchinson woman and her familiar, Mary Dyer, the infamous dead heretic.

His late Uncle Seaborn had long maintained that the man Foster had played a role in the Quakers incident of the early '60s.

Taken together, the collective evidence of Foster's past was of a certainty somehow related to the curse he was sure lay at the root of the madness now gripping Boston, Salem and even poor Ipswich.

But he put these facts aside for the moment.

Rubbing the ridge above his nose in blessed quietude Mather's thoughts flew to both his late uncle Seaborn and his deceased grandfather, that scion of early Boston, the famed Rev. John Cotton. An impression of their judgmental faces billowed up behind his closed eyes.

The room had gone silent as the minister had demanded – with a single exception: the verbal pollution, that filthy Indian tongue, was still being emitted from between the lips of the man sprawled in his coma on the settle.

It was unprecedented that a criminal like Foster, an enemy collaborator, should have come into Mather's possession. It was a clear sign of the Lord's favor, which he so earnestly sought at every waking moment.

Lord, how tired he himself had become!

Almost three in the morning now.

This was the darkest hour of all to the minister since it was well past the witching hour, when the door opened to the invisible world that existed just beyond the pale of the lives of good, ordinary men and women.

How much longer would this interrogation take? Mather winced at the idea that Fain's men had been listening these many hours.

Most of all, he grieved at the possibility that a spark may have been struck for the firing of future gossip about the renegade's familiarity with the strange ghosts that haunted the minister's family past.

He pondered, too, where things stood, admitting to the unseen voice that the hangings of recent days had rattled him. The voice in his head mocked him in return. With the great will with which he was blessed, he banished it.

Mather's hand idly reached into the ditty bag at his side, to the little personalized Bible he kept in it, a gift from Increase delivered with a father's kiss for his ordination. It was earmarked at Matthew 8:25-26, his text for the week's sermon. As a passage, it was one of his beloveds.

Mather read, lips silently moving, no stuttering now, "Lord, save us: we perish ..." (This they had begged Jesus Christ as Devil's storm raged. And He had told them ...) "Why are ye fearful, O ye of little faith?"

The minister's eyes grew heavy and he closed them. Soon, his own unremembered dreams carried him away. He clutched the little book ever tighter as he pursued them.

Fain's men, not even whispering, were hushed away by Tizzoo back to the kitchen area after her master passed out. The constable's assistant resumed his post by the door.

A dour look darkened the countenance of the brute Fain as

the Indian gibberish continued to burble out of the mouth of the dying man on the settle. The guard rolled his eyes and fingered his thick club as he wished himself into his wife's sweat-dampened bed this unholy hour.

Hopestill's imaginings were of a far less agreeable character.

His fevered mind remained in that dark forest of his agonized dreams, his cheeks still burning from where Oonoonunkawaee had brushed them with the fire stick.

For hours there, terrorized, he had refused to open his eyes, as the last time he did so it was to view the hideous leavings of Treadway's head protruding from the ground, reduced now to a smoking ruck of gore.

His arms had been pinioned behind him around a middling tree, and Borzugwon had made the cords unnecessarily tight, cutting off the circulation. In spite of the hell around him, Hopestill had fallen into a state of drifting, possibly a form of sleep, when he next became aware of a hand smelling of ashes curled around his face covering his mouth and under his nose, tightening there.

Brushing past him, from all sides now, since it was evident the camp had been surrounded, many silent pairs of feet padded into the clearing where the besotted Pequots lay snoring, arms and legs akimbo around the fire, which had been allowed to die down into a pit of glowering cinders, as alive as an eye. These winked at Hopestill as, gagged by the hand attached to the body crouching behind him, he watched more warriors than he could count creep into sight.

These Indians were garishly painted on chest, face and arms, with most bearing shaven heads bristling with woodpecker or crow feathers. Two of them carried heavy muskets of the old style with the cumbersome wheel-lock mechanism for igniting the powder in the pan. The rest were armed with clubs and axes.

At an unseen signal, the invaders fell upon the Pequots.

The resistance of the startled sleepers amounted to nothing more than a few wild outcries of distress. The deed was accomplished in mere minutes. Captured, Oonoonunkawaee's band was reduced to complete submission in the face of their enemies. They held their heads low to await the inevitable death coup.

Hopestill's hands were untied and he was hauled up by strong arms, blinking and dumbfounded.

Surrounded by three of the tallest, stoutest Indians among the new men, he could not be certain of what had just happened, although it was clear his life and fate were now in new hands.

He averted his eyes from the terrible thing that was Treadway, in plain sight still but unrecognizable as a human being.

The Pequots, no fight in them, docile as sheep, were stood up. Long yokes made of green, forked branches were fastened around their necks. They sang their death song, a mournful, tuneless, monotonous chant.

An Indian, smaller and darker than the Pequots, went from one to the other with a bag of lead powder mixed with mud with which he blackened the heads of the captives. Several of the band that had taken them jabbered menacingly at the Pequots while the paint was being applied, evidence there was much bad feeling between the two war parties.

At dawn's first light, the entire body pushed off and turned away directly west. This was easy to tell from the position of the rising sun behind them, which promised a warmer day than the ones previous.

The morning's sharp frost quickly thawed. The large party marched and marched, but in a steady and deliberate fashion with no hurrying – this outfit of strong, hardy men seemed to fear nothing. It took them two warmer and sunnier days before they reached the mighty river Hopestill came to know as the Merrimack.

There beside that beautiful blue ribbon, its surface shivering with the light autumn wind, the Indians threw down their packs and stopped to fish for the sturgeon, an enormous species he had never before laid eyes upon.

When one was taken under the gills with a trident, the spearman's partners on shore would scramble down the banks to take over and wrestle the primeval fish to ground. Each sturgeon's belly was full of black-gray eggs, which the sea-beast's captors scooped out by hand and ate raw.

That afternoon, the whole band feasted on the delicious flesh of the abundant catch. Hopestill relished the warm, roasted chunks divvied out to him served on a piece of birch bark plate. Wild plums, still in season, completed the meal. The yoked Pequots were thrown the fish heads and pelted with the fruit stones, which they haughtily disdained.

They continued along the banks of the great watery route for less than a day before being "hallooed" by several similarly dressed members of the same tribe, so identified by their liberal use of red dye on their bodies and accoutrements, the color a seeming predominate style among these particular Indians.

Many wore their shirts, some made out of European linen in the French style, hanging out and dyed red, or were adorned by a scarlet feather stuck in a scalp lock from which hung a long ponytail of hair liberally greased with animal fat.

This was the canoe guard and at their arrival a series of yells and joyous screaming arose, with much waving of weaponry, the clamor growing in intensity as the black-painted Pequots were led forth. The captives were roughly separated and flung into the bottoms of the waiting canoes. These were drawn up and ranged along the shoreline like a small flotilla.

Hopestill was assigned to his boat with the chief of the band, a brown-as-bean Indian named Wonnalancet. He knelt far forward in the gunwales, gazing upon the stunning vista of the river after they pushed off.

Along the wide banks, the sweetness of the grassland overflowed with honeysuckle and clover, the pleasing scent lingering in the breeze. Blue-black ducks and colorful waterfowl of all kinds rose up in flapping thousands as their approach sent these winged armies to flight.

The Indian next to Hopestill grunted while paddling, but his strong strokes seemed effortless. The boy held his tongue since he had reconciled himself to the impossibility of conversing with his new captors. These Indians lacked even the rough command of his own language that Oonoonunkawaee had displayed. Yet here and there they spared a few familiar words for his pleasure – "gun," "Injun," "hunt," "eat."

The raiders were flummoxed by Hopestill's name, though, since they couldn't pronounce it. On their first day on the march, Wonnalancet, the band's head man who had taken a fancy to him, kept trying and trying, but gave up the attempt. Pokes and grunts were substituted.

Hopestill was not resigned to die anonymously. While eating sturgeon, camped on the Merrimack, he turned to Wonnalancet and looked him in the eye.

"Robinhood," he told the Indian. He thumped his breast and repeated his new name with emphasis – "Robinhood!"

If he were going to his death or to some new torment why shouldn't he adopt an intrepid identity, the name of a childhood hero, entering into this strange new life of uncertain duration? The legend he remembered fondly from his youth in England suited his purpose admirably.

He was proud he had thought of it!

The more the idea took hold in him, the bolder he proclaimed it to the Indians. They, in turn, delighted in these sudden assertions and expostulations from the hitherto mild Englishman they had rescued from the torture of the Pequots. It gave them pleasure to see this new fire in the eyes of the young man.

After much trial, they were finally able to speak a fairly workmanlike version of the Sherwood Forest outlaw's name, and referred to Hopestill as "Robinhood" in their fashion after that. Indeed, for as long as his life among them.

Chapter Fifteen

A Son of Passaconnaway

The fleet of canoes sliced through the middle of the broad Merrimack in a straight line, their paddlers rhythmically cutting deep into the cold water, water so clear the pebble-laden tableau beneath them could be seen running on like an endless mosaic.

They were en route to Pennacook, the name of the place down-river to which the Indians repeatedly pointed. They kept well clear of any wooded islands.

Hopestill found it difficult to contemplate death in the midst of this boundless beauty and serenity. Yet there it was, underneath the surface, this question of what would happen to him when they got to where they were going.

His fear had, however, diminished considerably since his first day as property belonging to new hands.

He had not once been manhandled by Wonnalancet's men who used him far better than the Pequots. His share of the load was light – commensurate with his strength and health, considering both had deteriorated drastically after the original ambush of the Heard party.

Furthermore, he greatly admired the cohesiveness of this large band of fighters.

Even within the friendly territory of the Merrimack they kept up a strict guard, posting pickets far out from the line of march to give warning. Their silent mode of travel, too, was a revelation in comparison with the sloppy tactics employed by the Pequots. Such men, he supposed with unexpected optimism, might not be given to bouts of insane cruelty. This assumption provided a modicum of comfort although thoughts of his personal safety were becoming less and less important to him.

This was due to a rising anger that had been building inside Hopestill, and it competed for his full attention now that his fate hung in the balance once again. Not quite the rage of Achilles, perhaps, but a cousin to it boiled within like a kettle rattling over the flame, carrying with it a bitter reflux that threatened to gag him.

His capture – double capture now! – the agonies he had suffered, the sickening torture he had seen inflicted on a helpless man, this combined with all the frustrations and hardships of his life to date had been relentlessly displacing his natural mildness with the malignant, emotional curse of raw hatred, that, when experienced, filled his eyes to their tops with an unrequited fury he could scarcely contain. Yet already he was learning from the Indians. He kept his face impenetrable.

When he could bend his mind to the happier subject of hopefulness, he found there were good grounds for it. During the trek to the great river Hopestill's wounds had been personally seen to by the band's leader, Wonnalancet. Salve had been applied, not too roughly, to Hopestill's worst cuts and burns. The Indian had also given him a soft deerskin coat as a wrap for his torn shoulders, which protected him amazingly from the night cold while its texture was soothing against his tender skin.

Wonnalancet, while not a very large man physically, was amazingly athletic. Blessed with an intelligent countenance and a native kindness that transcended race, he had a sense of humor, too, that was not too crude – there was always some good-natured clowning around when the laughing leader joined any group.

On the river, though, Wonnalancet's face remained stern and determined. From his position in the lead canoe, he rarely looked back, or cast even a glance at the hovering ospreys that swooped out of the sky, launching themselves at the fish they spied. All the Indian's energy was bent on plying his paddle, repetitious as a machine.

The spindrift flung into their faces and onto their chests from the strokes dried quickly with the wind in their faces. The light air added to the speed with which they traveled. Hopestill looked forward, however perversely, to the resolution awaiting him ahead.

Just as the sun began its slow descent into the western sky and the shadows began to grow longer, the canoes sharply rounded a wide bend in the river. Without notice, the astonishing sight of a sprawling, chaotic village erupted into view.

This was unexpected. Suddenly, Hopestill's fear returned, his dread redoubled. His bowels grew loose, and the stink of his own waste soon assaulted his nostrils. The men behind him laughed.

Hundreds of shouting, gesticulating Indians of all ages rushed to crowd both banks as the canoes veered closer. They charged out of sturdy bark-and-branch wigwams that couldn't possibly have held so many. These conical structures dotted the large clearings in all directions. Musket shots rang out, seen at first by the pan flashes then followed by the odd, disconnected popping noise of bullets fired. Young women waggled their wailing babies, bound to boards, holding them high, old women shook tools and large branches at them while ululating in mad concert, a few more guns went off, then even more warriors hurled themselves into canoes from an island nestled in the river's bend to join the grand arrival, speeding to greet their brothers who had returned.

One by one, Wonnalancet's canoes steered onto the shelf of a flat, stony beach to the right, his Indians hopping out before they grounded, pulling their frail craft up onto the rough shingle in one effortless motion. A mass of Indians, men and women, now pressed them from three sides, babbling with a frenetic energy. A forest of hands reached out to grab Hopestill and pull him out of his canoe. From there, he was bundled along inside the gut of the mob, buffeted by bodies both reeking and sweet smelling. Some called out the name he had given himself, Robinhood – "Oahbenod!" is what it sounded like – as he was gripped in their embrace, held upright in the heart of the melee. His blond hair, plaited into a long tail by the Indians at their last camp, was stroked and touched by many fingers.

He could not see the Pequots who were in the following canoes, but he heard the renewed roar of the Indians shrieking at them as they were obviously led ashore behind him. Part of the crowd from his group broke away and surged to the captives even as he was led farther up the well-packed bank.

Turning his head to look back, Hopestill noticed a small knot of decidedly different Indians, more exotic-looking than even the Pequots. They stood on a small rise, aloof from the others, impassively watching the joyous scene unfolding before them.

Several of these strangers were decorated with heavy necklaces of shells wound round their necks in multiple strands. Colorful blankets with striking symbols woven or painted onto them covered their shoulders or were casually tossed over a powerful arm. Their heads, shaven save for a greased ridge at the crown, gleamed in the late afternoon glare. Their eyes, like the dead orbs within the rows of gutted fish to their left, pinned within an enormous framework of wooden slats to dry in the warm sun, were intent on the Pequots rather than Hopestill. Slowly, as in a body, they leisurely strolled downhill to join the mob of Pennacooks that had boiled up from the water's edge.

As they made their way there, the larger throng of howling men and women with Hopestill in its midst arrived at the center of a tidy, open green that had been swept clear. Its function was obviously as a common area where bigger gatherings could be accommodated.

Here Hopestill, while not bound or restrained in any way except by the constraint of being hemmed in by many curious bodies, was able, by dint of his height, to see the entry of yet another retinue into the crowd. This was a small knot of elders that had emerged from a well-built lodge-house higher up near the tree line. In front of it was a massive cooking pit over which hung three black kettles. Long log poles set in the earth nearby were pegged with the carcasses of gutted deer. The band of old men paused briefly to sniff at the contents of the kettles, then resumed their approach.

The mass of Indians parted to let them pass, showing every indication of a respect for their very evident authority, even though that authority was contained in the unlikely body of an ancient gnome wearing a gray wolf's head cap, gravely bent over but still with the full use of his sagging limbs. This elder of elders half-dragged, half-carried an intricately carved ceremonial spear that he used as a walking stick.

"Bashaba!" "Bashaba!" they cried out to him, pure delight written on their faces.

Their guttural glee revived that curious mixture of dread and fury which tore at Hopestill's emotions. It was all he could do to stop himself from screaming along with them.

The Indians backed away to create a path for their Bashaba

that led directly down to Hopestill. Stamping his spear, the chief abruptly stopped a few feet away from the white man.

He deliberately sized up the much taller figure of Hopestill, finishing by staring intently into the young man's disoriented eyes.

The mass of his followers grew silent except for a few loud voices coming from the rear of the crush of bodies.

Hopestill stood as straight as he could manage, nearly fainting with the effort to not show fear or any other kind of emotion.

The Bashaba smiled at him, then the little wizened figure raised his free hand slowly from the fold of his large blanket. The woolen wrapper slipped aside, betraying an age that must surely have made him 50 years old if not older. His puckered chest was covered in circles of varying sizes, painted in the darkest almagra, while a pair of thick green bars were smeared diagonally, left to right, from his shoulder to his sunken navel.

In the Bashaba's hand was an angry snake. Now revealed, it danced wildly in his grip.

The old gnome stroked the black, thick-bodied rattler with the spear's shaft while jabbering to Hopestill in the strange language of his new captors. Both men's eyes were locked into the other's. The snake, meanwhile, turned its head and looked at the old man in seeming agreement. Its long tongue flickered and licked the air, and its powerful tail curled around the loose folds of skin hanging from the Bashaba's scrawny arm.

At a word, one of the chief's seconds took the spear and the serpent. The old man advanced a pace forward and held out his left hand to within a foot of Hopestill's face. He opened it, uncovering in his heavily lined palm a shriveled leaf that he then crushed to bits.

The hand opened and closed, opened and closed. On the tenth opening, the powdery residue disappeared. On the eleventh, it was replaced by a wet green leaf in the full body of its life, as if it had just been plucked from a young beech.

The look on Hopestill's face at this magic was one of complete astonishment, a reaction that tickled the old man. The Bashaba's wry Asiatic face split into a playful grin.

He turned to the Indian behind him still holding the struggling reptile and addressed himself to the snake as if to explain what had just happened. The Indians around them took up the joke and laughed heartily. The chief lightly patted Hopestill's face, a surprising gesture that left the young man further nonplussed. A murmur of approval arose from the seething mob.

With a bit of a flourish, the old man turned away. The crowd again opened a path, allowing the chief and his entourage to move to greet Wonnalancet and his warriors who, with war clubs and hatchets in hand, stood surrounding the cowed, kneeling Pequots. Wonnalancet addressed his chief in a strong and steady voice, recounting, no doubt, their successful foray and equally successful return.

As the powerful raiding leader spoke, the small knot of strange Indians seen earlier by Hopestill sidled in closer to the Pequots.

One of that group, a wolfish looking warrior with exceptionally white teeth and mahogany eyes, stepped to the forefront of his companions and waited patiently to be recognized.

Indian women standing near Hopestill muttered "Magwak" under their breath with evident disgust.

The Bashaba ignored the Magwaks, as Hopestill assumed these warriors were called. Rather, the old chief listened intently to Wonnalancet, every so often nodding or grunting, as a father might listen to one of his progeny. And there was, upon consideration by Hopestill, a resemblance in both separated by many decades.

Behind the chief stood a pot-bellied Indian of middle age dressed more or less like an Englishman with long pants, no shirt and a floppy coat. His garb was topped off with a sort of slouch hat, much beaten up. This trailing Indian still held the old man's props, the writhing snake and the monster spear. When he spoke, very rarely, it was in a direct voice as if to clear up a point or two. He never took his eyes off the Magwak Indians.

These three, the Bashaba, Wonnalancet and the pot-bellied Indian, oblivious to the others around them, grew more animated as their conversation continued.

Then, following a long discourse without interruption from the chief, Wonnalancet made a wide sweep of his arm toward the Pequots.

He continued talking but in a more threatening tone, at which a strong murmur of disapproval arose from the nearest listeners. This angry murmuring was taken up in turn by all the other Indians until the gobbling of their language rose to a din.

A second Indian who had been with Wonnalancet's party when they had taken Hopestill, a man with an unpronounceable name and a sort of yellow lightning bolt blazoned across his chest, joined in the discussion, making his case in dynamic fashion, causing all heads to swing to Hopestill and then back to the Bashaba. With some final talk the parley ended abruptly.

Hopestill was shoved at the chief's group by many hands.

Wonnalancet approached him. He talked to the young Englishman in a mild voice but Hopestill could understand nothing of what he said.

He was led to the trussed-up Pequots.

Hopestill's insides twitched involuntarily, although he did not humiliate himself as he had done in the canoe. The little knot of men including the Bashaba now faced the Pequots.

The captives had been forced to kneel in a semi-circle, their hands bound behind them, the yokes replaced around their necks. Each stared straight ahead, expressionless and stoic. Several bore bloody wounds suffered in the surprise attack. Their faces were still blackened, rendering them even more satanic.

Oonoonunkawaee was one of these. This was the Pequot who had taken Hopestill in the Heard raid, and who had tormented him so sadistically. But the war chief was hardly a figure of terror now that his aura of invincibility had been shattered so easily by Wonnalancet's men.

Congealed blood caked the side of this once-formidable fighter's hatchet arm. His eyes had the glazed look of someone who had been struck a tremendous blow from which he had not fully recovered. The effect of surrender was so complete Hopestill had the distinct impression that if Oonoonunkawaee's hands were untied and the yoke removed, the Pequot would still grovel before the crooked-back ancient chief of the Pennacooks.

Yet when Oonoonunkawaee looked up and beheld his former captive towering over him he recovered his superior demeanor. The mask of hate replaced the face of submission.

And in that demonic stare, Hopestill could see the terrified eyes of poor, tortured Treadway reflected back at him as if they had been imprinted there.

Suddenly, the young man's ears filled, not with the growing clamor of the hundreds of Pennacook Indians surrounding him, but with the bleating of that human lamb in his death agonies, imprisoned in a world of pagan pain with even death's relief an impossible mercy.

Into Hopestill's right hand a war club was thrust.

The young man looked at this massive object with a sense of detachment, as if it weren't he to whom all were excitedly jabbering, but some other man.

The Bashaba pointed to Oonoonunkawaee and lightly swung his arm as if flicking at a no-see-um. At the same time, he intoned a very serious remark in his language to Hopestill that needed no translation since its meaning was brutally clear.

The club was polished and substantial but lighter than it looked. And rather than the usual round stone embedded in its head, this particular weapon was studded with the points of razor-tipped deer antlers so it was more in the line of a knight's mace. Its only function was to deliver a death blow.

Hopestill weighed it in his hand. Gripping it tightly by the handle he surveyed the anxious babbling heads around him before leveling his concentration on Oonoonunkawaee.

A sneer of defiance creased the Pequot's mouth and before he was even conscious of any thought to do this man harm, Hopestill reared back his arm and with all his strength sank the spikes of the club into Oonoonunkawaee's skull. Brain matter and blood sprayed everywhere. A bloodcurdling roar burst from the throat of Oonoonunkawaee's murderer. Hopestill screamed with the pent-up passion of a wounded animal.

But then, before anyone could think to stop him, Hopestill wrenched the war club out of the dead Pequot's head, lifted it again and struck at the uncomprehending, incredulous face of Borzug-won, who was yoked to the huge, still-twitching Pequot leader.

This second, uninvited blow sparked an immediate riot.

Bodies piled onto Hopestill from behind, slamming him to the earth and knocking the breath out of him. He could feel hands clawing to get at him. The chaos of fighting raged from all directions.

In the midst of this madness one voice, and Hopestill knew it came from the bellowing mouth of the pot-bellied retainer for the Bashaba since the man was draped completely over him, was haranguing them all in a tongue he could understand.

"Stop! Stop! Stop!"

The Indian, his body absorbing all manner of punishment meant for Hopestill, continued to plead.

"Passaconnaway need English son!" he screamed like a man raving.

In point of fact, everyone was raving.

Chapter Sixteen

Death Wish

The Mohawk delegation believed it had been disgraced twice by the Pennacooks. Wonnalancet's pre-emptive capture of Oonoonunkawaee's band was the first blow, the second and worst was Hopestill's theft of their remaining glory with his cowardly bludgeoning of the shawl-wearing Borzugwon.

The latter event had precipitated a melee in which seventeen warriors had been injured, but the worst hurt had been to Mohawk pride. These were, after all, representatives from the nation of the Keepers of the Eastern Door, the most feared within the Iroquois Confederacy. They had ranged a long way from their castles and longhouses on the river that bears the tribe's name in the colony of New York.

That they journeyed so far was due to their particular antipathy toward Oonoonunkawaee's men and to Pequots in general. These they regarded as an insolent tribe lacking in manners and obsequiousness. That along with promises of generous Dutch and English bounties for the killers' scalps led the Mohawk hunters to follow an extremely complicated trail of murder and outrage that ended in the heart of Passaconnaway's territory.

The Mohawks had failed to vanquish the Pequots, so they resorted to diplomacy with the Pennacooks to restore their lost respect. This was the necessary ingredient for peace among the nations of the people.

There in the fishing village at the bend of the Merrimack a solemn yet uneasy agreement had been reached with Chief Passaconnaway. With the sole exception of Oonoonunkawaee, the Pequot leader whose death was preordained, the remaining captives of his band would become the legal property of the Mohawks who had arrived in Pennacook hot on their trail but unfortunately too late.

True, it boded ill for the relations between Mohawk and Pennacook that the news of Wonnalancet's feat had arrived well before the return of Passaconnaway's son, his men and their prisoners. Yet even so, both sides had finally been able to put aside any residual rancor in order to strike a fair settlement that permitted the freed Englishman to take his symbolic revenge on the Pequot leader. This allowed Passaconnaway to prove to the English that his friendship with them remained inviolate. The Bashaba insisted on this non-negotiable term.

The Mohawks, assuaged with presents and expressions of love, agreed. Nominally at peace with the English due to their contempt for the Dutch and their hatred for the French, the proud Iroquois were not unmindful of Indian sensibilities in this part of their world. Privately, though, they believed Passaconnaway was behaving like a begging dog.

Then Borzugwon was murdered by Hopestill and the ensuing riot threatened to destroy all that had been achieved.

Although profuse apologies, promises of tribute and further demonstrations of loyalty averted outright war, the renewed undercurrent of bad feeling could not be diverted. There was now little more that could be said in the way of polite palavering and gift-giving that might ease the Mohawks' bruised feelings.

Just as dangerous for Hopestill's scalp was that more than a few Pennacooks were alarmed by Passaconnaway's balking at the Mohawk demands for all the Pequots. These tribesmen were loyal to Nanamacomuck, Wonnalancet's eldest brother, who was a warrior with a fierce nature and by virtue of his significant birth the hereditary leader of the great deer clan within the tribe.

Nanamacomuck feared Mohawk retribution in the wake of Hopestill's mad slaying of Borzugwon. This act he saw as a shocking affront to the most powerful of the Iroquois confederacy's tribes, one that could, if it so desired, destroy them on the Merrimack as easily as if they were geese on the water.

Nanamacomuck's faction lobbied strenuously to his father for offering Hopestill to replace the slain Borzugwon for the grand torture the Mohawks were preparing for the unlucky Pequots upon their return home.

Passaconnaway wouldn't hear of further appeasement.

He had absolutely no interest in losing his English protection in the form of the crazed, blonde-haired captive that Wonnalancet had opportunely redeemed from the bloody minded Pequots.

As he checked his oldest son, he reminded him that he, the Sagamore of the Pennacooks, had always counseled submission to the English Puritans and would always do so.

This was a truth no Pennacook could deny.

The whites, he told his sons and chiefs, could not be defeated, could never be defeated, and if the tribe was to survive in the years to come, it must make its peace with the whites and never break that peace, no matter what. Such talk frustrated and infuriated Nanamacomuck and his followers, yet they would not disobey the

Old Man of the Hills who could juggle with stones and talk to the rattlesnake.

Yet the shaky truce would hold for now. In the end, the talks concluded with the old chief putting on a juggling act with his three smooth rock balls, a show that never failed to fascinate them and ease their minds. Hopestill was kept out of sight.

Warily, the tribe turned out in force to watch as the Mohawks took their sullen leave of Pennacook with their three surviving Pequots, blackened in face and yoked at the neck. That night, led by Passaconnaway, his people held a ceremony in which they asked the Spirit for it to be an eternity before another Mohawk came among them. Oonoonunkawaee's and Borzugwon's smashed bodies, minus their precious scalps gifted to the visitors, were hauled away for the wolves.

Hopestill had been forcibly sequestered during these negotiations, taken to a lodge where dried hides were stacked higher than he was tall. The stink was outrageous. The fleas infesting these stiff, revolting boards hopped on him throughout his stay, causing him a great deal of torment, although eventually he was removed to a wigwam filled with the pungent smoke of wet logs that the lice did not appreciate.

His companion in isolation was the pot-bellied Jonny Findus, Passaconnaway's most loyal retainer and the first to jump on him at the beginning of the brawl since it was his duty to protect the Englishman from harm. Indeed, Jonny's bulk and Borzugwon's corpse had shielded Hopestill from the worst of the savagery, which was in any case limited to blows, gouges and bites due to the suddenness that had touched it off.

Jonny was one of the Bashaba's trusted aides not only because he knew how to milk a rattlesnake's venom, thus denuding it of most of its poison, but because he could speak passable English.

This he had learned after being taken as a young hostage by the Puritans during one of their frequent panics that an Indian uprising was imminent. He spent eight not altogether unpleasant years in Plymouth learning about the Holy Ghost and the proper way to turn a roast on a spit.

This experience in its entirety was a happenstance that worked out well for him the day Jonny decided to leave his owner. Not a single English voice challenged him when he departed, nor was he molested by animal or human as he somehow found his way back to Pennacook. The enormity of Jonny's feat impressed Passaconnaway to the extent that he took the boy under his wing and showed him some of his secrets, although not how to juggle with the stones.

As they sat in the smoke lodge, both blinking rapidly at the stinging clouds and staring off into space since they couldn't very easily make out anything too clearly, Hopestill asked Jonny what was to be done with him – his overriding fear being that he would be gifted to the Mohawks in reprisal for murdering Borzugwon. This horror the pot-bellied retainer waved away into the vapor.

"You return English. You say Pequots all dead. You say Passaconnaway's people loyal. You tell them, huh? You go home."

In response, Hopestill reflected on the emptiness of his life.

"I have no home," he said bitterly.

Jonny shrugged. "You have home. You live. Everywhere home."

Hopestill felt sick.

His wanton act of murder replayed in his mind with revolting acuity. He was ravaged in spirit and body, disgusted by everything he had seen and experienced in old England and new America. His filthy condition, the fleas crawling over him, his being covered with another man's blood and brain matter, his wounds, the smoke, his cowardly fleeing from Boston and his betrayal of Priscilla – everything about himself and his life to date repulsed him.

The inner violence he felt in his mind and heart erupted from his lips.

"I have no wish to go back. I wish to die."

To this, Jonny Findus had no answer.

In the days that followed, the departure of the Mohawks coupled with the demise of Oonoonunkawaee's band brought forth a general wave of good feeling.

Wonnalancet's taking of the Pequots ended the threat it posed for Puritan retaliation against the wrong Indians, namely the Pennacooks. This was a constant source of dread since it was well-established the whites did not distinguish among the tribes nor, as Passaconnaway had learned the hard way, seem to care which was the guilty Indian and which was not, so long as the deaths of red-skinned men resulted.

Also, it went without saying that the humiliation of the Mohawks, while causing a fright, had its beneficial side. Chiefly, it provided a source of amusement to Passaconnaway's people at the expense of the detested (and absent) Iroquois.

But the grave matter of Hopestill's return was another thing altogether. When his reluctance to be repatriated to the English became known there was an outcry.

Furthermore, this was only the prelude to a new round of objections when the gossip that is a prime source of information among tribal members gave rise to speculation that, as a possible solution, the Bashaba was considering adopting Hopestill into the tribe.

Even greater opposition arose from this.

Few wanted the Englishman to remain in their village a day

longer than necessary, since they argued not without validity that his presence was a standing threat, insulting as it was to the Mohawks.

Again, Passaconnaway refused to give in. As well pleased as he was with the advantages that accrued from the English-speaking Jonny Findus, the temptation of adopting a white man into his tribe suggested unthinkable possibilities for future security.

He had, for instance, begun planning to reach out anew to representatives of Dover, the nearest white settlement, in the wake of the Pequot raid that had killed Runny Jim Tunkett of Jim Heard's work party on the afternoon that Hopestill was taken. This was essential if a retaliatory raid on the Pennacooks was to be prevented.

It was Passaconnaway's belief, and Jonny Findus's as well, that the rescue of Hopestill along with proof of the capture of the real murderers would also work to the tribe's favor in the ongoing question of the establishment of a trading house near the village at the bend of the Merrimack.

The Bashaba had thus far held these negotiations at arm's length, for the sachem was wary the whites might use the post as a foothold on Pennacook land to steal it. Thus, held at a cautious distance was a powerful newcomer to the region, the white chief Walderne, who had recently settled in Dover.

As the days passed, Passaconnaway considered Hopestill's adoption with increasing seriousness. He began to more fully embrace this venture in hope it would serve as an impediment to a future war with the Puritan English the Indians could not possibly win.

By integrating the tribe onto the land as farmers and workers of the soil it might not be taken away from them and there would be no mostly one-sided blood spilling.

For this plan to succeed, the tribe needed tools and expertise, as well as seed for new crops, which could be obtained in the peaceful atmosphere in which trade flourished. Also, a truckhouse dedicated to trade, even one run by Walderne, would bring white protection closer to Pennacook, where it was needed to stem encroachment from the French and their allies, as well as the deadly Mohawks.

Passaconnaway's adoption scheme, at first a fancy, soon sprouted into a full-blown plan that grew out of Hopestill's spurning of all offers to return to the white community.

The turning point came when the Indians threatened him with expulsion into the forest and indeed, banished him there after he had frustrated the old man yet again.

Hopestill accepted this judgment without demur.

One frosty morning, he strode out of camp empty handed and bare-headed, walking away from them until he could travel no farther. Exhausted at the end of the day by his long hike, he sat down in the midst of the unknown wilderness and waited with a certain amount of longing for the end of his life in that green and white grave.

This would not be allowed.

Passaconnaway sent Wonnalancet to check on the white man's condition as soon as the sun rose on the following day. Thus, the Indian who first rescued Hopestill saved him yet again, finding the Englishman nearly dead of the cold and seriously dehydrated, although no permanent injury, save the loss of part of a toe from frostbite, was sustained.

Hopestill's desire for his own death was a mystery, and upon his rescue and return a source of intense tribal speculation. Yet his fortitude in the face of his own suffering impressed many.

The Pennacooks came to believe this white man carried a special kind of magic, a belief that was reinforced by the Bashaba's men who had settled on a less-subtle strategy, which was to adopt Hopestill into the tribe as Passaconnaway's own son. This was a radical idea perhaps, but one with a certain flair the old man relished since it tied up so many loose ends.

So on the appointed day, without any real acceptance on Hopestill's part, a number of warriors gathered around the tall young man, dipped their fingers in ashes and twirled the cornsilk colored hairs out of his scalp one by one, guffawing as they worked. They did leave one patch of hair at the rear of his head which they adorned with bits of shell and silver. Into the lock they stitched a single red cardinal feather.

Finishing, they yanked him standing, all the loose golden hair falling off his lap and into the dust. After removing his disgusting clothes, which caused nervous tittering among the women, Hopestill was led to the Merrimack and walked into it by the Indians, who playfully turned him over to six young women and four old hags. These all vigorously took hold of him, their cold wet hands causing him instant arousal and a healthy erection, delighting the tribe which had gathered to enjoy the spectacle.

Passaconnaway strode to the bank holding his snake and spear. The hilarity died down a trifle. The old chief waved his totems at the naked Englishman in the water, chanting for a great long while in a monotone that rose and fell as he lifted the spear and waved the serpent. When it was over, the village of Pennacook erupted with cries and screams of religious ecstasy.

Then came Hopestill's moment of true concern. This was when he was pushed beneath the surface of the clean water of the river by many forcible hands. These, along with others who splashed in to assist, reached down into the silt and assorted gravel of the river bottom to scrub him so vigorously it felt as if his skin was being flayed off.

As he thought they mean to drown him, Hopestill fought to surface. He finally broke the water with his face, gasping for air, choking and coughing. The Indians rushed to him in a great wave of humanity to carry him away to dry land for he was now one of them, reborn.

Chapter Seventeen

Tizzoo's Plan

The cinnamon breath of the woman beside him, exhaling on him, close to his face, the pure animal sensation of her heat, stimulated erotic memories within the sick old man huddled and shivering on the seat-bench.

Her heaviness, the feminine substance of her, brought Hopestill back yet again from his feverish visions in the overly warm room in the strange little Boston house.

These were stirrings all but absent since he had last lain with his wife, Sennaquinna, who possessed the most delicious taste among the two women he had known, really known, throughout his long life.

This one was different, though – foreign, completely unexpected, shameless.

Hopestill opened his eyes as the dream of his adoption and that of his wife dissipated like a waft of smoke. The blinking of a small but living fire flickered on and off in the hearth.

Across from him lay the sprawled form of the unconscious

Rev. Cotton Mather, mouth open, wig askew, gasping his snores into the room. Slumped to the floor against the entry door was the constable, Goodman Fain, chin compressed into neck, hands opened into relaxed claws.

All but one of Fain's men were nowhere to be seen, although the rhoncal chorus of heavy breathing and sputtering lips from the kitchen area explained the absence of guards. Only the head and shoulders of one was in sight, on the floor mid-way between the two rooms. The man's irregularly cut pumpkin-colored hair splayed out like the tendrils of a dead vine. Like the rest, he was passed out or asleep.

Hopestill couldn't remember until just then why it was important that he awaken. Then he knew. The woman had been speaking Pennacook to him, the same tongue in which he had been babbling aloud in his reverie.

"I giz 'em sometings in dey drinks to sleeps," crooned Tizzoo, reverting to her broken English as she carefully watched his eyes fluttering in amazement.

As she smiled at him without showing her vicious teeth, her hand gently stroked his penis under the blanket, occasionally squeezing the surprisingly alert member. Hopestill sighed with guilty pleasure.

Tizzoo was a big woman but little of it was fat.

Her darkness was a sensuous brown rather than the severe black, almost purple skin, of the few Negro slaves he had seen that had come from the continent of Africa. She was balanced on the bench next to him with one slippered foot on the floor, her other tucked up underneath. Her right hand cradled his weak head. They were as close as lovers.

Hopestill asked her in Pennacook, "How much danger are we

in? I am too weak to fight."

Tizzoo answered in the same birdlike whistling tongue, although not as competently or precisely, "I think very small amount catastrophe, my master. They sleep long time yet."

"I am not your master. I know you not."

"I know you not," she repeated, laughing very quietly.

"How come you to talk Pennacook?"

"Kancamagus," she said in the manner of a flirt.

"Kancamagus." Hopestill was truly taken aback.

Sadly, he shook his head in remembrance of Nanamacomuck's youngest son. This proud Pennacook warrior, Hopestill knew, had long ago succeeded to chief of his decimated tribe, a wild, dark spirit who had grown tall and lean and strong and mean, inhabiting an angry warrior's body.

And within that body, Kancamagus nurtured a slow-burning but eternal hatred for his adoptive uncle.

Tizzoo responded again in Pennacook.

"Kancamagus my lover for long time when he Boston slave here to Quaker man. Mather and his master, they different clans, but work together, understand? Kancamagus, me, lie together, talk together, many times. Pennacook easy for me. Like Carib a little bit."

"So you are Carib, not Africa?" Hopestill asked, using the English words since there were no comparative nouns in Pennacook.

"Ah, yes. Many years back, Capt. Eggington and the son of Walderne, that trading fellow you spoke, they and they men took Tizzoo and many others from my island, Youlou, and sold me here by and by," she responded.

Capt. Eggington he didn't know at all, but Hopestill narrowed his eyes at the mention of the Walderne name since he had borne witness to the magistrate's violent end in 1689.

Paul Walderne, the magistrate's son?

He also was now dead.

The son had played a pivotal role in the sensational murder of the white man Thomas Dickinson in 1667, at the much larger truck house the senior Walderne had finally established near the village at Pennacook with Passaconnaway's blessing and Hopestill's diplomacy. Yet Hopestill had lived to regret his role in opening up Pennacook land to the English, for it had led to disaster for his adopted parent and the members of his tribe.

The younger Walderne was slapped with a light fine by the jovial, familiar court in Boston for selling Indians hard drink in the elder Walderne's low-beamed tavern, while the magistrate himself was wrongly exonerated. Walderne's flunky Coffin was also fined minimally.

Naturally, the Pennacooks were outraged, especially given the full measure of justice they themselves had meted out to Dickinson's killer.

It had fallen to Hopestill to bring the killer, the rum-loving Nanamacomuck, Passaconnaway's eldest son and Kancamagus's father, a man who was also his Indian brother through Hopestill's own adoption, back to the village for trial.

There, Nanamacomuck died under the knife on the Bashaba's direct order to assuage the wrath of the Puritans. This caused an irreparable breach within the tribe, with the incident destroying Hopestill's status among the people.

The younger Walderne, an Indian revenge target, fled New Hampshire in the aftermath of Dickinson's murder to serve as a mate on one of his father's merchant ships. A trade voyage three years later ended with a wrecked xebec off the coast of West Africa and Paul Walderne's permanent disappearance.

Hopestill's fate was left hanging. To Kancamagus, especially, his adopted white uncle Robinhood-Hopestill became a deadly enemy, one to be either murdered at any opportunity or treated with extreme cruelty should he be unlucky enough to fall captive.

So Hopestill, too, was forced to escape from the region of Dover. He finally took refuge in Salisbury with his old friends, the Pikes and the Bradburys, while serving in the militia based there. He had since risen to ensign, despite his dark past.

Tizzoo was continuing to talk to him. "Where Kancamagus this day? He dead?"

She squeezed Hopestill gently as they conversed, but not so intensely as to make him spew, employing a trick with her practiced left hand to control him. Unaccountably, he found himself amused that his condition, poxed as he was, did not revolt her, although he smiled mostly due to the pleasure she was bringing him.

"Kancamagus long ways gone," Hopestill answered, weakly. "He and his band killed Walderne and many others ..." Here he waved his hand to indicate the faraway north of New Hampshire and Dover, "... thereaways. Never him come back here again."

He looked meaningfully at Tizzoo. "Except maybe dead," he added.

Tizzoo pulled her hand away abruptly. "Him, me, we had child. But child he too much like black man."

Her stare drifted to the wall beyond.

"Baby him die," she said harshly.

As she shifted her position, her large skirts and puffed-out petticoats ruffled like running water. They were dusty and covered in cobwebs from the loft, which she now idly brushed off. She lifted these up and over the sick man's hips and thighs, settling herself carefully so that he might slip into her.

Tizzoo haughtily considered the snoring minister across from them. She said to Hopestill, "You important man. My sir looking for you long time. He say you know why Devil play here. Say witches here, there …" she gestured, her fingers waving.

Around and around she moved, he her captive. "Many hanged up, dead. I see one witch, they take woman up into tree and drop her from rope. Her tongue hang out like this …" Tizzoo waggled her own tongue. "Man walk over and push it back into her mouth, with stick. I see this thing."

When Hopestill didn't respond, couldn't respond, she inquired politely, "You Robinhood, no? Kancamagus tell me Robinhood his uncle, is white man turn Indian. He say you betray Pennacook people to help Walderne when he tricked them in Phony Battle. Many die slaves then. Make him slave, too." There was no judgment in the tone of her voice, just matter of fact.

Without giving him an opportunity to answer, Tizzoo lifted the blanket and eyed the crude rendition of a blue arrow tattooed across Hopestill's chest. She circled her finger around the numerous pocks on his bare abdomen, as if they were islands in the stream.

"Kancamagus always angry," she said softly.

"Yes," he finally managed to answer. "Kancamagus always angry."

Hopestill looked into her foreign eyes, narrowed into slits, watching him watch her. Her dusky face up close was cratered with the tell-tale marks of the disease that now held him in its grip as tightly as she had retaken him under her dress.

She manipulated him into her. Hopestill let out a gasp of surprise. "How they catch you?" she asked, slowly moving over him.

He had to think. "They not catch me. I got sick. I lay for a long time outside prison house, then they took me …." – He could not remember the word for "hospital," or even if there was such a word in Pennacook – "… to the place for the sick. Very dirty place. Somehow Mather-men found me there. You say they were looking for me, yes?"

"Yes, looking for you. You must be some kind of sorcerer. They say you know about the curse on them."

"That's not why I am here."

That was not why he came to Boston at all. He had another reason to have returned to this cursed city of Puritans for the first time in, what was it, 50 years? Had it been that long?

Yet nothing had changed. He thought of the bodies along his journey south, still hanging in Salem Village, slung from the crooks of trees, necks snapped at that peculiar angle. The sight of the corpses stayed with him still. New England was a charnel-house, Hopestill thought.

"This is very dangerous, this thing we are doing," he managed to say in the midst of his increasing passion.

The bench creaked gently, like a small boat on a quiet sea. She moaned.

"I want new baby," Tizzoo said, "baby with yellow hair, hair like yours before it turned to snow."

Together they rode the bench silently before the lazy glow in the hearth, flameless now, nearly asleep in its bed of ashes.

They finished somehow that way, locked on the hard-backed settle-seat. When it was over she slid off him and scampered to the kitchen room, tittering with joy, for a freshly shucked cob with which to wipe herself.

Hopestill could barely move after his exertion and his eyes began to close with intense weariness. The funk of their extraordinary encounter was now reduced to a vague redolence in the air. It lingered for him to contemplate until her return.

When she did, a huge grin on her face, she did her best to make him comfortable again. She gave him something to drink, cleaned him off, and covered him once more with the blanket and her shawl. Tizzoo swayed her hips together in small circles.

"This help make new baby to be created," she informed him.

"Will a baby help you in any way?"

"Oh, yes, Robinhood. White baby for Tizzoo, white baby with yellow hair even better, be very good fortune. Maybe Tizzoo they take back to Youlou, then. Be away from here. This my plan."

This was her plan. He had no words for it. His own plan was shattered.

Major Pike, a comrade in arms for so many years now, had known what this return to Boston would cost Hopestill emotionally. Yet Hopestill had been happy to serve again on behalf of his courageous superior, perhaps the only man of God and law he had ever trusted.

Lying there, he took new hope from his thoughts of Pike.

The major had remained behind, still gathering evidence in Salisbury to save the imprisoned Mary Bradbury. He found himself talking aloud.

"Who is this Mary?" she asked. She had glided behind him, now standing over the settle, rubbing his neck sweetly.

"Who is this Tizzoo?" Hopestill answered dreamily.

He was suddenly all too aware of the absurdity of the shocking situation in which he found himself, having copulated with Mather's servant with what little strength he possessed right under the minister's snoring nose, when unexpectedly Fain became the first of the drugged bodies to begin moving.

Tizzoo's hands tensed around Hopestill's neck as they both heard Fain try to turn over.

The big watchman's unconsciousness was screaming to him about the incongruity of his position on the floor, leadenly spread against the door he was supposed to be guarding.

Fain's hands began to rub, animal-like, at his face as he sought to shake off the spell of his stupor. They could witness him trying to rebel against the potion placed in his drink by Tizzoo.

The enchantress, studying Constable Fain through narrowed eyes, resumed Hopestill's neck rub. She wasn't in the least alarmed, leaving her lover to speculate how many times she had pulled off her trick of putting men to sleep. After a few minutes, Mather's servant left Hopestill to move and straighten things up in the room.

She rearranged her master in his chair and smoothed out his wig, which had partially edged over one of his eyes. From the floor, she neatly reassembled the writing instruments, papers and other material so that nothing would alarm the minister when his eyes ultimately reopened.

Hopestill she treated most benevolently. She saw to all his needs, including holding Mather's drinking mug, with its residue of tampered cocoa, under him while he urinated. She tossed the mixed liquids into the fire. Wordlessly, they watched it hiss off the smoldering logs. She then replaced the empty mug on Mather's tray. Her face, Hopestill noticed, was composed, even serene.

Tizzoo fluffed out her wide dress, patted it down and flashed him a smile showing her teeth. Without a word, she began climbing.

He watched her vanish up the ladder into the loft.

Part II

A Tale Of Old New England

Chapter Eighteen

Sewall's Obsession and His News

Five days before the Rev. Cotton Mather was drugged into insensibility by his servant (whom he tolerantly suspected of being a slut), and five days before he felt fortunate to have purloined the Pennacook sorcerer Hopestill Foster (although dying and diseased) from the prison hospital, he received yet another urgent message from (that vexing man) Judge Samuel Sewall.

The minister was not in good humor to receive it. Judge Sewall's nervous equivocating at this unpropitious moment was eroding even Mather's firm resolve in regard to these increasingly problematic Satanist cases.

Nevertheless, he had repaired promptly to troubled Salem to meet his old friend, for Sewall was arguably as important as he in the culminating struggle in New England to defeat Satan and his minions.

Mather mused, as his chestnut gelding loped along to the assignation, that such persistent doubting, as was now Sewall's obsession, was much like the parable about the hands of a sinner duplicitously employed during Sunday sermon – the hidden hand working at unraveling a knot, ignoring Christ's message, the visible hand proclaiming its false innocence by resting on the listener's knee as if in rapt attention.

In his brief letter, the judge again complained that none of the accused was now admitting to his or her guilt. Bah! What did a judge expect from the lips of criminals?

Yet it was enough, conceded Mather, albeit with extreme irritation, to unnerve an already nervous man. And then there was, he grudgingly admitted to himself as he rode on, the inconvenient fact of the Little King of Hell himself, the defrocked George Burroughs, placidly dancing to Death's tune rather than taking ownership of his perverted dealings with Lucifer.

Oh, Sewall had cowardly absented himself from the occasion of Burroughs's hanging, yes, indeed he had.

But Mather was there at Gallows Hill the previous month, there to bear witness to the various ends of the latest batch of the unvirtuous, five in all that time.

He had taken Tizzoo with him on the whim that the sight might help ignite a Christian spark in the woman. Also, the sensation she created among the Salemites, which he pretended to ignore, bemused him in ways he couldn't explain.

In the end, the guilty received their reward for turning their backs on the Lord Jesus Christ and conspiring against the colony.

One of the witches sobbed, one prayed to whomever, one made an attempt, pitiful really, at begging, but they all choked on the rope. Yet Burroughs had made things difficult and the crowd grew surly at the end. Mather had had to think fast to salvage the afternoon from disaster.

He wrinkled his brow and nodded, albeit imperceptibly, as he rehashed in his mind Sewall's scrawled note that Tizzoo had handed him before he had set out on what promised to be another miserably hot afternoon.

Then, too, there was also the belated news of the Port Royal earthquake that Sewall (and just about everyone) was carping about.

Mather snorted. Hardly anyone in Boston or Salem, including Sewall, including himself, hadn't suffered through loss of Jamaican goods, property, or relations in that cataclysm. But rather than take it as a sure – no, a certain – sign that the very regions of the underworld were seething and convulsing in response to the hunting down of the shockingly extensive Salem-area coven, Sewall had the temerity to ask him, Mather, if it might not be a sign of a different sort.

Well, he would answer, if asked, that the death pangs of Devil would make him more a Devil than ever he was!

Sewall, in deference to Mather's past wishes, had called for their latest meeting to be on horseback along the narrow highway that ran against Salem's harbor.

The always cautious minister had once before impressed upon the judge they would seem less conspicuous than were they to just appear sitting at a table in one or the other's homes or just as suspiciously be seen together on the road to Boston. Why, it wouldn't take but a single indiscretion to set idle tongues wagging on the presumption that these two icons of the Bay Colony were acting in league with each other. No, a simple chance meeting on horseback was the thing. This way it might appear they had business together, which in fact they did.

Their rendezvous, to which Mather was the second to appear, had brought the minister to within a hundred yards or so of the beaten-down Brown's Marsh, which lay by the small shipyard wharf near the old Purchase house, now owned by the Bridges widow. It was a rather depressing land lot since the late woman's husband and the elder Bridges had never improved their scanty holdings to any degree before both had expired from the ravages of the bloody flux.

Sewall was already present, anxious to voice the fears of his tormented conscience, having arrived early and finding himself alone. He had dismounted, tied off his horse, and was pacing back and forth as Mather, a good horseman and characteristically arriving near the expected time, appeared at the top of the lane.

The judge was a jowly man with an appetite that oft times veered perilously close to the sin of gluttony, and he had trouble regaining his saddle after he espied the minister's form and horse bobbing down the dirt path. Succeeding only just in remounting before Mather's arrival, the judge was wheezing when he spoke. He curtailed the customary flattery to the point of rudeness, getting right to it.

"I needn't tell you, Cotton, how distressed I am to keep hearing about the circumstances of how Mr. Burroughs met his fate. The people won't stop gossiping about it. It must have been a shocking event. Shocking," ventured Sewall, his face abnormally puffy and pasty white.

Mather reflected for a moment before replying.

The impression of Satan's tough little minister before his August execution, calmly reciting the Lord's Prayer perfectly, one might even say elegantly, remained amazingly clear to his recollection. The crowd at the gallows tree had been deeply affected, too. Its muttering continued to be heard among little groups even after the final corpse had twitched his last and there had really not been the slightest attempt to disguise its seditious nature. Shameful.

"It was nevertheless a righteous sentence, Samuel," Mather replied authoritatively after allowing the judge's early flutters to die down. It was going to be necessary to reassure him after all.

Mather had gone through this before with several others who had heard about or seen Burroughs play his last dirty little trick. Even Abigail had broached the subject in her meekest voice. A glance had silenced his wife, but such would not be sufficient for Sewall.

Instead, Mather reminded his friend of the comic behavior exhibited by the other witch, Willard, to deflect the judge's thoughts off Burroughs.

"You recall hearing, though, how Willard's tongue had been seized by the Diabolic One?"

John Willard, a deputy constable, was a gibbet partner of Burroughs. He had been one of those accused and convicted of being an imp of Devil by that pathetic hag Margaret Jacobs, who now had recanted her testimony. Of course she wasn't to be believed, just as the defrocked Satanist Burroughs was not to be believed just because his master had freed his lips to blaspheme Our Lord with His prayer.

This, anyway, was the thrust of Mather's argument to Sewall, yet it did not wholly satisfy the man. So here was a dangerous moment, a very dangerous moment, equal at least to the crisis fomented by that other old woman, Judge Nathaniel Saltonstall. Saltonstall had months before tendered his resignation from the governor's own Court of Oyer and Terminer, created with typical brilliance by Mather and the other important Boston ministers to deal with Satan's attacks on New England.

Now here was Sewall, another member of that illustrious body, quivering like a partridge in gunsight.

Mather leaned into his horse hard enough to make the leather squeak before he continued.

He deemed that a bit of levity might lighten the judge's mood so he played the buffoon, just this once, in order to imitate Willard's stammer at his trial since it was so very like his own, except in Mather's case the affliction was conquerable because he had true faith and Willard had only Devil to rely upon and it led him to eternal damnation.

"Ah, ah, ah, ah, fah, fah, fah, fatha … d'ye remember?" Mather cruelly mimicked. "Then Hathorne said 'Yes?' and Willard, he continues, 'Ah, ah, ah, fah, fah, fatha' yet again, and Judge Hathorne, patience exhausted goes, 'Let us hear you now' and still, STILL, mind you, the wizard Willard could not say the Holy Words!"

Behind him, the poorly constructed black Bridges house stood unsteadily in the background sheathed in a sort of sooty mold, its rotting foundations forcing the walls to bulge outward. In appearance, the structure plumped like a fat spider listening to Mather's mockery.

"Aye, it is true," responded Sewall, unamused and still obviously shaken. "But next to swing there was little Burroughs, and HE could say it perfectly, beautifully, I keep being told. My heart is broken, my good Cotton, it is dashed now that he has hung. I think, where will this all end? Who isn't safe from the lure of demons if one of us, a Burroughs, can be corrupted as easily as a Moor?"

"As to that, my dear Samuel, I hardly need explain how true faith protects us, but only if we remain vigilant that Devil's ears are open to all we say and his evil knows no wormhole small enough to slither through for its meal of internal corruption. Heed my words, Samuel, Devil is by the wrath of God the prince of this world, and there are more devils in this wilderness than can be counted."

"I do not doubt, nay, even for an instant, what you say, Cotton. It is just that what I feel in my heart is that what gives me pause. Mr. Burroughs was one of us, one of The Chosen, one of the lambs beloved by the Great Giver. His wretched end has brought me to the edge of a chasm of doubt, I fairly do admit. Yet that is not why I wrote to you in such haste, my dear friend."

"No?" Mather worked especially hard to keep the look of sheer relief off his face from having been spared at least another hour of his valuable time trying to keep Sewall from bolting the court like that ingrate Saltonstall.

Sewall's face resumed its placidity in anticipation of the rewarding confidence it was now to share. "I have the word of a friend of a friend, you might say, that there has been a remarkable visitor to our Boston, and he is so disposed as to prevent his leaving our good town."

"You feel it might be an appearance that has some bearing on the matters at hand?" offered Mather. He tried to be nonchalant about Sewall's coy hint but his attention was riveted. It must have shown.

Sewall's face couldn't disguise how thoroughly pleased he was with himself.

"I believe so, if my intelligence is correct in that you continue to seek the Indian-dealer named Hopestill Foster, who once was, and perhaps still is, on service with the redoubtable Major Pike of Salisbury."

"Foster? Remarkable!" Mather was truly moved. "He is here?"

The minister could scarcely hear the rest of what Sewall was telling him over the pounding of his racing heart.

The younger Mather of the father-son ministerial team that dominated the Puritan world of America – his father Increase Mather still outshone him, as was only allowed by the Lord – was an avid collector of the lore of his peculiar universe. This he was assembling into a *Magnalia Christi Americana* to be the greatest book ever written, bar one.

Unhappily, Foster's unique contribution to Mather's tome had proven to be one of the most elusive to secure. The man rarely ventured anywhere near Boston.

It was common knowledge Foster had been embroiled in an immense scandal long decades before, a frightful episode that a careful investigator such as Mather might be able to trace all the way to the beginning of the discovery of the secret plots against his latter-day Israel-in-Boston.

But Mather's interest in Foster burned in him not just out of mere curiosity or because it was a quest long denied. Rather, it sprang from a deep well dug in his not-far-distant boyhood, from an innermost fear he had acquired that a confrontation with the man Foster might prove his own undoing.

This unease was reinforced on the occasion of his final meeting, exactly eight years before in 1684, with his late Uncle Seaborn Cotton, the pastor of the village of Hampton and one of the most awe-inspiring figures he had ever known.

Uncle Seaborn had introduced him to the strange story of the white man Foster and Foster's raising under the tutelage of a wicked Indian necromancer.

That was all most people had ever heard of Foster's strange tale. But Seaborn told him a great deal more.

His uncle regaled him with the story of how Hopestill Foster had stolen away from Christian Boston in the dead of night after fathering a monstrous child, a thing that had been expelled into the world shaped and looking like a twin to the creature that years later crawled from the womb of the witch Anne Hutchinson. The Lord, God bless His name, had destroyed both mother and monster with the help of savage hands.

The child-beast sired by Foster, Seaborn confided since it was a fact known only to a few, was quickly suffocated and buried. Years later, its pagan mother, Foster's illicit lover, the notorious Puritan-turned-Quaker Mary Dyer, was hanged for her reckless and wicked tongue that branded her as a scold to God. After Dyer's death, her monster's miniature corpse was discovered interred in consecrated ground! It was plucked from its casket and burned along with the corpse of its witch-mother.

It was the beginning of a long interest for Mather in the story of Foster. Yet there was more, he had learned. But what that unknown piece was, he had only been given a hint.

His intense curiosity notwithstanding, Mather was sternly warned by Seaborn not to look too deeply into the mystery.

This, too, made a profound impression on Mather, who was then barely 20, when he and Uncle Seaborn had enjoyed their memorable last talk.

Seaborn, with his one good eye and sour breath, had acquired the essence of a swallowed Jonah about him in his last year of life on this Good Earth.

His voice that gloomy afternoon had risen to an alarming pitch when he told his young nephew that it was the righteous, "The Righteous!" as he thundered, who had the most to fear from Devil. Cotton knew the warning was for him, and it made him tremble.

"Believe me, they that stand high cannot stand safe, nephew. Devil is a Nimrod, a mighty hunter, and common or little game will not serve his turn. He is a Leviathan, of whom we may say in Job 41:34, 'He beholds all high things.' Devil can raise a storm when God permits it, but as for those men that stand near Heaven, my Cotton, Devil will attack them with his most cruel storms of thunder and lightning. They that stand most high have cause to take most heed." Mather had never forgotten that last conversation.

Judge Sewall watched Mather's face change during this extremely brief interlude of introspection – become greedy he might have said uncharitably – at the prospect he presented his colleague of a meeting with Hopestill Foster.

It was wrong of him, he realized, but the judge relished delivering the rest of the news more than he should.

"I suppose I should tell you, Cotton, that the happenstance of Foster's visit to Boston has been interrupted, and not under fortunate circumstances."

Mather was jolted back into attention.

"Eh? How so, my dear Samuel?"

"The man collapsed in an extreme state some days back. I dare say it is the Small pocks from the description I received, and I am greatly distressed at having to tell you that they have been keeping him outside the gate in the infirmary hut although it is said that his remaining time is very short."

"You are not leading me a merry chase, Mr. Sewall? Surely, Foster was not in the prison?"

"He was in the prison most assuredly. But he was in the position of visiting a convicted witch …"

"You don't say! This is most astonishing!"

"… One of the Salisbury witches, Mary Bradbury."

Mather ventured, "The captain's wife?"

"More than that, minister, far more than that. Mrs. Bradbury is the dear friend of Major Pike. Foster was undoubtedly employed by him in contacting her. Precisely what they were about eludes me, however."

Chapter Nineteen

Cottonus Matherus

He ought not to have made light of Willard's fatal stammer, it was wrong of him to do so. That he had mocked a fellow human being who was now dead began to haunt him, at least a little.

This single somewhat distrusted thought picked at the Rev. Mather's mind as he watched Sewall's horse trot off past the nearly empty wharf with its haphazard pilings rotting slowly in the watery gums of the inlet. He knew, as he lavished on this conceit the attention it craved, that his cruel jest had burrowed a hole into his conscience. It was now lodged there like a worm.

It was disturbing enough to understand his behavior had been in terrible taste and completely out of character.

Was it a sin?

Mather jerked his head in absolute denial. He tried to concentrate solely on the news about Foster. This renegade was now inside his city of Boston. The Indian agent and known friend and ally of the demonic Quakers was operating openly and because of that was well within his grasp.

He understood he must act immediately before Foster slipped away – for all he knew Sewall's account of the man's illness could be some sort of feint. He knew men at the prison – the constable's assistant, Fain, although a foul-tempered, impious man, was a particularly ardent Puritan.

Yet Mather remained powerless to plot for the present moment. His horse jolted along but it was as if he traveled apart from the animal so lost was he in this unwelcome and unexpected new recrimination against himself.

He had tried to divert Sewall away from melancholy, and he had failed because the judge's mood had not been leavened in the slightest by Mather's aping of a dead man, even one as rotten as Willard.

Sinking lower in the saddle, the minister continued to brood. His behavior had been appalling. He tried to recall the youngish, less introspective Sewall of his Harvard years. Was this older Sewall a better Christian now, a better Christian than he?

Mather's horse, unaware of the tension above and having so long ago lost its urgency to cuddle up to a mare, had chosen its own route away from the meeting place with Sewall.

It had turned from the waterfront to meander up a small unnamed path, a cartway really, that led past the Bridges house into one of the oldest sections of Salem. Not far away was the haphazardly built home of William Becket's son, whose acquaintance Mather had made a few years before.

Pausing after expelling a hose-stream of hot horse water, the minister's mount next delivered a cascade of little brown apples into the lane. Mather kicked his heels to goad his dark bay forward out of range of the mess.

A little farther up on to his left, standing alone, was a mossy headstone half-sunken and crooked in the open field. Crows circled, cawing. This auspicious omen must be examined, he decided.

He slid off the animal and stepped into the little protective patch of wild barley that had sprouted up around the marker. The spiked tops of the plants waved gently in the soft south breeze that had for the previous few minutes been picking up and leaving off, like a man's breathing.

Mather bent down and peered closely. A June bug that he did not swat whizzed by his ear.

The tablet's strange angle had captured his attention as did the astonishingly legible carving.

As you are, soe were we

As we are, soe shall you be

The name of the deceased was either sunken below the soft ground or it may not have been there at all. He frowned on the latter practice, personally. There would come a day when the generations would forget those who went into the grave. It was as if it were not necessary anymore, since there had been so much death, to identify the one no longer here, only that beneath was the tomb door to the eternal void – or eternal life!

A scowl crossed Mather's face. It may have been that he pictured his moldering corporeal self, composting anonymously under a nameless stone in a barleyfield.

He sat down in the field next to the headstone and meditated on the buzz of insect life. If anyone was watching from the odd window opening no face showed to betray that interest in the minister's unusual dearth of manic activity. He caressed the stone. Its roughness and warmth were not unpleasant.

Sewall had been right to entertain his doubt, Mather decided. It was true enough the witch trials had become a burden on all of

New England. No one had been weighted down with it more than he.

Still, it was incumbent upon him to keep doing his best to maintain the official face of concern, and that face remained a mask of defiance against Satan's conspiracy, which was aimed at destroying the foothold of the saints fighting to reclaim the American desert. Mather knew that the people looked to him for reassurance.

If only Devil's slaves could be found, rooted out, hunted down, destroyed, eradicated and so defeated that they would never return, then all might be well and the dream renewed, the curse under which they lived lifted!

His fingers scraped lightly across the grave tablet's top. There was something familiar about its book-like feel, its weight. Around him, the little rough houses of Salem baked under the sun. He could sniff the scent of burning in the parched air, and his memories, seemingly unbeckoned, returned to that awful day in his youth when his family awoke to their house burning down.

His father Increase had trusted him with more than his life that morning, tasking young Cotton with saving the collected volumes of the wise men who followed in the footsteps of Christ. Bundled into the youngster's thin arms and carried out as the fire around him raged and smoked were some of his father's most precious jewels – a copy of Jerome's *De Viris Illustribus* and Gennadius's continuation, volumes of Epiphanius, Isidore and Prochorus, Melchior Adams's *Lives of Modern Divines* – almost a hundred or more of these heavy tomes he had himself personally saved.

Together, father and son watched with fascination and horror the conflagration that Increase had predicted for his city only weeks before from the pulpit of the old North Church. That day, the Rev. Increase Mather had chosen a verse from *Isaiah,* casting Boston in the role of Old Jerusalem with the words of the prophet:

"Thou shalt be visited by the Lord of Hosts with thunder, and with earthquake, and great noise, with storm and tempest, and the flame of devouring fire."

That edifice of the Old North Church, too, had been lost amid the flames that had made them all without warning homeless. It was truly, as his Papa had written in the diary from which Cotton had frequently stolen a glance, "a Fatal and dismall day."

This day in Salem felt fatal and dismal, too.

Again, his mind wandered about in the graveyard of his past.

Mather was only a few years older after the fire when he and Increase had ridden across the Dunster Street bridge into Cow Yard Lane and entered the rude square that contained Harvard College. He had arrived to take his entrance examination, and expecting some last-minute reminder to check his belongings, his Papa had turned to him and said, "My son, will you go with God and make us proud and be among us the most upright?"

Most fathers would have made it an order but Increase presented it as a question.

It was one he could readily answer in the affirmative. Ever since he could remember, this was what he had tried to accomplish – to be at the Lord's side and to be the most upright among His people.

At Papa's feet in his old study, Cotton had been a willing pupil and a brilliant student, memories that filled him with an almost inexplicable satisfaction. Under his father's tutelage, he had mastered science and medicine, the languages of antiquity, the philosophies of men.

He could speak Greek, Hebrew and was fluent in Latin, the language that Harvard demanded he speak at all times with the ease of a proficient scholar. He was extraordinarily proud, too, of the Latinized version of his name, "Cottonus Matherus," privately his most prized title since it showed he had conquered not only the texts but the tongues of the old prophets. This put him not above but on an equal plane with the luminaries who walked with Jesus Christ in the flesh at the very dawn of the Christian Age.

All of this he had achieved before he attained the age of 11.

However, for this and for other things, he had been rendered an object of derision at Harvard.

His fellow scholars had kicked him around mercilessly in his freshman year, particularly the seniors who sent him on endless fagging missions to fetch treats from the college buttery or to pick up personal items from the bootblack or the tailor.

Cotton hated being treated like a dog of a servant, but more than that it was the tormenting he received about his Papa that had driven him to despair. Increase's friendship and regard for President Leonard Hoar was well-known and resented among Cotton's classmates.

The students and scholars hated Hoar's exacting and severe manner. They detested the president's demands that every moment be used up and stuffed like a goose, that (and he could remember Hoar's exact words) "you should not content yourself with doing only that with which you are tasked but daily something more than your task."

Just as they hated Hoar, so they reviled Increase, Hoar's protector and chief advocate on the Board of Overseers, and so they detested the son and protégé, little Cottonus Matherus.

They called him names like "Cottonhead Blatherus," invented blasphemous puzzles in Latin for him to solve, had him fetch and get at all hours of the day or night, and especially when they could catch him, interrupted his prayers to have him procure trays of sweet rolls. More than slaps he received – they threw hot soup at him or poured it down his pants. One bully stood above the rest, a boy named Thomas Sargeant. He had taken the teasing of Mather to new heights, demanding that the youngster recite his lessons over and over again while standing on one foot holding a brimmed cupful of broth. When it inevitably spilled, Sargeant kicked him hard enough to make Cotton sprawl across the floor into the liquid mess while the other boys laughed.

He prayed harder than ever for the mischief to stop, and for the strength to bear the taunts and terrors. Worse was to come.

Bored and angry one dull afternoon, Sargeant, in the presence of the other boys, made light of Cotton's father, President Hoar and the Holy Ghost in such a disreputable way that to merely think about this outrage made Cotton cringe and cry and tremble. These displays of childish weakness drove the abuse Mather received to even further extremes.

Finally, the youngster could take it no more without informing a higher authority. At private instruction with Hoar to study the logic of Petrus Ramus, that saint and martyr, Cotton could no longer contain his misery.

After he had confided everything to his father's friend, the president stood up, face red and swollen, eyes bulging. Never had Cotton seen such inner violence exude from this ordinarily very even-tempered man.

Hoar dismissed Mather abruptly, almost angrily.

In a matter of days, there was evidence of something terrible coming down. Sargeant and the other students grew sullen and watchful. Their resentment of young Mather was palpable although he was now shunned rather than sadistically mistreated.

One horrible morning the dreaded moment arrived. The boys were called into the library upon pain of dismissal were they not to appear.

It was a terrible thrashing Sargeant received that day, a punishment made worse by the added humiliation of it having been delivered not by the presidential hand of Mr. Hoar but by the begrimed right paw of William Healy, the prison-keeper and a confirmed scoundrel.

Sargeant alternately screamed and twisted during his ignominious beating as the boys of Harvard looked on in shocked amazement.

Such brutal discipline administered by an outsider, unknown before at the college that tended to deal with its troubles internally, would soon be the widespread talk of the town and the gossip at church. That the flogging was laid on by the awful Goodman Healy turned it into a scandal of major proportions.

And Hoar was not yet done with poor Sargeant.

Praying over the prostrate, sob-wracked form of the boy, the thin-lipped president recited chapter and verse of Sargeant's many sins out loud for all to hear, including a repetition of the blasphemous insult the senior had made about the president, Cotton's father and the Holy Spirit.

Now there was no doubt that Hoar was going to get rid of the miscreant and throw him out of Harvard before the end of the term.

Sargeant wept and Cotton prayed.

He felt the eyes of all the boys upon him.

He could feel their hate.

It was about this time in his life that Mather's lifelong stammer, hidden very well by his clever enunciation tricks and sing-song delivery of his words, escaped its cage.

Cotton's prayers for himself were not answered and his standing at Harvard degenerated in the wake of the Sargeant incident. Moreover, his protector, Hoar, went into sharp physical decline.

After that terrible morning, a day never passed without a cruel look being cast in his direction or the hint of a vile remark uttered beneath the breath of a classmate.

From a curiosity as a boy wonder and ecumenical darling, and later, freshman victim, Cotton had slipped into a baser realm, that of "snitch" and "baby." His stuttering, random at first, now filled his mouth with fear almost every time he opened it to speak. This new fright all but killed off his natural-born loquaciousness, his most amiable trait and the one that disintegrated rapidly in the weeks ahead.

Cotton's life, measured as it was in the eyes of his peers, became intolerable. He dreaded contact with the other boys, and hid when he prayed as it was well known that to interrupt his private pleadings was the easiest way to provoke the "baby" into a fit of tears.

The abuse heaped on Cotton's narrow shoulders weighed the little boy down with the added guilt he felt at having brought on the illness that had felled President Hoar.

But Increase saw another force at work. The father believed most earnestly that it was Satan or one of his demons who had singled out his first-born for debasement. He saw Cotton's swallowing of his words, his choking on them and finally garbling them as if he were speaking in tongues, as proof enough of the underworld's influence in his son's case.

Increase's fears were confirmed when he had at last come to visit his son at the nearly empty all-in-one building that served as Harvard College.

There he found Cotton cringing in a corner of his room, blind to his father's presence so deep was he in his religious frenzy, stuttering over his devotions. Cotton's good black coat had been ripped up the back. His belongings were opened up to view and scattered about the dimly lit room as if flung by a rampage of imps. Without speaking a word, Increase swept the boy up and carried him out to the carriage.

They drove to the North End in silence, the boy miserable, the father devastated.

Chapter Twenty

All in the Family

A much older Mather, keenly aware of the necessity of a hasty return to Boston after his meeting with Judge Sewall, nevertheless lingered by the barleyfield tombstone.

It laid a spell on him, although he would not consciously have used a term of bewitchment to describe how touching the grave marker had so effectively seized his emotions. Through the stone, the minister felt himself dragged by an unseen hand back to important memories connected with the present.

And to the mystery man Foster.

Mather hugged the tablet, as the boy within him had hugged the knee of his beloved father Increase after his rescue from the hell of Harvard.

The youngster he saw again in his mind – himself – was damaged psychologically and emotionally. He was afraid to leave his house. He shrunk from loud noises. Most of all, he feared visitors, for they would ask questions of him, and he had lost command of his voice. Nothing but the most abject idiocy tumbled forth from his mouth when he deigned to speak, occasions which became ever more rare.

Each dawn, before breakfast, Increase and Cotton met in the father's library, clasped hands and sank to the floor to beg for Christ Jesus's intervention. The heads of father and son were often bent almost to the floor, pillows under tender knees in grudging concession to their shared pain of devotion and fasting.

But then, into this fever of constant prayer, came a memorable interruption.

To Boston one rainy afternoon in 1674, both of Cotton's uncles, the sons of the late Rev. John Cotton, the famed teacher and minister of old Boston, arrived for supper, an extraordinary event, for Seaborn Cotton pastored far to the north in Hampton while John Cotton the Younger spoke for the distant congregation of Old Plymouth.

Along with Increase, the brothers were the leading lights of that incredible union between the Mather and Cotton dynasties, a bond sealed with Increase's marriage to Cotton's mother, Maria. This still-beautiful, tender woman was the late Rev. Cotton's only surviving daughter so in effect, she was wedded to one luminary and sister to two.

Maria hovered at the elaborately carved doorjamb as the men talked quietly following their frugal meal of eggs and soft tack.

In her stillness that evening she retained the swan-like grace that had marked her from youth as a special child of the Lord. Whatever the men's differences with each other she, at least, was held in the highest regard. All her children adored her, too; when reading from the Book of Psalms, her voice was sweet as dulcimer notes.

Yet that night she was a silent swan watching the moon. No one could say exactly what she was thinking but then, this was her way.

At the head of the board upon which rested pewter mugs of good ale was Maria's husband Increase, a man just good-looking enough to turn heads.

Maria had met and fallen in love with Increase as a step-daughter in her future husband's father's house. Late in life, three years after the Rev. John Cotton's passing, his good friend the Rev. Richard Mather, the patriarch of the Mather family, had married Maria's mother Sarah, the Rev. Cotton's twice-married widow, in an extraordinary coupling that thrilled ecumenical Boston.

That evening, Maria watched her husband with veneration bordering on fascination.

Increase's wide-spread eyes were intelligent and sensitive, his demeanor polite and calm. There was something of the English gentleman in him that clashed with his thoroughly American roots, a fight that played out in a face which seemed to be constantly shifting from one semi-amused expression to the next. His voice ranged from chiding to confident, often in a single sentence, and it carried with it a commanding tone.

Beside her husband at his right hand was Maria's brother Seaborn, the late Rev. Cotton's eldest. Seaborn was six years older than Increase. Seaborn was so named because he was born at sea, screaming and lusty, aboard the *Griffin* during his father's daring flight from King Charles I's iron men in 1633.

Seaborn was not quite 41 on the night of their supper. He still retained the intense waspishness of appearance that so suited him for the semi-wilderness mission of Hampton village where he preached a mighty sermon every Sunday.

Beneath his firm little mouth, the distinctive, pointy, dagger-like beard he meticulously cultivated throughout his adult life had turned a dirty gray. This was in seeming sympathy with his cloud-like eyes, through which he had been having trouble seeing of late and so had taken to squinting when listening to another. Above the dagger-beard, Seaborn's mouth was pouty and seemed ready to argue at the least provocation, which he never found wanting.

The last of the trio of men at table was "John the Younger", the Rev. Cotton's second son, Maria and Seaborn's brother.

This John Cotton was Cotton Mather's most curious uncle.

In contrast to Increase, whose lighter side could not be hidden for long, and Uncle Seaborn, who while very serious could tolerate the occasional anecdote if it bore reference to themes limited to the seasons, Uncle John's cast of mind was usually as dark as the interior of a closed coffin.

John's nature, the family knew from experience, could take a very angry turn, for he had led a troubled life and blamed others for it, others whom he would not name, yet only refer to in oblique terms. And, as they all had come to understand, one would never talk to Uncle John about his famous father except when it was absolutely necessary to do so. No one ever asked him why this was.

Remarkably, young Cotton was permitted to linger with the men following this supper. Beside him, sitting upright although with bent face, was his first cousin John Cotton, Uncle John's son, a boy who, like his father, seemed immune to the joy of food or company.

As the men conversed, the two boys passively looked on, impressed though they were at these warships of God seated before them like a great faith armada.

The subject at hand before the men was the fate of the imposing Boston estate known as Cotton House, built for the patriarch himself back in the days.

That house and land, with more than an acre of choice garden, bore title to the Cottons inasmuch as it was a gift to the fabled minister of old Boston from a man of wealth and reputation at the time by the name of Sir Henry Vane.

A lavish gift indeed, but one that had devolved into an embarrassment.

Vane, the ex-governor of the Bay Colony, had fallen into marked disfavor before departing to England in 1637 at the height of the Anne Hutchinson scandal of that same year. An ardent Hutchinson supporter, Vane never wavered in his devotion to her. Nor did he return from England, where he died unmourned by Puritan Massachusetts.

By contrast, memories of the family patriarch, John Cotton the Elder, especially after his death, only grew sweeter with the passage of time. Among the church elite, the recall of Cotton's golden voice remained enshrined in all hearts.

Alas, some few still recalled his brief association with the hell-dwelling heretic Hutchinson and her detestable antinomianism. However, the late Rev. Cotton's role in that tawdry episode had for the most part long been forgiven and all but forgotten (even though Mrs. Hutchinson herself had not been forgotten and certainly not forgiven).

In Boston's infancy and John Cotton's time, Anne Hutchinson had dared to confront the established good men of the city and been paid back with the Judas silver she deserved.

Not only was her name cursed (and cursed still), but like Hutchinson's cohort Mary Dyer, another of her coven, Anne, had been said to have given birth to a devil's monster. This "*monstrum horrendum, deforme crasse*" as it was later labeled by Gov. Winthrop, who uncovered the dread conspiracy, was proof to all that both Hutchinson and Dyer had been impregnated by the same Satan.

The late, lamented Winthrop, Vane's successor, the Hutchinsons' closest neighbor, and Anne's mortal enemy, had written a spectacular description of these despicable oddities, and one much discussed. But this was not so much talked about in the Boston of Cotton Mather's youth as the delicacy of the matter was said to be much too nauseating for polite conversation.

As it were, the blighted Mrs. Hutchinson had perished in her exile somewhere far away in the wilderness of New York, a victim of savage hands, her living brood destroyed along with her.

From the Puritan point of view it was "good riddance to the mother of witches" as many said when reminded of her memory, and while some may also have wondered (privately, of course) how the estimable Rev. Cotton could have gotten so mixed up with that woman, in the days of Cotton Mather's boyhood the story had been relegated to a subject best left unbroached in the society of good Christians.

Vane's gift, Cotton House on Cotton Hill, that home of the legendary giant of modern Puritanism, had come attached with strings in the wake of Increase's marriage to the patriarch's daughter Maria.

Increase, although he had lived in the home with Maria and the children for a short period, had come to feel that he did not belong there at all since he did not consider himself to be the equal of the man who willed it in part to him through his beloved wife.

His was an uneasiness confirmed by the Rev. John Cotton's will, which had specified that upon the decease of his widow Sarah that the Cotton Hill estate be shared among his surviving children, who by then numbered only Seaborn, John the Younger and Maria (or, rather, her husband Increase).

Thus, the family dinner that evening was served in the dining room of the smaller but still very well-endowed house that Increase had been renting from the North Church, where he continued to preach every Sunday and lecture every Thursday. Lodging there, in his own home, his castle as it were, made Increase far more magnanimous than he might ordinarily have been that evening.

The urgent matter at Harvard was uppermost in the three men's minds so they talked of it first. Both Cotton brothers recommended that Increase see his way to succeeding the ailing Mr. Hoar as president. Increase demurred at this proposal, however, Maria's brothers did not push with the vigor they ordinarily might have exerted due to the more pressing matter of their inheritance.

So next to be conducted was the nettlesome remaining business of their still-intertwined family. This bore on the issue of the exact shares each would receive for the sale of the remainder of the Rev. Cotton's estate. While dreaded, this turned out to be all cut-and-dried stuff, with the formal agreements decided with surprising good will.

Last, there was the matter of the old Cotton House on Cotton Hill to be finalized. The grounds and house lay in the very heart of Boston town, and after Increase and his family had moved out, the estate was all but empty.

All but empty, that is, save for the sickbed room in which dwelled the ailing, very elderly Widow Sarah – Sarah Hawkredd Story Cotton Mather – the now thrice-married, notoriously close-lipped *grande dame* of the family. The only other tenant was Sarah's single nursemaid and servant, a giant African named Titus whose frizzed white hair stood up like broom straws and whose gaunt body resembled jerked meat.

Both Seaborn and John had paid their respects to their aged mother upon arrival in Boston. However, they chose, perhaps out of habit, to impose on their brother-in-law that afternoon and evening rather than on their mother's less-than-generous hospitality.

In any event, Mistress Sarah never left her house.

The widow was in her last years, and possessed as she was of a clear hand and clear mind, she had little use for visitors even though they were of her own flesh and blood.

It was a touchy subject before the inheritors, this matter of the Widow Sarah Mather.

With all due delicacy and respect, the men debated the widow's current presence on Cotton Hill and the likelihood of it remaining in the hands of its last owner for any length of time. It was only logical, then, that the widow's increasingly dim prospects for better health – naturally, bearing only on the question of her continued hold on property that desired selling in a very urgent way – was raised.

As the matter warmed, the men were briefly interrupted with cups of warm cocoa, steeped delectably by Increase's young new slave, a rather attractive brown girl with a shapely figure named Tizzoo.

Tizzoo had been pressed on Increase as a gift from a slave trader married into the family, Capt. Jeremiah Eggington, whose business associate was a Dover man, Paul Walderne. The captain was widowed from Maria's late sister Elizabeth, considered by all to have been the dearest flower of the Cotton family.

Increase accepted the gift reluctantly. He didn't care to own a slave for one, and he didn't especially care for Capt. Eggington, a cruel man who grossly mistreated his chattel, for the other.

The men waited for Tizzoo to withdraw, upon which Increase said to Seaborn, "You know this man Paul Walderne's pap, Major Richard Walderne, I apprehend, dear brother?"

Increase chose to overlook John the Younger's trailing eye trained on the retreat of his amply endowed servant.

"Richard Walderne? Very well, very well," said the man born

at sea, the eldest of the late Rev. Cotton's living children.

Seaborn, shorter than the other two in stature yet sturdily built like a good chest, puffed with pride at being able to confirm his association with father and son Walderne.

"He is the magistrate at Dover, near my Hampton Village. A very pious man of Christ. Very pious. Very diligent in his duties."

"He is a sawyer as well, I hear," said John the Younger. "A wealthy one."

"Aye, he does well," agreed Seaborn. "A military man he is, too. He knows how to skin a heathen as well as a Christian."

Increase considered the remark. "What happened, I wonder, to his son Paul, from whom I acquired my Tizzoo? Would you know, Brother Seaborn? There has been all kinds of talk at the waterfront regarding a shipwreck or, perhaps, an Algerine pirate attack near black Africa."

Answered Seaborn, "What I know is Paul was an individual unsuited to land or to this shore in particular. He is said to have perished at sea but whether, like the prophet, he will return, I am very much in ignorance. I myself rather doubt the Lord will make further use of him, I fear, or provide another illustrious providence for your collection, Increase."

The jest referenced Increase's book, *Illustrious Providences*, published to wide acclaim. Seaborn held out his drink to his brother-in-law to show it was all in sport. Increase clinked cups and nodded his favor.

Uncle John the Younger took a long sip of Tizzoo's hot chocolate and made his own point with the near-empty container.

"Our Heavenly Lord made good use of the man's father though, did he not, Seaborn? Was not the elder Walderne the magistrate who turned out the miserable Quakers from Dover some dozen years back?"

"Indeed he was!" Seaborn acknowledged. "I had the good fortune to witness their dismissal from our fine village of Hampton and it was a glorious day for the Lord I will most certainly attest."

Increase leaned forward to ask, "Yet it is said these children of Satan escaped their full retribution."

Seaborn pursed his smallish mouth. His dagger-beard point dipped to his chest.

"Those hags were finally paid in full, I do assure you both," the eldest brother answered with a certain amount of relish.

Almost in the same breath, Seaborn thumped his empty cup on the table and his voice turned bitter as the rankest vinegar.

"Aye, paid in full, the heretics were, but it was justice delayed thanks to the meddling and interference of three scoundrels from Salisbury who saw fit to pervert God's law against sinners!"

Chapter Twenty-One

A Notorious Case

Young Cotton and his cousin John looked at each other surreptitiously, both boys unwilling to betray by word or sign to their elders their astonishment at not having been asked to leave the table and the room. Nor did Maria leave, as would ordinarily have been her custom. Without a word, she took her usual seat by the fire, hands in lap, eyes glistening.

"Mind you these fanatics," Uncle Seaborn warned the boys of the Quakers.

"They have the energy of the old serpent. In them we see the vomit cast out in the bypast ages, licked up again by these seducers for a new digestion, once more exposed for a poisoning of mankind."

"Well put, brother Seaborn," said John the Younger. His eyes, unnoticed except by Maria, continued to search for the return of Tizzoo.

There followed a spirited discussion of the faults of the Quakers and their many evil provocations against the chosen Puritans, faults that Seaborn took great pains to justify that led in a wholly rational progression to the very stern measures against them put into place by leaders such as Richard Walderne of Dover.

The subject of the Quakers was one area, at least, where the brothers could agree, for it was accepted among them without question that this strange imported sect was the worst cabal of heretics and disbelievers ever seen in North America, rivaling even the Roman Catholics of New France for perfidy and sin.

The Quakers were inspired by their leader, roundly reviled by all around the table, a wily fellow still at large named George Fox. Fox was an English zealot who, it was said, once had the ear of the Lord Protector Cromwell himself.

It was at this point that Uncle Seaborn observed in a simpering aside to his two young nephews that since the Restoration it was not only possible to have the ear of Cromwell in the England of that day, but "the entire head if one should wish it."

The boys and Uncle John were politely amused, but Increase, no true friend to the crown, was not.

"I will not make merry on a dead man's head, no matter whose," Increase asserted. After staring them all down, he continued with his eye on Uncle Seaborn.

"They claim that Scripture does not tell people of the Trinity, if you can imagine that," said Seaborn, darkening in face with the recollection. "Deny it completely, they do! I remember as if it were indeed yesterday when that trinity of themselves, the very worst of the lot, three harlots, three ugly hags, came before me in our fair village to receive their due."

"By the writ of the righteous Goodman Walderne, of whom we have previously spoken," added John the Younger.

Seaborn brushed away a few non-existent crumbs from his

cravat. "Indeed, a wonderful fellow, industrious the magistrate is and a great friend to the Bay Colony as well, I will most vehemently add. He was very handy when it came to dealing with those devil-driven creatures!"

Warming to the subject, Seaborn related his joy at observing Devil thrashed out of the wretches when they came through his Hampton that frigid afternoon 12 years before.

"They sang out that day!" he exclaimed with a triumphant note. "Constable Brike laid on with a will and a heavy arm, as God's my witness."

Seaborn turned to his sister, who had not said a word thus far. "My dear Maria, I would spit next if you would permit me to sully your clean floor."

"As you wish, dear brother."

Seaborn waved her assent away.

"I will not do so, as much as I wish to. But the events following Hampton anger me still."

The dagger-bearded brother launched into a tirade of disgust that Magistrate Walderne's writ for extreme punishment had been negated as soon as in the next town.

"It was all the doing of that headstrong Mr. Pike of Salisbury, with the aid of a conspiracy, mind you, that yon Quakers later escaped to bedevil New England anew upon recovery from their stripes, yes, and it was a queer group of allies that otherwise reputable men like Major Pike and Capt. Tom Bradbury had gathered unto them that day, I might add," Seaborn said, pausing just then to draw in air through his nose like a bull ready to charge. He snorted it out.

"The oddest was this man Hopestill Foster …"

Here, Seaborn's brother, John the Younger, went pale.

Increase, appearing as if he were rummaging through old trunks in his mind for this misplaced name, bobbed his head rapidly without speaking.

"Hopestill Foster, Hopestill Foster," he said searchingly, in an undertone. Behind him, Maria bowed her angelic face.

"Yes, the renegade Indian trader," responded Seaborn. His face was bright with anger.

"As I have since learned, it was this Foster who had arranged for the subversion of the writ in Salisbury that resulted in the release of the three heretics. And after only the briefest acquaintance with the lash of justice!"

"Yes, yes," said Increase. "Paul Walderne, the magistrate's son, did speak of that man Foster."

Cotton's father's brow furrowed. "When did I last did see young Paul, God rest his soul? It was after Tizzoo was given me along with a set of plate from the isles. We talked briefly about his new career as an officer on his father's vessel. It was Paul Walderne who told me that the man Foster was also to blame for the murder in his father's truck house near that Pennacook savage's village ..."

"A notorious case. Notorious!" seconded Seaborn.

"Certainly it was that," John the Younger interceded. "Yet wasn't it Paul Walderne whom the court censured for Tom Dickinson's death?"

"Paul, certainly," said Seaborn, finger pointed in the air. "But I beg to say the older Major Walderne himself was acquitted of any misdeed by the court, as indeed he should have been. Why, the major was in Dover when Thomas Dickinson was fatally stabbed from behind by that Indian."

"God help us," said Increase. "It was a drunken brawl, a terrible thing. A white man died."

"I myself am a man who thinks not commerce in strong liquors is to be always abhorred," huffed Seaborn. "What would we drink, elsewise?"

"Well, such is not to be given to the red men, in any event," said Increase. "It makes them to lose their senses, such senses as the devils have, in any respect. And it was on that point, I believe, the major and his son were prosecuted, was it not? And was not the major's right-hand man, his clerk Peter Coffin, fined twenty pound, eh?"

"True enough," said Seaborn, "although the real culprit as has been identified to my satisfaction was Foster, whom I most sharply recall when those Quaker hags came through. He was a tall, seedy man, with yellow hair. It's a wonder the Indians didn't take his goldy locks from him when they had the chance. Instead, why, he became one of them!"

Increase spoke up.

"My word, this man Foster has been in the thick of it. He is a bit of a legend in the northern woods ..."

Seaborn interrupted and poked his finger at Increase, a habit the brother-in-law detested but endured for the sake of his dear Maria, who hated to hear him complain about Seaborn's bad habits.

"Worse, the court took no notice of this cur, and he escaped into the woods again, where he hunts among those fiends. I could tell you more about this rascal than you'd ever want to know, believe me!"

With that knowing pronouncement, Seaborn turned his gaze to his young nephews and opened his mouth to say further, but at that point, John the Younger, who had for the most part been sitting at his place with a deepening scowl etching his features, unexpectedly shot his brother such a wicked glance that the boys, startled by its intensity, pressed backwards in their seats as if in fear a mortal blow would be struck.

Seaborn thrust his old face with its threatening beard at his brother.

In a milder voice, he conceded in a tone of retreat, "But I don't think that's a discussion that's fit for their ears, or the ears of anyone at this table – or beyond. Indeed, I have said too much already."

At that, Maria, silent before then, let out her breath with an audible hiss. Managing a wan smile, she excused herself from the men of God and their children, and left the room.

In the sudden absence of his sister, Seaborn visibly seethed at having been cut off in mid-tirade.

Grasping the table board as if to break off a piece, he blurted out, "Devil's at work with that Foster. He is an unholy man, a fornicator, in alliance with the filthy Quakers and the painted serpents of the woods!"

"Well you might be appalled and repulsed," Seaborn continued, turning to address his nephews particularly, while waving at John the Younger as if to calm his brother. "Well you might.

"Now imagine, if you will, delivering a sermon, as occurred in Dover, and having a ranting Quaker hag walk into the service completely devoid of clothes, blowing her stinking breath in your face while mocking the Lord's Holy Day and laughing at the idea that our Jesus will not arise in a Second Coming. That is the likes of which we have had to deal with. Why, it begged to be a revolution of the heretics. My mouth is dry – may I get a glass of sherry, my dark angel?"

Tizzoo, who had peered in to see if she was needed by the

family, covered her mouth behind two hands and tittered silently with her eyes.

For the moment, as refreshments were replenished around the table, the discussion left Dover and Foster and returned closer to the Boston of 1674.

It seemed that once again there had arisen a renewed horror in the city over deteriorating relations with the Indians, a fear that had never gone away, not even after the vanquishing of the Pequots back in Old Winthrop's day.

Increase and Seaborn turned to John for answers since the younger brother was an experienced hand with these dangerous natives. Prior to receiving the call to mount Pastor Raynor's former pulpit in Plymouth, the second son of the famous Rev. John Cotton had preached to the Wampanoags at Noepe, which some called Martha's or Martin's Vineyard, a desolate, flat wasteland plentiful only in oysters, lobsters and Indians.

While no one even so much as alluded to the circumstances under which Uncle John had been coerced to minister to Indians on that lonely island, this aspect of his life was not far from any of the minds around the table.

Even the boys knew of John's lecherous secret and his shame, since his temporary excommunication from the First Church the year before little Cotton was born – the year the Quakers were whipped through Seaborn's Hampton, actually – was common knowledge. He had since been restored to grace, however.

Uncle John was less pessimistic about the prospect of Indian troubles than the family would have expected.

He even dared to suggest that if the red race were handled gently, like children instead of brute animals, there would be no trouble at all.

"There are Wampanoags and there are Wampanoags," Increase replied with a grim tone to his voice. "The reason I raise this point is that I have heard of grave troubles. Know you an Indian named Sassamon, John?"

"Sassamon is a Christian, brother Increase. Indeed, he is a pupil of the Rev. Elliot as is my recollection."

"I believe this Sassamon resides in Dorchester," said Seaborn.

"As you both know," Increase continued, "I hear many things, including what has been hushed up. But it is coming out, I fear. That is why all the talk of massacres and bloody deeds are in the gossip."

Both brothers and both children were enrapt.

"Pray continue" they said as one.

"A powerful sachem has arisen among the Wampanoag tribe by the name of Metacomet, who bears a Christian name as well – Philip. Sassamon has brought word that a monstrous conspiracy now exists among the devils of the woods. He says they are stronger than we can know. He says they aim to wipe us all out to a man and drain the blood pouring from our mutilated corpses into the great ocean. A Jerusalem we shall become, a bleeding state."

And here Increase bowed his face. "I don't know if that we don't merit a rebuke from our Lord," Increase continued, introspectively. "For if we go on to provoke Him, what can we expect but the extreme punishment?"

Chapter Twenty-Two

Tongue-tied

The men droned on and the boys were finally dismissed to bed. Increase kissed Cotton on his forehead and bade his son to say his prayers. Uncles Seaborn and John expressed their utmost wishes for a restful slumber, too.

The suggestions were successful. Increase's house, filled from top to bottom with guests and servants, the rather pleasant smells of cooking, and the murmuring of talk, made for a warm and comforting environment that induced sleep as readily as if it had been delivered in a draught of powered poppies. Cotton ultimately drifted into one of the deepest sleeps he had ever known that night.

Yet at first, the boy was restless and unhappy. Eyes wide open, he recalled that evening with a deep sense of shame. He had hardly spoken a word to anyone so sure was he that he might slip and begin to spit out his language in a welter of slobber.

His cousin John, after prayers, had already turned in and was peacefully whimpering and sputtering his little snores beside him in the bed they shared.

Cotton begged God silently for the same tranquility. He had read his verses in Greek yet even the heroic language of Alexander could not calm his mind. He lay still, closed his eyes with good intent and then, suddenly, he was gone.

In the midst of that azure deep of sleep, Cotton imagined he was being led by a large paternal figure to a pulpit before a great multitude. Acres of straining faces were screwed up in keen anticipation for his forthcoming lecture.

It seemed to him that he floated a thousand yards over those faces and heads, happily at first, but then with increasing apprehension that this journey would end behind the lectern. At that dread spot, the leading hand would release his and leave him there alone, which is what transpired in his dream.

He stared out before them all with his notes arrayed in perfect squares before him. The text he could not clearly make out although it seemed to him that it might be something from *Ezekiel* (he could not be sure, much as he might concentrate). He understood, with a pathetically keen awareness, that it was time for him to speak, to deliver the sermon of his life – the one that would make his reputation and be the talk of generations.

Yet he could not utter a sound, a peep or a squeak.

The restlessness of his nightmare audience increased.

They were so kind, so caring. They wanted him to succeed. He could see it in their eyes. Most of all, he understood, they wanted to hear the endowed son of their great teacher, Increase Mather. They wanted to bathe in the powerful voice of the father's inheritor, the certain recipient of the mantle passed on by the most blessed family in New England.

Instead, Cotton flapped his lips to emit a great nothingness.

He willed the sounds and words to come out. He knew exactly

what he must tell them. Yet his voice had left him. And not just his voice – neither noises nor groans could he produce from his vocal cords. His tongue lay wedged in the back of his mouth, choking him.

He wanted to die there, victim of a stroke or a bolt from Heaven. The increasingly louder sighs of patient waiting bedeviled his ears. The mute forms of his shadowy listeners fidgeted astride their cold, bare benches. The helpful faces in his audience grew alarmed. He could hear them ask each other, "What is the matter with our Cotton? Why can he not speak? This is very strange!"

It was in this state of near-apoplexy that the boy found his voice.

In a strangled yelp that roused his sleep-sodden cousin John, Cotton sat straight up, wild-eyed, gasping for air. He felt about his throat to ascertain if his head were still attached to his young neck, a process his relation watched with trepidation.

"Cotton! Cotton!" Young John cried out in alarm. "You must awaken!"

Cotton pulled himself upright in the bed, blinking in amazement at his good fortune of God's grace in releasing him from his nightmare. He hummed to hear himself make a noise, then ventured a few words, which came out fine.

It was with profound relief that he said without more than a hint of stammer, "I assure you, my good John, I am returned in this world now and extremely glad of it."

The boys sat up together, blinking and rubbing their eyes. The house was silent in Cotton's little attic corner of it where the two boys temporarily shared a room.

John said, "I am so very relieved you are all right, cousin. You alarmed me so. I myself was having a pleasant vision. I believe James the Apostle may have played a part in it. Or was it Saul of Tarsus?"

A good-natured boy, sweet in temper and fair in looks although a good deal shorter and a bit on the portly side, Cousin John also was possessed of many other virtuous traits – including the happy one of not taking up more of the bed than was his allotted share.

Of all the cousins, Cotton and he were the closest. But John's lot in life was proving to be a more uphill climb – while two years older than Cotton, Cousin John's prospects seemed poorer by very much.

His father, the Rev. John Cotton the Younger, the son of the famous minister in the days of the founders whose testimony had helped wreck the heretic Anne Hutchinson, had not risen like a star in his ministry career. Rather, the minister's son had fallen like an angel.

In Uncle John's past was a scandal that provoked his excommunication from the church – a ruinous dalliance with a married woman, since exiled. Although John himself was spared that fate, and was later reinstated at the insistence of Increase and other elders – who argued that the great Rev. Cotton's legacy must not be tarnished in such a fashion if there remained any hope at all of saving the son – John the Younger was still looked upon with askance by most.

He was considered with suspicion by many to be a "black Puritan," a wrong-hearted man, and a failure to be scorned. Had his father not been the senior John Cotton, the Younger's time in the colony would have been a short one leading to the pillory, or worse, to the sinful snake pits of atheist Rhode Island.

It was as a result of Uncle John's struggles that his son John, Cotton's cousin, had been accorded a seat at the dinner table that evening. One of the points of discussion had to do distinctly with the boy's future.

Uncle John had lost many years of advancement due to the cloud over him created by his excommunication. Most humiliatingly, he had been forced to accept a long missionary posting to Martha's Vineyard in the service of Christianizing the Wampanoag. The experience had not made Uncle John's fortune by any means, and thus it remained to be seen whether his son could afford to remain in Boston and enroll in Harvard.

The three-quarters moon in the sky beamed its light through the single diamond-shaped pane set like a jewel in the attic room's south wall. It illuminated the two shining young faces as they talked about diverse issues for nigh upon an hour in low tones inasmuch as they were both now wide awake.

Cotton felt completely at ease in talking with his cousin. So much so, that he had to pause only now and again to sort out his words beforehand before speaking them. His stammer was being held at bay in magnificent fashion.

It was then, as they exhausted the ordinary subjects that were on their minds, that John became quieter and more introspective.

"Maria is very beautiful," John remarked. "She must be the most wonderful mother to you."

Cotton was touched by the unexpected sentiment, and said so.

"Father talks about her quite often," John continued. "He is very much admiring of her, in her qualities as a sister. My new sister, Mariah, is named for her. But Cotton, I do beg your leave to discuss such matters, as Father's thinking about our family leaves me very much disturbed, sometimes."

"How so, John?"

"He is very much resentful of our late renowned grandfather, for one thing, and blames that sainted man of God for all manner of ills for which he has suffered, for another."

"I have never heard ought but good about our grandfather and thus I am very much surprised to hear you speak thusly," said

Cotton, a little put off.

"Please, cousin, I do beg of you to not think the less of me for mentioning it. I would not do so otherwise were it not very much on my mind in this evil late hour."

John paused as if hesitant to go on.

"Cotton, has your Papa ever talked about his sister, our late aunt, Elizabeth?"

"Aunt Elizabeth, Capt. Eggington's wife? No, she has never been the subject of a conversation between us," Cotton replied honestly. Late as it was, he believed he could talk into morning, relieved as he was at the sudden flight of his stammer. "She had gone to be with the Lord our God 'ere I was born."

John said, "Yet she retains a fascination for my father for which I cannot account. They must have been close indeed."

Cotton considered the line of questioning, and reached back into his past.

"I believe I may have seen a portrait of her once."

"A portrait!" exclaimed John. "We Mathers and Cottons are very down on these likenesses, which ape the creative hand of our Lord, as I am told. It is rare indeed to see one in New England. Yet you have seen one of our aunt? How extraordinary!"

Cotton tried to concentrate. "It was definitely Elizabeth," he finally decided. "I saw it in Grandmama's house at Cotton Hill. Just the once."

He explained to John that this nearly forgotten visit took place a few years previously, not long after the Rev. Mather, Mistress Sarah's third and last husband, expired after an agonizing bout of the stone.

After the pastor had passed on in his misery, his widow had

removed back to Cotton Hill in Boston, her previous residence.

On that one occasion, Cotton had been taken to an unfamiliar small parlor room by the bizarre form of the servant Titus to await his Mistress Sarah's descent from the upstairs region of the old Cotton home. There, he was to receive the gift of a book for his birthday.

It was a room that had hitherto been closed off to Cotton as a young boy during the time when Increase's family had lived briefly at Cotton Hill. So it was natural his interest was rekindled by its unexpected availability that day.

As it so happened, Cotton did not fear Mistress Sarah as did the other young children in the extended family. Yet he did see in his double-grandmother a figure to be reckoned with.

When on the rare happenstance he was in her company (which wasn't often, he being away at Harvard or preparing his lessons or in prayer and she confining herself to her room in the old house) he addressed her as "Ma'am," and she to him as "Young Mr. Mather."

Interestingly, on those occasions, she smelled vaguely acidic to him, much as he imagined the odor of dried-up leaves one sometimes saw congealing at the bottom of glass bottles in the window of the apothecary. This peculiar scent, rather than off-putting, appealed to that smidgen of a scientist in him.

And the scent was thick in that room which, other than a small bench seat and a smallish box covered with a rectangular carpet, was otherwise as bare as a beech in winter.

Except for one new object. This was a painting of a pretty girl of an indeterminate young age.

In the girl's hand was a gaily beribboned white feathered fan. Around her neck was a double-strand of pearls. Fastened to her collar was a small cameo of a strange man.

It was while he was scrutinizing the painting that footsteps and creaking boards recalled to him the true purpose of his visit.

Cotton returned to his seat.

After a few polite sentences, his curiosity piqued him to ask Mistress Sarah about the painting. Rather than answer him directly, she had stared him down with a single word.

"Elizabeth."

His grandmother ventured nothing further and, given her manner, Cotton felt it best not to inquire any more into the matter except to wonder privately at the exceptionalism of it all. There was a well-stated prejudice in the family against graven images, which included paintings of people and various likenesses.

Cotton sighed.

"That is all I know of Aunt Elizabeth, cousin," he said to Cousin John.

"I know more," John answered. "Or rather, I should say that Father knows more."

Chapter Twenty-Three

Uncle John

That same evening, as the boys conversed under the black canopy of Boston's night, less than a quarter-mile from her step-son Increase's home, the grand widow Mistress Sarah Hawkredd Story Cotton Mather tossed and turned with the groans of age, burdened with a profound melancholy that refused to relent.

Her bedroom was the room where she had given life to all her children born in America save Seaborn, yet it was not a great comfort to her to be in it when the moon fell and the quiet of the city was as a graveyard.

The inexplicable sadness she bore weighed like a heavy chain hammered into her past, binding her there. As a consequence, she declined most invitations and extended only a very few herself, these being mostly of a legal nature having a bearing on the distribution of her outward estate.

Her inward estate, as she called it, she left to the hands of her faithful Creator and Redeemer.

Precisely what her mental affliction stemmed from, no one

could say, yet it was clearly not from any loss she had suffered among her husbands. Mistress Sarah was well aware of the grave's limitations on marriage.

More to the point, she was in full accord with her second husband John's – the great patriarch – admonitions to those widows who exhibited immoderate grief over temporal separation, such as she had suffered thrice among husbands and many times among children.

She had well learned from the eminent and departed Rev. Cotton to "not look too much upon this affliction of death" and to avoid "inordinate love" in life. Such sentiments, he once told her, were not to be relied upon, adding helpfully (he assumed) that in such cases where mortal beings are parted from each other by the will of the Lord, "there is a far greater love that will be theirs to share in the years hence, a love which nothing can dissolve."

Perhaps it was with such advice in mind that Mistress Sarah, whenever in public, which was infrequent, was otherwise notable for her severe black dress in which she was always seen those last few years. Its opaque fabric admitted no particle of her flesh to the outside save the outline of her sharply etched, lemony face. Even that was a rare sight for the sun or the sons of man.

However, little if any critical note was taken of the widow's extreme desire for seclusion. Neither was her absence even from the sermons delivered by her stepson Increase to be remarked upon.

By virtue of her extraordinary linkage to the two men considered Boston's greatest ministers, the widow was preserved from reproof and at the same time reserved for the greatest respect and admiration.

For if any in Boston proper were said to enjoy the unwritten protections of Puritan *lèse majesté* it was the mysterious Mistress Sarah.

Her stepchildren, which accrued to her in the course of her final marriage, were all the issue of the Rev. Richard Mather's late first wife Katherine. These were, by that evening in late 1674, widely scattered in the here and now, or among the quick and the dead.

The fate of Mistress Sarah's natural born children was a trail more difficult to follow.

There was said to be a single daughter through the late Goodman Story, her first husband in England, although whether she existed at all was a matter of speculation. Mistress Sarah had chosen to remain silent on the point except in her will, which she had preserved in secrecy until the day it would be needed (very soon now, it was expected).

As to the six others, these all by John Cotton who was by then himself deceased, three were, as Mr. Cotton liked to say, "in Heaven where all true happiness is forever."

Two children, Sariah Cotton and her brother Rowland, were cruelly taken from their parents by the Small pocks at a very young age.

Another daughter, Elizabeth, the wife of a commerce trading man, Capt. John Eggington now of Barbados, died during a tragic complication of the childbirth. It was Elizabeth's death in 1656 at age eighteen, out of all the others, that was said to have caused the widow Sarah the most remorse.

Her grief, worsened by her failure to heed the late Rev. Cotton's caution against taking exceeding delight in the company of the living, was palpable. It may even have been then that she took to wearing complete and utter black in her outfit, a habit that she even wore at her third wedding, this to the Rev. Mather, celebrated just days after her Elizabeth had been entombed in the old graveyard.

Elizabeth's death did bring into the world a grand-daughter, so named Elizabeth also. This child – who may have been the girl in the portrait Cotton had viewed and who remarkably resembled her late mother – was cared for at the Rev. Mather's fine home with the help of Mistress Sarah herself. Yet heartbreak struck again within a few years when the dear little girl went to be with Christ Jesus before her eighth year had been fully lived.

That was in 1664, a little more than a year after Cotton was born to Increase and Maria.

Following the loss of her grandchild Elizabeth, Mistress Sarah began a relentless slide into seclusion that rarely brought an invitation of admittance.

In short, it was a large and complicated family tree the boys shared, and as the widow Sarah, their grandmother, lay on her bed of nails at Cotton Hill, the two cousins, Cotton and John, sat in the dark shadows on the edge of Cotton's bed in his loft.

The light was non-existent since the moon had waned.

"I can hardly keep it straight in my mind," declared John upon an especially troublesome point about the heritage of his cousins.

"Well, as to your question about our Aunt Elizabeth," replied Cotton, "I have no memory of her, nor our poor cousin Elizabeth Eggington, her daughter. They went to Heaven e'er I could know them, sadly."

The subject exhausted, a thought came to Cotton. Had he considered it further, he might not have expressed it. Yet it escaped his innocent lips.

"I know Uncle John has suffered a great deal," Cotton said gently to his cousin.

"Far more than you know, dear Cotton," answered John. The boy picked at the ticking of the rough mattress thrown over the twisted yards of ropes that served for a bed frame.

Sensing there was more to know, and being insatiably curious in his nature, Cotton delicately inquired as to whether John's father might be "in difficulties" again, implying that, perhaps, this was behind his cousin's odd conversation about long-dead family members.

"I have heard many nights my father and my mother fighting, after which he would depart from their room and sit before the fire weeping," said John.

"It is not so unusual in marriages," said Cotton. As close as he was to his Papa, Cotton was often privy to the counseling Increase gave couples in the course of his ministry. So he knew that within marriage there was both joy and sorrow, as much of both as the Lord allotted.

"No blows were struck, I hope?" Cotton ventured.

"Nay, nothing of the sort. Yet my father on that night and many others I have seen was bowed to the ground with a great sadness. Once, after we had been among the Indians on the Vineyard ..."

"That must have been exciting!"

"It is not what you expect at all, dear Cotton. These are not savages and yet they are not wholly Christian, either. And they were devoted to Mr. Mayhew's son, who was then presumed dead, my father having replaced him there on that desolate island, you see. Where was I?" John made a face.

"Among the Wampanoag."

"Yes. I remember it had been a very trying day, the Wampanoag had so many questions. Old Mr. Mayhew that day had rejoined a man and wife and there was much anger, I'll tell you. The Indian man was a fornicator and she absolutely did not want him back in her house. It is the custom that she would be able to marry another man. But Mr. Mayhew was insistent that the vows of God must be reforged, and so he did just that. Father then had to explain why an Indian who broke the law wasn't punished and was instead rewarded and the wife punished."

Cotton nodded in sympathy with Uncle John's dilemma.

"I tried to accompany Father when he went from village to village even though he preferred I stayed in our home and work on my studies. He so admires you, Cotton, and hopes that I will be as brilliant a scholar!"

Cotton was pleased to hear such praise and told John so.

"We were returning home through a patch of woods after that eventful day when Mr. Mayhew forcibly interfered with the tradition. There was a large sitting stone along the path and Father just gave out a big sigh and sat down. Usually he wouldn't stop like that, just sit down and stop. He said, 'John, I can't tell you how very bereft I feel at this moment. Forgive me, son.' Not knowing what else to say, I said, 'Father, I forgive you.' He reached out to touch me."

John pushed a hand through his thick, auburn hair. Cotton waited for him to continue.

"Father said, 'John, you know it is a very grave sin to lie.' I said, 'I know that, Father. You had me learn that in our catechism together.' He began to cry anew. I asked why he was so troubled, was it the Indians or Mr. Mayhew, and he said no, it was because that day reminded him of the lies he said he was told by his father, our grandfather."

To say Cotton was astonished and dismayed would not be the half of it.

"Surely Uncle John could not believe such things about grandfather!" he exclaimed.

John looked at Cotton firmly. "Says I to myself the exact same thing. But Father was very adamant in his belief and could not be dissuaded from it. I asked for particulars but he would not hear of it. That same evening we had come home, Father took some of the broken-up furniture that was left from the late young Mayhew and started the pile of old wood afire outside. Father then went into our home and brought back a wooden box from our possessions and threw it onto the blaze. Tears ran down his face as it was consumed."

"What was inside the box?" asked Cotton.

"Letters. Grandfather's letters and papers regarding the heretic Anne Hutchinson. Mother came out to watch and I heard them talking about them. Grandfather had asked Seaborn to destroy these things long before, but my uncle had desisted, out of some terrible fear, I believe, and sent the bundles on to my father. That evening Father had resolved to fulfill his promise to Seaborn. I begged him to tell me what the letters said, but he refused. He finally said he hoped, with their destruction, that the story of our Aunt Elizabeth would perish in the flames along with the lies."

"You quite astonish me with such a tale," said Cotton, taken aback.

Taken aback, and feeling more than a little upset that he had been led into a conversation that had taken such a turn against his grandfather. Feeling thus, Cotton was brought up short and issued an abrupt admonition to his cousin to cease the narrative. Indeed, Cotton became openly hostile for the first time to John.

Cotton's late grandfather, the first Rev. John Cotton, was a man he had been brought up to revere and admire as an icon. Moreover, it was a love double-reinforced since it had been instilled into Cotton by a Papa he admired more than any other save the Lord.

"Don't be cross with me, cousin, I beg of you," said John, recognizing with horror the gulf that had suddenly opened between them.

"I cannot help but feel we are in dangerous territory and I wish to hear no more of this, ever," Cotton said, finally, after consideration.

John replied, a little bit put out himself by Cotton's abrupt manner, "I will never speak of this again, Cotton. But I was brought to mind of it this past evening, at table, when that man Hopestill Foster's name was raised, and I could see the look on Father's face, which reminded me of his past sorrow. The night he burned Grandpapa's letters was the only other time I ever heard of the man, when my father spoke of him to my mother and told her that he hoped never to hear of that name ever again."

They returned to their pillows very unhappy with each other after that, and it was a long while before the bliss of sleep welcomed either boy, but this time, the seductions of Morpheus claimed Cotton first.

John still had a bit of tossing and turning to do.

He was quite put out by his cousin's dismissiveness about the sensitive subjects he had dared to discuss, and felt himself slighted.

After some restless minutes, he resolved to never bring the matter up again. The idea brought him a certain calm.

Nor would he, John resolved as his waking moments were ending, even mention to Cotton the most interesting part of his story.

This was the fact that his father had, that day in the woods on Martha's Vineyard, at the last minute pulled out of the fire, before it could be in the least scorched, a single fat letter of Grandpapa's.

He knew where it was hidden, too, but a great fear kept him from opening it.

Chapter Twenty-Four

As to the Matter of Time

Trotting to Boston rather briskly now from his meeting in Salem with Judge Sewall and toward his fateful rendezvous with the man Hopestill Foster, his reveries almost complete, the Rev. Cotton Mather was struck by the peculiarity of the memory of his Aunt Elizabeth – brought back to life and mind as it were, like a resurrection.

He and Cousin John had never spoken again of their night's conversation, and had since become estranged from each other's company. Nevertheless, Mather now decided he would, upon the completion of his interrogation of the wretch Foster – God willing! – revisit the matter with his father. Was it possible that he himself was now bewitched, tormented by his family's past? He wouldn't put it past Devil.

The thought greatly distressed him, but it was not the only recollection that disturbed his churning mind. The idea of Foster finally within his grasp had revived the horror of the Dover-area massacre in which Richard Walderne was slaughtered, a bloodbath that held an uncanny fascination for the minister.

Mather was less inclined to think of that portentous calamity as a tragedy. Rather, the minister saw in the old man's disgusting murder and mutilation at the hands of those Indian fiends and allies of Foster, a warning from King Lucifer himself. Walderne's obscene demise in 1689 along with the destruction wrought at Cochecho would be the prelude to another fatal round of great ills which were now besetting the Massachusetts Bay Colony and its neighbors.

Not since King Philip's War had there been such uprisings of the red devils from the woods!

Their new outrages took place not just throughout New England but in New York and farther south where the idolatrous antichrists of New France, secure in their Canadian lairs, ventured out like wolves in the night, bloodying their maws wherever opportunity presented.

York in the province of Maine had been disemboweled by the French and their bloodthirsty allies on Candlemas in the present witchy year of 1692, while only two winters before that Fort Schenectady in New York had been all but wiped out on a most frightful February night. Only one man, who had run nearly naked through a snowstorm clear to Albany, had lived to bear the tale of the massacre.

With an angry wave of his hand swatting at the distracting images, Cotton banished all these irrelevant thoughts.

His focus narrowed.

Judge Sewall's intelligence about the man Hopestill Foster, that he was in Boston, in custody and in no condition to escape, was of the utmost importance.

Certainly, what Foster knew about Walderne's murder intrigued the historian and appalled the minister in him. But those were secondary considerations. It was the secrets Foster might know about Cotton's own family that threatened to burn a hole through his heart.

Rounding Gallows Hill, the Rev. Mather winced and bit his lip lightly. The graves of the witches hanged there a few weeks before, including the warlocks Burroughs and Willard, were nearby. He imagined he could smell the turned earth wherein they lay.

Mather's mind plotted the arrangements he needed to make with Constable Arnold at the prison.

He had wharf property that he had procured from the estate of a dead Quaker where an interrogation could be held without drawing too much attention.

Yes, he thought, that would do very well.

The minister now rode hard, his horse already hotly lathered, on the good south road.

There was not a moment to lose.

As to the matter of time, so urgent then for Mather riding away from Salem that warm late summer afternoon in '92, this commodity was of no particular value to the Pennacook chief Kancamagus at that exact moment.

Chief Kancamagus, the grandson of Passaconnaway but better known to the English as John Hogkins, was leisurely eating his meal in front of his dwelling in the Indian town of Odanak, far to the north.

Kancamagus-Hogkins was a runaway slave, a murderer, and a renegade with a small fortune attached to his head – literally, there being no scalp money to be had for a case such as his. Proof of death in the form of that head was the only acceptable receipt.

Yet "John Hogkins" was no more alive than an empty rattlesnake skin.

That thin veneer of English flesh known as Hogkins had been flayed off by the hand of the one who had inhabited it for two long, humiliating years as the servant of the late Caleb Boelkins, a Boston Quaker as soft as risen dough who erroneously believed that inside every pagan lived a useful slave.

Kancamagus shifted his haunches as he grabbed another greasy handful of mashed corn and fat augmented by the shreds of venison pounded into it. And as the Rev. Cotton Mather deliberated on massacres and such on his hurried journey back to Boston, Kancamagus pondered the fates that had led his small band to its current plight as wards of the French Father King.

This took away his appetite. Abruptly, the strongly built Indian stopped chewing and put the horn bowl aside. The woman behind him whisked it away immediately.

The Pennacook remnants Kancamagus now led were a pitiful lot. Fewer than a dozen warriors with slightly more than thrice that many women, children and old men, they were despised in Odanak, which the French called St. Francis.

There, barely tolerated by their Abenaki brethren, they lived in squalor outside the stockade walls protecting the Jesuit chapel within. Around them, Odanak's wigwams, huts, rude houses and fort stood on the bluff above the raging river that flowed into the turbulent St. Lawrence.

Still, life was not so onerous as it once had been.

Since the years following the disastrous "Phony Battle," the catastrophe to the Pennacook that was the final tragedy that flowed from Metacomet's defeat in King Philip's War in 1676, Kancamagus and his people had found a saving branch on which to cling.

The largess of the French race, of which its resident Jesuit *abbés* were the vanguard, eased the disaster of displacement from traditional hunting grounds. These white men were responsible for the gunpowder and tools the Abenaki received, and supplies from nearby Quebec heaped in their big bateaux flowed much more regularly now that war had returned to the frontiers.

Whenever these heavy boats crunched into the landing below the town, the leaders of the various clans, including Kancamagus, were called inside the stockade to hear the messages of the White Father's sons who dwelled in New France. These orations were treated with respect out of deference for the presents that inevitably followed.

In general, most of the speeches ordinarily consisted of peaceful greetings and well wishes from the King of France to His children, who at Odanak were for the most part the various tribes of the Abenaki gathered there. Far more important, the Frenchmen concluded these affairs with the distribution of presents. On very rare occasions there was salt to be had in little barrels and leather bags filled with colored glass beads. There was that, yes, but this new war with the English meant that weapons were brought in, too.

The firing of a musket with a loud pop announced that a new council was convening. Kancamagus stood up and joined the others shuffling through the perpetually open gates of the fort and onto the parade grounds. Along the way he shifted his blanket about his shoulders and over his arm like a Roman strolling to the ancient senate.

From gossip heard on his walk Kancamagus learned that a boxload of the new-style muskets so coveted by the warriors was to be distributed that day, very welcome news.

The dog-wheel action of the old guns was a great hindrance in the field. So much so that the more skilled of the men in the ancient ways still preferred the silent flight of the bow and arrow, although there was no question about the weapon for close-in fighting – the hatchet was the tool of choice. Kancamagus possessed three such killing axes but on a war party he brought only the one with the wicked impaling spike opposite the razor-bladed front edge.

The Indians took their places and sat down in the dust before the great log pole, Kancamagus being off to one side, far from the place of honor before the speakers. This was of no import to the Pennacook chief. Now that his tribe was dying out like the Pequot, status mattered not at all to him.

He snatched a pinch of snuff from a little painted box and stuffed it into his right nostril. The box, a possession of his late master, was decorated with a miniature painting of a Dutch girl carrying a yoke of flowers looking up at someone unseen in a window. The keepsake gave him pleasure since he had taken it after wetting his knife in the rich man Boelkins's belly, holding it in and twisting it until the man's death groaning faded away.

Sitting next to Kancamagus at the council fire was the chief of the Kennebecs, Bomazeen, who wore around his neck a string of stiff human fingers. Kancamagus offered the small, wiry man the delicate snuff box per the English custom, but Bomazeen turned his face away as if a dog had approached. A contented Kancamagus took no offense at this slight.

After the welcoming addresses from the French officers, there came the ineluctable harangues from the priests. The chiefs and honored warriors listened with expressions arranged in ceremonial gravity about the continuing necessity to drive the English Puritans into the fathoms of the endless lake. Grunts of approval ensued.

However, when the French who would accompany them on the new raids were praised, Kancamagus could see the backs of some men stiffen in the way they do when an insult is given.

The Abenaki needed no paternal encouragement to raid. Their forays brought them goods and especially captives to kill or sell as their whims desired. Besides, making war on the English was far preferable to fighting other Indians who knew how to make war back on them. A single Indian had been known to leap from the woods and frighten an entire troop of English men.

As the Frenchman in his dirty white uniform lectured them, with the trade goods and gifts arrayed behind the officer as incentive to stay and listen in polite silence, Kancamagus smiled.

Behind his eyes lived his happy revenge dream.

He relished reliving it when of necessity he must sit and listen to any of the white Frenchmen.

In it, the corpulent, naked Walderne screams like a sow as he, cut by their knives, struggles in the chair-throne they had heaved atop the massive trading room table the night of the Cochecho massacre. Indian faces sprayed bright red reflected the joy of their work.

Before they toppled the dying Walderne to impale him on his own sword, Kancamagus had cut off the major's pig-like right hand. This was the one that had so often cheated them when it weighed down the fur scales. Then he and the others had partaken of the major's beating heart. What was left of the organ was tossed into the corner with the other body bits that had been sliced off.

Walderne deserved his doom because he was the author of the Phony Battle and the miserable lot of the Pennacook tribe that followed.

Kancamagus's brow narrowed at the memory of the Phony Battle.

This sight, different from that of his revenge dream triumph in Walderne's cabin, was an old vision now. Still, it came sharply into focus behind his glazed-over eyes while the Frenchman clucked on in his chicken-noise language.

Before the day of trickery and betrayal in Dover destroyed

them during Skamonkas – that first week of September 1676, the month of the corn harvest – the Pennacook were still formidable. Not powerful, but formidable.

Sixteen years later, in 1692, they were nothing.

Passaconnaway's children and grandchildren had been reduced to a handful of warriors living from raid to raid and compelled to shoulder insults from others.

But worse, far worse, their glory and that of their ancestors was shared among a decreasing of men whose stories would one day never be repeated except in another place that has no relation to this world.

It was true, of course, that well before his tribe's obliteration, Chief Passaconnaway had left them forever.

His body drooping with old age, it was said the legendary Sagamore had ridden away on a great sled pulled by wolves over the ice-frozen Merrimack to the place where warriors go when they die. The people wept. This was in the white man's year of 1672, four winters before the Phony Battle.

Kancamagus sneered at the legend that had grown up around the death of the old chief, his grandfather. Yet what did it matter what the people believed? He knew the Bashaba's politics had destroyed the tribe long before the crooked hands of Walderne and Robinhood dealt the fatal blows.

A sled it was that dragged Passaconnaway's flesh-on-bones skeleton out of Pennacook village, but the conjurer was dead on it, stiff as a bone. The feathers that adorned his lank hair stuck out like those of a grouse hen, ridiculous looking almost. It was all Kancamagus and the other adult warriors of his clan could do to stifle their disrespect.

The women might sing of a sled drawn by wolves, since there

were wolves, many of them in the following nights, but the Pennacook people could not fail to hear the brothers of dogs playing in the burial ground, fighting over the meat of Passaconnaway.

Kancamagus's uncle Wonnalancet, the blood-brother of Robinhood, had become chief with the Bashaba's final blessing. After that, two were always at his side – Robinhood, the adopted white man Foster who was his brother in blood, and Passaconnaway's old retainer Jonny Findus, the little fat man who by then was so disturbed in his mind that he talked only to the sky.

Wonnalancet trusted Robinhood. No matter. Kancamagus knew that trust to be suspect as the love of a serpent. And as it was bound to be, that same trust failed his uncle, too. The yellow-haired Englishman taken into their tribe as Passaconnaway's son was also the paid lackey of Walderne.

Robinhood pretended to love the Pennacook but Kancamagus knew better. He had listened always to the wise counsel of Nanamacomuck his father until those lips were sealed forever by order of the Bashaba. His father was killed to prevent some new retribution by the whites. Passaconnaway's order was womanly, beyond cowardly.

What could those impotent English have done to them? Their soldiers held no fear for Pennacook warriors. Even the small Pequot band that had captured Robinhood when he was a stripling had terrorized white settlements for years with impunity.

Nanamacomuck was dead, his father was dead. Passaconnaway's true son was a token life paid for drinking Walderne's strong waters.

To the son, Nanamacomuck's crime was not that he had killed a white in that fat major's truck house, a structure filled with Pennacook furs obtained by trickery and deceit. His father's crime was that he was drunk with English rum when he had carved the white man Dickinson nearly into two halves.

The boy Kancamagus implored his father not to return to Pennacook with Robinhood's band. He beseeched him to remain out of the camp and challenge Passaconnaway's power. Yet his father merely looked upon his son with the milky eyes of a cow dimly aware of the descending mallet. Then he had walked back to the river town with Robinhood's men – returning to his doom.

Wonnalancet supplanted Nanamacomuck as chief because Passaconnaway was as frightened of Kancamagus as he was of the whites. Nor would the old man forget or forgive the hatred Kancamagus held for the Sagamore's appeasement of the English.

And so Passaconnaway gave the blessing to his blood uncle and sealed the doom of the Pennacooks. Kancamagus knew Wonnalancet would follow the same dishonorable path of appeasement until they were all farmers like the English that King Philip's warriors butchered in their fields.

And so as he mused, the animated Frenchman at St. Francis droned on to his listeners, who were as silent stones squatting before him.

This pale white French spoke now of the vast brotherhood of the tribes in Canada gathering on the frontiers to strike not only the Puritan English but the Iroquois dogs who skulked at their heels. At the appropriate pauses, the Abenaki assemblage dutifully murmured its approval.

Kancamagus's ears listened to the talk noise but his eyes did not see anything except what was in his thoughts.

Chapter Twenty-Five

Phony Battle

It was shameful to remember such days, but the Pennacook people had lived in fear, like rabbits caught out on the snow, during the final months of Metacomet-Philip's war on the whites in the year 1676.

Even so, some Pennacooks, including Kancamagus, had fought with the Wampanoag and Nipmuck alongside King Philip until the tide had turned and the Puritans regained the upper hand. This the English were able to do with the assistance of traitorous friendlies like the Mohegans who were able to smoke out ambushes and track down the war's leaders. The Christian Indians, drunk with Jesus love, also hunted them to their death.

Kancamagus was a young warrior then, in the prime of his life. He was foolhardy, certainly, brave beyond measure, but hatred roiled his bowels and enraged his heart.

The glowing core of that molten enmity was directed at his uncle, Robinhood, the white man adopted by Passaconnaway before Kancamagus was born. Robinhood, whom the English called Hopestill, had been the instrument of death for his beloved father as well as the agent who betrayed his tribe to Walderne in the shameful Phony Battle in which no enemy was killed.

It was after an apprehensive mid-summer feast that Chief Wonnalancet told the Pennacooks they must journey to Dover during Temezownwas, at the time of the gathering of the crops when the corn was at its peak.

Walderne had summoned the tribe. He had learned from his spies that the ranks of the Pennacook were swollen with fighters from King Philip's decimated Indian army, and the white chief demanded a census be taken of its members.

Kancamagus, barely able to walk, was among these refugees. He and what was left of his war party had drifted back to the main Pennacook village on the Merrimack at the war's chaotic close. He had been painfully wounded by a lead ball that had plowed an agonizing, deep red furrow across his abdomen and right forearm. The flesh around the edges was jagged, but the rip was as straight and neat as a corn row. He sewed himself together with deer gut.

Chief Wonnalancet, posturing, welcomed his nephew back, although both knew there was a gorge between them as wide as the watery one in the mountains to the north, in sight of the great stone face, where Passaconnaway had taken them hunting when Kancamagus was a child.

The supplicant Kancamagus made no trouble for his uncle. He was humbled by his wound which made him weak, and thus was wary of antagonizing his enemies within the tribe. Still, his soul boiled with loathing at the changes that had been wrought in his former home during his absence.

Since he had been made chief, Wonnalancet not only had aped Passaconnaway's policies of appeasement, he had embraced them like a woman in her heat. As did Passaconnaway before he disappeared from the world, the new chief rejected the arguments of Kancamagus out of hand.

Playing the woman to the English, though, had done the tribe little good.

In the immediate aftermath of the war the village had nearly doubled in size as the survivors of the Puritan and Mohegan slaughters limped in and increased the population almost daily. It was inevitable that such large numbers of rootless, unfamiliar Indians would attract the attention of the English, and they did.

Wonnalancet began receiving written messages (which Jonny Findus read to him) from the Puritans in the hand of Major Richard Walderne. These ordered him to appear before the English and explain what was going on at Pennacook.

Kancamagus smelled the trap. He implored Wonnalancet to leave Pennacook and retreat deeper into the woods but in this he was countered by Robinhood and Jonny Findus, who were in direct negotiations with the strongman of Dover, Walderne.

Robinhood could boast of much stature within the tribe before its fall. He had since his adoption taken a Pennacook woman to be his wife and had fathered two boys by her, although by the time Philip's war began in 1675 the woman and sons had died. Since then, Robinhood lived apart from the tribe on the edge of Pennacook territory between Walderne's Dover and the Indians. He became the ambassador between the races, although he was neither liked nor trusted by a majority of either.

Wonnalancet paid every heed to Robinhood, though. Every heed.

At the thought of his white uncle, Kancamagus's mind leaped to the present. His hand instinctively felt for his knife and his forefinger lightly brushed the razor-edge. How he longed to slide it into that man's flesh.

Wonnalancet forbade any Indian to stay behind. He insisted that all come in to Cochecho on the appointed day so that the English could have no excuses on which to lay blame on the Pennacooks. Whoever had come into the village, even fresh from Philip's disastrous war, was obliged to make the journey.

The chief told the restless among them to have no fear, that Wonnalancet and his Indians were under the direct protection of Walderne. To further ease their trepidation, he encouraged them to bring goods to barter since Robinhood informed them there would be a trade fair held in the great field beyond Walderne's house.

But Kancamagus decided to bring only his war hatchet. He ordered his wives to hide.

So it was that the last great trek of the Pennacook to the east was arranged.

And it was, as Kancamagus had suspected, a trap.

Greeting the arriving Indians at Cochecho was the big-bellied white chief Walderne. As the Indians filed in from the great cornfields, he could be seen holding up his right hand, standing as tall as he could make himself. From afar, Wonnalancet returned the salute.

Kancamagus looked for Robinhood but failed to catch sight of him.

What he could not know was that in order to prevent another double-cross of his plans, Walderne had sent Foster far into Maine on an expedition to mark the most magnificent of the white pine and oak for the masts and planks of the Royal Navy. For his services to the crown (and a well-placed bribe), Walderne had obtained a King's Warrant for the great northern forests. Foster's absence was one of the many reasons for Walderne's exceptionally good humor that day.

Kancamagus, who hadn't seen Walderne since years before

the war, observed from the distance that the white chief had grown even more plump during the interval, like an Albany Dutchman. Fearing discovery as a fighter for Metacomet he hung back as the Indians walked closer to the fort.

Walderne, a dumpy man when he was out of uniform, did look splendid that afternoon.

He drew himself up in his finest major's regalia. His red coat's brass buttons and ceremonial gorget gleamed in the sun. A spray of lavender was sewn onto his ornamental sash and a fine sword hung by his right hand. This dropped to rest on its hilt, a subconscious reflex perhaps, as the Indians advanced nearer.

Walderne needn't have fretted.

Wonnalancet's Pennacooks and their guests were suitably impressed with their reception. Whatever tentative misgivings they might have held were soothed by calming memories of their late Bashaba and his enduring friendship with the Puritans. That Wonnalancet was continuing Passaconnaway's policies helped make most feel secure in the presence of their white friends.

There was, however, a reticent quality to their final approach due to the presence of two long rows of soldiers and colonists standing at parade rest on either side of the wide field. Each cohort was captained by a dismounted leader who stood by the side of his horse.

The instinct of some of the younger Indians, those whose memories of the Bashaba were of the shortest duration, was to bolt. A jabber of nervous excitement burbled amongst them since the number of whites nearly exceeded that of the Indians, the majority of whom had never seen more than a handful of colonists together in any one place.

Wonnalancet, sensing that wave of unease, went among them

to pour his calming oil on their waters, but still, the chief himself was amazed.

Such an impressive contingent of armed white men had never been assembled so far north. There were many more men in the field then there were in all of Dover. He reasoned these must have come from as far away as Salisbury, or even Boston, the terrifying white man's town described with awe by Jonny Findus.

The Indians held back at first, declining to advance, waiting to see if Wonnalancet and his family showed any hesitancy or fear but the chief was brave. A touch of concern, perhaps, passed like a shadow across his handsome face but on he strode, walking across the field proudly, erect, to clasp hands with Walderne, who moved a few steps toward him to pump the chief's arm vigorously.

With that gesture the concerns of the Indians melted away. Also tempering any remaining apprehension was a long row of benches and raw mill boards piled high with refreshments both liquid and solid. Behind these, tended by teams of unarmed white men stripped down to their shirts in the heat, copper cauldrons atop blazing cordwood fires overflowed with boiling corn and meat. Wonnalancet and Walderne, arm in arm, walked to the fort-house with the Indians following their leader.

Kancamagus hung back with the cautiousness of an old deer as the Pennacooks swarmed to the food, ripping away chunks of venison, turkey and duck and holding these high in celebration.

He refused to partake. Instead, he watched the soldiers on both sides of the clearing, his right hand curled around his war axe. Mindful of his tell-tale wound, Kancamagus wrapped his blanket tightly around him even though the afternoon sun was at its most sweltering. Thinking of Robinhood again caused his stomach to heave.

Being far removed from each other, the whites and Indians,

except for the chiefs, didn't mix – but the rum flowed freely in both camps.

Earthen jugs had been set around for passing. The male Indians took their fill of the fiery drink, as did some of the wives. Wonnalancet, who did not care much for watered-down rum or even stronger drink, quaffed his share. And everyone helped themselves from the cauldrons without invitation, dipping into the boil as many times as they could stand it for fistfuls of vegetables and meat to wolf down.

The white soldiers had relaxed from their earlier attentive posture. As the banquet continued, they stood or sat in groups, laughing and looking to their equipment. From the size of the bone heap scattered before them on the ground, it was obvious they had feasted earlier.

Quick work was made of the meal. The slops from the remains were flung to the dogs of both races. Then Walderne climbed unsteadily onto the long board that served as a table.

He kicked away the mugs and earthen bowls near him to address the Indians and the whites by proclaiming all to be brothers seeking peaceful existence with each other. Jonny Findus translated the major's speech, punctuated with belches. The Pennacooks who listened murmured appreciatively. Others had fallen asleep after gorging themselves.

Kancamagus took notice when Walderne proposed an entertainment, which the major termed an "exhibition."

Jonny Findus fumbled as he had no similar word in Pennacook. In his translation he substituted the word "game" instead, bringing to mind the frenzied stick-and-ball sport the toughest young men would play sometimes. It was a rough game in which arms were broken and heads were split open, but it was an entertainment beloved by the Indians.

However, this was not what Walderne had proposed. The Indians and the whites would fight a sham battle in the clearing, he declared. Both sides would fire over the heads of the others and be judged by their chiefs for their spirit in the contest. Walderne paused for the translation and smiled when he detected the clear delight seen in the faces before him.

He then announced there would first be a demonstration of the cannons, which caused many reclining Indians to stand back up in pure astonishment.

Some had heard of this remarkable weapon, which was said to fire with the authority of a dozen or more muskets, although none but those who had been in Philip's War had ever seen one put to use. The Indians were keen to hear it make thunder and witness its lightning, and set to whooping in anticipation of this delight.

Walderne stepped down from the table and led a dozen strong Pennacook men to one of the two field pieces, which they patted and touched as if it were a beast to be won over.

The major personally picked up the drag lines and laid the thick ropes over the shoulders of the Indians, motioning where he wanted the artillery to be positioned. Wonnalancet, seated on the ground amid a pile of duck bones, laughed at the sight. Other Indians joined in the good-natured ribbing. The whites, still positioned far enough away to pose no threat, watched from their vantage point at the outer edges of the clearing.

Jonny Findus accompanied the major as he gave his explanation to the Indians. Walderne pointed out the touch hole where the piece was to be fired, and then went through the motions, as he explained the operation of loading to the pudgy translator. As he was so engaged, a playful white man, one of those tending the fires, snuck up and poked a burning splinter near the cannon's top. It went off with a massive explosion.

The bucking carriage narrowly missed crushing Walderne, but it did not miss the legs and arms of four Indians, who were shockingly wounded. They looked at their broken, spurting wounds with detachment, as if what had just destroyed their limbs was occurring in a delusion. A hundred yards away, a stick of Indian men and women who had been struck by the fired cannon ball also went down. Plowing into them the projectile dropped the figures like wind-blown stalks.

Almost all of the Indians lazing about on the ground were sodden with drink and meat. They jumped to their feet as if suddenly deranged by the tragedy and the blast, converging upon the inert, smoking weapon in a lunatic mass of pumping arms and legs. Once some of them fired their guns into the air, the rest began shooting their muskets at the innocent sky or at nothing. They fired and screamed and ran around in mad circles.

In the disorganized frenzy that followed, no one noticed that Walderne had slipped away. Nor did the Indians comprehend at first the two lines of colonial infantry that had neatly formed up on either side of the field, and that had begun to advance upon the Indians from both directions.

The soldiers walked forward at a steady pace, their heavy muskets leveled.

Not all had bayonets, but those that had them had affixed the razor steel to their gun barrels. Although to many an Indian the white faces had before looked similar at a distance, the closer the enemy marched toward them the more the wild differences among the dangerous faces leaped out. The hats, the shirts, the footwear of the English were all different. The wild patches of color sewed into the buckskins or linen shirts on each advancing fighter were anything but festive. Instead, the oncoming whites with their stitched clothes, black teeth and barbaric beards had an aura of crazed lethality, barely contained.

On the verge of being surrounded almost by default, their imminent dilemma filled the Indians with horror. They saw now they were trapped between two lines of heavily armed and advancing soldiers. They understood their own muskets, having all been fired off for the most part, were now useless.

"Passaconnaway!" some wailed. Others cried out to invoke the old magic, "Bashaba!"

Falling back, crowded upon themselves like rats chased into a wall, the Pennacooks became hopelessly intermingled. Some were half-drunk, others were sick with fatigue and nauseous from having eaten too much.

Bewildered, leaderless, they began to sit down, first some, then most, to await the ending that they felt, that they *knew*, had been predestined, arranged, decreed.

Chapter Twenty-Six

The Quaker Boelkins

Kancamagus, slow to escape, was seized by Capt. Charles Frost's soldiers within minutes of the surrender. He was separated from the others, marched down river, and manhandled into a whaleboat by Frost and four of his most ferocious-looking men, real killers. He knew better than to resist.

Behind him, the demoralized Pennacooks were bound together into a long, miserable line. Vicious fighting broke out among the whites over Indian muskets and possessions as their officers ineffectually hectored the miscreants. His last sight of the battlefield was of an ashen-faced Wonnalancet sitting alone amid the bawling women and children. They staggered around him in ignorance of his melancholy as if he were a stone. Nor did any soldiers bother to guard the invisible chief of the Pennacooks.

After shoving off, the chaos behind Kancamagus receded into the noise of the rapids speaking to his ears as the pilot ran the vessel into the placid Fore, which emptied into the mighty Piscataqua. Angry water sawed at the craft with little razor waves.

He thought of jumping overboard and trying to swim for it but his guards hemmed him in. In any case, furtive glances told him that Frost, a dour, unhealthy man but with an intelligent look about him, was anticipating the move. He calculated, too, his suppurating belly wound combined with the rigors of his recent journey would undo him should he attempt anything nearly so rash. So he crossed his arms and legs, closed his eyes and let the wind buffet his face as the bulky craft flopped forward in the choppy waters.

Frost had his men turn into the dismal landing known to the English as the Point of Graves. Kancamagus could see this was one of those curious places where the whites buried their dead underneath pieces of the stones that stood. A musket barrel was shoved viciously into his back and a grunted order made him step out onto land. He did so.

Surrounded by the headstones and his enemies he accepted his fate. The hard men barked questions at him, pushed him around violently, slapped his face. His nose was suddenly smashed with the flat of a hatchet. He sank down to his knees, stunned. He comprehended but a smattering of their English, but he understood enough to know that two of them wanted to murder him then and there while the other three, including the man Frost, wished to keep him alive.

Frost screamed something at him. When he failed to answer, his skull was cracked from behind, much too hard, by the force of a musket stock. He heard one of the men say in English "He's a dead Indian" before he began to tumble over a waterfall that never ended. A knife ripped into his back, but its destructive force felt only like a harmless kick. He imagined himself crying out, yet oddly enough did not hear his voice.

Time had passed, he was certain of that, perhaps many days, before he opened his eyes again. He was in a room in a white man's house that reeked of fresh resin.

Covered to his neck by a soiled shroud, he was lying on his back along a board, his hands down at his sides. Around his middle and upper arms a strip of cloth wound gently underneath the wood. It was not an uncomfortable position. His head had been rendered immovable, however, by the clever use of an open-top box that had been built around it on three sides. The thick cloth cushioning his pounding head was sodden with fluid, probably blood.

As Kancamagus gathered his wits about him, a white face bent over his to remark, "Thou art awake, it seems. Hmmmm." The man had been chewing cloves.

It was a face of indeterminate age and a curious one, with almost as many warts as whiskers, and it belonged to an eager head that bobbed this way and that as it sniffed in examination. A flat beaver hat, sweated through and through, was tied around it as if it might scamper away at the least chance.

Kancamagus shrank from the man only to discover that any movement shot a lightning bolt of pain into his back. "Thou hast been cruelly used," warned his examiner. "Please to lie still."

The Quaker Boelkins straightened with a grimace as his hand searched his waistcoat pocket. Taking a deliberate thumbful of snuff from an exquisitely painted little box, he planted the pinch up his nostrils. He looked for help from behind him in translating his sentiments. There, a young woman with features as soft and light brown as doeskin was hovering.

Her hair was hidden by a bright scarf, but several of her teeth gleamed like knives sharpened to tiny ivory points. When she saw the Indian stare at these oddities, she clamped her lips. She spoke timidly to him in a crude form of Abenaki that was only barely intelligible.

"Be careful" were her final words in his tongue, although a discrete expression of concern relayed to him far more than what she said.

Kancamagus closed his eyes. He knew enough English from listening to Jonny Findus over the years to gather that he had been stabbed and left to die. He also discerned from the conversation of unseen others in the room that he was somewhere in the English castle town called Boston among people who knew his name, and that his whereabouts had become known to others who wanted to harm him further.

What he did not know, what he couldn't know just then, was that he was now a slave, and the white beast who had taken ownership of him, Caleb Boelkins, had just profited massively from the sale of the Pennacook Indians captured at Cochecho. These were already en route to Barbados, shackled head-to-head amidships, awash in their own vomit and filth.

Judged enemies in the employ of the late King Philip in a massive, single, rote trial in a Boston wharf warehouse, the special court decreed these bewildered natives to be Crown property. Within minutes of its opening, and with astonishing speed, Caleb Boelkins arranged to have the full lot of nearly 300 shipped off to the steaming British Caribbean slave island since, as "chance" would have it, a sleek sloop owned by his employer, Capt. Jeremiah Eggington, one fitted out for the trafficking of human beings, was standing by in the next dock over "in the event of such an eventuality," as Boelkins told the sullen magistrates. The solicitors found the Quaker's presence at court almost as distasteful as the pathetic Pennacook rabble, until they were personally assured all would be privy to a share of the profits, once booked.

None of this would be known to Kancamagus until many weeks had passed. In his present state of helplessness, he conceived of the odd figure of the Quaker dressed all in black as a sort of holy man or healer, which he was and wasn't. Boelkins was no physician, but he was skilled in patching up flesh and healing broken bones for the glory of God, true, but mostly for the glory of his purse.

His most celebrated exploit (in his own mind) was cheating some Hebrews representing the Dutch West India Company who had ensconced themselves at Barbados waiting for an incoming shipment. The Hebrews were hoping to snap some of these up for a quick return to the new plantations bearing fruit in the Virginia colony and no doubt win a weighty addition to their collective purse.

However, not amenable to being cheated, the heavily bearded buyers had been on the lookout for signs of a virulent flux that was abounding at the time, one that left a telltale white discharge running down the legs of the half-dead cargo. Boelkins, who fortunately had been aboard Eggington's ship when it landed at Saint Michael that particularly affluent evening, contained the crisis by stuffing up the anuses of African blacks who hadn't yet expired. A plaster of oakum did the trick.

That was then, of course. His acquisition of Kancamagus was proving to be less of a windfall and more an act of stupidity on his part.

A fluke delivered the Indian to Boelkins when Capt. Frost suffered a seizure of conscience and reminder of his duty to carry Kancamagus to Boston per Walderne's orders. So Frost sent back two of his men to the graveyard to carry the body away before it was discovered.

To their disgust, they found a little bit of life left in the wounded warrior, but then they figured if he lived they could sell him. So they threw his mangled body into the boat, nearly breaking his neck in the bargain, and took him to Kittery. There, a fast shallop sped them to Boston and Quaker Boelkins, well known to them as "the slave doctor."

Through these criminals, Boelkins learned the identity of Kancamagus, as well as the interesting fact that the Indian had a huge price on his broken head.

Under other circumstances, he would have collected the bounty for himself in a trice. That is, until he heard in the same breath that Major Richard Walderne was the one anxiously hoping to present Kancamagus to the governor for Bay Colony justice. The Quaker Boelkins honed a very fine hatred toward Walderne.

This was not merely because the Dover magistrate and military leader was a man for whom no Quaker in New England bore even a modicum of love.

It was one thing entirely that Walderne's brutal hounding of Boelkins's sect on behalf of the Puritans knew no bounds. It was quite another that the wealthy Dover trader was the instrument by which Boelkins's older sister Alice Ambrose – one of the three Quaker women whipped out of Dover in '62 – had been crushed in spirit and body, a lovely amaranth destroyed in the grip of an iron gauntlet.

The brother loved his sister. More, he worshipped her. Alice meant everything to him. And she had been tortured and scourged and driven out of her mind by Walderne and others of his cruel stripe.

One of the earlier followers of George Fox, Alice converted to his teachings to embrace her inner light. This she discovered within her breast with all the fervor of a true saint, which she was in her brother's devoted eyes.

Alice and her poor husband Alan were among the earliest Quaker loyalists who dutifully suffered with the peregrinator Fox around England, happily sleeping in muddy ruts, enduring taunts and threats, starving at times. Somehow, through all those trials, she survived, grew stronger and became determined to take Fox's call of faith to America in search of initiating new Friends. It was through Alice's exhortations that Boelkins reined in, for a short time, his own restless spirit and turned it to Christ.

The death of their parents was quickly succeeded by the demise of Alice's husband Alan following that kind man's sickening ordeal at the hands of a county sheriff and his wife, both infamous for their antipathy toward the Foxites. They imprisoned Alan Ambrose in a small hole that opened fifteen feet above the ground in the middle of a stone wall. Forced by necessity to clamber up and down the slippery rocks to fetch his meager food, he fell to his death one morning. Alice, numb with grief, determined her calling was to be an ambassador for Fox to the intolerant Puritans of New England.

Caleb Boelkins, by that time a reluctant Friend, discovered Alice's plans too late to stop her. Her abrupt leaving was a painful blow to him, and he fretted over his next course.

Boelkins was prosperous then by current standards, having turned his parent's modest estate into the makings of a shipping clerk's post for himself in Liverpool. Politically astute, he avoided taking sides in the civil war, angering neither Roundhead nor Parliamentarian, and steering well clear of the quarrels between men that were likely to get one killed.

From shipmasters, he grew alarmed by reports of how bad things had become for the Quakers in Puritan New England. Anxious to trade the stink and nightmares of England for those of the New World, he took passage in one of Capt. Eggington's ships, the *Fair Falcon,* making the chance acquaintance with its master that would serve his purposes in America, and began his hunt for his sister.

Through the help of other Friends, whose network in New England was as efficient as a secret society, he found Alice in 1663 in Boston, the year after her ordeal-by-whip, barely alive, a scarred skeleton maniacally determined to carry on her work.

He pleaded with her, begged her to go back to England with him after all she had been through. She refused. Weeks later, she vanished again, this time without a trace.

The last he heard, she had been tried by another Puritan court in Virginia and sentenced to further brutality at the whipping post and was reduced once more to an insensate, inert form under the lash. From sources in that colony, Boelkins learned Alice's wits were completely beaten out of her this time, leaving her mind tormented in madness with visions of death and Christ. He could learn nothing further.

Boelkins wept for her and swore his vengeance in mute rage. His search for Alice lasted for years, but she had disappeared from life as if she had never been. In his grief, he and Eggington forged a partnership in the slave trade that consumed him with guilt.

Then Kancamagus came into his life.

For a day, the Quaker reveled in his discovery, and fancied any number of ways in which his dangerous Indian might somehow be put to use in his employ. Unlike all but a smattering of his co-religionists, Boelkins had no scruples against utilizing violence against others provided it was carried out by unclean hands.

But there was a problem.

He was not yet a rich man, or as rich as he wanted to be, and thus much was demanded of his time. So within days of buying the wretched Indian from Frost's craven associates, he regretted it most sincerely to himself, especially as Kancamagus's prospects of recovery dimmed by the hour.

It was at the nadir of his expectations that a saving grace with extremely sharp teeth intervened. As one of the esteemed Rev. Increase Mather's curious servants, Tizzoo was well-known to Boelkins.

He was the purchasing agent who completed the paperwork for her sale to the minister, but the truth was that in many ways she still belonged to him – the man who sold her.

Increase Mather's loathing of Quakers was pronounced, but the minister tended to overlook the occasional weed in his garden if it could be proven useful to him, and Boelkins certainly was useful in his multiple business capacities in the employ of Increase's brother-in-law Eggington.

The captain was even less scrupulous about Quakers. He actually preferred them to any of the scrofulous Puritan clerks he was sometimes forced to utilize in Boelkins's absence.

Since Eggington lacked most of the Puritan virtues of religious discrimination, he early on recognized the Quaker's unique ability to squeeze the quicksilver out of a gold piece, and the clerk's expertise with the slave trade that was swelling the population of Barbados added an extra fillip to his value.

Quaker Boelkins was not a man who kept all his thoughts to himself. When he appeared to have reached a dead end with the unwanted Indian and soon wished him only to be gone from his house, he raged around his kitchen, overturning kettles and tossing pots.

It was during one of these fits that his frequent visitor Tizzoo promised Boelkins that not only could she heal this handsome warrior, but with her special knowledge of the old craft from her homeland she could convert him into a pliable tool to do Boelkins's bidding.

Chapter Twenty-Seven

A Little Death

The Quaker was highly susceptible to Tizzoo's suggestions as he was fond of the attention she lavished on him when they chanced to be alone, which was not an unusual occurrence at that time, even in a city as destitute of possibilities for love as Puritan Boston.

Tizzoo's situation was complicated.

Minister Increase had accepted Tizzoo as a gift on a whim from his wife's brother-in-law. He was intrigued with the slave's teeth and her pleasant, pleasing manner, and all the possibilities these presented by way of conversion to Christ Jesus. Still, it pained his heart to have any dealings with the poor blacks, Increase told the captain (who related the conversation to his Quaker partner), since they were all either sickly, homesick, or mistreated. Yet the minister required another helping hand for his beloved Maria, and a brown girl servant might be a blessing.

It turned out to be not so.

Maria Mather was uncharacteristically unnerved by Tizzoo, and thought it wrong for her to be in their godly home, especially when Increase had to be away in England for long periods.

So by and by, Tizzoo was unofficially added to Mistress Sarah Story Cotton Mather's household at Cotton Hill, which in the final regretful years of that old woman's life amounted to only one other tenant – a single towering, nearly fleshless black slave, Titus, to whom, out of boredom and perhaps spite, the old woman confided everything. The freakish looking Titus, a saved Christian completely devoted to the needs of his increasingly senile mistress, paid little attention to Tizzoo's comings and goings.

In the months following the brutal assault that felled Kancamagus at the Point of Graves after the Phony Battle, Tizzoo assumed the responsibility of nursing the Indian back to health. She did so with the blessing of her secret lover, the Quaker Boelkins, who himself nursed the idea of owning a dangerous man in his employ who could be used with discretion to settle some of his accounts.

Boelkins was not himself a violent person. The idea of using physical violence to stamp his brand on Kancamagus gave him pause. Instead, he saw the fruit of Tizzoo as a much sweeter lure to further his aims.

He encouraged the alluring slave of the Rev. Increase Mather to attend whenever possible to his new resident man-servant, to whom he accorded a respectable Anglican name, John Hogkins. This the Quaker pronounced "Hawkins," but misspelled it in the register to further obfuscate the chain of possession by which Kancamagus came to be with him.

Gradually, over months, the Indian slave Hogkins regained the use of his limbs, which had withered in the course of his recovery. However, he continued to be prone to sudden vomiting due to the incessant vertigo suffered from the near-fatal knock on his head. That meant he had to be helped about, which Tizzoo was more than willing to do.

The two killers in Frost's employ who had peddled the dying Indian to Boelkins returned some weeks after they had brought him in. Their intent was to blackmail the Quaker when they learned Kancamagus was still alive and unsold. In turn, the Quaker promised to denounce them and have them arrested for rescuing a public enemy who needed to be dealt with in the strictest way. In due time, the three Englishmen ultimately reached modest terms.

In the streets, Puritan blood-ardor ran high against the tribes. During the course of Kancamagus's recovery two of his companions who had warred with him in the field with King Philip and were caught in the net of the Phony Battle were hung up on trees in public and left to disintegrate there, consumed by clouds of crawling green flies.

Tizzoo related this to the newly minted John Hogkins during their almost daily meetings together at the Quaker's house. She had further let slip that Montowampate, the Sachem of Saugus, a relation to Kancamagus by marriage, was one of those kidnapped from the field of the Phony Battle, enslaved and shipped to Barbados to be worked to death in the broiling sugar fields. This outrage was almost too much for Kancamagus to bear, but he swallowed his fury because he did not wish to frighten the woman upon whose tender mercies he had grown pathetically dependent.

Frailness of limb was foreign to him, bewildering and incomprehensible.

He had never lacked for vitality, surviving over his lifetime the rigors of brute combat as well as the strength-sapping attacks of illness with amazing vigor. Still, there in the Quaker's house in the strangeness of the English castle-town, he was reduced to moving about with the doddering deliberateness of Passaconnaway in the senile Sachem's last days.

Even more debilitating to his spirit was that he was so keenly aware of this. After one especially exhausting day achieving nothing more than standing up again after fainting, he imagined himself slipping away from his life, much as a wounded deer hops on only three good legs into the tree line, the following wolves dancing behind, their long tongues lolling wetly out of their jaws in anticipation of the blood they would soon taste.

Kancamagus began to compose his death song. Tizzoo refused to let him sing it.

She forced him to eat and drink, badgering him like a common scold to move around in the newly built little side room. This he did as much as the long chain on his right leg would allow. The Quaker Boelkins was a very careful man.

In truth, they had little time together alone, but they made the most of it. In the first few weeks following his healing, while the Quaker was away from his small shack tucked amid the rat's nest of buildings, cargo and chandlery accumulating along the ever-busier waterfront, they began to communicate on a more intimate level.

This was possible because Tizzoo, although not unfamiliar with the Abenaki dialect employed by Kancamagus, enjoyed a certain proficiency with the language of the Wampanoag. This was the result of a happy coincidence.

Whenever he was in Boston visiting his brother-in-law Increase, the Rev. John Cotton the Younger, the disgraced son of his famous minister father, would use Tizzoo to practice speaking the Wampanoag words he had learned while working with the praying Indians of Martha's Vineyard and at Mashpee Village on Cape Cod. The servant listened raptly to this handsome white man in hopes of kisses that were promised with the minister's eyes and moving lips but never delivered.

For his part, John Hogkins/Kancamagus could understand a great deal more of English and Wampanoag than Tizzoo knew of his tongue. His war party had consisted of Indians from many New England tribes, and they had taught themselves how to understand each other through linguistic shortcuts easily learned.

So soon, with the ties of language, mutual need, and a deepening sexual attraction, Hogkins and Tizzoo became very attached to one another in those early months together. Not surprisingly, they also became secret lovers, although not so secret that Quaker Boelkins didn't guess what was going on.

Yet, with a businessman's indulgence, he welcomed it as long as it led to the taming of his pet Indian – although he did worry that the comely Tizzoo's frequent visits to his house would arouse an angry response from the influential Mather family. Any Quaker, even the lapsed, indifferent example Boelkins presented to society, stood on *terra infirma* in Puritan Boston.

Yet he needn't have concerned himself to any extent. Tizzoo could afford to attend to Hogkins because she was not much needed or wanted in Mistress Sarah Mather's house. Her presence there was hardly noted, or if it was, it was mostly ignored.

Having been lent to the family matriarch by the Rev. Increase Mather, whose wife was glad to be rid of her disturbing presence, Tizzoo was happy enough in the employ of her new mistress. She grew even more delighted once she realized that the only man of the house, the slave Titus, was not to be master over her. She was just another piece of furniture to him, a curious object forgotten as soon as they were apart.

However, when they were together, things were altogether a bit different.

Titus was a veritable fountain of information, about not only the white people who controlled Tizzoo's destiny, but about the most powerful white families of them all, the Cottons and the Mathers.

Titus was a legendary figure in a city where freakish black giants commanded supreme awe.

At nearly six-and-a-half-feet tall, Titus was one of the tallest men in Boston, and one of its frailest, too, resembling a sort of human praying mantis. Cheekbones bulged from his face like a ship's spars, while atop his high, narrow face, a ball of frizzy gray-white hair exploded from his scalp in panicked peaks anchored to his head.

Slavery, as a state of existence, meant nothing to Titus. He was in thrall to his mistress, the widow Mather, and she was equally emotionally dependent on Titus. There were no secrets she didn't share with him, although it must be stated that Titus, while pretending to be literate in the white man's language, in many instances did not fully comprehend all that was told to him in confidence.

His frequent "Ay'm" and "Nay'm" were merely devices that allowed him to get by with a general sense of what was required, or to show he was not completely stone-deaf.

As in the matter of the small black bottle that the wizened old lady kept by her bedside, for instance.

Titus tried very hard to understand the white woman's story about the little bottle but since he did not, he would interject a word or two at the appropriate time.

Had he been able to make sense of it, Titus would have found it a most fascinating tale.

Its sad story had taken place decades before, in the 1630s, when Titus's frightful frizz was the color of obsidian in the Africa of his youth, and an unborn Tizzoo was years away from chasing land crabs marching up the brilliant white sand of her native island, Youlou.

The occasion of its telling was in the course of one of those disturbing, dreamless states the ancient Mistress Sarah was prone to when sleep refused to invade her bedroom and conquer her.

In the great loneliness that overwhelms the mind in the dead of night, she called out to Titus to sit by her side, hold her bony hand and listen to her story.

"Dear, dear heart," the lady murmured to her attendant, imagining herself to be comforting him rather than otherwise.

"Ay'm," replied Titus, nodding in his most solicitous manner

The black bottle she clasped within her ancient left hand. This she twirled about and around with laudable dexterity, a tiny earth of her life spinning on its axis.

Within its impenetrable glazed bowel it contained her greatest secret, a fabulous and amazing story that she could never let go even though all its loose ends, or so she had supposed, were tied up and sunk into the depths of time.

Inside the room that night they talked in the blackness. The room was hot, stifling, yet even so Mistress Sarah's translucent skin was cool to the touch as Titus stroked her face with a hand that was remarkably gentle and soft.

Mistress Sarah's gray eyes, now turned luminescent in her advanced age, glowed with the moisture of her heartfelt tears.

"I was stricken, my dear heart. Would I have perished was my prayer to the Almighty."

Such talk alarmed Titus. "No, no, mum! Say not, say not."

"Yes, perish!" she insisted. "Perish! A demon was growing inside of me, clawing for escape, churning my womb into blood for its bathwater, and I was so alone, so alone."

Her voice faltered and she moaned. Titus himself began to tear up in sympathy with her tone of unfathomable loss.

"I fears me some terrible t'ings," the servant agreed.

She had been so ill then, when the story in the bottle was born, so very ill, that turbulent year of 1637, when her beloved second husband John Cotton was being attacked and savaged by the hierarchy of his own church.

The rumors of an affair between her John and the heretic Anne Hutchinson had been flung at her every day from every corner through looks, insinuations, hints and taunts.

She braved them as if she were a fortress under siege, but there was no real escape in the Boston of yesteryear, a close community where everything was known, and secrets, even if kept, were Devil's, at work like a worm in one's soul.

Swollen with a life inside of her, convinced it was a demon clawing to get out in the midst of the Boston scandal, the woman then known as Sarah Cotton had succumbed to all her fears and had sought out the horrible midwife Goody Hawkins, pleading for a cure for the safe delivery of a healthy Christian baby that would bring no shame to her John, or to her family.

The potion to get her through her trials had been delivered by Goody in the little opaque bottle, left in a flowerpot at the height of the new moon.

It was the potion in the same vial that she, that late night, held up to Titus.

"Behold Devil himself," she cried out to the black man.

He shrank from the sight, trying to ward it off with the deeply lined palm of his hand.

She recounted to his uncomprehending ears how her ingestion of the substance had produced an immediate reaction, roiling her bowels and causing her to vomit copiously upon the bed and the floor.

For days, she lay in agony. John was inconsolable, fearing her death and that of the child. Then, when all hope was lost, her water broke.

They had no choice. Mistress Anne Hutchinson, the same, the outcast, John's supposed paramour, was called to the Cotton home and Sarah's side that desperate evening.

With Anne came that other evil one, Mary Dyer.

Her eyes darting frantically from face to face in a hopeless search for good tidings, Sarah's terror redoubled when, below her, an expression of terror shattered Anne's good looks.

"Push, my dear Sarah, push for the love of God and get it out," Anne had whispered, a note of hysteria in her voice.

Mary Dyer urged her to breathe deep.

John had stood stock still, biting the back of his hand. The husband could not even find the nerve to pray.

The room had become super-heated, as if they were in hell.

Then, out it came, dead.

Worse than dead.

The old woman Sarah turned to Titus in a helpless state. Her eyes welled up. The hand on his tightened fiercely. Had he wanted to draw away from his mistress's pain, he could not.

"Elizabeth," she moaned. "Oh, my Elizabeth."

Chapter Twenty-Eight

Major Pike is Worried

Alone at last, Major Robert Pike slumped forward on the smooth, varnished, reworked stump that served for a chair in Ensign Hopestill Foster's tidy little cabin, ensconced on the western edge of the major's magnificent Salisbury farm. He pressed his massive, vein-knotted hands into his face. These held the thick, yellowing letter his grandson Wymond Bradbury had stolen. It remained unread.

It was helpful to blot away the light in order that he might compose himself before going outside again. He could not bear to face his daughter Sarah, Wymond's mother, in such an advanced state of personal distress.

After a bit his eyes hurt so he put his hands in his lap and willed them to remain there. He looked at the letter, now a bit crumpled, letting it fall out of his hands. In a low voice he spoke into the emptiness.

"No good thing can come from this."

A line of daylight that had broken in through a crack in the wall danced on his knee. He wobbled the lighted leg back and forth, playing with the sunbeam out of a childish whim to forget his troubles. The chair, he noticed, a clever, cut-in design by his old friend Foster, was substantial, even comfortable. He would sit there longer if he could. Such distracting thoughts lasted only seconds, however.

Often, under the pressure of similar strains in his adult life, Pike had secretly hoped to die before he broke into pieces. That way, the people wouldn't pity him, or make excuses for his unmanly behavior, and his headstone would bear no blemish. This old wish still held its power, he found.

The major had been the rock of Salisbury and the much larger venue of Norfolk County in Massachusetts for so long that it seemed impossible he would ever shatter, but the cracks were there and he knew each fissure as well as he knew his own children, some of them dead now, the Lord rest their souls.

Pike thrust a glance to the closed cabin door in front of him. Beyond were Sarah and the scout Colin Edgerly, who awaited Pike's orders.

Edgerly was a good man. He had matured remarkably since joining the train-band as a 16-year-old, learning almost as much woodsmanship from Foster as from Pike. The old man and Edgerly were good friends, interesting because Foster had so few.

Old man. Pike smiled at the term. Few were as old as he, inside and out.

He listened to Sarah talking in low tones on the other side of the door.

His daughter was impatiently awaiting her father's stepping outside again, he having abandoned her to escape inside Foster's little home on the pretext of fulfilling a private request by the missing man.

"I insist upon passing, Mr. Edgerly!"

Sarah's demand made him wince. He could imagine the conflicted younger man straightening, barring the way to the door and beyond, to the woman's father.

That door, part of that low-framed cabin with its clean pegged walls, stood on the edge of the common bordered by Pike's well-managed farm. The major had in his youth ripped this land from the grip of the wilderness.

More than a working farm, the Pike acres since the days of King Philip's War had become the *de facto* parade ground for the militia so miserly allotted to Pike's command by the paranoid Bay Colony government. Yet despite the ever-present actuality of war that haunted the frontiers, there were hardly enough men at Pike's disposal to send out on patrol let alone form up on parade. Very few of his men remained now that the frenzy of getting the harvest home had reached its peak.

It was, to face facts, a sorry situation for the old man designated as commander-in-chief of the forces of northern Massachusetts, New Hampshire and Maine east of the mighty Merrimack.

The Colony had appointed him following the murder of Walderne at Cochecho three years before in 1689, but it had studiously neglected to provide any flesh, muscle or fat for the bones of his sorry command. Making matters worse, the yeomen refused service if it meant leaving their farms and women undefended.

So the frontier and its inhabitants still burned at the hands of the French and Indians, while the best Pike's few men could do when dispatched was to give the remains a Christian burial. Sad work it was, when most of the time less than a dozen full-time militia served at the major's beck and call.

Pike leaned back in Foster's chair and mentally counted the numbers he could deploy that day in his absence if he went south, as he was now wont to do. The figure he arrived at greatly displeased him.

He hung his head.

Outside, the conversation between Edgerly and his Sarah had ended. Obviously they were waiting for him to emerge again. He stood up, straining his aching knees and looked around at the sparseness of the cabin, which was a much different place without Foster.

Ensign Foster, no longer welcome in Dover by white or Indian, had been offered this small share of land to tenant because of the many valuable services he had performed over the years for the county and for Pike himself. The scout's home served both as a rallying point and field headquarters for the officer staff, such as it was, when needed.

Now the cabin was empty because Foster was missing, having not come back from the selfish, personal mission to Boston upon which Pike had employed him, even though he was sick.

Foster's disappearance inside that city gone mad was proving to be the worst disaster in a long line of personal crises that hemmed Pike in from every direction. He thought of himself as threatened like an army that had been outgeneraled and cut off from its line of communications, awaiting only the fatal, last blow.

Pike had been hammered by such blows. Two evenings previously, Capt. Thomas Bradbury, his great good friend and old Salisbury neighbor, collapsed in his arms.

Tom was prostrated by grief and anxiety about his wife Mary who, in Pike's opinion and in that of every good man and woman in Salisbury, represented the flower of womanhood.

Alas, Mary's virtues mattered less than her crimes in the eyes of the state, and so Goodwife Bradbury, for all her godly years as a wife and mother, had been condemned to Boston prison in chains, there to await death. She would be hung for a witch in the coming days. Pike's hands balled up into fists at the horrible vision.

In a desperate bid to save Mary's life, a delegation from Salisbury, good friends of Tom Bradbury all, had signed a petition imploring the witch-hunting Court of Oyer and Terminer to free the woman. Pike himself had written a strong letter of support. Their arguments went unheard, and were taken by the court's representatives in the meanest way, supposing that a sniff of rebellion might be discerned in the protest.

Having been rudely rebuffed in Boston in such a threatening manner, the Salisbury freemen who dared to sign had implored Pike to act that very morning, for without his protection they, too, stood in danger of being implicated in the witchcraft mania that had taken root in Salem and was spreading north.

Moreover, just for having dared to put name to paper, their farms and livelihoods stood as much at risk from the witch hunters as from the depredations of the French and Abenakis.

And then there was the wedding, the sorry wedding.

A rapid, angry knocking on the door caused Pike to jump.

He opened it and there stood Sarah, his eldest. The sight of creeping old age upon her plain face, so evident in the daylight that framed her lean and determined form, frankly startled him into silence. She resembled, more than he could ever admit in his heart, her mother, his beloved first wife of the same name, gone now like so many of his friends and enemies.

Pike had been about to redress Edgerly for permitting the disturbance, but when the scout stared expressionlessly right through him it was clear as a lace curtain to Pike that Sarah had impulsively decided to act and that Edgerly had declined to forcibly prevent her from doing so.

Then, irresistibly, a wave of tenderness washed over him.

"Sarah, my dear," he said in a fatherly tone. "Ensign Foster's affairs needed my most urgent attention."

She allowed him no respite.

"Our family's affairs require an ever-greater share of your attention, I'm sure," she told him. Behind her, Edgerly bit his lip.

Pike took his daughter's arm as he stepped out over the cabin threshold. With his other arm, he shooed the scout to retreat toward the fence. On its other side, the bull Elias placidly chewed under the umbrella of the warming sun.

"What are we to do about Wymond's letter?" Sarah demanded.

"The letter is not Wymond's," Pike reminded her sharply. "It is the stolen property of the Rev. John Cotton and thus, in the nature of things, evidence of a mortal crime and sin against the commandment of God."

The fire of Sarah's words burned in her eyes, the same intense brown eyes of her mother.

"My son is guilty of a crime only if the procuring of evidence that will save an innocent woman from being murdered is called a crime in days such as these!"

Pike held up the neatly folded letter, sealed and resealed numerous times considering the amount of wax staining its exterior.

"Think, Sarah. What evidence is this? You cannot read it, since it is written in Latin. It is stolen goods is all. What use is it? Do you insist I read it, and become complicit in your and Wymond's crime?"

Sarah flew at him, aiming to snatch the letter back. "I cannot read the Roman tongue, to be sure, Father. But let's not be deceived. Wymond knows its worth. His beloved has sworn to its immeasurable value and the secrets it holds about the Cotton family. It is our only hope!"

"There may be other means ..." Pike began weakly.

"There are no other means, Father. The court in Salem Town has spoken. You know there are no other means."

"I have sent Mr. Foster on his mission. We must hear what he has to say."

"Hopestill has been gone too long. He was overdue a fortnight ago. He has been swallowed up in the net laid cunningly – aye, too cunningly – by the witch hunters."

At which she drew a deep breath, pulled her arm from his and turned to face him.

"Satan himself would be ashamed at what some decree need be done in the name of our Lord."

Pike was just as angry that moment.

"I daresay Satan would look askance upon a theft. A theft from the house of a man of God and church. A theft from the very parlor of Wymond's father-in-law to be. No, Satan would not be very much ashamed of such an act."

Sarah, widowed twice and in fragile condition ever since her second husband John Stockman's death, withered under her father's set glare.

Pike understood in that moment the punishing strain that afflicted his daughter. With pity in his heart he would not spare for himself, he kissed her at-first unyielding forehead, then took her in his arms as she wept out the bitter salt within.

The terrible storm that now threatened to overwhelm them had not broken upon the announcement that Wymond's wedding proposal to Mariah, the beautiful daughter of the Rev. John Cotton the Younger, had been accepted.

No, that December day so many months before had been one of the most joyous occasions the Pike household had experienced in a long while.

Sarah had rushed to her father's house with the news. Martha, Pike's second wife, clasped her step-daughter's hands and kissed them. Together, the family gave thanks on their knees. After the meal and the sharing of a very little brandy, they had bundled up, the weather being fair and not too bitter, and their destination not too far distant, to inform the Bradburys of their joy.

Wymond was named for his father, Tom and Mary Bradbury's eldest son, who perished at sea when he and Sarah were but new-lyweds, and with their son less than a year born.

Fatherless, the boy had come into his own as both a cooper and a farmer, with holdings that were quickly becoming the envy of Salisbury's young men. And during those formative years, his grandfather the major and he had become as close as father and son.

Mariah Cotton had cousins living in nearby Amesbury, and Wymond had chanced to meet the girl when she had visited after her father had accepted an invitation to guest-preach in his late brother Seaborn Cotton's old pulpit at Hampton.

An encounter along the road near Salisbury, that so many years before had delivered the poor Quakers to be whipped, brought those dear hearts together. True love had never so quickly entwined two young passions as it did during that chance meeting.

Wymond quickly sought the assent of Mariah's parents, and received the blessing to a marriage that would unite the Bradburys to the Cottons, binding two of the most prominent names in New England through matrimony. It would bring into the fold, too, through the Pikes, a family of equal acclaim.

But what should have been a joyous time spiraled calamitously into an intense personal tragedy for the families who were to be united in Christ's love for eternity.

The arrest of the groom Wymond's grandmother Mary rocked Salisbury and astounded New England.

With the arrest of Goodwife Bradbury, one of the colony's foremost members had been infamously indicted in the burgeoning Salem witch scandal.

Not just indicted, but now in the wake of Hopestill Foster's disappearance, Mary Bradbury had been branded a criminal by the state and a danger to the community, no longer seen as a woman of faith and Christ, but as a consort of Devil who stood convicted in a shocking decision.

Chapter Twenty-Nine

Witch's Brew

Pike called for his black horse Buttons just after sundown and set out for Boston as the last glimpse of the orange orb twinkled out in the west.

He was accustomed to traveling at night when on personal business, both for caution's sake so as not to be seen and for an old prejudice against breaking the Sabbath. Earlier in his life he was accused of journeying before the sun had set on the holiest of days, and it had cost him dearly in reputation and expense at court. So even though it was not the Lord's Day, Pike still preferred to wait until there was no question about the day having expired before he took to horse – especially on so dangerous a journey.

With a flick of the reins and touch of the spur Buttons knew where to go. He soon found his way to Thomas Bradbury's farm, Pike's first destination, and a familiar stopping-off point for the major inasmuch as Bradbury's was not too far distant from the road to the ferry across the Merrimack.

It was dark as the inside of a pastor's coat when horse and rider turned up the path. A gargantuan red oak that marked the property line was the lone sentry.

The little lane led to Bradbury's barn, the largest in Salisbury, with its three-quarters slanting roof and stone foundation. An overpowering smell of new hay drying in the fields beyond lent the air a sweet scent. Pike dismounted and squinted into the gloom as he led the stallion to an open stall. He forked in some straw from the large pile in front of the harnesses and watched Buttons chew.

"That's for a good lad," he said to the horse, patting its twitching withers.

The flicker of a light caught his eye. Turning, Pike could see Bradbury walking toward the barn, carrying a candle lamp that framed the man's serious face in a circle of yellow.

"God's blessing to you, Robert," called Bradbury, passing under the massive beechwood lintel from which the barn doors were suspended.

"And to you, Thomas," Pike returned, with real warmth in his voice.

Wings flapping, hooves and claws scritching the wood, the livestock in the barn moved into the corners and up into the rafters. Nervous animal eyes watched the white-haired men as if they, too, wished to know how things would turn out.

Pike's dearest friend planted himself gently on a barrel's top. The breath whistled out of his mouth involuntarily when he finally settled.

Like Pike, Capt. Thomas Bradbury was feeling aged and worn out. Even so, Bradbury, a learned man, could always be counted on, Pike knew. For that reason he would confide his plan of action, only lately conceived.

Their time together spanned the uncertain decades of war and peace, decades during which insanity, cruelty and disorder often ruled the brutal wilderness in which they had made their lives.

It was a time, though, when just one or two men could make a difference. So it was that Pike and Bradbury represented in the hearts and minds of many people in Salisbury and Norfolk County the granite wall protecting if not civilization itself, then its essence.

Between them, they were the millstones that helped grind out a level measure of justice and equity for the people. Each had been elected over and again by their fellow freemen to preside as chosen leaders in the community's military, judicial and political affairs.

In their time together there wasn't a dispute over a jot or a tittle of common law they hadn't encountered, or that had eluded their sensible solutions in the course of their duties as village and county officers.

Pike and Bradbury were inseparable in war and peace, natural leaders that the men and the women of Salisbury and beyond looked to without question.

More than that, they were friends, real friends, friends who depended on each other, carried each other, shared their blessings and soon, friends whose fortunes were to be joined through a marriage that united the families of their children.

That night, however, they had no one to look to – except themselves.

Pike reached up on a shelf for the saddle blankets stacked above.

These he tumbled down into the dust and made a place for himself. Bits of straw clung to his clothing and hat, which he had kept on his head out of long habit. Sarah and Martha were forever reminding him to remove it indoors, but neither of Pike's most important women, his oldest daughter and his second wife, were there in Bradbury's barn.

"You are going to fetch Foster." Bradbury said it as a statement of fact.

"Aye," Pike replied.

"No word, then?"

"None."

"I had thought of going myself."

"'Twould be too dangerous for ye, Thomas. You'd be taken up for a witch yourself now, I don't doubt it."

Bradbury rubbed his brow, as if the melancholy that had overwhelmed him the other day in Pike's presence needed to be restrained from emerging. He said after a bit, "It's a sort of madness, is it not, Robert? Only Devil himself could dream up such a scheme to ensnare a good woman like my Mary."

Pike considered how to respond. Under no circumstances could he risk bringing anyone else on his mission to Boston.

As a magistrate now, Pike was a powerful man to be sure, but power in Pike's case was no talisman. He had long been regarded as a gadfly at best, a potential enemy at worst, by the hard-core Puritans holding sway in the Bay Colony. Pike was resented as one who, while chafing at the least chain that bound his personal liberty, was unwilling to submit absolutely to the shackles of Christ's word. That made him, if not an outright enemy, then a man to be watched. Yet he remained a hero to many and thus, dangerous.

They watched him from afar with spies sent to Salisbury. They watched him with the help of informers who lived nearby. They would sweep him up like a bit of dust if they felt threatened by him again, and Pike knew it.

Some independent thought stirred his hand and it moved to the letter pinned inside his shirt. With a will, Pike scratched his arm instead.

Finally he spoke. "I hear things, as you know, Thomas. There's a small lass chained up like a dog in the Boston prison, daughter of the convicted witch Good, a slight thing of four years, maybe five."

Bradbury shifted uncomfortably.

Pike continued, "Sarah Good was hanged but she cursed from her rope that the judges would choke on blood. So they fear her little girl would do them harm as a spectral imp and they chain her tight as a Quaker. A little girl, mind you. There she squats in her filth all the day, prey to pirates and thieves locked up in that stinking den, and all of her reason is no doubt gone from her brain. No, Thomas. Boston is dangerous, and all else twixt here and our good Salisbury is a mousetrap."

Slowly shaking his head, Bradbury wiped his knee, his voice filled with an uncharacteristic anger. "That would be young Dorcas Good. I hear things, too, Robert. So they'll leave the girl to rot, no doubt, in Arnold's jail, like my Mary!"

"Your Mary they would do no better," said Pike. It was a terrible thing to say, but he said it.

His friend stared into space. "It's a witch's brew that is a-stir."

Pike nodded knowingly at the term.

He had little inkling of how far gone were the Puritans of Salem and Boston in their witch madness until he was ordered, that spring, in his capacity as the member from Salisbury of the Board of Assistants to the General Court of Massachusetts, to take depositions in the strange case of Susannah Martin of nearby Amesbury.

This poor woman, like Mary Bradbury, was the object of hysterical accusations that Pike privately felt were detestable. Yet as a strict believer in the law he had no choice but to record these ridiculous testimonies asserting that the woman had, for instance, tormented a variety of barnyard animals and men. One of these alleged victims, the obnoxious, apelike carpenter of those parts, Barnard Peach, swore that Goodwife Martin had come in through his window one night and bent him around like a hoop. Then she laid on him and bit his fingers. Pike had a difficult time containing his astonishment at the charges, not at how absurd and unbelievable their depiction, but that such complaints could be lodged at all by a sane mind.

Even more extraordinary than the details of the accusations themselves were their otherworldly nature. The woman's accusers were reporting that the perpetrator of these crimes was not the flesh-and-blood *ipsa corpus* of Susannah Martin, but her spectral form, which had somehow departed from her body to commit the heinous acts for which she was charged.

Pike dutifully deposed the available witnesses in his jurisdiction, who in his opinion were as unsavory a collection of untrustworthy delators and informers as he had ever seen. Yet, ultimately, that was not for him to judge. The law required him to put their complaints into strict, legal form for the court, and he did so.

And, that very May of 1692, on the basis of the so-called evidence that Pike helped to collect against the woman, the court at Salem had hanged Goody Martin along with four others, including Sarah Good, the mother of the little witch in chains.

A cow lowed and clomped its hooves. Buttons, startled, skittered at his rope's end. The men looked at each other. Bradbury spoke first.

"What can we do?"

"I have given it much thought, Thomas. If they have taken Hopestill Foster I will not gain a chance to argue the matter, I fear. Long have they sought him."

"Perhaps that the man has died is a horrible thought I had last night. He was most unhealthy when last I saw him at your place."

It was true, Pike agreed.

"I should not have sent him, and for that I bear a burden. His reputation is such that he is marked after all these years, still. But I thought it best. We must know where Mary is."

And Pike knew the best man for such a dangerous job, sick or no, was his chief scout, Ensign Hopestill Foster.

The hellholes to which Mary Bradbury would have been taken after being pronounced a witch and condemned to die were three – Ipswich jail, Salem jail or Boston prison. Yet each city was crawling with watchmen who would challenge any stranger, since the insanity of the witches' scare had heightened the tension in all of New England.

Of the three, only tiny Ipswich village, to the south of Salisbury and to the north of Salem and Boston, held any hope for the sort of precipitate action that Pike had been so fond of in his lost youth, but was still prepared to take.

More to the good, Ipswich was the home of Mary's side of the family. As such, there was a strong network of Perkins brothers who might be depended upon if Mary were transferred to that town.

Bradbury was thinking along the same lines.

"John Perkins was up to visit last week. They have watched for Mary to be brought to Ipswich, but the court is keeping her hidden," he told Pike eagerly, alive to the possibilities of rescue. "He said his sons would take Mary if there was a way. It was all I could do to prevent him from riding to Boston."

"It would surely have been the death of them all," replied Pike. "You have done them a good turn through your wise counsel. I appreciate how difficult that must have been, Tom."

The old major stood up and stroked the flank of his horse. For some minutes he was lost in thought. Finally, he spoke in a quiet voice.

"Thomas, there is now a better way."

"By all means, speak of it."

"You can read and write in the Latin form as well as ever you could?"

Bradbury brightened for the first time. "Must you ask? I had the language of Caesar beaten into me like a threshing."

Pike handed him the letter Wymond had stolen from the Rev. John Cotton the Younger.

The red wax that sealed it was broken anew.

The two friends spoke long into the night.

As they conversed, many miles to the south in Boston, where imaginary devils and demons ruled the minds of men, inside the house the Rev. Cotton Mather had procured for his interrogation of the prisoner Hopestill Foster, that same night had been a long one, too.

Foster, his unexpected recovery from a bout of the Small pocks almost spent, was the only man awake before the dwindling fire inside the hearth. The others, including Mather himself, remained drugged by Tizzoo's potion.

In the dim light of the sputtering candles, Foster watched the watchers.

The constable's assistant Goodman Fain was not about to get up any time soon. Nor were the rest of them, it appeared. The snuffling symphony of drugged men cast under the spell of sleep continued. Fain snorted, gasped, jerked up once, eyes open, then slowly crawled back into his dream.

Hopestill's sweats resumed. He shrugged off his thin coverings, but could not so easily shed the living nightmares of his past that flickered on and off.

No escape was possible. He eyed the doorframe, partially blocked by the somnolent bulk of the watchman. He couldn't have forced his way past even if he had the strength to get up and walk, which he didn't, not by a long shot.

Hopestill knew his fate was sealed up within the rough-hewn walls of this deadly house. He could accept that here, at last, he would come to his end.

What he couldn't abide, there in his helplessness, was the idea that he had failed Pike in this, his last mission for the man.

He had failed him and he had failed her. That was the heavy burden he bore, in addition to the disease that was killing him.

The wife of Pike's dearest friend, Mary Bradbury was, like himself, alone and with faint hope of rescue. When he last saw her, she was chained like a dog in a Boston prison hole, next to that insane, gibbering child, awaiting the noose of the tarred hanging rope.

This good woman he had first met so many decades before, at the end of that terrible day along the Dover-Hampton Road, from where the Quaker women were saved. It was a rescue in which Hopestill had played a major role, acting on behalf of Pike and Bradbury, both of whom had sickened of the relentless persecution of the strange religious sect.

In the midst of a winter storm, when the rescuers finally reached Salisbury, Mary had taken the sufferers into her home. While treating the women's deep cuts and open wounds caused by the brutal beatings, she had taken this cruelty so deep to heart that the Quakers were compelled to console *her*.

Hopestill appeared later, stamping his icy boots in her doorway with a shamed-faced look. But Mary had embraced him as might his sister or his mother – or Priscilla – pronouncing him "brave, stalwart and beautiful" for having helped secure the deliverance of the three battered women.

Unaccountably, Hopestill had wept like a child then, so complete was the emotion he felt of being welcomed by another of his race after a life of self-imposed isolation.

That was thirty years before. Now, he drew himself up on the rack of Mather's settle in horror at the thought of Mary Bradbury in such utter distress, and he unable to help her.

Mary was, like Hopestill, elderly now, nearing 80, only a bit younger than their mutual friend and neighbor Major Pike. Incredibly at this late date in her life, but maybe not so incomprehensible given the times, Goodwife Bradbury had been judged a witch.

This verdict, as it were, had been rendered on the flimsiest, most improbable evidence imaginable, a fabrication of hurtful lies conjured up out of a lifetime of political animosities calculated to bring down Pike and the Bradburys.

Hopestill, then sick as a calf but not yet broken out in the telltale pocks that would lead to his collapse and arrest, had bribed himself a visit into the Boston prison to meet with the frail woman he had always called "Miss Mary."

This familiarism was a liberty she not only allowed, but an endearment she let on that she enjoyed very much from Hopestill, who had become the Bradbury's close family friend.

Hopestill had gasped when his eyes had adjusted to what light there was in Arnold's miserable holding cell.

Almost twenty prisoners were packed into what effectively was a large dirt hole, with Mary Bradbury shackled alongside that poor, little girl in the foul den. Human scat was everywhere. The trapped air was miserably humid and oppressive, reminding Hopestill of the old *Lyon* and its stinking straw, rife with vermin and excrement as it was by the end of his miserable boyhood voyage to Massachusetts.

The two old friends clasped hands when they laid eyes on one another. Hopestill had done his best to comfort the lady, but she was in sore need of clean linens and decent food and drink. Through the kindness of Pike he had been able to smuggle into the jailors some silver coins for Mary's needs, but there was no guarantee they would be used in that way.

He remembered her fair skin, stretched to an unnatural thinness, almost windowlike in its translucence.

She had smiled. "Thou hast brought me hope, Ensign Foster." Since her encounter with the Quakers, Miss Mary had taken up some of their ways, including their peculiar form of address.

"It is little enough that I bring, miss."

"It is enough for now. I sorely needed it. But you are not well."

Hopestill had to stand very still then in front of her, as a sudden wave of chills shook him to his core. Her cries for help rang in his ears. The child beside her screamed out alarm in a high-pitched keening.

"Pocks! The Small pocks!" shrieked a prisoner who looked in, upon which the rest of the denizens of that black hole took up the cry. That was the last he saw of Mary Bradbury.

He bowed his head. The fire in Cotton Mather's hearth flickered out.

Chapter Thirty

The Purloined Letter

Devils, the devils of time, gnawed at Pike's mind as he cantered down the familiar road to Salem and Boston after leaving the ferry above Newbury. He was in a race to save a life, probably two.

Pike knew for a certainty Mary Bradbury could not survive much longer, in whichever hole she had been stuffed.

Earlier that summer, he had stopped to briefly watch the disgusting prison at Ipswich being enlarged.

Little better than a pit in actuality, its muddy, unhealthy interior was dug into the side of the slow-moving, mosquito-infested river beneath it. By now, it was almost certainly overflowing with the excess from the Salem and Boston gaols. She might be among them, or she might be dead.

Thoughts of Mary's plight tormented him. Aboard the disheveled, garbage-strewn ferry across the Merrimack earlier that morning, Pike's stomach had churned with anxiety. It ate at him still as he bounced in the saddle on the road to Salem.

Adding to the queasiness in Pike's midsection was the knot

of tension left over from the crossing after leaving Bradbury's farm as dawn broke. That part of the journey had been awkward and potentially dangerous.

Operating the rafts across the river were the two Carr brothers, James and Richard. Both of these scoundrels had testified against Mary by furthering the preposterous tale that she had bewitched their brother John, causing his death some years before.

James ran one stage of the ferry from the road's end at Salisbury to the big island in the middle of the river, while Richard operated the second raft waiting at the south end of the island, completing the journey across the Merrimack to Newbury.

These lanky men, careless in their dress and language, were strange people, as strange as their late father George.

It was George, Pike knew, a man as defiant and set in his ways as anyone the old major had ever met, who had forbidden John from courting pretty Jemima True out of some ancient vexation against the Trues, an order that proved a death blow to his mentally infirm son. Yet the girl would never have had him in any case, and she was doubly afraid of his brothers. More than once Mary, a friend and relative to Jemima, had warned them away from pestering her. That was an insult never forgiven, earning Mary the blame for John's fatal melancholy.

Pike said nothing to James Carr as the craft steered to the large wooded island in the middle of the river, yet he felt the other's eyes on him the whole time. The veteran soldier kept his hand on the butt of his hidden pistolette until they made shore.

Sensing the feel of James's eyes on his neck until he passed out of sight, Pike walked his horse along the brush-heavy path to the south ferry. A rough-looking man with a disfiguring white scar across the back of his neck, having arrived from the Newbury side, passed him by along the path, trailing his horse. Both men politely touched their hats in turn. Pike remembered him as one of Capt. Frost's old company from Philip's War, but only after they were well past each other.

At water's edge, the second raft bobbed, awaiting Pike. Buttons stepped onto the roped logs as gingerly as a dancer, sinking it fetlock-deep momentarily into the placid river. Pike splashed aboard followed by a savagely grinning Richard Carr, who stepped in behind the major.

They shoved off. Richard Carr leered at Pike, and asked too many questions. Pike answered none of them. He was prepared against any blackguarding by the brothers.

"You travel alone, Major? Just you and your horse, eh?" crooned Richard, as much to the wide river as to Pike. The ferryman threw an apple core at Buttons purposely just beyond reach of the horse's tether. Pike kicked it into the water.

Across the Merrimack, taking his leave with barely disguised disgust, Pike rode hard for Salem along the long, lonely road that led past little Rowley and its graveyard. The Carrs no doubt would report his leaving, but it was of no concern to him now. The time for action had come.

Past Rowley and its farms, at the outskirts of Ipswich, Pike picked a path he knew that led around that small village and kept well to the west. He had no intentions of stopping, or being stopped.

It remained an uneventful ride as he neared Wenham and the striking, shining lake of the same name that glistened like a giant tear just to the southwest of the tiny hamlet.

He slowed the tiring Buttons to a walk as the silvery-black sheen reflected horse and rider, a mirror's image that Pike could not resist even in his haste.

By water's edge he dismounted to let Buttons drink deeply and browse for the fiddleheads he so loved from that spot. Alas, these were no more to be found in that dry summer, but Buttons found other delectables soon enough.

Once, Pike had taken his first wife Sarah to visit Boston and stopped here to refresh. It had been a mild spring that year, he recalled. Blissfully had they kissed in a moment that was as fresh in his mind as was the touch of their lips that blessed afternoon so many Mays ago.

He put his fingers in the water and stirred, the image dissolving. Not too far to Salem Towne, Pike calculated, squinting into the late September sun.

From the saddle bow, the old major hefted his travel bag and carried it to the water's edge. He sat down on a large stone that slanted away from the water, one he had reclined on many times before.

The purloined letter inside his shirt burned against his bosom. Memories of the previous day came flooding back.

After seeing his bereft daughter Sarah back to her farm in the company of Edgerly that afternoon, Pike had gone into the house to prepare for his journey. Martha had anticipated him by laying out his things on the bed. There were few words that needed to be said as she cooked supper.

"You'll be going away tonight?" was all she had asked.

"Yes, my dear."

He kissed her cheek, went into the room they shared, quietly shut the door and withdrew from his coat the Cotton family letter stolen by his grandson Wymond. Turning it over once, he began to read from the neatly written Latin inscription that flowed in black ink across the folded outside paper. It wasn't terribly difficult to decipher.

"John, you must be the son who obeys this command. I cannot."

It was inscribed by Seaborn Cotton, obviously, as it bore the late minister's initials with the notation that it was posted from Hampton and was to be delivered to Seaborn's brother John in Plymouth. There was also a reference to an enclosed packet of other materials (which was missing).

Pike examined the reddish seal binding the folded edges of the papers. He discerned it had been broken at least twice and then refastened with wax of a slightly duller hue.

Resolved, he forced the newer seal and read the shocking confession, or as much of it as his rudimentary familiarity with the ancient tongue of the church had allowed.

Concentrating hard, Pike sat down on the edge of the bed. His free hand gripped his knee.

There were two letters, actually, both bearing the date of Oct. 31, 1652. They were of very fine paper vellum, in perfect condition after nearly 40 years. Pike turned them over and discerned the faintest watermark of a rose showing through the center of the pages.

The single page that was the first letter was a detailed set of instructions to Seaborn from his deceased father, the elder Rev. John Cotton, that famous minister and teacher of Old Boston, having fled there from England in 1633.

In a firm hand, the father ordered the son, upon the forthcoming event of the father's death, which the Rev. Cotton stated in a poignant aside that he fully expected before the winter of that fatal year 1652 to conclude, to destroy the contents of the packet enclosed with the letter of instruction, as well as the pages Pike was holding in his right hand.

That packet, the elder Cotton wrote Seaborn, contained the

entirety of the father's private collection of personal papers and materials pertaining to the great controversy of 1637 and of the following year involving Anne Hutchinson and the independent women's meetings over which she presided.

These were all, the minister sternly commanded his son, to be "put on the fire."

Pike squinted at the Latin order again – *"super ignem."* It was underlined for emphasis. He could see where tiny dots of ink had sprayed the paper where Cotton had pressed too hard on the quill.

But this command, according to his note written on the outside of the original letter of instruction, Seaborn the eldest son, for whatever reason, could not bring himself to carry out.

Rather, Seaborn had forwarded the entirety, the two letters and presumably the missing packet of materials, to the next son in line, to his younger brother John, whom Pike wryly reminded himself was soon to become Wymond's father-in-law.

Pike next took up the second and much longer letter, also addressed to Seaborn and forwarded by the older brother to John.

This one bore a note in Seaborn's writing as well.

"Burn this one first."

The major read only a little bit into it before receiving the shock that sent him reeling.

This second letter made it terribly clear why the elder Rev. Cotton wished these vital histories expunged.

Cotton had written his son Seaborn, "I fear with all my heart to tell this story, but I now fear only Christ's judgment were I to fail at clearing my breast before I must leave you. Nor could I die in good conscience with my beloved first-born in ignorance of the Almighty Truth, which conquers all."

The confession the dying minister had to make to his son concerned the awful events of the year 1637, and in particular that dreadful winter.

It was then the political and ecumenical storms around Anne Hutchinson had broken upon Boston and New England, with he, John Cotton, liable to be torn to shreds in the winds that blew.

Matters had come to a head that portentous year, after Hutchinson's brother-in-law, the Rev. John Wheelwright, had preached a seditious sermon against the most conservative of the Puritan clergy. Wheelwright was banished from Boston in March.

Then, in May, the pro-Hutchinson governor Henry Vane was swept out in a bloodless coup by John Winthrop, the champion of the hard-line ministers. These launched a full-scale political and social offensive against Hutchinson and her followers, an attack culminating in a sensational trial that saw Cotton's most devoted follower put under sentence of banishment to take effect the following spring.

The next target was to be Cotton himself.

The Rev. John Cotton stood accused at that moment in all but name of condoning the actions of the heretics who were now being rounded up, disarmed, stripped of their property and otherwise intimidated by Gov. Winthrop and the powerful social forces that had coalesced behind him.

A grim choice awaited him – denounce Anne Hutchinson or share her fate. But then came a miracle of the Lord.

Cotton's wife Sarah had become pregnant.

The couple, recounted the minister to his son, had tried so hard to have a baby in order that such physical evidence of their love might counteract the unspoken but horrible conjecturing then taking place within the city.

This gossip supposed that he, Cotton the minister, was in thrall to Mrs. Hutchinson, and that the teacher and his leading lady acolyte were themselves illicit lovers.

In the letter, Cotton swore to his son that such was not the case.

But he could not deny Anne's abiding love for him.

Anne, Cotton wrote, possessed a soul as sweet and pure as any angel. It was in that love that she conceived a plan to rescue her teacher and "another one" in order to follow Christ's example by taking the punishment of ostracism, exile and condemnation completely upon herself.

In order to spare Cotton, to save his good name and his eminent "works of grace," his loving disciple was prepared to bear it all for his sake, to drain from the cup every last bitter dreg of acrimony and hate.

Such was the crushing weight of his sin, the sin of being weak and afraid, John Cotton wrote Seaborn, that it was driving the very breath out of him as he approached his deathbed.

And thus the Rev. Cotton had acquiesced to a plan that rescued him but lost Anne Hutchinson forever.

The crisis came about at the moment of Sarah's delivery in early December.

Sarah had been so frantic, so obsessed with the idea of conceiving at the height of the Hutchinson affair, that in order to guarantee a healthy pregnancy at the proper moment, unbeknownst to him, Cotton's wife had resorted to soliciting a midwife's vile potion.

Its consumption produced both a miscarriage and a monster.

Cotton wrote there was no need to go into those terrifying details, which haunted him nightly, since all of New England knew of the case by now.

But what New England did not know was that the creature was his and Sarah's creation.

Cotton wrote of his agony that night. He described his morbid fears that, if it were discovered, Sarah's birthing of such an ungodly thing would mean their ruin and the destruction of everything he had spent his life working for.

As for his wife Sarah, her terror at this ghastly birthing had "unhinged her mind" and came close to deranging him, too, he admitted to Seaborn.

At the first evidence that night that something was terribly wrong, he had sent for Anne at once and she arrived in company with Mary Dyer, her closest friend. Their counsel at Sarah's bedside proved a godsend, or so it seemed.

The foul birth, in all its horror, passed swiftly, like a sudden nightmare. Cotton held his wife's hand and blocked her view as the two women behind him scooped up the remains of the sickening mess that had passed through the birth canal.

Quickly, before it could be discovered, they hid the dead monstrosity in Mary Dyer's basket, all the while keeping up, behind tightly closed doors, the pretense of a long and difficult childbirth.

At that critical moment, Anne told John Cotton she knew of a child, a healthy girl, born as God would will it that very night! Earlier that evening, she had attended this birth.

But that child, too, was damned, wrote Cotton.

This baby girl, conceived out of wedlock, had been created within the shame of a union between the unmarried daughter of a soapboiler and the disgraced indentured servant who lived with them.

The family was of the Rev. Hooker's church, many years now since removed to Connecticut, but on that December night in 1637 they prepared to leave Boston imminently to escape the shame of what they knew would be a ruinous scandal. The mother of the girl especially wanted no part of the new baby. She had sworn in front of Anne and Mary that she would kill it with her own hands if it were not taken away.

And thus, God had prepared the way, Anne told her pastor – him, John Cotton.

As an intimate of the family fully versed as to their plight, Anne knew that the mother who delivered this normal baby girl was in fact that moment dying of complications from the birth.

A tragedy, Anne had said, but one that the Lord himself had prepared to lead the Rev. Cotton out of danger.

As to the father of that baby, the servant boy, the family hated him and wished him gone.

They were determined to send him deep into the wilderness, as far away from Boston as was possible, with good chance that he might die there and be forgotten, and had made arrangements to be rid of him.

Pike's skin tingled with alarm. He stood up and exclaimed, "Hopestill!"

His cry brought Martha into the room. She looked at him and he stared back.

Both were afraid to speak. The major cradled the tell-tale letters to his chest.

Chapter Thirty-One

Spectral Evidence

The remainder of the birth plot was fairly simple to carry out from that point, although the question of the sanity of the Rev. Cotton's wife, Sarah, proved to be a major impediment.

Pike, reading intently, had held the late minister's letter up to the light carefully to peer at it closely. The writing, clear to that point, became muddled, as if the author were in a fever.

At last the old major was able to make sense of it again, although Tom Bradbury, with his superior understanding of Latin, in reading it afterwards during their night meeting in his barn, later brought out many of the more salient points that Pike had originally missed.

Several times during his own reading from it, Bradbury pronounced himself staggered by Cotton's confession.

"I am not sure I can go on, Robert," he protested. "I feel profaned. Surely we are compounding a sin here. These words frighten me."

Pike assured his good friend that they were acting in accordance with God's will. "Else we wouldn't be reading it at all, Tom," he reminded him.

The Rev. Cotton's letter continued.

Even though the full physical deformity of her dead baby was not revealed to her, Cotton's wife Sarah lapsed into an unbalanced state – she knew things had gone terribly wrong, and she shrank from all attempts at consolation, and fell to raving and muttering like a Bedlam inmate.

Above all, she could not comprehend the meaning of the presence of the disgraced Anne Hutchinson and her cohort Mary Dyer in their bedroom.

"Her shame, I now see, was mine," Cotton had written.

Fortunately, in another part of the house, their two young children, Seaborn, then four years old, and Sariah, two, remained mercifully fast asleep, watched in silence by Anne's oldest daughter, who was also kept in ignorance of the plot. And the house on Cotton Hill, at that time in Boston's young history, enjoyed a certain privacy that permitted the ongoing subterfuge to proceed.

The husband had given his wife a strong dose of brandy and a drop of laudanum, which Sarah swallowed as eagerly as if it were the poison she had earlier begged for. Soon after, she tumbled into unconsciousness while the two women and Cotton talked over their next move.

After what seemed an eternity of indecision, Anne and Mary left the house with the absurdly light remains of the grotesquery that was the Cotton's dead child.

Several hours later, the pair, shivering with the cold of that night, returned with another basket in which, wrapped in thick red swaddling, squirmed the most perfect baby girl any of them had ever seen.

"I presented our new daughter to your mother when she awakened," read Cotton's narrative, "and the light in her eyes, which I had thought extinguished forever, began to glow anew. Your sister Elizabeth had been reborn that night by God's grace."

Anne and Mary left the house again, this time to return to the soapboiler's property, which lay along the Roxbury Road, to announce their success at placing the child "in a good home" as they told the distraught family.

The women were followed thereafter by John Cotton, who left Anne's daughter to watch over the house and sleeping children, warning the girl not to disturb his wife and new daughter under any circumstances.

Cotton, through pre-arrangement with Anne and Mary, remained at a distance from Sandyman's property. Eventually he met in the road the soapboiler, the father of the young girl Priscilla who had given birth out of wedlock.

From Goodman Sandyman, the Rev. Cotton learned that everything Anne had said was true, and that the boy responsible for the family's disgrace had, in fact, been sent away that very evening, less than an hour before, by small craft.

"Thank the Lord for holding back the blasts of winter," Cotton prayed. He promised the soapboiler that all would be taken care of, but the man remained bereft.

It was then the Rev. Cotton, his own heart breaking at the grandfather's grief, revealed to Sandyman that his daughter's child was given to replace another's.

That "other," the minister told Sandyman without revealing the paternity of this last-named horror, was "a spawn of Devil."

Sandyman was thunderstruck by that news. As Cotton wrote Seaborn, the soapboiler had grabbed him and swore that he had told this same falsehood to the boy to scare the wits from him.

"Was it Devil speaking, then, through me?" Sandyman demanded. Cotton had no answer for the man, God's wisdom having deserted him. And so they had parted, the sad sound of Sandyman's sobbing haunting the minister's ears.

Thus, it remained only to bury the remains of John and Sarah Cotton's monster.

In order to accomplish this last part of their long night's work, the three of them – John Cotton, Anne and Mary – hurried through sleeping Boston to the deserted churchyard, where they sought out the resting place of the stillborn child miscarried by Mary Dyer some six weeks previously.

The rude cairn lay in plain sight. Due to the frozen earth, the little casket remained above ground at the edge of the cemetery, protected from the hunger of wolves by a rock heap. Several larger coffins, beneath a barrier of snow-covered stones, were stacked close by. Formal burial in the ground would take place after the spring thaw.

Laboring under the moonlight, the three quickly uncovered the box containing Mary Dyer's dead child. Opening the lid, they prayed for the soul within. Mary finally stood aside, her resolve faltering, and it fell to Anne and John Cotton to shake the ghastly contents of their basket into the coffin. It gave them pause, the enormity of their deed, Cotton wrote in his faltering hand.

They replaced the stones, unseen by anyone as far as they knew, and prayed again, with the greatest sincerity, in the dark, hands clasped. With scarcely another word, they departed the consecrated ground of the churchyard and returned to their respective homes, each burdened with their thoughts.

"I would have given God my life there and then, my son," the letter to Seaborn had concluded, "but the Lord was not prepared to take it from me, even then, for the choice that I made and the things I had condoned. We swore amongst us like the blackest Satanists the most solemn oath, which Anne forever kept. Even Mary Dyer, who was later accused of being the mother of the beast, evidence of which they found in the spring, kept her vow of silence, such was her contempt for Gov. Winthrop and the church for having turned their backs on Anne.

"Anne Hutchinson was determined to save my ministry at all costs to herself and so she did. What she could not salvage was my conscience, which torments me unto the grave. And so to this reward of death I cannot go without the story being told. Sarah, your mother, has quite completely obliterated it from her thoughts and we have never mentioned it, even between us, thanks be to the Heavenly Father who cares for his lost sheep. And your sister, Elizabeth, God bless her soul, remains as innocent as the lamb of Christ. It is God's will, truly, that it is thus.

"So I ask only this: Know the truth, and bury it with you, my dear son, for it is part of us now. I have arranged for all the rest. Forgive me, as I know Our Father has done, and Christ be with you now and for always."

The sun was getting low and the still, late afternoon September air abnormally warm, when Pike walked Buttons up to the rude outskirts of Salem Village.

"Rain," his inner farmer voice spoke. Pike looked up into the cloudless sky. It had been a very dry season thus far and he hoped his weather intuition was accurate.

The friendly door of Nathaniel Ingersoll's Ordinary was at the corner of the turn, which took the North Road, as it was then known, into Salem proper if traveling that far into the town. Pike wasn't.

He knew some of the spurious witch hearings had been held at Ingersoll's, but he was well acquainted with its touchy owners, and they were fond of him. Here he would refresh and discover what he could.

Before entering the yard, he cast a glance behind him where, a stone's throw away, was the training field where the major would meet with the other military commanders from northern Massachusetts. He halted for a moment, thinking of the dead boys' faces he had sent into the forests and swamps of New England never to return.

He shook his head as if to fling these images aside. Ingersoll's was where he had gone to console himself when he was in Salem passing through to Boston. He had many a glass of their excellent cider there in happier times, too.

Now he sought information.

Pike led his horse to the stables in the rear looking for the boy, but he was nowhere to be found. The barn, though, was nearly full of mounts, plus a fat sow, too lazy to get up, and some chickens. He found Buttons a bit of hay and a nice corner in which to munch it.

Coming around to the front of the large house, he expected to hear a great deal of commotion issue from within, but it was as quiet as if a wake were in progress. With a deep sigh, Pike entered wearing his hat, as was his habit from the days when the Quakers refused to doff theirs.

The interior of the taproom was dark, cold and strangely sober for a licensed house.

Furrowed farm faces turned toward his.

Those quickly looking away recognized the tall, leathery old man as an exalted agent of the Bay Colony government while a small minority of curious gazes lingered submissively. But Pike's own eyes sought the first familiar figure they settled on, a bulky, middle-aged man sitting by himself in a bit of a corner wedge created by an odd architectural mishap within the wall.

"Your honor," he said to Judge Samuel Sewall, hovering over him. The judge looked up out of his sherry glass.

Sewall was a large man with a bulbous nose, half the age of Pike, but he seemed shrunken and old nevertheless. He attempted to raise himself up in greeting, but Pike bade him with his hand to remain seated.

"Magistrate and Major Robert Pike," said Sewall. "Surely, it is my honor, sir. You are here, no doubt, for the pressing of Corey, eh? And the hangings?"

"The pressing of Corey!" replied Pike in astonishment.

The room behind him went mute. Pressing was an ancient punishment inflicted in cases where the defendant refused to plead. The incriminated was forced to lie on the ground, a board was laid upon his chest, and a deathly load was added, crushing rock by crushing rock, until the accused pled – or expired.

Sewall scrunched his shoulders together in disgust. "Pressed like a *pâté* of goose or a confit of duck, he was. I have never seen the like, as God's my witness. Furthermore, he called for more weight every hour. If you have come to see it, you are too late. His last call was, well, his last."

"I have not come to see it," Pike said, biting off his words.

"You are too soon for the hangings, then. That will be on the 'morrow, if you're an early riser. Corey's widow will be among 'em. But I see I have piqued your interest, sir."

"You have my full attention, I do assure you."

"I have only the greatest respect for you, Major Pike, as you well know. Pray have a seat."

Sewall indicated the ledge by the window, adjusting his small table to allow his visitor to take advantage of the narrow perch next to him.

The judge bent his flushed face to Pike's ear.

"I am reassessing things," he whispered. "Your letter to the court in regard of Mrs. Bradbury and the other witches I found to be compelling if not influential."

"Mrs. Bradbury is not a witch, your honor," Pike whispered back. Despite his caution, the eyes of the taproom were upon both men now.

"Tut, tut," replied Sewall in a louder tone. "She is a convicted witch at that."

He took a taste of his fortified wine, searching Pike's face for the inevitable protest. None came. Sewall leaned over again, his voice hushed.

"Yet I concede the court, this court, may have been prone to mistakes in such regards. The matter of the use, or misuse I might say, of spectral evidence in the proceedings has become of particular interest to me. It was well stated in your letter defending Mrs. Bradbury. Come, let us stroll outdoors to see the evening sun set."

Sewall drained his glass. He rose from his seat and the men walked to the door. Pike waved to the innkeeper, already hurrying over with a glass for him, but they were outside before he could intercept them.

The pair strode, arm in arm, some ways before stopping.

"I have lost some friends these days past, Robert. Capt. John Alden, you are acquainted with, I'm sure. Accused of witchcraft, and the court persuaded by the testimony of the bewitched and ready to rule. Alden has managed to make his escape from the Boston prison, I have heard." At this, Sewall looked at Pike knowingly.

The judge went on. "Your letter to the court has had an effect on me, I do admit. I committed the salient line to memory. You wrote, 'There may be innocent persons that are not saints, and their innocence ought to be their security, as godly men's, and nobody question but Devil may take their shape.' A brilliant, if I may say, logic."

Pike bowed. He replied, pressing home the point, "It follows that only Devil may assume a spectral, out-of-body form, if it be seen. How else may it be so? And how may a person be convicted upon the word or deed of the Author of All Lies?"

"Alas, there is truth in that," replied Sewall. "Ah, doleful, doleful witchcraft."

"We are all caught up in his talons."

"Just so. Just so. Well, you may put your mind at ease for now about Mrs. Bradbury. Safe she is in Boston, although poorly in health, I suppose, even though they have removed her chains. Your man was able to give the gaolers some money for her care is my recollection."

"My man Hopestill?" ventured Pike cautiously.

"Ahem. Indeed."

Pike's face showed its deep concern at Sewall's tone and expression, so the judge hurried to explain.

"He has been inquired after, I might add."

"Inquired after? By whom?" Pike instantly regretted his eager tone.

A guilty look spread over Sewall's face, but he resolved to make a clean breast of it, confiding the information he had advanced to his friend the Rev. Cotton Mather, whose abiding interest in the man Foster and his career was well-known between them.

"At first I feared for Mr. Foster's life, however," Sewall added. "I was told he exhibited all the signs of being stricken with the Small pocks. It was in the company of Mrs. Bradbury that he was taken ill. Now it is my understanding he has recovered sufficiently to undergo a preliminary examination of sorts."

Pike gripped Sewall's arm. "Have you knowledge of Ensign Foster's whereabouts at this moment, your honor? It is of vital import that I reach him."

"As it so happens …" he glanced at Pike, who removed his hand from Sewall's arm, "… I just this day heard from Cotton Mather. He has written to ask me to discuss with my brother Stewart the possibility of obtaining a number of trial documents. I expect him here tomorrow, actually, for the executions."

"I would go to Boston now, tonight, to see him."

"Then I expect you will find him in his temporary offices at the Quaker Boelkins's house, near the wharf."

"I do not know this Quaker Boelkins."

"Alas, it is only a name attached to a property later acquired by the minister. The house's namesake was pitilessly murdered by a renegade Indian some years previous, shortly after Philip's War. Shocking, genuinely morbid. Will you step back inside and sup with me before you depart?"

"If my company would please you, I agree. I feel done in," said Pike.

"Then you shall have a meal and good drink, major. I will also write you a pass to get you into Boston this night. The watchmen can become very dangerous creatures after the sun retreats, eagerly looking for Devil and his agents."

Chapter Thirty-Two

Escape of the Witch

"Horses!" shouted Constable Fain, peeping through a crack at the bottom of the door. He was the first to be roused by the clattering on the loose cobblestones outside.

The burly warder clambered up from the midst of a second horrible night's repose, lashing out with his boot at those within range. The constable's man called Orange'ead barely moved when struck, with only the pumpkin-colored tendrils of his hair crawling through the thick dust of the floor in response.

"Two horses, your worship! A black one and a, a, pale white one!" an agitated Fain called again to the Rev. Cotton Mather, slumped over in his chair. Mather's eyes slowly widened. He was dreaming of his father.

Awake, he could see very little. The fire had gone out. The room's blackness was barely dispelled by the inadequate sputtering of a single flickering taper. Dark's blanket had yet to be lifted in spite of the hours that had passed. Such nightmares! A part of his waking mind recalled he had to attend a set of hangings in Salem that day.

Before rising from his seat, the minister had the presence of mind to remove his writing tray, notebooks, pens, ink pot and cup, all heaped on his lap by Tizzoo after a second night's gleanings of useless stories, legends, tall tales and utter nonsense from the poxed, delirious renegade Foster.

A great pounding on the door shook the little house.

"Open it!" demanded Mather, his head throbbing.

He stepped over to the settle, to where Hopestill Foster lay motionless, and placed a hand upon the damp forehead to ascertain whether there was life in the inert body. The blood still flowed in the liar's veins. Behind him, Tizzoo padded halfway down the ladder, hanging on almost upside down like a bat and peering into the gloom of the room.

Fain's men, stupid with sleep, gathered around their boss as he opened the door. In the outline against the oncoming dawn a tall old man with a rigid military bearing stood there.

He said behind him, "Good job, Dogged Pease! We are here!" A dimly seen figure, a rangy, bushy haired man who was the middle-aged stable boy at Ingersoll's, bootless atop his pale horse, touched his tricorne hat.

Turning to face Fain, who blocked the opening with his bulk, the old soldier announced himself with authority.

"Major Robert Pike, commander of the troops of Norfolk County and a sworn magistrate of the Massachusetts Bay Colony."

Fain stared at him with a wholly idiotic expression.

Pike barked at the imbecilic face, "One of my officers, Ensign Hopestill Foster, is here. Get out of my way!"

Alarmed, Mather swept to the door in his disheveled state, brushing aside Fain to face the fierce presence standing just outside.

"I am at your service, major, even at this unholy hour. Pray, enter, please. Tizzoo, see to the fire and the candles!"

"Rev. Mather," Pike said respectfully, brought up short.

He had suspected Mather might be present, but he was surprised nevertheless at seeing the minister in such a disreputable part of the city at such an ungodly time of night.

He continued with overwrought courtesy, "It is my honor again."

Mather nodded. "You do me honor as well, major, or should I say, 'cousin,' since we will be relations after the wedding of your Wymond and my uncle's Mariah."

He stepped aside for Pike.

Tizzoo had hurriedly set to re-lighting the room with the remaining candle. Exploring the ashes of the fire with a poker and adding a log, she soon had it brightening the little room.

Pike spied the unconscious, embarrassing form of the nearly naked Foster, wrapped in Tizzoo's shawl, and brushed past Mather wordlessly and discourteously. The minister winced, surprising himself yet again with the uncomfortable sensation of a sense of shame.

Touching his friend, Pike instantly drew back, startled by the manifest starkness of the disease. He looked over at Mather, who smiled wanly.

"This is highly irregular," Pike told him.

The minister, who had regained command of himself, chose to dissemble. "If you have had the pocks, there is no reason to be fearful. Ah, I see you have been afflicted in the past!"

Pike involuntarily touched the old scars on his face and throat.

The minister continued, a bit bolder. "I assure you Mr. Foster's presence here is necessary, major. New England is in crisis. This man has the information I need."

Pike straightened. "Indeed?" he remarked in a tone more severe than Mather expected.

"Oh, yes," replied Mather defensively.

Pike returned to Foster, standing over him. With his back to Mather he touched his hand to his coat.

"I would aver that the information you need is in my breast pocket, sir."

The minister's heart fluttered. He retreated a step. "What do you mean?" he asked.

Pike turned and took three measured paces toward Mather, as if he were commencing a duel. He motioned with his head to Fain and his scruffy crew of cohorts.

"Send these vile men away immediately," he commanded.

Fain and his crew had been watching from the area around the entrance to the other room with slack mouths. Their brute, silly expressions seemed to register no intelligence about the meaning or import of Pike's appearance or words. Worse, a gathering collective stink hung about the men's legs like a cloud of dung mist.

The Rev. Mather weighed his options.

"Mr. Fain. Take your men outside."

He dangled a small purse at the warder.

"Your pay is here. Let order be kept. You shall have it shortly." He motioned with his head to get out.

"That it will, your grace," answered Fain, a smile brightening his ugly face. Hefting his cudgel, he herded his astonished people through the door.

Pike looked over at Tizzoo, who had glided to Foster and was now wiping his face with a rag. She had come down the ladder with her own ratty quilt, which she wrapped with tender care around the shivering sick man.

"What about her?"

Mather stayed composed. He worked his jaw back and forth to control the stammer he felt rising from his increasingly nervous gut. "Tizzoo can barely understand English. However, she makes excellent chocolate, if I may offer you a pot."

Pike ignored the offer. "I will nonetheless address you in Latin. Slaves know far more than a master suspects, as Pharaoh learned to his dismay in Egypt."

"The stirring saga of the Jews in the book *Exodus*. Quite right," Mather bowed.

"Prepare yourself, then. Read this," Pike said, withdrawing a sheaf of loose papers from the inside of his coat.

Cotton reached eagerly for these as he would a plate of hot biscuits, then withdrew his hand fearing a burn. Stinging, too, was his petty teacher's annoyance with Pike's gross misuse of the old tongue.

"Rather *perlego* than *lego*," he lectured, crossly.

"You recognize the hand?" Pike asked, his phrasing again in the poorest Latin. "It is that of Thomas Bradbury, whose writ is known in every public record in Salisbury for its beauty. But this paper contains not beautiful things, but rather awful deeds."

Mather folded his arms in refusal. "What interest would any writing of Thomas Bradbury, the husband of a convicted witch and, I dare say, a suspect himself, hold for me?"

"This is a fair copy," Pike said, holding the papers, "of another letter, an original letter, which is here, next to my heart, where it shall remain safe. Your grandfather John Cotton's most closely held secret is contained within."

Mather bristled in righteous anger. He pointed a finger at Pike.

"Theft, a mortal sin! And I need not quote you chapter and verse, major!"

For the first time, Pike smiled. He replied in the King's good English.

"I have borrowed what's needed, which is called necessity, and to which I need not cite the appropriate verse." His face darkened again. "Read it, and be quick about it."

Then he added, "but sitting down is my advice."

Mather sat as directed. He read slowly at first, then his eyes narrowed as he devoured the Bradbury copy with a sense of shock and awe such as he had never before experienced, not even once, over the course of a remarkable life filled with a providence of wonders.

When the minister had finished, his hands dropped to his lap.

"History will damn me, damn my family," Cotton Mather whispered to the room.

Pike advanced to the stricken, downcast man of God and hunter of witches, tempted to wring his goose-white neck. Instead, he glanced at the poor figure of Hopestill, fussed over by a terrified Tizzoo.

His good friend, so cruelly abused by time, circumstances and fate, lay inert on the bench, used up, nearly broken. He returned his gaze to Mather.

"Aye, history may well damn ye!" Pike snarled. "But it will not be because of what is in this letter."

With that, the old major snatched the Bradbury copy from Mather's limp hands, crumpled the papers up, and tossed the wad into the flames where the crinkly mass crackled like Devil's own laughter.

Before him, Mather, a man he had met three previous times, once as a child prodigy, the second as a young minister and now, in maturity, a powerful icon, was reduced to an empty husk.

Pike explained in a quiet voice, "I don't care about history. I care about the present and the people in it."

Mather continued to stare absently at the fire. The great secret he had sought was now his, and it was a curse upon his very being.

"Look ye, here, Reverend." Pike knelt down to face Mather. "The letter I still carry will return with me, all its terrible history contained within as if never seen by my eyes or those of Mr. Bradbury. But in return you must give up my man here into my safekeeping, as well as secure the release of a good woman named Mary."

Mather's voice remained small, like a mouse voice.

"Impossible," he said tonelessly. "Impossible."

"It is not impossible," replied Pike.

Then he explained how it *was* possible.

And so it was, much later that same day, that an open cart carrying the prisoner Mary Bradbury, the convicted witch of Salisbury, passed through to the north of Salem, its high wheels creaking as if they would break off at every revolution.

To the south of the road it was taking, inside Salem itself, the grim deeds of the hangman were in progress at a most dismal site in the village, attended by almost all who lived in those parts, and by Cotton Mather himself.

Mather had ridden along with them, wearing a long, sour face, from Boston to Salem. Near Gallows Hill, where Mather had turned off, eight witches in all were meeting their doom, among them the newly widowed Martha Corey, whose husband Giles had been pressed to death only days before under a weight of stones.

Those who continued north averted their eyes.

The driver of the cart containing Mrs. Bradbury was the deputy sheriff of Ipswich, John Harris, who had only three fingers on his left hand. He would very much have liked to have detoured into Salem to enjoy the spectacle. Also, to nip a bit of witch rope was to ensure an endless skein of good luck.

But he had his orders.

Curious orders they were, too, from the constable of the Boston lock-up and from the eminent Rev. Mr. Mather himself.

Harris's prisoner was being sent away north to Ipswich for "a thorough examination" by "a special expert in supernatural matters."

These worthies, his little writ of paper stated, were to determine whether the indescribably happy old woman sitting next to him was indeed the actual Mrs. Bradbury and not a spectral apparition that had wantonly assumed her form to commit heinous acts.

Naturally, Deputy Sheriff Harris was frightened out of his wits at the prospect of sharing a cart seat with a familiar of Lucifer, no matter how harmless the alleged compatriot appeared to be.

He had at first insisted his passenger be contained in a shut-up box around which a stout length of iron chain was wrapped, iron and chains said to be certain proof against bewitchment.

However, at the last moment, his personal safety was guaranteed by the escort of a second cart behind his in which the reins were held by one of the deadliest soldiers in New England, old as he might have been at that time, the estimable Major Robert Pike of Salisbury. And, until they reached Salem, the legendary minister Cotton Mather himself was available to ward off any incipient evil.

After leaving accursed Salem, Pike assured Harris that no witch would accomplish any mischief in his sight that day since he had dealt with many of those evildoers over the years and vanquished them all. As it happened, the major was himself on a journey north, riding the entire way with the bald-headed deputy sheriff, accompanying folk on their way to the frontier.

This was all well and good, but Harris had gotten a look at the strange pair in the bed of the major's cart, and he didn't much care for the couple he saw back there. And that demon child with them … well, it was enough to make a person think twice before shutting his eyes.

To begin with, there was the corpselike figure of a grinning old man who was experiencing the Small pocks by all appearances. And this poor fellow was attended by an even odder sight, a brown servant woman (whom he had to admit privately possessed a very comely appearance for one so dark). The ill man lay nearly buried in a deep pallet of yellow straw. The woman sat by his right hand, holding it. Nor were they the worst of it. Peeping forth from the straw in which she had buried herself, was a ratlike little girl with burning eyes.

A fair ways down the road, the drivers stopped both carts to refresh.

In one brief instant, when Harris reached behind his seat to fetch his bit of biscuit for lunch, the dark woman in Pike's conveyance unnerved the deputy sheriff by flashing him a quick smile behind which might have been a mouthful of devil teeth. Harris blinked his eyes three times, then touched wood.

When they had resumed their journey, Harris thought on it.

After a few more miles, he estimated he may have been mistaken. In any event, after that, he reckoned he was safer where he was, riding with the presumed witch, than with the bizarre trio in the rear of the major's cart.

The travelers proceeded along the road to Ipswich as the day progressed, a day that was growing ever darker and more dismal with the threat of rain.

Harris dreaded a cart ride in the rain since it meant they might get stuck, and it was while he was preoccupied with his new concern that four horsemen appeared, spreading out to flank the narrow road ahead of him. They were a few miles south of Ipswich then.

Deputy Sheriff Harris was acquainted with all of these men, three of whom were named Perkins, which was the witch Mary Bradbury's maiden name far back in time, so he wasn't unduly alarmed.

He hauled up on the leather leads and waited for the major's wagon to catch up.

Pike called across from his seat, "You may proceed on to town, Deputy. These good men will accompany us to the proper authorities in this matter elsewhere, at a secret location."

Harris said nothing as the witch known as Mrs. Bradbury was helped into the major's cart, taking her seat next to him. Just then, the child screamed aloud, raising the hair on Harris's neck. Leaping from the cart's rear, the pitiful figure jumped up on the seat board and wormed her way into the woman's elderly arms, burying her face there.

The deputy chewed on his lip, turning things over in his jumbled mind. But what could he do? He had his written orders in hand allowing for the transfer of custody, signed by the great Rev. Mather – signed with such a seemingly angry scrawl that it nearly ripped the paper.

The cart with Mrs. Bradbury and the men riding alongside raced away to the north, Major Pike's whip cracking the air. The black woman in the back sat upright in the straw and waved gaily to him as they departed.

As he watched, Deputy Harris thought it most curious that when Mrs. Bradbury had moved to the other cart, the major had allowed himself to be hugged and fussed over to such an extent by the dangerous criminal whose custody Harris had just relinquished.

And then there was that apparition of a child …

"Most odd," he muttered under his breath. "Most odd."

Pike's cart with its five occupants, and the horsemen accompanying, got smaller as they disappeared over the small hill that led around the village and on to Rowley, three miles distant.

Harris watched until they were no longer to be seen.

He remained motionless in the road for a good while. A few sprinkles of rain spattered on his round shoulders and bare head, which he smeared with his three-fingered hand.

His guess was the old Bradbury woman was not a witch. Yet he supposed his betters were right, that this was a matter for the experts, who were trained to look further into things. He pondered for a few moments to think of what experienced minds actually knew about such matters, and it made him shudder.

All was now very quiet on the darkening road.

Mentally, and this was very difficult for him, the deputy added up the various totals of the cost he would submit to the court to meet his expenses. Four shillings ought to cover it, he decided. It was more than he deserved, but a man's family has to eat.

Harris flicked his little switch at the horse's flanks. It trotted a few feet, then stopped.

The mottled horse, a purchase from his wife's overbearing brother, was an incorrigible dawdler.

"Get going, you devil," he commanded.

1697: A Desecration

Kancamagus crawled a bit farther before he gave up and sank his face into the warm, dark earth. Not without a sense of irony did he realize he lay dying within a day's walk from the old field where the Phony Battle took place and the Pennacook tribe was destroyed so many summers before.

The wound in his upper back astonished him. He knew it was massive, gaping and gushing his blood. What he did not feel was pain, since the shock deadened nearly all physical sensation except around his face.

His band had deserted him, left him behind, not wishing to linger any more in this beehive of angry white hornets. Kancamagus heard them have an argument as to whether he was going to die soon, but that quickly ended with the decision to flee and flee quickly by Sagamore Sam, who had assumed leadership.

Unhappily, they left without anyone volunteering to cut his throat. And since no one was in favor of shooting him in the head to finish him off because they feared the report of a gunshot would put them into even greater jeopardy, they had taken off into the fields of tall corn without a word to him.

A trip over the exposed root of an old beech tree by the Indian directly behind him was what felled Kancamagus. The warrior's gun went off and the destructive blast ripped into the meat of his back, shredding his skin, which hung in red tatters around the entrance wound.

As he lay in the dirt, Kancamagus knew he shouldn't even be alive, but this was just passing fortune. He would soon become another spirit of the forest once his blood ran out of his body, which would be any time now.

He might die alone, but he would not die completely unavenged.

By chance, he had heard of the scarred-neck white man who had knocked him in the head and stabbed him at the Point of Graves all those years ago. The discovery of that man had also led to the intelligence that his hated captor during the Phony Battle, Capt. Charles Frost, was living in close proximity.

Kancamagus led a raiding party to the little collection of dwellings in Maine the whites called Elliot Village and waited for their chance. This they seized on a church day, and when the English issued out of their praying place, they were fallen upon and slaughtered. Frost died screaming, as did the man with the scar.

This was a great moment for Kancamagus, but it was quickly spoiled by the arrival of other white men, causing his warriors to run away before they were finished with their work.

That night, the Indians hid out in the nearby woods. The mood of the band was sullen. Sagamore Sam and the other warriors argued with him to quit the scene of the raid, but Kancamagus refused their entreaties. So they skulked in the vicinity, waiting until the English put the body of Frost into the ground on a hill near their God place.

That same night, under their chief's direction, they dug up Frost's mutilated corpse, impaling it on a sharpened tree trunk near the open grave. The ghastly thing was arranged so it seemed to be standing up when it was found.

Only then would Kancamagus give the order to retreat, but he now led them toward a second raid he planned to carry out before their return to Odanak.

This one he would relish even more than the murder of Frost and the scarred man because their next target was hidden so deep in the woods of the north that Kancamagus would have days in which to enjoy himself without fear of interruption.

However, Kancamagus's band had been seen passing near Cochecho and was hotly pursued by a patrol of whites. It was during their mad dash for cover that the last chief of the Pennacook was mortally wounded.

His anger and regret at realizing that he would never be able to take his revenge on his white uncle Robinhood and his former lover Tizzoo produced a nauseating bitterness in the warrior's mouth.

He thought of Tizzoo and their time together in the white's castle town of Boston. Mostly, he recalled with disgust her holding out to him the tiny black bottle that the slave Titus had lent to her from the old woman's house.

This bottle, his lover had promised, contained the magic of a powerful birth that would produce a chieftain to lead all the Indians of the forest.

She drank from it and destroyed their child. That night, an enraged Kancamagus murdered his master, the Quaker Boelkins, and escaped his English skin forever.

Kancamagus thought of these things but soon it was hard to think at all.

His senses were fading away. He listened to the birds singing and the squirrels scolding. He tried hard to understand but it was impossible. He dreamed he saw Passaconnaway, his grandfather. The old conjurer held his snake, talking to it, and Kancamagus listened intently to divine any meaning. But the rushing in his ears grew louder, to a crashing din, and it carried him away like a river.

The remaining Indians of his band led by Sagamore Sam bypassed Hopestill Foster's cabin by many miles.

Now that Kancamagus was dead and his revenge dream dead with him, they wanted nothing to do with the old sorcerer who dwelled there under the stone face of the haunted mountain where ghosts walked.

Robinhood, they knew, was the son of Passaconnaway, the great chief of the Pennacooks.

Reputed to be one who knew all the terrible secrets of the magic once practiced by the legendary sachem of the tribe, even in old age the adopted white warrior was a man to be feared.

Also, this devil lived with a brown witch, it was said, who had escaped from the Puritans of Boston. She, too, had many powers of evil, so it was best to let them alone.

Soon, the old man would die.

Soon, the woman would be eaten by wolves.

Soon, the little cabin in which they lived would return to the forest in which it was set, watched and protected by the unblinking gaze of the god's face embedded in the granite cliff surrounded by clouds.

The Indians, running on, never gave them another thought.

Unaware of her escape, the former slave Tizzoo, unwillingly given as a gift by Mather to Pike to care for Foster, worked in the extensive garden she had planted around their cabin.

Hopestill had removed to this far-off place in the New Hampshire woods following his recovery from the Small pocks in the spring after the year of the witch hunts.

He favored his old haunt, where he used to dwell when he worked for Walderne back in the days, because it lay well to the north of Dover and Cochecho. He had had to abandon it and flee after Walderne betrayed him and the Pennacooks at the sham fight at the end of Philip's War.

Now he had returned, and it suited Hopestill well because he had no wish to live among any people ever again.

Major Pike had asked most endearingly for Hopestill to remain at his place on the farm at Salisbury, but this he would not do, and although they had parted forever, they had parted the best of friends.

Hopestill had agonized over his decision, but the story Pike told him, how his first love Priscilla had died in ignorance of his fate, killed any chance of his remaining within the bounds of his old world.

The truth, when it was told to him, broke his heart. He learned how their little girl had been taken from them the night he was forced on that frozen, dangerous passage to Maine.

Pike discovered that Elizabeth – his and Priscilla's daughter, given to the Cottons – had died in childbirth in 1656. Pike also found out that Elizabeth's only child, whom she also named Elizabeth, had died of the Small pocks eight years after her young mother passed away.

What tore at Hopestill was that he could not see these pieces of himself in his mind, and never would in this life.

On the day of Hopestill's departure, the Bradburys, Captain

Tom and Miss Mary, came to see him and Tizzoo on their way, weighing their wagon down with a heavy load of gifts, clothing, seed, tools and a fat dairy cow to follow behind.

Tizzoo drove the wagon and Hopestill had ridden the fine white mare the Bradburys had given him. He turned back to wave, and they were all waving to him. The little girl, now grown a bit taller, whom he had first seen shivering in chains, clung to Miss Mary's apron.

He faced forward once more in the saddle and never looked back. His final departure was from the company of all white men, forever, and he would not retreat from his decision.

On the afternoon that Kancamagus lay dying, Hopestill reclined while sitting within the door frame of his cabin.

He had been very tired of late, and was too fatigued to hunt that day.

So he sat in one of the comfortable chairs he had made and tried to find his strength again.

The effort of dragging the chair to the open door of the cabin had greatly fatigued him, and so he basked in the rays of the warm July sun to recover.

It was then, sitting there, that a greater weariness than he had ever known washed over him, like the unexpected impact of a wave from the mighty salt ocean.

He struggled against it, much as he struggled against the Indian baptism he had received in the Merrimack's depths the day he was adopted into his Pennacook family.

It felt like a heavy hand holding him down under the water, but it was a gentle hand and a strangely comforting one, and as it increased its hold over him, Hopestill could barely keep his eyes open.

He concentrated with much difficulty on Tizzoo's broad back as she worked outside in the garden, pulling up weeds. Her linen shirt was sodden with the sweat of her labor.

She has a kind heart and a good soul, Hopestill thought.

Softly, so softly he wasn't even sure he was making any sound at all, a song struggled to emerge from deep within him, from the depths of his being, from a place he knew but couldn't remember, and he began to sing.

The End

Appendix

Chronology

1620 – Hopestill Foster born in Exeter, England.

1632 – Voyage of the *Lyon* to America.

1635 – (August) Hurricane lays waste to Boston.

1637 – Priscilla Sandyman taken ill; formal persecution of Anne Hutchinson for heresy begins; Hopestill exiled to Maine.

1640 – Hopestill captured by Pequots; adopted as a son of Passaconnaway into the Pennacook tribe.

1662 – The whipping of the Quaker women stopped by Hopestill Foster, Robert Pike and Thomas Bradbury.

1663 – Cotton Mather born to Increase and Maria Mather.

1667 – The murder at Walderne's truck house. Kancamagus's father Nanamacomuck sentenced to death by Passaconnaway.

1674 – Cotton Mather leaves Harvard; the Cotton and Mather families convene in Boston.

1675 – King Philip's War devastates New England.

1676 – Metacomet, 'King Philip,' is defeated and killed; the 'Phony Battle' destroys the Pennacooks; Kancamagus is captured and enslaved by the Quaker Boelkins.

1689 – Richard Walderne is murdered in Kancamagus's Cochecho raid.

1692 – Mary Bradbury sentenced to hang as a witch as part of the Salem witchcraft insanity; Hopestill captured by Cotton Mather.

1697 – Hopestill and Kancamagus die on the same day, July 4.

Afterword

Author's Notes

IT WOULD BE A POOR STUDENT of 19th century American poetry who fails to recognize within this novel the echoes (the rather loud echoes, admittedly) of John Greenleaf Whittier's "How the Women Went From Dover," which was my inspiration.

Quaker, abolitionist and fierce foe of tyranny, Whittier put the darkest possible edge on the face of Puritanism in a body of work that shows his deep and abiding interest in exposing to a new generation their forefathers' legacy of bigotry, misogyny and intolerance. The Quakers during the mid-1600s in New England were persecuted and brutalized by the government of North America's first and hopefully last theocracy.

We owe much to Whittier for having revived what precious few memories are retained of an almost forgotten hero, Robert Pike (1616-1706), who figures so prominently in our adventure.

Pike's daring rescue of the whipped Quaker women is marked with a modest memorial in his hometown of Salisbury, MA, if celebrated nowhere else other than in this book and Whittier's poem.

A faded newspaper clipping from the public library there shows that the 1662 episode was once re-enacted, albeit not very realistically, in a show of civic pride.

The fearless major deserves greater renown than history has given him.

Pike was a champion of individual liberty at a moment in time when to speak out meant risking everything. He cared not, openly challenging the theocracy that ruled over him and his neighbors. This he did with a true patriot's conviction that abhorred injustice in every form.

Magistrate, court officer, farmer, military leader, rescuer of Quakers, an aged Robert Pike took on his greatest battle during the witch hysteria that swept 1692 Salem and its neighboring venues. Pike's brilliantly reasoned letter to witch judge Jonathan Corwin was rightly termed "courageous" by one of his biographers, Roland L. Warren.

Writes Salem historian Chadwick Hansen, "The crux of Pike's position was his view that afflicted persons were subject to diabolical torments; that making evidence of such torments was accepting the word of the Devil; worse, that accepting such evidence was holding commerce with the Devil, and therefore in itself (is) a kind of witchcraft."

Alas, Pike's letter and all his best efforts were not able to effect the escape of Mary Bradbury, a close friend of the major's and the wife of his dearest companion, Thomas Bradbury.

Yet Goodwife Bradbury eventually did somehow slip her confinement in the Boston prison to which she had been condemned to await her hanging after conviction of the charge of witchcraft. She was in fact the only convicted Salem-associated witch sentenced to die to have escaped from prison – and her doom – although others who were not yet legally proven guilty did manage to find a way out of Boston, notably Capt. John Alden, Judge Samuel Sewall's friend.

And while Mary herself was not a notable historical figure, readers of great science fiction will be very relieved to know that, perhaps as a consequence of her mysterious getaway, an ancestral line that later produced the novelist Ray Bradbury remained intact because of it.

The circumstances surrounding Mary Bradbury's escape, followed by her disappearance for a few years – to ultimately resurface in colonial life as if nothing much had happened – was never documented. With the blast of heat produced by the fiery witchcraft hysteria having dissipated in the late fall of 1692, the smoking ruins of the scandal left a wealth of embarrassment that few then living wanted to poke through in the aftermath.

With the story of the Quakers told, I was free to imagine how Mary was able to cheat the death rope, and to paint out to the edges of the canvas of that first, terrible American century, so filled from beginning to finish with the unsparing pain of men and women trying to carve a life and future out of what they saw as an unholy wilderness while, co-existing so uneasily with the whites, the Native Americans of Passaconnaway's and Kancamagus's tribe watched their paradise stolen by hard men like Richard Walderne. When you next travel the "Kancamagus Highway" in New Hampshire, please ponder the irony of the ride.

The chapters involving the Pennacook, Pequot and Mohawk people have disturbing elements in them, two points upon I'd like to touch.

Regarding the infamous cruelty of the treatment of captives, while this varied according to tribe, it was unquestionably a lamentable part of the history of that time, which is all I care to say about it, other than it mirrored in many respects the horrors inflicted upon all the races then living by their own peers.

So our friend Cotton Mather was correct, indeed, to suspect there were monsters abroad in his world doing Satan's work – only these were human monsters.

In respect to the so-called "Phony Battle," historical accounts do not give us any solid information of exactly how the Pennacook were tricked that fateful 1676 day near Cochecho. I imagined the scene taking place just as I described it, a plan by Walderne to lull the tribe into his confidence, discharge their weapons and face defeat at the hands of troops well-placed to exploit their fatal predicament.

The murder of the white man Thomas Dickinson in Walderne's drinking tavern, which he pushed all-too-close to Pennacook lands to entice the Indians, was based on a historical court record.

Richard Walderne was a true man of his times, unfortunately so in many respects, as it seems probable that, after being killed by Chief Kancamagus in the horrible fashion described – probably in retaliation for the Phony Battle catastrophe – some of Walderne's children seem to have adopted the name of Waldron, which was an alternate spelling of his name found in some accounts.

Hopestill Foster, and the others named Hopestill Foster of that era and later, did exist – just not in the fictional guise or form in which I created my tormented hero. Encountering the name, I appropriated it in order to animate the body I believed necessary to perform the heavy lifting of pushing the story from the 1630s well into the 1690s, and the lad acquitted himself well.

The Sandyman family, too, was a literary device, accomplishing the mission of getting Hopestill to New England and fixing him into the beginning of his troubles. The major themes of that early American experience, particularly the Anne Hutchinson and Rev. John Cotton saga, are based on well-known accounts, and it was fairly easy to imagine the extreme depression and desperate anxiety that must have motivated Sarah Cotton to desire a child be born at the height of that strange episode when all of Boston must obviously have been smirking about the relationship between her husband and his most ardent advocate.

Among the many helpful volumes of material that I relied upon for this part of the narrative were Larzer Ziff's *The Career of John Cotton, Puritanism and the American Experience,* (Princeton University Press, 1962), and the amazingly wonderful *The Correspondence of John Cotton,* (The University of North Carolina Press, 2001), edited by Sargent Bush, Jr. It was within the latter volume that I was rewarded with the happy discovery (from the story's point of view, of course) that, upon his death bed in 1652, the Rev. Cotton had ordered all of his Hutchinson-related papers and letters burned to ashes.

Undoubtedly, there will be some confusion about the "monster births" episode within the narrative. For this part of the story, we have Hutchinson-hating Bay Colony Gov. John Winthrop and his mean-spirited diaries to thank for all the nastier bits of gossip.

Winthrop, whom I suppose was the Fox News/Bill O'Reilly of his time, plotted his way back into office at the height of the Hutchinson controversy to make hay of it, dredging up in its aftermath the most lurid conspiracy theories about what, in all probability, were libelous myths designed to smear the reputations of both Hutchinson and her leading acolyte, Mary Dyer.

For more on this, I urge readers to consult the wonderful 1990 paper published by the Massachusetts Historical Society, edited by Valerie Pearl and Morris Pearl, entitled, *Gov. John Winthrop on the Birth of the Antinomians' 'Monster': The Earliest Reports to Reach England and the Making of a Myth.* Equally enlightening for me was Anne Jacobson Schutte's *Such Monstrous Births: A Neglected Aspect of the Antinomian Controversy* (University of Chicago Press,

Renaissance Quarterly, Spring, 1985).

The primary Salem events have produced many fertile sources for the historian and writer. I utilized many of these, particularly the excellent David Levin-edited volume, *What Happened in Salem?* (Harcourt, Brace & World, Inc., 1960); Chadwick Hanson, *Witchcraft at Salem* (George Brazillier, Inc., New York, 1969); and Frances Hill, *The Salem Witch Trials Reader* (Da Capo Press, 2000), the latter proving most helpful in sorting out a few tricky timeline matters.

Cotton Mather and his father Increase figure prominently, and I am indebted again to David Levin for his remarkable *Cotton Mather: The Young Life of the Lord's Remembrancer, 1663-1703* (Harvard University Press, 1978); Michael G. Hall, *The Last American Puritan, The Life of Increase Mather* (Wesleyan University Press, 1988) and, last but not least, Cotton himself, author of a lifetime of deadly screeds, exhortations and observations.

Mather's speech disorder was good for a few chapters' worth of depth to his character, and for that I thank not only Levin again but Carol Gay for her fine paper, *The Fettered Tongue: A Study of the Speech Defect of Cotton Mather* (American Literature, Vol. 46, No. 4, 1975).

Very helpful, too, was the Len Travers-edited *The Missionary Journal of John Cotton, Jr., 1666-1678* (Massachusetts Historical Society, 1978), although here I need to state the usage of the term "the Younger" in the novel to describe the Cotton family pedigree was by my own choosing. I like to think even back then no one wanted to be called "Junior."

It must also be noted that few sources of primary information were more invaluable to me than the *New England Historical and Genealogical Register*, whose volumes I devoured like a heaping plate of Ipswich fried clams. Likewise, the yellowed pages of the *Essex Antiquarian* were most beneficial for helping to recreate the feel of old Salem. Both publications are, literally, gold mines.

Treasure troves, too, were the genealogical departments of several important West Michigan institutions that I utilized heavily – Muskegon's Hackley Public Library, Grand Haven's Loutit District Library, and Holland's Herrick District Library. What great gifts they are to the reading public. Likewise, a tip of the hat to Carolyn Tremblay of the Dover (NH) Public Library, for providing me with a copy of the invaluable map from Mary Pickering Thompson's *Landmarks in Ancient Dover* (Dover Historical Society, 1892).

I am indebted equally as much to the curators of the fabulous Thomas Prince Collection within the Boston Public Library, which graciously afforded me a rare view of many original letters from Cotton Mather and his contemporaries, and to Hope College's Van Wylen Library in Holland, Michigan, for its astonishing collection of rare books in the religion field.

My earliest readers helped me avoid many pitfalls. Chief among these were my extraordinarily patient wife Maxine, and my daughters Tracy, Rae and Natalie. Many others were critical to the effort, notably the late Richard Maher, Sr., Andrew Burns, John Stephenson and Robert Burns.

However, my task would have been impossible without my great friend and editor, West Michigan writer Bill Garrigan, who helped shepherd all of the rewrites into this final version.

Thank you, Bill.

Thank you, too, to amateur historian and archeologist Richard Lunt of Dover, New Hampshire, who was my guide to many of the settings and scenes in that neck of the woods. No writer could have asked for a better companion in the field.

Finally, my gratitude to my agent Roger Rapoport, whose unflagging encouragement carried me on, and to Garn Press publisher and editor Denny Taylor for her tireless professionalism, insightful criticism, and kind enthusiasm for my novel. Were all writers this blessed.

David Joseph Kolb

Grand Haven Township, MI

June 1, 2015

28850330R00197

Made in the USA
Middletown, DE
30 January 2016